Grace Livingston Hill

Lo, Michael

BARBOUR
PUBLISHING

© 2000 by R. L. Munce Publishing Co., Inc.

Edited and updated for today's reader by Deborah Cole.

ISBN 1-59310-675-0

Published by Barbour Publishing, Inc., P.O. Box 719, Uhrichsville, Ohio 44683, www.barbourbooks.com

Our mission is to publish and distribute inspirational products offering exceptional value and biblical encouragement to the masses.

ecpa Member of the
Evangelical Christian
Publishers Association

Printed in the United States of America.
5 4 3 2 1

Chapter 1

$\mathcal{T}$he crowd had gathered at a great stone house on Madison Avenue. An automobile stood before the door. A beautiful little girl, not yet three years old, in white velvet and ermine, with her dark curls framed by an ermine-trimmed hood and silk rosebuds, came out of the door with her nurse for her afternoon ride. The nurse stepped back to the hall for the wrap she'd dropped, leaving the baby alone, her dark eyes shining under the straight dark brows, as she looked gleefully out on the world. At that instant, as if by magic, the crowd assembled.

It might be better to say that just then the crowd focused on the particular house where the baby daughter of the president of a great defaulting bank lived. More or less all morning, men had been gathering, passing the house, looking up with troubled or threatening faces toward the richly laced windows, shaking menacing heads and muttering imprecations. But there had been no disturbance and no concerted crowd until the child appeared.

The police had been more or less vigilant all morning but had seen nothing disturbing. The inevitable small boy had also been in evidence, with his instinct for excitement. Mickey with his papers often found himself in that quarter on bright mornings and would search for the child's starry eyes and dark curls in the windows of this particular house.

But the man with the evil face on the other side of the street, resting his hand against the lamppost and sighting the baby with a vindictive eye, had never been seen there before.

Mickey noticed him first. Circling him innocently, he'd heard his imprecations against the rich, caught the whispered oath as the child appeared, and seen the man's ugly look. Alarmed, he crossed to the other side of the street, his eye on the offender, and was the first to see the covert motion, the flash of the hidden weapon, and fear the worst.

"Hi, there! Mickey! Look out!"

An alert voice called from a huddled group of urchins in the front of the crowd, but too late. The boy flashed past without heeding, straight up the stone steps where the child smiled at the crowd. Holding his bundle of papers high, with the late morning sunlight catching his tangle of golden hair, Mickey flung himself in front of the little one. The revolver's sharp *crack* from the opposite curb was simultaneous with their fall. Mickey's own ragged, neglected little body, receiving the bullet intended for her, went down with her as she fell.

Then all was confusion.

A child's cry—a woman's scream—a police whistle—the crowd's angry roar, like a pack of wild animals that had tasted blood. Stones flew from men whose wrongs had smoldered in their breasts and bred a fury of hate and murder. Women were trampled upon. Two of the plate-glass windows crashed as the flying missiles entered the magnificent home.

The chauffeur attempted to drive the car around the corner but was held up at once. He discreetly got out of the way, leaving the car in the hands of the mob who swarmed into and over it, disfiguring it in their wrath. Then came the noise of exploding tires, ripping of leather cushions, groaning of the machinery as the mob took vengeance on the car to show what they'd like to do to its owner.

Gone into bankruptcy! He! With a great electric car like that and servants to serve him! With his baby attired in a queen's trappings and his house swathed in lace that had taken the eyesight from many poor lace-makers! He! Gone into bankruptcy and slipping away scot-free, while the men he had robbed stood helpless on his sidewalk, hungry and hopeless because the pittances they'd put away in his bank, the result of slavery and sacrifice, were gone! And they were too old, too tired, or too filled with hate to earn it again.

The crowd surged and seethed, snarling, throbbing, desperate—leaderless and more dangerous.

The sight of the child with her dancing eyes and happy smiles, "rolling in luxury," called to mind their own puny darlings, grimy with neglect, lean with want, and hollow-eyed with premature knowledge. Why should one child be pampered and another starved? Why did the bank president's daughter have any better right to those wonderful furs and the exultant smile than their own children? A glimpse into the rooms beyond the sheltering plate glass and drapery showed even greater contrast than they'd dreamed between this home and the bare tenements they'd left that morning, where the children were crying for bread and the wives shivered with cold. Their every breath cried out for vengeance, and with brute instinct they sought to hurt the man through his child, because they had been hurt by the wrong done to their children.

The policeman's whistle had done its work, however. The startled inmates of the house had drawn the child and her preserver within the heavy carved doors and borne them back to safety before the mob could force its way in. Amid the outcry and disorder, no one noticed that Mickey had disappeared until his small band of companions set up an outcry; but even then no one heard.

The mounted police had arrived and were issuing orders. They arrested, handcuffed, and marched away the man who had fired the shot. They ordered the people right and left and rode their horses ruthlessly through the masses. Law and order had arrived, and the downtrodden could only flee.

The square was soon cleared and guarded by a large force. Only the newspapermen came and went without challenge. The threatening groups of men still hovering about withdrew farther. The wrecked automobile was patched up and taken to the garage. The street quieted, and by and by workmen came to install temporary protections where the window glass had been broken.

Yet through it all the ragged newsboys stood their ground in front of the house. Until the quiet was restored, they evaded each renewed command of officer or passerby and stayed there, whispering now and again in excited groups and pointing up to the house. Finally a tall policeman approached them.

"Clear out, kids!" he said, not unkindly. "You hear me? You can't stay here any longer."

Then one of them wheeled around. He was the tallest, with a fierce freckled face and flashing black eyes in which the evil passions of four generations looked out upon a world that had always been harsh. He was known as Fighting Buck.

"Mickey's in dare. He's hurted. We kids can't leave Mick alone. He might be dead."

Just at that moment, a physician's runabout drew up to the door, and the policeman fell back to let him pass into the house. Right after him followed the bank president in a closed carriage attended by several men in uniform who escorted him to the door and touched their hats politely as he vanished inside. Around the corners, scowling faces haunted the shadows, and murmured imprecations were scarcely withheld in spite of the mounted officers. A shot was fired down the street, and several policemen hurried away.

"Mickey's in dare. He's hurted. I seen him fall. Maybe he's deaded. We kids wants to take him away. Mickey didn't do nothin'. He jes' tried to save der little kid. Mickey's a good 'un. You get the folks to put Mickey out here. We kids'll take him away."

The policeman finally attended to the ragamuffins' pleading. Two or three newspapermen joined the knot around them, and the story was presently written up with all the racy touches writers of the hour knew how to use. Before night Buck, with his fierce black brows drawn in helpless defiance, was adorning the evening papers in various attitudes as the different snapshots portrayed him, and the newsboys, bootblacks, and good-for-nothings standing around him figured for once in the whole city's eyes.

The small band held their place until forcibly removed. Some were barefoot and stood shivering on the cold stones, their grimy faces blue with anxiety and chill.

The doctor came out of the house just as the last one, Buck, was being marched off with a loud protest. He eyed the boy and quickly understood the situation.

"Look here!" he called to the officer. "Let me speak to the youngster. He's a friend, I suppose, of the boy that was shot?"

The officer nodded.

"Well, boy, what's all this fuss about?" He looked kindly, keenly into Buck's black eyes.

"Mickey's hurted—mebbe deaded. I wants to take him away from dare," he burst forth. "We kids can't go off 'n' leave Mickey in dare wid de rich guys. Mickey didn't do no harm. He's jes tryin' to save de kid."

"Mickey. Is that the boy who took the shot in place of the little girl?"

The boy nodded and looked anxiously into the doctor's face. "Yep. Hev you been in dare? Did youse see Mickey? He's got yaller hair. Is Mickey deaded?"

"No, he isn't dead," said the physician, "but he's pretty badly hurt. The ball went through his shoulder and arm and came mighty near some vital places. I've just been fixing him up comfortably, and he'll be all right after a bit. But he's got to lie very still right where he is and be taken care of."

"We kids'll take care o' Mickey!" said Buck proudly. "He tooked care of Jinney when she was sick, an' we'll take care o' Mickey all right. You jes' brang him out, an' we'll fetch a wheelbarry an' cart him off'n yer han's. Mickey wouldn't want to be in dare wid de rich guys."

"My dear fellow," said the doctor, quite touched by the earnestness in Buck's eyes, "that's very good of you, I'm sure, and Mickey should appreciate his friends. But he's being taken care of perfectly where he is and can't be moved. It might kill him to move him, and if he stays where he is he'll get well. I'll tell you what I'll do," he added as he saw the lowering distress in the eyes before him. "I'll give you a bulletin every day. You be here tonight at five o'clock when I come out of the house, and I'll tell you how he is. Then you needn't worry about him. He's in a beautiful room lying on a big white bed and has everything nice around him, and when I came away he was sleeping. I can take him a message for you when I go in tonight, if you like."

Half doubtfully the boy looked at him.

"Will you tell Mickey to drop us down word ef he wants anythin'? Will you ask him ef he don't want us to get him out?"

"Sure!" said the doctor, amused. "You trust me, and I'll make good. Be here at five o'clock sharp and again tomorrow at a quarter to eleven."

"He's only a slum kid!" grumbled the officer. " 'Tain't worth-while to take so much trouble. 'Sides, the folks won't want um botherin' round."

"Oh, he's all right!" said the doctor. "He's a friend worth having. You might need one yourself someday. What's your name, boy? Who shall I tell Mickey sent the message?"

"Buck," said the child gravely. "Fightin' Buck, they call me."

"Very appropriate name, I'd think," said the doctor, smiling. "Well, run along, Buck, and be here at five o'clock."

Reluctantly the boy moved off. The officer again took up

his stand in front of the house, and quiet was restored to the street.

In the great house, meanwhile, consternation reigned.

The nursemaid had reached the door in time to hear the shot and see the children fall. She barely escaped the bullet herself. She was an old family servant and therefore more frightened for her charge than for herself. She had the presence of mind to drag both children inside the house and shut and lock the door immediately, before the seething mob could break in.

The mistress of the house fell in a dead faint as they carried her little daughter upstairs, and a man and a maid followed with the unconscious boy. The servants rushed about, while the housekeeper telephoned the bank president what had happened and sent for the family physician. No one knew yet who was hurt or how much. Mickey had been brought inside because he blocked the doorway, and they needed to shut the door. If it had been easier to shove him out, the nursemaid would probably have done that. But, once inside, humanity bade them look after the unconscious boy's needs. Besides, no one knew yet exactly what part Mickey had played in the morning's small tragedy.

"Where shall we take him?" said the man to the maid as they reached the second floor with their burden.

"Not here, Thomas. Here's no place for him. He's as dirty as a pig. I can't think what come over Morton to pull him inside anyway. His own could have tended to him. Besides, such is better dead!"

They hurried on past the luxurious rooms belonging to the lady of the mansion and up the next flight of stairs. Nora passed by the bathroom door where the full light of the hall windows fell on the grimy figure they carried and uttered an exclamation.

"He's not fit fer any place in this house. Look at his clothes.

They'll have to be cut off'n him, and he needs to go in the bathtub before he can be laid anywheres. Let's put him in the bathroom, and you call Morton. She got him in here, and she'll have to bathe him. And bring me a pair of scissors. I'll mebbe have to cut the cloes off'n him—they're so filthy. Ach! The little beast!"

Thomas, glad to be rid of his burden, dropped the boy on the bathroom floor and left to call Morton.

Nora, with little knowledge and less care, took no thought for her patient's life. She was intent on making him fit to put between her clean sheets. She found the tattered garments none, too tenacious in their hold to the little half-naked body. One or two buttons and a string were their only attachments. She pulled them off gingerly and, holding them at arm's length, took them to the bathroom window where she pitched them down into the paved court below that led to the kitchen regions. Thomas could burn them or put them on the ash pile. She was certain they'd never go on again and wondered how they'd held together this long.

Morton hadn't come yet, but Nora, discovering a pool of blood under the bare shoulder, lifted him quickly into the white bathtub and turned on the warm water. There was no use wasting time and getting blood on white tiles she'd have to scrub. She wasn't unkind, but she hated dirt. Supporting the child with one arm, she scrubbed him with the other hand. The shock of the water, cold at first, brought consciousness to the boy for a moment in one long shuddering sigh. The eyelashes trembled on the white cheeks, and his eyes opened. He gazed wildly on the strange surroundings, the water, and the vigorous Irishwoman who had him in her power.

He threw his arms up with a struggling motion, gasped as if with sudden pain, and lost consciousness again, relaxing once more into the strong red arm that held him. At this critical moment Morton entered the bathroom.

Morton was a trim, apple-cheeked Scotswoman of about thirty years, with neat yellow-brown hair coiled on top of her head, a cheerful tilt to her freckled nose, and blue eyes set in rosy cheeks. Integrity exuded from her being, flamed from her cheeks, spoke from her stubborn chin, and looked from her trustworthy eyes. She had been with the bank president's baby ever since the star-eyed creature entered the world.

"Och! Look ye at the poor wee'un!" she exclaimed. "Ye're hurtin' him, Nora! Ye shouldn't have bathed him the noo! Ye should've waited the docthur's comin'. Ye'll mebbe kin kill him."

"Ach! Get out with yer soft talk!" said Nora, scrubbing more vigorously. "Did yez suppose I'll be afther havin' all this filth in the nice clean sheets? Get ye to work an' he'p me. Do ye hold 'im while I schrub!"

She shifted the boy into the gentler arms of the nurse and splashed even harder. Then suddenly, before the nurse could protest, she'd dashed foamy suds on the golden head and was scrubbing that with all her might.

"Och, Nora!" cried the nurse in alarm. "You shouldn't 'a' done that! Ye'll surely kill the bairn. Look at his poor wee shoulder a bleedin', and his little face so white an' still. Have ye no mercy at all, Nora? Rinse off the suds at once an' dry him softly. What'll the docthur be sayin' to ye fer all this, I can't think. There, my poor bairnie," she crooned to the child, softly drawing him closer as though he were conscious. "There, my bairnie, it'll soon be over. It'll be all right in a minute, poor wee b'y! There—"

But Nora did her work and made the little lean body glistening white as polished marble, while the heavy hair hung limp like pale golden silk.

The two women carried him to a bed in a large room at the back of the house, not far from the nursery, and laid him on a blanket, with his shoulder stanched with soft linen rags.

Morton was softly drying his hair and crooning to the unconscious child, begging Nora to put the blanket over him lest he catch cold, and Nora was still drying his feet, unmindful of Morton's pleading, when the doctor entered with a trained nurse. The boy lay white and still upon the blanket as the two women, startled, drew back from their task. The body, clean now and beautifully shaped, might have been marble except for the delicate blue veins in wrists and temples. In spite of signs of privation and lack of nutrition, the boy showed strength in well-developed muscles, and it went to the heart to see him lying so helpless, with his drenched gold hair and his closed eyes. The white limbs didn't quiver, the lifeless fingers drooped limply, the white chest didn't stir with any sign of breath, and yet the curved lips hadn't altogether gone white.

"What a beautiful child!" exclaimed the nurse involuntarily as she came near the bed. "He looks like a young god!"

"He's far more likely to be a young devil," said the doctor grimly, leaning over him with practiced eyes and listening to the quiet chest. Then he started back.

"He's cold as ice! What have you been doing to him? It wasn't a case of drowning, was it? You haven't been giving him a bath at such a time as this, have you? Did you want to kill the kid outright?"

"Och, the poor wee b'y!" sobbed Morton under her breath, her blue eyes drenched with tears. "He's like to my own wee b'y I lost when he was a baby," she explained in apology to the trained nurse who wasn't, however, regarding her.

Nora had vanished, frightened, to consult with Thomas. Morton brought the things the doctor called for and showed the nurse where to put her belongings. And after everything was done and the boy was comfortable and brought back to consciousness, she stood at the foot of the bed and smiled at him when he opened his eyes.

His eyes were dark blue but wide with brave fear as he glanced about on the strange faces. He looked like a wild bird, whose instincts held him still because he saw no way of flight. He looked from side to side in the room and made a furtive motion to rise from the pillow. And in his glance were the gentle harmlessness and appeal of the winged thing that has been caught.

"Well, youngster, you had a pretty close shave," said the doctor jovially, "but you'll pull through all right! You feel comfortable now?"

"Poor wee b'y!" murmured Morton, her eyes drenched again.

The boy looked from one to another doubtfully. Suddenly he remembered and understood. He looked about the room and toward the door. His eyes turned to the doctor with a question, but his lips formed no words. He looked at Morton and knew her for his baby's nurse. Suddenly he smiled, and that smile seemed to light up the whole room, filling Morton's heart with joy. It seemed to her it was the smile of her own lost baby come back to shine upon her.

"Where's—de little kid?" He searched Morton's face anxiously as he framed the eager question.

"She's safe in her own wee crib takin' her morning nap. She's just new over," answered the woman reassuringly.

Still the eyes weren't satisfied.

"Did she," he began slowly, "get—hurted?"

"No, my bairnie, she's all safe and sound as ever. Your own self saved her life."

The boy's face lit up, as if to say, "Then I'm glad." But not a word did he speak.

"You're a hero, kid!" said the doctor huskily. But the boy knew little about heroes and didn't comprehend.

The nurse bustled up to take her place at the bedside, and Morton and the doctor left, the doctor stepping again into the lady's room below to see if she was feeling quite herself again after her faint.

The nurse leaned over the boy with a glass and spoon. He looked at it curiously. It was a situation entirely outside his experience.

"Why don't you take your medicine?" asked the nurse.

The boy looked at the spoon again as it approached his lips and opened them to speak.

"Is—"

In went the medicine, nearly choking the boy, but he understood and smiled.

"A hospital?" he finished.

The nurse laughed.

"No, it's only a house. They brought you in when you were hurt out on the steps. You saved the little girl's life. Didn't you know it?" she said kindly, her heart won by his smile.

A beautiful look rewarded her.

"Is de little kid—in this house?" he asked slowly, wonderingly.

"Oh, yes, she's here," answered the nurse lightly. "Perhaps they'll bring her in to see you sometime. Her father's very grateful. He thinks it showed wonderful courage for you to risk your life for her sake."

But Mickey understood nothing about gratitude. He only understood that the beautiful baby was in the house and might come there to see him. He settled to sleep with an occasional glad, wistful glance toward the door, as the long lashes sank on the white cheeks, for the first sleep the boy had ever taken in a clean, white, soft bed. The prim nurse, softened for once from her precise attention to duties, stood and looked upon the sleeping child's face, wondering what his life had been and how the future would be for him. She half pitied him that the ball hadn't gone nearer the vital spot and taken him to heaven before he missed the way, so angelic this face appeared in the soft light of the sickroom.

Chapter 2

Starr Endicott, sleeping in her lace-draped crib on her embroidered pillow, knew nothing of the hate and murder that rolled in a wave on the streets outside and had almost blotted out her life. She didn't know that the three notable families whose names were interwoven in her own and whose blood flowed in her tiny veins represented the great hated class of the rich and that those upon whom they'd climbed to this height looked upon them as an evil to be destroyed. Nor did she know that she, being the last and in her name representing them all, was hated most of all.

Starr Delevan Endicott! It was engraved on her tiny pins and locket, on the gold circling her finger, on her brushes and combs. It was embroidered on her dainty garments, coverlets, and cushions, and crooned to her by the adoring Scottish nurse who came of a line that knew and loved an aristocracy. The pride of the house of Starr, the wealth of the house of Delevan, the glory of the house of Endicott—weren't they all hers, this one beautiful baby who lay sleeping in her arms to tend and to love. So mused Morton as she hummed.

Oh, hush thee, my babie, thy sire was a knight,
    Thy mother a ladie, both gentle and bright—

And what did Morton care that the mother in this case was neither gentle nor bright, but only beautiful and selfish? It made the child dearer that she had her love to herself.

And so she laid little Starr in her crib; and the boy, her

preserver, from nobody knew where and of nobody knew what name of fame, lay sleeping also. And presently Delevan Endicott himself came to look at them both.

He came from the turbulent world outside and from his fretting, petted wife's bedside. She had been fussing at him for letting a bank in which he happened to be president do anything that would cause such a disturbance outside her home, when he knew she was so nervous. Not one word about the step that had stood for an instant between her baby and eternity. Her husband reminded her gently how near the baby had come to death and how she should rejoice that she was safe. But her reply had been a rush of tears and "Oh, yes, you always think of the baby—never of me, your wife!"

Sighing, the man had turned from his fruitless effort to calm her and gone to his little daughter. He'd hoped his wife would go with him, but he saw the uselessness of that. The little girl lay with one plump white arm thrown over her head, the curling baby fingers just touching her cheek, flushed with sleep. She looked like a rosebud among the rose and lacy draperies of her crib. Her soft, dark curls and long, dark curling lashes brought out each delicate feature of her face. The father, as he gazed down upon her, wondered how any creature, no matter how wicked, could desire to put out this life. His little Starr, his one treasure!

The man who had tried to do it—could he have intended it, or was it only a random shot? Those who saw judged it intention. The father's quickened heartbeats told him it was, and the thrust had gone deep. How they must hate him, and how they would have hurt his life irretrievably if the shot had done its work. If that other atom of human life hadn't intervened!

Where was the boy who had saved his child? He must see him at once. The gratitude of a lifetime should be his.

Morton divined his thought, as he stepped from the crib

after sweeping his lips over Starr's cheek. With silent tread she followed her master to the door.

"The poor wee b'y's in the far room yon," she whispered, and her tone implied that his duty lay next in that direction.

The banker had often noticed this gentle suggestion in the nurse's voice; it reminded him of something in his childhood, and he invariably obeyed it. He might have resented it if it had been less humble, less trustfully certain that of course that was what he meant to do next. He followed her direction now without a word.

The boy had just fallen asleep when he entered and lay as sweetly beautiful as the little beauty he'd left in the other room. The man of the world paused and exclaimed in wonder. He'd been told a little gamin had saved his daughter from the assassin's bullet, but this child's features were as delicately chiseled, his form as finely modeled, his hair as soft as any scion of a noble house might boast. He, like the nurse, felt that a young god lay before him. Mickey had always impressed a stranger thus, even when his face was dirty and his feet bare.

The man stood with bowed head and gazed upon the boy to whom he felt he owed a debt he could never repay.

He recognized the child as representing that great unwashed throng of humanity who were his natural enemies, because by their oppression and by stepping upon their rights when convenient he'd risen to where he now stood and could maintain his position. He had no special feeling for them, but this boy was different! This spirit-child with the form of Apollo, the beauty of Adonis, and the courage of a hero! Could he have come from the hotbeds of sin and corruption? Surely not! He must be of good birth. Inquiry must be made. Had anyone asked the child's name and where he lived?

Then, as if in answer to his thought, the dark blue eyes opened. He found them looking at him and started as he realized it. Yet he couldn't summon words but met the child's steady searching gaze, as if the eyes would see and understand the principles on which the man's life rested. The man felt it and had the sensation of hastily looking at his own motives in the light of this child's look. Would his life bear that burning appealing glance?

Then, unexpectedly, the child's face lit up with his wonderful smile. He'd decided to trust the man.

Never before in his proud and varied experience had Delevan Endicott encountered a challenge like that. It beat through him like a mighty army and took his heart by storm. It was the challenge of childhood to the fatherhood of man. With a strange new impulse the man accepted it and, struggling to find words, could only answer with a smile.

A good deal passed between them before any words were spoken, a good deal the boy never forgot and that the man liked to return to in his moments of self-reproach; for somehow that boy's eyes called forth the best in him and made him ashamed of other things.

"Boy, who is your father?" the man asked huskily at last. He almost dreaded to find another father owning a noble boy like this—and such a father as he would be if it were true he was only a street gamin.

The boy still smiled, but a wistfulness entered his eyes. He slowly shook his head.

"Dead, is he?" asked the man, more as if thinking aloud.

But the boy shook his head again. "No, no father," he answered simply.

"Oh," said the man, and a lump gathered in his throat. "Your mother?"

"No mother, never!" came the solemn answer.

It seemed he scarcely felt that either was a deep lack in his assets. Likely fathers and mothers weren't on the average desirable kindred in his neighborhood. The man reflected and tried again.

"Who are your folks? They'll be worried about you. We should send them word you're doing well."

The boy looked amazed. Then a laugh rippled out.

"No folks," he gurgled. "On'y jest de kids."

"Your brothers and sisters?" asked Endicott puzzled.

"None o' dem," said Mickey. "Buck an' me're pards. We fights fer de other kids."

"Don't you know it's wrong to fight?"

Mickey stared.

Endicott tried to think of something to add to his moral homily but couldn't.

"It's very wrong to fight," he reiterated lamely.

The boy's cherub mouth settled into firm lines.

"It's wronger not to, when de little kids is gettin' hurt an' de big fellers what ought ter work is stole away they bread, an' they's hungry."

It was an entirely new proposition. It was the challenge of the poor against the rich, the weak against the strong, and from the lips of a mere babe.

"I'd fight fer your little kid!" declared the young logician. He seemed to know by instinct this was the father of his baby.

Ah, now he had touched the responsive chord. The father's face lit up. He understood. Yes, it was right to fight for his baby girl, his Starr, his one treasure, and this boy had done it, given his life freely. Was that like fighting for those other unloved, uncared-for, hungry darlings? Were they then dear children, too, of somebody, of God, if nobody else? The boy's eyes were telling him in one long look that the world of children at least was kin, and the father felt that in mere decency of gratitude he must acknowledge so much. Poor hungry babies. What if his darling were hungry! A sudden longing seized him to give them bread at once. But at least he would shower his gratitude upon this one stray defender of their rights.

He struggled to find words to let the child know this, but the tears in his eyes spoke for him.

"Yes, my boy! You did fight for my little girl. I'll never forget it as long as I live. You saved her life, and that's worth everything to me. Everything, do you understand?"

At last the words rushed forth, but his voice was husky, and those who knew him would have declared him more moved than they'd ever seen him.

The boy understood. A slender hand stole out from the white coverlet and touched his. Its outline, long and graceful, spoke of patrician origin. It was hard for the man of wealth and pride to realize it was the hand of the child of the common people, the people who were his enemies.

"Is there anything you'd like to have done for you, boy?" he asked at last, because the depth of emotion was more than he could bear.

The boy looked troubled. "I was thinkin', ef Buck an' them could see me, they'd know 'twas all right. I'd like 'em to know how 'tis in here."

"You want me to bring them up to see you?"

Mickey nodded.

"Where can I find them, do you think?"

"Buck, he won't go fur, till he know what's comed o' me," said the boy with confidence in his friend. "He'd know I'd do that fer him."

Then honor and loyalty must exist among the lower ranks of men—at least among the boys. The man of the world was learning a great many things. Meekly he descended the two flights of stairs and went out to his own front doorstep.

There were no crowds anymore. The police were still on duty, but curious passersby dared not linger long. The workmen had finished the windows and gone. The man felt little hope of finding the boys, but somehow he had a strange desire to do so. He wanted to see that face light up again. Also, he had a curious desire to see these youngsters from the street who could provoke such loving anxiety from the hero upstairs.

Mickey was right: Buck wouldn't go far until he knew how it was with his comrade. He had moved off at the officer's word when the doctor promised to bring him word later, but he didn't intend to let a soul pass in or out of that house all day that he didn't see. So he set his young pickets here and there about the block, each with his bunch of papers, and arranged a judicious change occasionally, to avoid trouble with the officers.

Buck was standing across the street on the corner by the church steps, making a lively show of business now and then and keeping one eye on the house that had swallowed up his partner. He wasn't slow to perceive he was being summoned by a man on the steps and ran eagerly up with his papers, expecting to receive his coin and maybe a glimpse inside the door.

"All about der shootin' of der bank millionaire's baby!" he yelled in his most finished voice of trade, and the father, thinking of what might have been, felt a pang of horror at the careless words from the gruff voice.

"Do you know a boy named Buck?" he questioned as he paid for the paper that was held up to him and searched the unpromising face before him. Then he marveled at the sullen, sly change on the dirty face.

The black brows drew down forebodingly; the dark eyes reminded him of a caged lion ready to spring. The child had become a man with a criminal's face. There was something frightful about the defiant look with which the boy drew himself up.

"What if I does?"

"Only that a boy in here," he said, motioning toward the door, "would like very much to see him for a few minutes. If you know where he is, I wish you'd tell him."

Then came a change more marvelous than before. The

whole defiant face became eager, the black eyes danced with question, the brows settled into straight pleasant lines, and the mouth softened.

"Is't Mickey?" he asked earnestly. "Kin we get in? I'll call de kids. He'll want 'em. He allus wants der kids."

He placed his fingers in his mouth, stretched it, and issued forth a sound that might have come from an exulting fiend's mouth, so long and shrill it was. The man on the steps, his nerves already wrought to the snapping point, started angrily. Then suddenly around the corner at a swift trot emerged three ragged youngsters who came at their leader's command swiftly and eagerly.

"Mickey wants us!" explained Buck. "Now youse foller me 'n' don't say nothin' 'less I tell you."

They fell in line behind the bank president and followed, awed, within the portal that unlocked a palace more wonderful than Aladdin's to their astonished gaze.

Up the stairs they slunk, single file, silently and sleuthlike over the polished stairs. They skulked past open doors with frightened defiant glances, the defiance of the poor for the rich, born and bred from hunger, cold, and need of every kind. But they took it all in and for many days gave embellished details of the palace where Mickey lay. It seemed to them that heaven itself could show no grander sights.

In a stricken row against the wall, with sudden consciousness of their ragged caps in hands, grimy hands behind them, they stood and gazed upon their fallen hero-comrade.

They'd perhaps never seen his face clean before. His white robe seemed of unearthly whiteness. It dazzled them. His newly washed hair shone on his head. They saw him gathered into a different world from any they knew. How could he ever be theirs again? How could it have happened in the few hours since Mickey flashed past them and fell martyr to his kindly heart and saved the wicked rich man's child? Buck's brows drew together in his densest frown. He felt that their Mickey was having some terrible change come upon him.

Then Mickey turned and smiled at them and in his familiar voice shouted, "Say, kids, ain't this grand? Say, I jes' wish you was all in it! Ef you, Buck, an' the kids was here in this yer grand bed, I'd be havin' the time o' me life!"

That turned the tide. Buck swallowed hard and smiled his darker smile, and the rest grinned sheepishly. Grandeur and riches hadn't spoiled their prince. He was theirs still and wanted them. He'd sent for them. They gained courage to look around the spotlessly clean room—at the nurse in her crackling dignity; the dish of oranges she promptly handed to them and of which each in awe partook a golden sphere; the bright flowers Morton had placed on a stand by the bed; the pictures hanging on the walls; and then back to the white bed that held their companion. They couldn't get used to the whiteness and cleanness of his face and hands and bright gold hair. It burned like a flame against the pillow, and Mickey's blue eyes seemed darker and deeper than ever before. To Buck the children had given their obedient following and looked to him for protection, but after all he was one like them, only a little more fearless. To Mickey they gave a kind of farseeing adoration. He was fearless and brave like Buck, but he was something more. In their superstitious fear and ignorance he seemed to them almost supernatural.

They skulked silently down the stairs like frightened rabbits when the interview was over, each clutching his precious orange. Not until the great doors had closed upon them did they utter a word. They had said very little; Mickey had done all the talking. When they'd filed down the street behind their leader and rounded the corner out of sight of the house, Buck gathered them into a little knot.

"Kids, I bet cher Mick don't be comin' out o' this no more. Didn't you notice how he looked jes' like the angel o' the monemunt down at the cemetery?"

The group took on a solemnity that was deep and real.

"Anyhow, he wanted us!" spoke up a curly headed boy with old eyes and a thin face. Mickey had always defended him. He bore a hump on his ragged back.

"Aw! He's all right fer us, is Mick," said Buck, "but he's different. Old Aunt Sal said one day he were named fer an angel, an' like as not he'll go back where he b'longs someday, but he won't never fergit us. He ain't like rich folks what don't care. He's our pard allus. Come on, fellers."

Down the back alley went the solemn procession, single file, till they reached the rear of the Endicott house, where they stood silent. At a signal from their leader, each grimy right hand was raised, and each ragged cap taken off and held high in the air toward the upper window, where they knew their hero-comrade lay. Then they turned and marched silently away.

They were in place before the door whenever the doctor came, and they always went around by the way of the alley afterward for their ceremonial good night, sometimes standing solemnly beneath the cold stars while the shrill wind blew through their thin garments. But as long as the doctor brought them word, or as long as the light burned in the upper window, they felt their comrade hadn't gone yet.

Chapter 3

Heaven opened for Mickey on the day Morton, with the doctor's permission, brought baby Starr to see him.

The baby, in her nurse's arms, gazed down upon her rescuer with the unprejudiced eyes of childhood. Mickey's smile flashed upon her, and she answered with a joyous laugh. The beautiful boy pleased her. She reached out her hands to greet him.

The nurse held her down to the bed. "Kiss the wee b'y— that's a good baby. He took care of baby and saved her life when the bad man tried to hurt her. Kiss the wee b'y and say 'thank you.' "

The saving of her life meant nothing to Starr, but she obediently murmured, "Tank oo!" as the nurse had drilled her to do before she brought her. Then she laid her moist pink lips on cheeks, forehead, eyes, and mouth in turn, and Mickey, in ecstasy, lay trembling with the newness and pleasure of it. No one had ever kissed him before. Kissing was not in vogue in the street where he existed.

Thereafter, every day until he was convalescent, Starr came to visit him.

By degrees he grew accustomed to her presence enough to talk with her freely as child with child. Her words were few and her tongue as yet unacquainted with the language of this world. But perhaps that was better, for their conversations were more of the spirit than of the tongue, Mickey's language, of circumstance, being quite unlike that of Madison Avenue.

Starr brought her wonderful electric toys and dolls, and

Mickey looked at them in awe, yet always with a kind of rare indifference, because the child herself was to him the wonder of all wonders.

And every day, when the nurse carried her small charge away after her frolic with the boy, she would always lift her up to the bed and say, "Now kiss the wee b'y, baby Starr, and thank him again fer savin' yer life."

And Starr would lay her soft sweet mouth on his as tenderly and gravely as if she understood her obligation. At such times Mickey would watch her bright face as it came close to his, and when her lips touched his he would close his eyes as if to shut out all else from this sacred ceremony. After Starr and Morton were gone, the nurse would look furtively toward the bed and note the boy's still face, his eyes closed as if to hold the vision and memory longer. At such times her heart would draw her strangely from her formality to touch the boy with a tenderness unnatural to her.

Other times Mr. Endicott would come and talk briefly with the boy, just to see his eyes light and his face glow with that wonderful smile, and think what it would be if the boy were his own. Always Mickey enjoyed these talks, and when his visitor was gone, he would think with satisfaction that this was the right father for his Starr. He was glad she had a father. He'd often wondered what it would be like to have a father. Not that he felt a great need for one. He'd taken care of himself since he could remember and felt quite grown-up, and fathers usually drank. But a baby like that needed a father, and he liked Starr's father.

But the dearest thing now in life for him was little Starr's kisses.

To the father, drawn first by gratitude to the boy who had saved his child's life, and afterward by the boy's own irresistible smile, these frequent visits had become a pleasure. There had been a little boy before Starr came to their home, but he had lived only a few weeks. The memory of that golden, fuzzy head, the little fingers, the blue eyes of his son still lingered bitterly in the father's heart. When he first looked upon this waif, the notion seized him that perhaps his own boy would have been like this had he lived, and a strange and unexpected tenderness entered his heart for Mickey. He kept going to the invalid's room night after night, pleasing himself with the thought that the boy was his own.

This notion took such strong hold on the man's heart that he considered adopting the child and bringing him up as his own—this, after he had by the aid of detectives thoroughly searched out all that was known of him and found that no one owned Mickey or seemed to care what became of him except Buck and his small following. Meanwhile the child, well fed, well cared for, happier than he'd ever dreamed of being in his hard life, rapidly convalesced.

Endicott came home one afternoon to find Mickey down in the reception room dressed in black velvet and rare old lace, with his golden hair, which had grown during his illness, tortured into ringlets. An adoring group of ladies had gathered about him as he stood with troubled, almost haughty mien and gravely regarded their sentimentalities.

Mrs. Endicott had paid no attention to the boy before this, and her sudden interest in him came from a changed view of him as he sat up in a big chair for the first time, playing a game with Starr. His big eyes and beautiful hair attracted her at once, and she lost no time in dressing him up like a doll and making him a show at one of her receptions.

When her husband remonstrated with her, declaring that such treatment would ruin the spirit of any real boy and spoil him for life, she shrugged her shoulders indifferently.

"Well, what if it does? He's nothing but a foundling. He should be glad we were willing to dress him up prettily and play with him awhile."

"And what would you do with him after you were finished? Cast him aside?"

"Well, why not?" she said with another shrug. "Or perhaps we might teach him to be a butler or footman if you want to be benevolent. He'd be charming in a dark blue uniform!"

The woman raised her delicate eyebrows, humming a light tune, and her husband turned from her in despair. Was it nothing to her that this child had saved her baby's life?

That settled the question of adoption. His wife would never bring up the boy into anything like manhood. It was different with a girl—she must of necessity be frivolous, he supposed.

The next morning an old college friend entered his office, a plain man with a pleasant face, who hadn't gone from college days to a bank presidency. He was only a plain teacher in a struggling Florida college, and he came soliciting aid for the college.

Endicott turned from puzzling over Mickey to greet this old friend he hadn't seen for twenty years. He was glad to see him. He'd always liked him. He looked him over critically, however, from his successful-New-York-businessman point of view. He noticed the plain cheap business suit, worn shiny in places, the shoes well polished but breaking at the side, the sprinkling of gray hairs. Then his eyes traveled to his friend's kind, worn face, and he couldn't help feeling somehow that the man was happier than he was.

He asked many questions and found pleasure in hearing about the other's family and their happy united efforts to laugh off poverty and have a good time anyway. Then the visitor told of the college, its struggles; its great needs and small funds; how its orange crop, a large part of its regular income, had failed that year because of the frost; and they needed funds to carry on the work that school year. Endicott found his heart touched, though he didn't usually give large amounts to anything.

"I'd be glad to help you, Harkness," he said at last, "but I've got a private benevolence on my hands that will take a good deal of money, I'm afraid. You see we've narrowly escaped a tragedy at our house—" And he launched into the story of the shooting and his indebtedness to Mickey.

"I see," said the professor. "You feel you owe it to the lad to offer him a better life, since he freely risked his life for your child's."

"Exactly!" said Endicott. "I'd like to adopt him and bring him up as my own. But I don't think my wife would feel as I do about it, and I'm not sure I'd be doing the best for the boy. To be taken from one extreme to another might ruin him."

"Well, Endicott, why don't you combine your debt to the child with benevolence and send him down to us for a few years to educate?"

Endicott sat up interestedly.

"Could I do that? Would they take so young a child? He can't be over seven."

"Yes, we'd take him, I think. He'd be well cared for, and his tuition in the prep department would help the institution along. Every little bit helps, you know."

Endicott suddenly saw before him the solution to his difficulties. He entered eagerly into the matter, talking over rates, plans, and so on. An hour later it was settled. Mickey was to take a full course with his expenses prepaid and a good sum placed in the bank for his clothing and spending money. He was to have the best room the school afforded, at the highest price, and study music and art and everything else offered, for Endicott meant to do the handsome thing by the institution. The failure of the bank of which he was president hadn't affected his private fortune.

"If the boy doesn't seem to develop an interest in some of these branches, put some deserving one in his place and put him at something else," he said. "I want him to try everything, to develop the best in him. So we'll pay for everything you've got there, and that will help out some other poor boy perhaps; for of course one boy can't do everything. I'll arrange it with my lawyer that the payments shall be made regularly for the next twelve years, so that if anything happens to me, or if the boy runs away or doesn't turn out worthy, you'll keep on getting money just the same, and someone else can come in on it."

Professor Harkness went away from the office with a smile and in his pocket three letters of introduction to wealthy New York businessmen. Mickey was to go south with him the middle of next week.

Endicott went home that afternoon with a relieved mind, but in his heart he found a surprising reluctance to part with the boy.

When he told Mickey he was sending him to college and explained to him that an education would enable him to become a good man and perhaps a great one, the boy's face was grave. Mickey had never felt the need of an education, and the thought of leaving New York gave him a sensation as if the earth were tottering under his feet. He shook his head doubtfully.

"Kin I take Buck an' de kids?" he asked after a thoughtful pause and with a lifting of the cloud in his eyes.

"No," said Endicott. "It costs a good deal to go away to school, and there wouldn't be anyone to send them."

Mickey's eyes grew wide with something like indignation, and he shook his head.

"Den I couldn't go," he said decidedly. "I couldn't take nothin' great like that and not give de kids any. We'll stick together. I'll stay wid de kids. Dey needs me."

"But, Mickey—" Endicott said, looking into the large determined eyes and settling down for combat. "You don't understand, boy. It would be impossible for them to go. I couldn't send them all, but I can send you, and I'm going to, because you risked your life to save Starr."

"That wasn't nothin' 't all!" declared Mickey.

"It was everything to me," said the man, "and I want to do this for you. And, boy, it's your duty to take this. It's everybody's duty to take the opportunities for advancement that come to them."

Mickey looked at him thoughtfully. He didn't understand the large words, and duty meant to him a fine sense of loyalty to those who had been loyal to him.

"I got to stay wid de kids," he said. "Dey needs me."

Feeling it was useless to argue against the calmly stated fact, Endicott began again gently, "But, Mickey, you can help them a lot more by going to college than by staying at home."

The boy's eyes looked unconvinced, but he waited for reasons.

"If you become an educated man, you can earn money and help them. You can lift them up to better things, build good houses for them to live in, give them work to do that will pay good wages, and help them be good men."

"Is you educated?"

Thinking he was making progress, Endicott nodded eagerly.

"Is that wot you does fer folks?" The bright eyes searched his face.

The color flooded the bank president's cheeks and forehead.

"Well—I might—" he answered. "Yes, I might do a good deal for people, I suppose. I don't know if I do much, but I could if I were interested in them."

He paused. He realized the argument was weakened. Mickey studied his face.

"But dey needs me now, de kids does," he said gravely. "Jimmie, he don't have no supper most nights less'n I share, and Bobs is so little he can't fight dem alley kids. Sometimes I gets a flower off'n the florist's back door fer little sick Jane.

Her's got a crutch and can't walk much anyhow. And cold nights me an' Buck, we sleeps close. We got a box hid away where we sleeps close an' keeps warm."

The moisture gathered in the banker's eyes as he listened to the story. It touched his heart as nothing ever had. He resolved that after this, his education and wealth should at least help these slum friends of Mickey to an occasional meal or flower or warm bed.

"Suppose you get Buck to take your place with the kids while you go to school and get an education and learn how to help them better."

Mickey shook his head slowly. "Buck, he's got all he kin do to git grub for hisse'f an' his sister, Jane. His father is bad and kicks Jane and don't get her nothin' to eat. Buck, he has to see after Janie."

"How would it be for you to pay Buck something so he could take your place? I'll give you some money you may do with as you like, and you can pay Buck as much as you think he needs every week. You can send it to him in a letter."

"Would it be as much as a quarter?" Mickey held his breath in wonder.

"Two quarters if you like."

"Oh! Could I do that?" The boy's face fairly shone, and he came and threw his arms about Endicott's neck and laid his face against his. The man clasped him close and would fain have kept him there, for his well-ordered heart was deeply stirred.

Thus it was arranged.

Buck was invited to an interview. But when the silver half-dollar was laid in his grimy palm, and he understood that others would follow and he was to step up into Mickey's place in the community of the children while that luminary went to college to be educated, his face wore a heavy frown. He held out the silver sphere as if it burned him. *What! Take money in exchange for Mickey's bright presence? Never!*

It took a great deal of explanation to convince Buck that anything could be better "fer de kids" than their own Mickey, now and forever. But he was quick to see where the good lay for Mickey, and after a few plain statements from Mr. Endicott, no longer demurred. Buck was willing to give up Mickey for Mickey's good but not for his own. But it was a terrible sacrifice. The hard face knotted into a fierce expression when he came to say good-bye. The long scrawny throat worked convulsively; the hands gripped each other savagely. It was like handing Mickey over to a different world from theirs. He confidently promised to return to them as soon as the college completed its mysterious education and live with them as in the past, sleeping in Buck's box alongside him and taking care of the others when the big alley kids grew trouble-some. But somehow an instinct taught them he would never return again. They'd had him and would never forget him, but he would grow into a being far above them. They looked vin-dictively at the rich man who had perpetrated this evil device of a college life for their comrade. It was the old story of the helpless poor against the powerful rich. Even heartbeats didn't count against such power. Mickey must go.

They went to the station the morning Mickey was to depart and stood shivering and forlorn until the train was called. They listened sullenly while Professor Harkness told them that if they wished to be fit to associate with their friend when he came out of college, they must begin at once to improve their opportunities. First they must go to school and study hard, and then their friend in college would be proud to call them friends.

They didn't think it worthwhile to tell the kind but igno-rant professor that they had no time for school and no clothes to wear if they had the time or inclination to go. Schools were everywhere and free, of course, but it didn't touch them. They lived in dark places and casual crannies, like weeds or vermin. No one cared whether they went to school. No one suggested it. They would have as soon thought of entering a mansion and insisting on their right to live there as to present themselves at school. Why, they had to hustle for a mere existence. They were the water rats, the bad boys, the embryo criminals for the next generation. The problem with any who thought of them was how to get rid of them. But of course this man from another world didn't understand. They merely looked at him dully and wished he would walk away and leave Mickey to them while he stayed. His presence made it seem as if their companion had already left them.

It was hard, too, to see Mickey dressed like the Fifth Avenue boys, handsome trousers and coat, a thick overcoat, a hat on his hair that had always been capless, thick stockings and shining shoes on his feet that had always been bare and soiled with the street grime—and gloves on his hands. This was a new Mickey. "The kids" didn't know him. In spite of their best efforts, they couldn't be natural. Great lumps arose in their throats, lumps that never dared arise for hunger or cold or curses at home.

They stood helpless, and Mickey, sensing the trouble, thought to give his comrades some clothing article as a remembrance. Mr. Endicott came upon the scene in time to keep Mickey from taking off his overcoat and enveloping Buck in its folds. He was eagerly telling them Bobs should have his undercoat, Jimmie his hat, and Jane his gloves, and only his stockings and shoes were left for Sam. But he gave them willingly. He saw no reason why he couldn't travel hatless, coatless, barefoot, and bare-handed; for hadn't he gone that way throughout his existence? It was a small thing to do for these friends he was leaving for a long time.

The bright face clouded when he was told he couldn't give these things away, that it wouldn't be fair to the kind professor to ask him to carry with him a boy improperly dressed. But he smiled again trustfully when Endicott promised to take the whole group to a clothing house and fit them out.

They bade Mickey good-bye, pressing their grimy noses against the station gate bars to watch their friend disappear from their lives.

Endicott himself felt like crying as he came back from seeing the boy aboard the train, knowing he wouldn't meet the bright smile that night when he went home.

But it wasn't the way of "the kids" to cry when tragedy fell among them. They didn't cry now. When he returned to them, they regarded the banker with lowering brows as the originator of their bereavement. They had no faith in the promised clothing.

"Aw, what's he givin' us!" Buck had breathed under his breath. But to do Buck credit he hadn't wanted to take Mickey's coat from him. When their comrade went from them into another walk in life he must go proudly appareled.

Endicott led the huddled group away from the station to a clothing house and amused himself by fitting them out. The garments weren't of as fine material or elegant a cut as those he'd purchased for Mickey's outfit, but they were warm and strong and wonderful to their eyes. One by one the grimy urchins went into a little dressing room, presently emerging with awe upon their faces to stand before a tall mirror surveying themselves.

Endicott presently bade them farewell and, with a conscience at ease with himself and all mankind, left them.

They issued from the clothing house with scared expressions and walked solemnly a few blocks. Then Buck called them to a halt before a plate-glass show window.

"Take a good look at yersel's, kids," he ordered, "an' we'll go up to the park an' shine around an' see how ther swells feels. Then we'll go down to Sheeny's an' sell 'em."

"Sell 'em! Can't we keep 'em?" demanded Bobs, who had never felt warm in winter in his small life.

"You wouldn't hev 'em long," sneered Buck. "That father o' yourn would hev 'em pawned afore night. You better enjoy 'em awhile, an' then git the money. It's safer!"

The children with wisdom born of their unhappy circumstances recognized the truth. They surveyed themselves gravely in their fleeting grandeur and then turned to walk up to the aristocratic part of town, a curious procession. They finished by rounding the Madison Avenue block, marched up the alley, and gave the salute with new hats toward the window where their prince and leader used to be. He was no longer there, but his memory was about them, and the ceremony did their bursting hearts good. Their love for Mickey was the noblest thing that had so far entered their lives.

Jimmie suggested they must let Jane see them before they disposed forever of their elegant garments. So Bobs, minus coat, hat, stockings, and shoes, was sent to bid her to a secluded retreat at the far end of the alley. He hurried back ahead of her tapping crutch to don his fine attire before she arrived.

Little Jane, with sallow face, unkempt hair, and tattered clothing; shivering in the cold twilight, stood and watched the procession of pride as it passed and repassed before her delighted eyes. The festivity might have been prolonged, but the voice of Bobs's father reeling into the alley struck terror to their hearts. They scuttled away to the pawnshop, leaving Jane to hobble back alone to her cellar and wonder how it would feel to wear a warm coat like one of those.

"Say!" said Jimmie as they paused before the shop door and looked reluctantly down at their brief glory. "I wisht we could keep jest one coat fer Janie!"

"Couldn't we hide it some'eres?" asked Sam, and they all looked at Buck.

Buck, deeply touched for his sister's sake, nodded.

"Keep Jim's," he said huskily. "It'll do her best."

Then they filed proudly in and gave up their garments to the human parasite who lived on other men's souls. They came away bearing the one coat they'd saved for Jane, each treasuring a pitiful bit of money which seemed a fortune in their eyes.

Jane received her gift with true spirit, skillfully hid it from her inhuman father, and declared that each boy should have a turn wearing the coat every Sunday at some safe hour; so deep satisfaction reigned among them. Their grandeur wasn't departed after all.

Meanwhile, Mickey, in his luxurious berth in a sleeper, smiled drowsily as he thought of the fine new clothes his friends must be wearing and then fell asleep to dream of little Starr's kisses on his closed eyelids.

Chapter 4

$\mathcal{M}$ ickey entered a new world of blue skies, songbirds, and high, tall pines with waving moss and dreamy atmosphere, with plenty to eat and wear and with light and joy and ease.

Yet the world bewildered the boy, and for the first week he stood off and regarded it suspiciously. True, there were no dark cellars or freezing streets, no drunken fathers or frightened children or blows or hunger or privation. But this education he'd come to seek, so he might return to his own world and better it, wasn't a garment one put on and exercised in so many times a day. Nor was it a cup from which one drank or an atmosphere one absorbed. It was a strange, imperceptible thing got at in some mysterious way by a series of vague struggles followed by sudden and almost alarming perceptions.

For a time it seemed to the boy, keen though his mind, that knowledge was granted only to the few, and his was a mind that would never grasp it. How, for instance, did one know how to make just the right figures under a line when one added a long perplexity of numbers? Mickey the newsboy could tell like a flash how much money to return to the stout gentleman who occasionally gave him a five-dollar bill to change on Broadway. But Mickey the scholar, though he knew figures and could study out with labor easy words in his papers, had never heard of adding up figures in the way they did here, long rows of them on the blackboard. He needed private instruction before he could enter classes.

Professor Harkness himself undertook the task and gradually

revealed to the child's neglected understanding some of the rudiments that would enable his further progress. The sum paid for his tuition necessitated that the boy advance reasonably, for his benefactor had made it understood he might someday visit the institution and see how he was progressing. Some great pains were taken to enlighten Mickey's darkness.

Nor could the boy understand the discipline that ruled everywhere. He'd always been a law unto himself, his only care being to keep out of the way of those who would interfere with this. Now he must rise with a bell, stay in his room until another bell, eat at a bell, and even play ball when the recreation bell rang. It was hard for an independent spirit to get used to all this, and while he had no mind to be disorderly, he often directly disobeyed the law from sheer misunderstanding of the whole regime.

The boys' dormitory was presided over by a woman who, while thorough in all housekeeping arrangements, had certainly mistaken her calling as a substitute mother for boys. She kept their clothes in order, their rooms aired, their stockings darned, and their lights out at exactly half-past nine. But her grim countenance forbade any familiarity, and she never thought of gaining the confidence of her rough, but affectionate, charges. Mickey never felt like smiling in her presence. He came and went with a sort of high, unconscious superiority that almost irritated the woman, because she wasn't great enough to see the child's unusual spirit and as a consequence didn't win his heart.

But he didn't miss her lack of motherliness, for he'd never known a mother and wasn't expecting it.

The professors he grew to like, some more, some less, always admiring the most those who seemed to deal fairly with their classes—fairness being judged by the code in use among "the kids" in New York. But that was before he knew the president. After that his code changed.

His first interview with that dignitary was on an afternoon when he'd been overheard by the matron using vile language among the boys at the noon hour. She hauled him up with her most severe manner and told him he must answer to the president for his conduct.

As Mickey had no conception of his offense, he went serenely to his fate, walking affably beside her, only wishing she wouldn't look so sour. As they crossed the campus to the president's house, a blue jay flew overhead, and a mockingbird trilled in a live oak nearby. The boy's face lit with joy, and he laughed gleefully. But the matron only looked more severe, for she thought him a hardened sinner defying her authority and laughing her to scorn. After that it was two years before she could believe anything good of Mickey.

The president was a noble-faced, white-haired scholar, with a firm, tender mouth and understanding eyes. He wasn't the kind who won by great athletic prowess; he was an old-fashioned gentleman, well along in years, but young in heart. He looked at the child of the slums and saw the angel in the clay.

He dismissed the matron with a pleasant assurance and took Mickey to an inner office where he let the boy sit quietly waiting a few minutes till he finished writing a letter. If the pen halted and the kind eyes studied the child's beautiful face, Mickey never knew it.

The president asked the boy to tell him what he'd said, and Mickey repeated innocently the terrible phrases he'd used, phrases familiar to him since boyhood, conveying statements of facts that were horrible but nevertheless daily happenings in the corner of the world where he'd brought himself up.

With rare tact the president questioned the boy, until he made sure there was no inherent rottenness in him. Then kindly, but firmly, he laid down the law and explained why it was right and necessary for such a law. He spoke of God's purity. Mickey knew nothing of God and listened with quiet interest. The president talked of education and culture and made matters very plain. When the interview was concluded and the man asked the boy for a pledge of good faith and clean language from then on, Mickey's smile of approval blazed forth, and he laid his hand in the president's readily enough and left the room secretly admiring the man. The whole conversation had appealed to him deeply.

Mickey sought his room and laboriously spelled out with lately acquired clumsiness a letter to Buck:

> *Dear Buck we mussent yuz endecent langwidg enny moor ner swar. God donte lyk it an' it ain't educated. I want you an' me to be educate. I ain't gone to, donte yoo ner let de kids.*
>
> *Mickey*

In due time, according to previous arrangement about the monthly allowance, this letter reached Buck. He tracked the doctor for two whole days before he located him and lay in wait till he came out to his carriage, when he got up his nerve to hand over the letter to be read.

The doctor, deeply touched, translated as best he could. Buck's education had been pitifully neglected. He watched the mystic paper in awe as the doctor read.

"Wot's indecent langwidg?" he asked with his heavy frown.

The doctor took the opportunity to deliver a brief sermon on purity, and Buck, without so much as an audible thank you but with a thoughtful air that pleased the doctor, took back his letter, stuffed it into his ragged pocket, and went his way. The man watched him wistfully, wondering whether Mickey's appeal could reach the boy and, sighing, went away to try to make a few things better.

That night "the kids" gathered in front of Jane's window, for she was too weak to go out with them, and Buck delivered a message on ethical culture. Whatever Mickey, their prince, ordered, that must be done, and Buck was doing his level best, although for the life of him he couldn't see the sense in it. But thereafter none of "the kids" was allowed to use certain words and phrases, and swearing gradually disappeared from their conversation. It would have been a curious study for a linguist to observe just what words and phrases were cut out and what allowed to flourish unrebuked; but nevertheless it was a reform, and Buck was doing his best.

With his schoolmates Mickey held a high position from the first. His clothes were good, and he always had a little money to spend. One of Endicott's wishes was that the boy should be like other boys. It meant something among a group of boys, most of whom were the sons of rich fathers. Moreover, he was brave beyond anything they'd seen, could fight like a demon in defense of a smaller boy, and didn't shrink from pitching into a fellow twice his size. He could tell all about the New York City baseball and football games, knew the pitchers by name, and yet didn't boast uncomfortably. He could swim like a duck and dive fearlessly. He could outrun them all by his lightness of foot and was an expert in gliding away from any hand that sought to hold him back.

His peculiar street slang didn't trouble them in the least, nor his lack of class standing, though that presently became a thing of the past. Mickey, as soon as he understood the way, marched up the hill of knowledge, taking in everything handed to him and assimilating it. It began to look as if no leftover courses in the curriculum might be given to some other deserving youth. Mickey would need them all. The president and the professors became deeply interested in this boy without a past. Everywhere, with everyone, Mickey's smile won his way, except with the matron who hadn't forgiven him because her recommendation of his instant dismissal from the college hadn't been accepted.

The boys hadn't asked many questions about him nor been told much. They knew his father and mother were dead. They thought he had a rich guardian, perhaps a fortune coming someday, but they didn't care. Mickey never spoke about these things, and a strange reticence about him made them dislike to ask him questions, even when they knew him well. He was entered under the name Endicott; on questioning him, Professor Harkness found he could lay no greater claim to any other surname and called him that until he could write to Mr. Endicott for advice. He neglected to write at once and then, the name having become fastened upon the boy, thought it best to let the matter alone since there was little likelihood of Mr. Endicott's coming down to the college, and it could do no harm. He never thought out possible future complications, and the boy became known as Michael Endicott.

But his companions, as boys will, thought the matter over and rechristened him "Angel." So Angel, or Angel Endy, he became, to the end of his college course.

One delight of his new life was his outdoor freedom. A beautiful lake spread its silver sheet at the foot of the campus slope, and here the boy revelled in swimming and rowing. The whole country around was filled with wonder to his city-bred eyes. He attached himself to the natural sciences teacher and took long silent tramps for miles. They penetrated dense hammocks, gathering specimens of rare orchids and exquisite flowers; they stood motionless and breathless for hours watching and listening to some strange wild bird; they became familiar with slimy coiling serpents in dark bogs and green lizards and black velvet spiders; they brought home ravishing butterflies and moths of pale green, gold, and crimson. Mickey's room became a museum of curious, wonderful things, and he an authority on a wide range of topics.

The new life with plenty of wholesome food, fresh air, good sleep, and happy exercise was developing the young body into strength and beauty, even as study and contact with life were developing the mind. Mickey grew up tall, straight, and strong. In all the school, even among the older boys, was none so perfectly developed. In his face were strength, simplicity, and character. With the acceptance of his new moral code according to the president, a look of high moral purpose had grown. No boy in his presence dared use language not up to the standard. No boy with his knowledge dared do a mean or wrong thing. And yet, in spite of this, every boy admired him and was more or less led by him. If he'd been one whit less brave, one shade more conscious of self and self's interests, one bit conceited, this would not have been. But from being a dangerous experiment in their midst, Mickey became known as a great influence for good. The teachers saw it and marvelled. The matron saw it and finally, though grudgingly, accepted it. The president saw it and rejoiced. The students saw it not but acknowledged it in their lives.

Mickey's flame of gold hair grew more golden and flaming with the years. When his ball team played in a nearby town, Mickey was sighted by the crowd and pointed out at once.

"Who's that boy with the golden hair?" someone would ask a team member.

"That? Oh, that's the Angel! Wait till you see him play!" would be the reply. And he became known among outsiders as the Angel with the golden hair.

At a game a listener would hear, "Oh, see! There'll be something doing now. The Angel's at bat!"

Yet in spite of all this, the boy lived a lonely life. Giving himself continually to those about him, receiving in turn their love and devotion, he yet felt set apart from them. Occasionally some boy's father or mother, or both, or a sister or little brother would come down for a trip through the South. Then that boy would be excused from classes and go off with his parents for perhaps a week, or they'd visit him every day. And Michael would look on and see the love-light beaming in their eyes. That would never be for him. No one had ever loved him like that.

Sometimes he would close his eyes and try to return in memory to the time he was shot and the wonder of the soft bed, the room, and little Starr's kisses. But the years were multiplying now, and room and nurse and all were growing dim. Only Starr's kisses remained, a delicate fragrance of baby love, the only kisses the boy had ever known.

One day, when a classmate had been telling of his father's arrival and what it would mean to him, Michael went into his room and, locking his door, sat down and wrote a stiff school-boy letter to his benefactor, thanking him for all he'd done for him. It told briefly, shyly, of a faint realization of what he'd been saved from, showed a proper respect and desire to make good, and touched the heart of the busy man who'd almost forgotten about the boy. But it didn't hint of the heart hunger which had prompted his writing.

The next winter, when Michael was seventeen, Delevan Endicott and his daughter, Starr, took a flying trip through the South, stopping for a night and day at the college.

The president told Michael of his expected coming. Professor Harkness had gone north on school business.

The boy received the news quietly enough, with one of his brilliant smiles, but went to his room with a tumult of wonder, joy, and almost fear in his heart. Would Mr. Endicott be as he remembered: kind, interested, and helpful? Would he be pleased with the progress his protégé had made, or would he be disappointed? Would there be any chance to ask after little Starr? She was a baby still in the boy's thoughts; yet of course she must have grown. And so many things might have happened—she might not be living now. No one would think or care to tell him.

Baby Starr! His beautiful baby! He exulted that he'd flung

his useless life once between her lovely presence and death! He'd do it again gladly now if that would repay all her father had done for him. Michael the youth was beginning to understand what that meant.

His other friends, Buck, Jimmie, Bobs, and the rest, were still enshrined in his faithful heart, though their memory had dimmed with the years. Faithfully every month the boy had sent Buck two dollars from his pocket money, his heart swelling with pleasure that he was helping those he loved. But only twice had word come back from that far city where he'd left them. In answer to the letter the doctor had translated for them, a brief laborious epistle had come, terse and to the point, written with a pencil stub on the corner of a piece of wrapping paper and addressed by a kind clerk at the post office where Buck bought the stamped envelope. It was the same clerk who usually paid to the urchin his monthly money order, so he knew the address. To indite the letter Buck went to night school two whole weeks before he could master enough letters and words to finish it to his satisfaction. It read:

Deer Mik WE WunT
Buck

The significant words filled the boy's heart with pride over his friend whenever he thought of it, even sometime later. He had faith in Buck. In his mind Buck seemed to be growing and keeping pace with him, and he never dreamed that if Buck saw him now he wouldn't recognize him.

When Mickey had been in Florida several years, another letter came from Buck addressed in the same way, and little better written than the other. Night school had proved too strenuous for Buck; besides, he felt he knew enough for all practical purposes, and it wasn't likely he'd need to write many letters. This occasion, however, called for one.

Dear Mickey,

Jany is DEAD sHe sayd tell yo hur LUV beeryd hur in owr kote we give hur ther wuz a angle wit pink wins on top uv the wite hurs an a wite hors we got a lot uv flowers by yur money so yo needn sen no more money kuz we ken get long now til yo cum.

BUCK

After that, though Michael had written as usual every month, for some time no reply came, and the money orders were returned to him as not called for. Buck in his simplicity evidently took it for granted Mickey wouldn't send the money and came no more to the office. At least that was how Michael solved it, and in his heart he vowed to hunt up Buck the minute he was through at college and free to return to New York and help his friends. Meanwhile, though the years had dimmed those memories of his old life, and the days went forward in study, he always kept in view his intention of one day going back to better his native community.

But Mr. Endicott's coming was a great event to the boy. He could scarcely sleep the night before the expected arrival.

Prior to the evening meal, the through train from New York reached the station. Michael was given the privilege of going to meet his benefactor.

Tall and handsome he stood on the platform as the train rushed into the town, his cheeks glowing from excitement, his eyes bright with anticipation, his cap in his hand, and the last rays of the setting sun glowing in his golden hair. When Endicott saw him he exclaimed mentally over his strength and manly beauty, and more than one weary tourist leaned from the open car window and gazed, for something strange and compelling about Michael reminded one of an angel.

Chapter 5

*M*ichael met Mr. Endicott unembarrassed. His early New York life had given him a self-poise that nothing seemed to disturb. But when the father introduced his young daughter, the boy caught his breath and gazed at her with deepening color and intense delight.

She was here then, his Starr! She'd come to see him and looked as he would have her look. He hadn't realized before that she'd be grown up, but of course she would, and the change in her didn't shock his memory. The clear white of her skin with its fresh coloring was the same. New York life hadn't made it sallow. The roses were still in her cheeks. Her eyes were the same, dark and merry, and looked at him straight, unabashed, with the ease of a girl trained by a society mother. Her dark curls were longer, hanging to the slender waist and crowned with a fine wide Panama hat. She gave him a little gloved hand and said, "I'm afraid I don't remember you very well, but Daddy has been telling me about you, and I'm very glad to see you."

She was only a little over twelve, but she spoke with ease and simplicity, and for the first time in his life Michael felt self-conscious. She was so perfect, lovely, finished in expression and movement. She looked at him intelligently, politely curious, and no longer with baby eyes. He couldn't help wondering what she must think of him, and for a few minutes he grew shy before her.

Mr. Endicott was surprised and pleased at the boy's appearance. The passing years had easily erased the tender feelings

Mickey the street urchin had stirred in his heart. This visit to
the school and college wasn't so much because of the boy, to
whom he felt he'd discharged his duty, but because of the repeated invitations of Professor Harkness and the president. It
didn't go against him to see the institution he'd from time to
time contributed to, with his liberal allowance for the boy's
education. It was convenient for him to stop, being on the
regular route he'd planned for his southern trip. He'd left his
wife at Palm Beach with her fashionable friends and, with
Starr as his companion, the father toured the Orange Belt with
a view to investments. It suited him to stop off and receive
the thanks of the college; so he stopped. Not that he was a
heartless man, but so many things in his world made him forget, and most of us appreciate a little pleasant adulation.

But when Michael stood before him with the deference of
more than a son, his heart suddenly leaped back to the day
when he'd first gazed upon the little white face on the pillow,
when the blue eyes had opened, and Mickey had smiled.
Michael smiled now, and Endicott became aware at once of
the subtle fascination of that smile. And now the thought presented itself, *What if this were my son! How proud I'd be of him!*

Michael was indeed good to look upon, even to the city
critic's eyes. Endicott had left orders with his tailor for a full
outfit to be sent to the boy, spring and fall, or suitable plain
clothing for a schoolboy, little realizing how unnecessary it
was to have dressed him so well. The tailor had taken the
measurements sent to him yearly in answer to the firm's letter
and kept Michael looking as well as any rich man's son
desired to look. Not that the boy knew or realized. The
clothes came to him, like his board and tuition, and he took
them well pleased and wrote his best letter of thanks each
year as Professor Harkness suggested. But he had no idea that
part at least of his leadership power with the schoolboys was
due to his plain though stylishly cut garments. This fact

wouldn't have counted for anything with boys who had been living in Florida for years, for any plain decent clothes were thought fit, no matter how they were cut. But the school's patronage was at least half rich men's sons sent south for a few years to a milder climate for their health. These as a rule, when they came, had exaggerated ideas of the importance of clothes and prevailing modes.

So Michael didn't look like a dowdy country boy to his benefactor but presented a remarkable contrast to many boys Endicott was acquainted with at home. Something about Michael, even as a small lad, commanded marked attention from all who saw him. This attention Endicott and his daughter gave now as they walked beside him in the sunset glow and listened as he pointed out the various spots of interest in the college town.

The institution boasted of no carriage, and the single horse car that traveled to the station belonged to the hotel and its guests. The walk wasn't long, however, and gave the travelers an opportunity to breathe the clear air and feel the evening stillness.

Starr, walking on the inside of the board sidewalk, looked down at the small pink and white and crimson pea blossoms growing everywhere and then up at the tall pines and felt an awe. Her only day at Palm Beach had been so filled with hotels, people, and automobiles that she'd had no opportunity to realize the land's tropical nature. But here in this quiet spot, where the tiny station, the post office, the grocery, and a few scattered dwellings, with hotel lights gleaming in the distance, seemed all there was of human habitation, she suddenly realized the difference from New York.

Michael had recovered his poise as soon as she no longer faced him, though he was profoundly conscious of her presence on her father's other side. But he talked easily and well. Yes, the hotel held five hundred guests and was pretty well filled at this season. Some distinguished people were stopping there. The railroad president's private car had stood on the track for a few hours last week. That car over on the side belonged to a steel magnate. The other one had brought the wife of an inventor. Off toward the sunset were the school and college buildings. No, they couldn't be seen until one passed the orange grove. Too bad there was no conveyance. But the one little car turned off toward the hotel at this corner, and the school's one beast of burden, a mule—Minus, by name, because he wasn't so many things—was lame today and couldn't be requisitioned to bring the guests from the station.

Mr. Endicott felt he was drawing nearer to nature in this quiet walk than he had since he was a boy and visited his grandfather's farm. It rested and pleased him, and he was charmed with his protégé. His frank, simple conversation was free from all affectation or from any hint of his low origin. The man felt already that he'd done a good thing in sending the boy here to be educated. It was worth the little money he'd put into it.

Starr watched Michael shyly from the shelter of her father's side and listened to him. He wasn't like the boys she met in New York. He was fine-looking and possessed both strength and kindness in his face. Above all, his smile and firm chin made her feel he was nobler than most she knew. Something about him made her know he had a greater purpose in life than his own pleasure. Not that she thought this out. Starr had never learned to think. She only felt it as she looked at him and liked him at once. Moreover, she sensed some glamour about the boy, for her father had just told her how he'd saved her life when she was small. She felt a prideful proprietorship in him that made her shy in his presence.

At the college president's gate, on the edge of the campus, the president came out with his apologies. He had been detained on business at the county seat ten miles away and drove home with a friend whose horse was slow. He was sorry not to have shown courtesy to their honored guests by meeting them at the station. Endicott walked with the president after the greetings, and Michael dropped behind with Starr and eagerly pointed out to her the buildings.

"That's the chapel, and beyond are the study and recitation rooms. The next is the dining hall and servants' quarters, and over on that side of the campus is our dormitory. My window looks down on the lake. Every morning I go swimming before breakfast."

"Oh, aren't you afraid of alligators?" Starr asked, startled.

Michael looked at her with a tender protectiveness.

"No," he answered without laughing, as other boys would have at her girlish fears, "they never bother us here. Besides, I'm sort of acquainted with them. I'm not afraid of them. Nothing will hurt you if you understand it well enough to look out for its rights."

"Oh!" said Starr, eyeing him in wonder. As if an alligator had rights! What a strange, interesting boy. The idea of understanding an alligator. She was about to ask how understanding the creature would keep one from being eaten up when Michael pointed to the crimson west.

"See!" he said. "The sun is almost down. Don't you love to watch it? In a minute more it will be gone, and then it'll be dark. Hear that evening bird? *'Tit-wiloo! Tit-wiloo!'* He sings sometimes late at night."

Starr followed his words and saw the sun slipping like a ruby disc behind the fringe of palm, pine, and oak bordering the lake below the campus. She saw the wild bird dart from the thicket into the clear amber sky above, utter its sweet weird call, and drop again into the fine brown shadows of the living picture. And she watched as the sun slipped lower to the half now, and now less than half.

Breathless they stood and let the two men go on ahead,

while they watched the day turn into night. The brilliant crimson poured itself away to her lands, till only a rim of glowing garnet remained; then, like a living thing dying into another life, it, too, dropped away, and all was night.

"Why! How dark it is!" exclaimed Starr as she turned and found she could scarcely see his face. "Where's the twilight? Is anything the matter? I never saw it get dark all at once like this!" She peered around into the strange velvet darkness.

"No, that's all right," Michael assured her. "That's the way we do here. Almost everybody from the North speaks about it at first. They can't understand it. It's the difference in the position of the sun, nearer the equator, you know. I'll show you on the chart in the astronomy room if you like. We haven't any twilight here. It would seem odd. You wouldn't know when night began and day ended. I don't remember it when I lived in New York. Look up there! That's the evening star! It's come out for you tonight—to welcome another—Starr!"

They walked silently through the warm darkness, with Michael touching the young girl's elbow distantly, reverently, to guide her, until they entered the circle of light from the open door, and matron and teachers came out to welcome the young stranger and bring her into the house.

Michael lingered a moment by the door, watching her as she went, her sweet face wreathed in smiles, with the matron's thin arm around her and a new, gentle look upon that one's severe countenance. He watched until they mounted the stairs out of sight.

Outside, he removed his cap and stood looking up at the star, communing with it perhaps about the human Starr that had come back to him out of the shadows of the past.

And she was a star. All who saw her acknowledged it. He marveled as he recalled the change in the matron's face and because of her gentleness to the little girl forgave her all she hadn't been to his motherless boyhood.

Starr came down to dinner in a few minutes radiant in a rosy dress of soft Eastern silk, girdled with a fringed scarf of the same and a knot of coral velvet in her hair. From the string of pearls about her white neck to the dainty point of her slipper she was exquisite, and Michael watched her with open admiration. The long lashes drooped shyly over the girl's rosy cheeks, and she was pleased.

She sat at her father's side to the president's right, with Michael across the table. He bore well Endicott's scrutiny as his keen eyes searched the boy's face throughout the conversation.

That evening passed like a dream, and Michael lay awake again that night anticipating the next day. At last he had some people who in a way he might call his own. They'd cared to come and see him after all the years! His heart swelled with joy and gratitude.

The guests attended chapel exercises with the students the next morning, and Michael saw with pride his companions' eyes turn toward the beautiful young girl and then at him almost enviously. The color mounted into his young face, but he sat so quietly no one would have guessed the tumult running riot in his veins. He felt it was the happiest day of his life.

After chapel, the guests were shown about the college buildings and campus. The president and Endicott walked ahead, Michael behind with Starr, answering her questions.

They'd been through all the classrooms, the gymnasium, the dining hall, servants' quarters, and dormitories. They'd visited the athletic grounds and the tennis courts and walked by the lake, where Michael had taken them out for a short row. Returning, they were met by a professor who suggested they hear some of the classes recite and so turned their steps toward the recitation hall.

"I think you must be very brave," Starr said. "To think you saved my life that way when you were just a little fellow!"

She looked up, her face full of childish feeling.

Michael smiled at her and wondered if any eyes were as beautiful as those before him. The president's daughter was stout and a romp; she never took time to look at the boys. And the professors' daughters were quiet and studious; they paid little attention to the boys.

"I want to thank you for what you did," Starr continued. "Only I can't think of any words great enough to tell you how I feel about it. I wish I could do something to show you how I thank you."

She lifted her eyes again to his. They were entering the school's large hall now.

"Isn't there something you'd like that I could do for you?" insisted Starr, following him into the empty chapel where Mr. Endicott and the president stood looking at a tablet on the wall by the farther door.

"Your father has done everything for me," said Michael sunnily, with a sweep of his hand that seemed to include him, his garments, and his mental outfit. He turned his blazing smile upon her, thus speaking more eloquently than words.

"Yes, but that's Papa," said Starr impatiently, softly stamping her dainty foot. "He did that because of what you did for him saving my life. I'd like to do something to thank you for what you did for me. I'm worth something to myself, you know. Isn't there something I could do for you?"

She stood still, looking up into his face anxiously. The two men had passed through the farther door and on to the recitation rooms. The girl and boy were alone for the moment.

"You have done something for me. You did a great deal," he said, his voice almost husky. "It was the greatest thing anybody ever did for me."

"I did something for you! When? What?"

"Maybe you don't remember it, but I do. I was getting well from the shot at your house, and your nurse used to bring you up to play with me every day. Always, before you went away, you used to kiss me. I've never forgotten that."

He said it quite simply as if it were a common thing for a boy to say to a girl. But his voice was low as though the depths of his soul were stirred.

The color flooded Starr's cheeks.

"Oh!" she said, embarrassed at the turn in the conversation. "But that was when I was a baby. I couldn't do that now. Girls don't kiss boys, you know. It wouldn't be proper."

"I know," said Michael, his own color heightening now. "I didn't mean that. I wanted you to know how much you'd done for me already. You don't know what it is never to have been kissed by your mother or any living soul. Nobody ever kissed me that I know of but you."

He looked at the little girl with such a grave, sweet expression, his eyes so expressive of the long lonely years without any woman's love, that, child though she was, Starr seemed to understand. Her young soul went forth in pity, and tears sprang to her eyes.

"Oh! That's dreadful! Oh! I don't care if it isn't proper—"

And before he knew what she was about to do, the little girl tilted to her tiptoes, put up her dainty hands, caught him about the neck, and pressed a warm, eager kiss on his lips. Then she sprang away frightened, across the room and through the opposite door.

Michael stood still in bewilderment. The compelling of her little hands, the pressure of her fresh lips lingered with him. Tears gathered in his eyes, but he didn't know it. He stood with bowed head. Nothing so sacred, so beautiful, had ever entered his life. Her baby kisses had been half unconscious. This kiss she gave because she wanted to do something for him. He didn't attempt to understand the joy surging through his heart and pulsing in every fiber of his being. His lonely, unloved life was enough to account for it, and he was only a boy with a brief knowledge of life. But he knew enough to enshrine that kiss in his heart as holy, not even to be thought about carelessly.

When he roused himself to follow her, she'd disappeared. Her father and the president were listening to a recitation, but she was nowhere to be seen. She had gone to her room. Michael went alone to a thicket by the lake.

She met him shyly at dinner, with averted gaze and a glow on her cheeks, as if half afraid of what she'd done. But he reassured her with his eyes. His glance seemed to promise he would never take advantage of it. His face wore an exalted look, as if he'd been lifted above the earth, and Starr, looking at him wonderingly, was glad she had followed her impulse.

They took a horseback ride to the orange grove that afternoon—Mr. Endicott, a professor, Starr, and Michael. The president had borrowed the horses from some friends.

Michael sat like a king on his horse. He'd ridden the college mule bareback every summer, and riding seemed to be as natural to him as any other sport. Starr had been to a New York riding school and was accustomed to taking her morning exercise with her father in the park or accompanied by a footman. But she sat atop her Florida pony as happily as though he'd been a shiny, well-groomed steed of priceless value. It seemed unusually delightful to her to ride with this nice boy through the beautiful shaded road of arching live oaks richly draped with old gray moss. Michael stopped by the roadside, where the shade was dense, dismounted, and plunged into the thicket, returning in a moment with two or three beautiful orchids and some long vines of yellow jessamine whose perfume filled the air. He wreathed the jasmine about the pony's neck, and Starr twined it about her hat and wore the orchids in her belt.

Starr had never seen an orange grove before, and the trees were loaded with fruit, green and yellow, and set about by blossoms. She tucked a spray of blossoms in her dark hair under the edge of her hat, and Michael looked at her and smiled in admiration. Mr. Endicott, glancing toward his daughter, caught the look and recalled the time when he'd found the two children in his drawing room being made a show for his wife's guests. He sighed half in pleasure, half in foreboding. What a beautiful pair they were, to be sure, and what had the future in store for his little girl?

On the way back they skirted another lake, and Michael dismounted again to bring an armful of great white magnolia blossoms and dainty bay buds to the wondering Starr, and then they rode on slowly through the wooded road.

"I wish you could be here next week," said the boy wistfully. "It will be a full moon then. The best time to ride through this place is on a moonlit evening. The moonbeams make little ladders of the jasmine vines."

"It must be beautiful," said Starr dreamily.

Then they rode for a few minutes in silence. They were coming to the end of the overarched avenue. Ahead of them the sunlight shone clearly like the opening of a great tunnel framed in living green. Suddenly Starr looked up gravely.

"I'm going to kiss you good-bye tonight when we go away," she said softly.

Touching her pony lightly with the whip, she rose out into the bright road, with the boy, his heart leaping with joy, not far behind her.

Before supper Mr. Endicott had a talk with Michael that went further toward making the fatherless boy feel he had someone belonging to him than anything yet.

"I think you've done enough for me, sir," said Michael, respectfully opening the conversation as Endicott came out to the porch where the boy was waiting for him. "I should begin to earn my own living. I'm old enough now," he said, holding his head up proudly. "It's been very good of you all these years—I never can repay you. I hope you'll let me pay back the money you've spent on me, someday when I can earn enough."

Michael had been thinking this speech out ever since the president told him of Endicott's expected visit. But somehow it didn't sound as fine to him when he said it. It had seemed the only right thing to do when he planned it; but as he looked into Mr. Endicott's kind, keen eyes, his own fell in troubled silence. Had his words sounded ungrateful? Had he seen a hurt look in the man's eyes?

"Son," said Endicott after a pause, and the word stirred the boy's heart strangely. "Son, I owe you a debt I never can repay. You gave me back my little girl. I think I have at least a father's right in you at any rate and mean to exercise it until you're twenty-one. You must finish a college course first. When will that be? Three years? They tell me you're doing well. The doctor wants to keep you here to teach after you've graduated, but I thought you might like to come up to New York and have your chance. I'll give you a year or two in business, whatever seems to be your bent when you're through. Then we'll see. Which would you rather do? Or perhaps you'd prefer to let your decision rest until the time comes."

"I think I'm bound to go back to New York, sir," said Michael, lifting his head. "You know, sir—you said I was to be educated so I might help my friends. I've learned, of course, that you meant it in the broader sense than just those few boys, for one can help people anywhere; but still I feel as if it wouldn't be right for me not to go back. I'm sure they'll expect me."

"Loyal to your old friends still? Well, that's commendable, but I imagine you'll scarcely find them congenial now. I wouldn't let them hang too closely about you. They might become a nuisance. You have your way to make in the world."

Michael looked at his benefactor with troubled brows. Somehow the man's tone disturbed him.

"I promised," he said simply. Because there had been so little in his affections, Michael had cherished that promise through the years. It stood for principle and loyalty in general.

"Oh, well, keep your promise, of course," said the man easily. "I think you'll find the discharge of it a mere form."

A fellow student came across the campus.

"Endicott," he called, "have you seen Hallowell go toward the village?"

"He just went out the gate," responded Michael pleasantly.

Mr. Endicott looked up surprised. "Is that the name you're known by?"

"Endicott? Yes, sir, Michael Endicott. Wasn't it your wish? I supposed they'd asked you. I had no other name I knew."

"Ah! I didn't know," replied Endicott.

There was silence for a moment.

"Would you—shall I—do you dislike my having it?" asked the boy, delicately sensitive at once.

But the man looked up with something like tenderness in his smile. "Keep it, son. I like it. I wish I had a boy like you. It's an old name and a proud one. Be worthy of it."

"I will try, sir," said Michael.

The guests ate an early supper, and then Michael walked through another sunset to the station with Starr. He carried a small box in which reposed a tiny green and blue lizard for a parting gift. She'd watched the lizards scuttling away under the board sidewalks or changing their brilliant colors to gray like the boards so they might not be observed. She was interested in them and charmed with her gift. This particular lizard Michael had trained to eat crumbs from his hand, and it was tame.

The two said little as they walked along together. Each was feeling what a happy time they'd spent in one another's company.

"I'll write and tell you how the lizard is," said Starr, laughing, "and you'll tell me about the funny and interesting things you're doing, won't you?"

"If—I may," said Michael.

At the station a New York acquaintance of the Endicotts invited them to ride in his private car which was on the side track waiting for the train to pick it up. Michael helped Starr up the steps and carried the lizard into the car as well as the sheaf of flowers she insisted on taking with her.

Some ladies inside welcomed Starr effusively, and Michael, suddenly abashed, laid down the flowers, lifted his cap, and withdrew. A sudden blank had come upon him. Starr was absorbed by people from another world than his. He would have no opportunity to say good-bye—and she'd promised. But then of course he shouldn't expect her to do that. She had been very kind to him.

He was going down the steps now. An instant more and he would be in the track cinders.

A sudden rush, a soft cry, caused him to pause on the car's second step. It was Starr, standing just above him, and her eyes were shining.

"You were going without saying good-bye," she said with reproof in her voice.

Her cheeks were rosy red, but she stood her ground courageously. Placing a soft hand on either cheek as he stood below her, his face almost level with hers, she tilted his head toward her and touched his lips with her own pink ones, delicately as if a rose had swept them.

Simultaneously came the sound of the distant train.

"Good-bye, you nice, splendid boy!" breathed Starr and, waving her hand, darted inside the car.

Mr. Endicott, out on the platform still talking to the president, heard the oncoming train and looked around for Michael. He saw him coming from the car with an exalted look upon his face, his cap off, and the sun sending its golden beams over his hair.

"Son, I'm pleased with you," he said, catching his hand

heartily. "Keep it up, and come to me when you're ready. I'll give you a start."

Michael gripped his hand and blundered out some words of thanks. Then the train was there, and Endicott had to go.

The two younger ladies in the car, meanwhile, were plying Starr with questions. "Who's that magnificent young man, Starr Endicott? Why didn't you introduce him to us? I never saw such a beautiful face on any human being."

A moment more and the private car was fastened to the train. Starr, leaning from the window, waved her tiny handkerchief until the train had thundered away among the pines, and nothing was left but the echo of its sound. The sun was going down, but it didn't matter. Sunshine filled the boy's heart. She was gone, his little Starr, but she'd left the memory of her soft kiss and bright eyes, and someday, when he was finished with college, he would see her again. Meanwhile he was content.

Chapter 6

*T*he joy of loving-kindness in his life and a sense that somebody cared seemed to stimulate Michael's mind to greater energies. Whatever he did, whether studying or playing, he did with all his might.

The last year of his stay in Florida, a department of scientific farming was opened on a small scale. Michael presented himself as a student.

"What do you want of farming, Endicott?" asked the president, passing through the room during the teacher's first meeting with his students. "You can't use farming in New York."

In the kind old president's mind was perhaps a hope that the boy would linger with them, for he'd become attached to him in a silent, undemonstrative way.

"I might need it sometime," answered Michael, "and anyway I'd like to understand it. You said the other day that no knowledge was ever wasted. I'd like to know enough at least to tell somebody else."

The president smiled, wondered, and passed on. Michael continued in the class, supplementing the study by reading agricultural magazines and government literature on the subject. Agriculture had had a strange fascination for him ever since a noted speaker from the North had come and told the students that the new field for growth today lay in getting back to nature and cultivating the earth. Michael, as usual, wanted to know if that statement was true, and if so, why.

The three years flew by. Michael won no few honors, and

the day came when he'd completed his course and, as class valedictorian, went up to the old chapel for his last commencement in the college.

He sat on the platform looking down on the kind, uncritical audience assembled for the exercises and didn't see a single face come for his sake alone. Many were interested in him because they'd known him through the years and because he bore the reputation of being his class's honor man and the school's finest athlete. But that wasn't like having someone of his own who cared whether he did well or not. He found himself wishing that even Buck might have been there— Buck, the nearest to a brother he ever had. Would Buck have cared that he'd won highest rank? Yes, he'd have been proud of him.

Michael had sent out three invitations to commencement, one to Mr. Endicott, one to Starr, and one addressed to Buck, with the inner envelope bearing the words "For the kids." But no response had come to any of them. He'd received back the one addressed to Buck with "Not Called For" in big pink letters stamped across the corner. It had reached him that morning, just before he stepped onto the platform. He wished it hadn't come till night; it gave him a lonely, almost forsaken feeling. He was "educated" now, at least enough to know what he didn't know, and no one cared.

When Michael sat down after his oration amid a storm of hearty applause, prolonged by his comrades into something like an ovation, someone handed him a letter and a package. A mistake was made at the post office in sorting the mail, and these weren't put in the college box. One of the professors going down later found them and brought them up.

The letter was from Mr. Endicott, containing a businesslike line of congratulations, with a hope for the recipient to come to New York if he still felt like it, and a check for a hundred dollars.

Michael looked at the check in awe, reread the letter carefully, and put both in his pocket. The package was tiny and addressed in Starr's handwriting. Michael saved that till he reached his room. He didn't want to open it before any curious eyes.

Starr's girlish letters had been few and far between, and the last year they'd ceased altogether. She was busy with life—finishing school, dancing school, music lessons, and good times. Michael was a dim, pleasant vision to her.

The package contained a scarfpin of exquisite workmanship. Starr had pleased herself by picking out the prettiest thing she could find. She had her father's permission to spend as much as she liked on it. It was in the form of an orchid, with a tiny diamond like a dewdrop on one petal.

Michael looked on it in wonder, the first suggestion of personal adornment ever to come to him. He saw the reminder of their day together in the orchid; studied the beautiful name, "Starr Delevan Endicott," engraved on the card; then put them carefully back into their box and locked it in his bureau drawer. He'd wear it the first time he went to see Starr. He was very happy that day.

The week after college closed, Michael drove the college mule to the county seat ten miles away and bought a small trunk. It wasn't much of a trunk, but it was the best the town afforded. In this he packed all his worldly possessions, bade good-bye to the president and the professors who hadn't already gone north for their vacations, took a long tramp to his old haunts, and boarded the midnight train for New York.

The boy felt an independence which kept him from letting his benefactor know of his intended arrival. He didn't wish to make him any unnecessary trouble, and though he'd now been away from New York for thirteen years, he felt certain he could find his way about. Some things one may learn even at seven are never forgotten.

When Michael landed in New York, he looked around him with vague bewilderment for a moment. Then he started out with assurance to find a new spot for himself in the world.

He had no baggage but his trunk to hinder him. He'd discovered the trunk could remain in the station for a day without charge. He carried only a handsome raincoat and umbrella, part of the outfit the tailor had sent him that spring, so he picked his way unhampered across Liberty Street, eyeing his former enemies, the policemen, and every little urchin or newsboy with interest. Of course Buck and the rest would have grown up and changed some; they wouldn't likely be selling papers now—but—these were boys such as he'd been.

He bought a paper from a ragged fellow with a pinched face, and a strange sensation came over him. When he left this city he was the newsboy, and now he had enough money to buy a paper—and the education to read it! What a difference! Not that he wanted the paper now, though it might prove interesting later, but he wanted the experience of buying it. It marked the era of change in his life with tremendous contrast. Immediately his real purpose in having an education, to uplift his fellow beings, vague during the years, took form and leapt into vivid concern, as he watched the newsboy's skinny legs scrambling across the muddy street under the horses' feet and between automobiles, in imminent danger of his life.

Michael had thought out what he'd do, and he proceeded to carry out his purpose. He had no idea what a picture of well-groomed youth and manly beauty he presented as he marched down the street. He walked like a king, and New York abashed him no more now than it did before he left. Some spirits are born that way. He walked like a gentleman, unafraid.

He had decided not to go to Mr. Endicott until he found lodging somewhere. An innate delicacy had brought him to this decision. He wouldn't put one voluntary burden upon his kind benefactor. Born and bred in the slums, from where did this feeling come?

Michael threaded his way through the maze of traffic, instinct and vague stirrings of memory guiding him to a quiet shabby street where he found a dingy room for a small price. Dangers that might have beset a strange young man in the city were materially lessened for him because of his wide reading. He'd read about New York whenever he found something in the back of an old magazine, comparing it with his faint memories, until he knew the relation of things to one another pretty well. A stranger less versed might have gotten into most undesirable quarters.

The boy looked around his new home with a strange sinking of heart, after he'd gone out to get something to eat and arranged for his trunk to be sent to his room. It was tiny and not overclean. The faded wallpaper had an ancient floral design. The one window looked out to brick walls, chimneys, and roofs. The city noise clattered in, and the smells and heat made it almost stifling to the boy who had lived thirteen years in the South's sunshine and outdoor freedom.

The narrow bed looked uninviting, the bureau washstand was cheap, and the mirror above it reflected a warped image, disturbing even the least vain. Michael wasn't vain, however, and thought little about himself. But the room with its soiled carpet was depressing. When his trunk was placed between the bureau and the bed, there would be scarcely room for the one wooden chair. It wasn't a hopeful outlook. The boy removed his coat and sat down on the bed to whistle.

Life—grim, appalling, specterlike—rose before his mental vision, and he spent a bad quarter of an hour trying to adjust to his surroundings. His previous sunny philosophy struggled with the sudden reality. Then his trunk arrived.

As he opened the trunk a whiff of the South issued forth.

He caught his breath with a keen homesickness. His school days were over, with the joy of that companion-filled life passed. He hadn't known such aloneness as now in this city.

The last thing he'd put in his trunk was a branch of mammoth pine needles. The breath of the tree brought back all that meant home to him. He caught it up and buried his face in the plumy tassels.

The tray was filled with flags, pennants, photographs, and college paraphernalia. Eagerly he pulled them out and spread them over the lumpy bed. Then he grabbed his hat and rushed out. In a few minutes he returned with tacks, pins, and a small hammer. In an hour he'd changed the atmosphere of the whole place. Not an available inch of bare wall remained with its dirty wallpaper. College colors, pennants, and flags were grouped about pictures, and over the unwashed window was draped Florida moss. Here and there, apparently fluttering on the moss or about the room, were fastened beautiful specimens of semitropical moths and butterflies in gaudy colors. A small stuffed alligator reposed above the window, gazing down on the scene. A large alligator skin was tacked on one wall. One or two birds' nests fastened to small branches hung here and there.

Michael threw down the hammer and stood back to survey his work, sighing with relief. He felt more at home now with the photographs of his fellow students smiling at him. Opposite was the baseball team, strong and sturdy; to the right the glee club with him as their leader; to the left a group of his classmates, with his special chum in the midst. As he gazed at that kind face in the middle, he could almost hear his voice calling to him: "Come on, Angel! You're sure to win out!"

Michael felt better and hung up his clothes and arranged his effects on clean papers in the rheumatic bureau drawers. These were cramped quarters but would do until he was sure of earning some money, for he wouldn't spend his little savings more than he could help now and wouldn't depend any longer on Mr. Endicott's benevolence.

When his box of books arrived, he would ask permission to put some shelves over the window.

So he cheered himself as he put on his best garments, for he intended to arrive at Madison Avenue about the time his benefactor reached home for the evening.

Michael knew little of New York ways and less of society's habits; the few novels he'd read were his only instructors on the subject. He was going entirely on his dim memories of the habits of the Endicott home during his brief stay there. As it happened, Mr. Endicott was at home when Michael arrived, and the family was dining alone.

The boy was seated in the reception room gazing about him with his usual unconsciousness of self, when Endicott entered bringing Starr. A second time the man was deeply impressed with the fine presence of this boy from obscurity. He didn't look out of place even in a New York drawing room. It was incredible, though of course a large part of it was due to his city-made clothing. Still, that wouldn't account for his ease of manner, graceful courtesy, and instinct for saying the right thing at the right time.

Endicott invited the lad to dine with them, and Starr eagerly seconded the invitation. Michael accepted as eagerly and moments later found himself seated at the elegant table beside a beautiful, haughty woman who stared at him coldly and said nothing to him throughout the meal. The boy looked at her half wonderingly. It almost seemed as if she resented his presence; yet of course that couldn't be. He had the highest idea of this whole family. No one belonging to Starr could have anything but a lovely spirit.

Starr herself seemed to feel her mother's disapproval and spoke little, but she smiled shyly at Michael now and then when her mother wasn't noticing. Starr was sixteen now, slender and lovely as she'd given promise of being. Michael watched her, satisfied.

At last he turned to the mother, in her cold grandeur, and with earnestness and deference in his voice said, his glance still half toward Starr, "She's like you, and yet not!"

He said it gravely, as if it were a great discovery to them both, and he felt sure it was the key to her heart, admitting he admired the beautiful girl.

Mrs. Endicott froze him with her glance.

From the roots of his hair down to the tips of his toes he felt it—her resentment of his daring to express an opinion about her daughter, or even in having an opinion. For an instant his self-possession deserted him, and his face flushed with mingled emotions. Then he saw Starr's look of distress as she struggled to reply for her silent mother.

"Yes, Mama and I are often said to resemble one another strongly," she said with a tremble in her voice that roused the boy's manliness.

He flung off the oppression settling down on him and listened attentively to what Endicott was saying, responding gracefully, intelligently, and trying to convince himself it was his inexperience with ladies that caused him to say something inappropriate. He made no more personal remarks after that.

Endicott took the boy to his den after dinner. Later Starr slipped in, and they talked a little about their beautiful day in Florida together. Starr asked him if he still rode and would like to ride with her in the park the next morning when she took her exercise. It was arranged in her father's presence and with his full consent that Michael should accompany her in place of the groom who usually attended her rides.

Mrs. Endicott came in as they were making this arrangement and called Starr sharply out of the room.

After their withdrawal, Endicott questioned the boy about

his college course and living habits. He was pleased to hear Michael was independent enough to secure lodgings before coming to his house. It showed a spirit worth helping, though he told him he should have come straight to him.

Endicott was leaving on a business trip for a week and told Michael to enjoy himself looking around the city during his absence. On his return he should present himself at the office at a certain time when he would put him in touch with something that would start him in life.

Michael thanked him and went back to his hot little room on the fourth floor, happy in spite of heat and dinginess and a certain homesick feeling. Wasn't he to ride with Starr in the morning? He could hardly sleep for thinking of it and of all he had to say to her.

Chapter 7

When Michael arrived at the appointed hour the next morning, he was shown into a small reception room by a maid and waited there a full half hour. Finally he heard garments rustling in the distance and, a moment later, became aware of a cold stare from the doorway. Mrs. Endicott, in an elaborate morning dress, was surveying him through a jeweled lorgnette, her chin tilted, a look of scorn on her face. She must have noted the grace of his movements as he rose to greet her. Yet for some reason this only seemed to increase her dislike.

No welcoming hand was offered in response to his good morning, and no answering smile displaced the woman's severe expression as she confronted the boy, slowly paralyzing him with her glance. No word did she utter.

But Michael possessed great self-control and a keen logical mind. He saw no reason for the woman's rebuking attitude and concluded he must be mistaken. Rallying his smile he asked, "Is Miss Starr ready to ride, or have I come too early?"

Again the silence became impressive as the cold eyes looked him through before the thin lips opened. "My daughter is not ready to ride—with *you*, this morning or at any other time!"

"I beg your pardon, ma'am," said Michael, now deeply astonished and unable to fathom the woman's strange manner. "Have I misunderstood? I thought she asked me to ride with her this morning. May I see her, please?"

"No, you may not see Miss Endicott! And I consider your coming here at all a great impertinence. Certainly my husband has fully discharged any obligations for the slight service he assumes you rendered many years ago. I've always wondered if you did more harm than good. Of course you were only a child and couldn't do any heroic thing then. Probably if you'd kept out of things the trouble never would have happened, and your meddling simply gave you a wound and a soft bed for a while. In my opinion, far more has been done for you than you deserved, and as far as my daughter is concerned the obligation is discharged."

Michael had stood immovable while the woman uttered her harangue, his eyes growing wide with wonder and dark with a manly shame for her as she went on. When she paused for a moment, she saw his face was white and still like a statue, but something in the depth of his eyes held her in check.

With calmness and deference, although his voice rang with honest indignation, Michael spoke. "I beg your pardon, Mrs. Endicott, but I've never felt there was the slightest obligation resting on any of this family for the trifling matter that occurred when, as you say, I was a child. I feel the obligation is entirely the other way, of course, but I can't understand what you mean. How is my coming here at Mr. Endicott's invitation an impertinence?"

The woman looked at him with contempt as if it were scarcely worth the trouble to answer him; yet something about him demanded an answer.

"I suppose you're as ignorant then," she answered cuttingly, "as you seem to be honest. I'll explain. You're not fit company for my daughter. It's strange you don't see that for yourself! A child of the slums, with only shame and disgrace for an inheritance, and brought up a pauper! How could you expect to associate with a gentleman's daughter? If you have any respect for her, you should understand it isn't for someone like you to call on her and take her riding. It's commendable that you've improved what opportunities have been given you, but it's the height of ingratitude in a dependent to take on the airs of an equal. You might as well understand you can't do it. I simply won't have you here. Do you understand?"

Michael stood as if rooted to the floor, horror and dismay growing in his eyes and stupor trickling through his veins, as though the full meaning of her words had been slow to reach his consciousness. Yet outwardly his face was calm, and only his eyes had seemed to change and widen and suffer as she spoke. Finally his voice came to him.

"Madam, I didn't know," he said in a stricken voice. "As you say, I am ignorant."

Then lifting his head with a challenge, as he would whenever he had to face a hard situation, his voice rang clear and undaunted: "Madam, I beg your pardon. I'll not offend this way again. It was because I didn't understand. I wouldn't hurt your daughter in any way, for she's been the only beautiful thing that ever came into my life. But I'll never trouble her again."

The bow with which he left her, marching past her into the hall and out of the door where he'd once laid down his boy-life freely for her child, could have been no more gracefully or dramatically effected if he'd been some great actor. It was natural and full of dignity and reproach, and it left the lady feeling smaller and meaner than she'd ever felt in her rose-colored, velvet-lined existence. Somehow the contempt she'd prepared for crushing the lad, he suddenly flung from him as a hated garment and walked from her presence, leaving it wrapped about her.

"Well, really!" she gasped at last when she realized he was gone and her eloquence not finished. "Well, really! What right had he to leave like that without my permission? Impertinent to the end! One would suppose he was a grand duke. Such airs! I always told Delevan it was a mistake to educate the masses. They simply don't know their place and won't keep it."

Nevertheless, the woman was shaken. Michael had made

her feel as if she'd insulted a saint or a supernal being. She couldn't forget how the light had sifted through the depths of his great eyes as he spoke those last words, and she resented the ease with which he'd left her presence. It was too much like a victor's departure and not like one crushed back into his natural place. She was cross all day.

Starr meanwhile was lingering upstairs waiting for Michael. She was purposely kept busy in a distant room by her mother and wasn't told of his coming. An hour passed beyond the appointed time, and she grew restless and disappointed, then annoyed and almost angry that he'd so easily forgotten her. But she didn't tell her mother, and the old Scottish nurse who would have been her confidante had been sent on an errand to another part of the city.

Thus, as the days went by, and Michael came no more to the house, the girl thought he didn't want to come, and her disappointment and mortification were succeeded by a haughty resentment, for her mother's teaching had shown some result in her character.

Michael had entered the Endicott mansion a boy with a light heart and a happy vision of the future. He walked out an hour later, a man with a heavy burden on his heart and a blank vision of the future. So much had the woman wrought.

As he walked from the house, his head drooped, and his spirit was troubled within him. He went as one in a terrible dream. His face had the look of an angel newly turned out of paradise and for no fault of his own, an angel who bowed to the supreme mandate, his life crushed within him. People looked at him strangely and wondered as they passed. It was as if sorrow were embodied suddenly, looking through eyes intended for love. For the first time Michael, beloved of his companions for his unselfishness, was thinking of himself.

Yet even so no selfishness was in his thought. It was only as if that which had always given him life and the breath of gladness had suddenly been withdrawn from him and left him panting, gasping in a wide, unexpected emptiness.

Somehow he found his way to his room and locked the door.

Then the great spirit gave way, and he flung himself on the bed. He didn't seem to have an atom of strength left to move or think or even breathe consciously. All his physical powers had deserted him, now in this great crisis when life's foundations were shaken to their depths and nothing seemed to be anymore. He couldn't think it over or find a way out of the horror; he could only suffer it, fact by fact, as it menaced him slowly throughout that day.

Gradually it became distinct and separated itself into thoughts so he could follow it.

First was the fact, like a great knife that severed soul from body, that he might not see Starr or have any more to do with her. So deeply had this interdiction taken hold upon him that it seemed in his agitation he might no longer even think of her.

Next, following in stern, logical sequence, came the reason for this severing of soul: the fact of his lowly birth. Coming as it did, out of a trustful life that had never questioned much about his origin but had sunnily taken life as a gift and thought little about self, with the bluntness of a cruelty, it had cut and hacked in every direction what was left of either soul or body. And it left no hope of putting things together again.

That was how it came as the boy, without a friend in the world to whom he could turn, lay and took it.

Gradually out of the blackness he began to think back to his own beginning. Who was he? What was he? For the first time in his life, though he knew life more than most boys he'd associated with, he felt shame concerning his own birth, and it scorched its way into his soul.

He might have thought of such a possibility before perhaps, if his very youngest years hadn't been hedged about by a beautiful notion that sprang from the brain of an old Irishwoman in the slums, whose heart was wide as her ways were devious. One day when little Mickey had run an errand for her, she said, "Shure, an' then, Mickey, yer an angel sthraight frum hiven an' no misthake. Yer no jest humans like the rist av us; ye must av dhropped doon frum the skoy." And from that it went forth that Mickey was the child of the sky, and that was why no one knew who his parents were.

The notion had guarded the boy's weird babyhood and influenced more than he knew his own thought of existence, until life grew too full to think much on it.

Out of the darkness and murk of the slums Mickey's soul had climbed high, and his ambitions reached up to the limit-less blue above him. It had never occurred to him that his upward movements might be restricted. He'd taken others to be as freehearted and generous as he. Heir of all things, he'd breathed the atmosphere of culture as though it were his right. Now he suddenly saw he had no business climbing. He was about to mount a glorious height from which he was sure other heights were visible, when a rude hand brushed him back and dropped him down as though he were some crawling reptile at the bottom of things. And worst of all he might not climb back. He might look up; he might know the way up again. But the honor in him—the only bit of the heights he'd carried back to the foot with him—forbade him to climb to the heights of glory, for they belonged to others, those whom fortune favored and on whose escutcheon was no taint of shame.

And why should some souls be more favored than others? What had he, for instance, to do with his birth? He wouldn't have chosen shame, if shame there was. Yet shame or not he was branded with it for life because his origin was enveloped in mystery. The natural conclusion was that sin had had its part.

Then through the boy's mind tumbled a confusion of ques-tions more or less unanswerable, in the midst of which he slept.

He seemed to have wandered out into the open again with

the pines he loved above him and underneath the springy needles with their resinous softness. He lay looking up into the changeless blue that covered the heights, asking the tumultuous questions that throbbed through his heart, asking them of God.

Silently the city noises slunk away and dropped into the ceaseless calm of the South. The breeze fanned his cheek, the pines whispered, and a rippling birdsong touched his soul with peace. A quietness came down on his troubled spirit, and he was satisfied to take the burden laid upon him and bear it. Peace was on him when he awoke, far into the next morning.

The hot June sun steamed into his stuffy room and fell across the bed. He was sodden and heavy with the heat and the oppression of his garments. His head ached, and he felt as nearly ill as he'd ever felt. The specter of the day before confronted him in its torturing baldness, but he faced it now and looked it squarely in the eyes. It wasn't conquered yet, not by any means. The sharp pain of its newness was as great, and the deep conviction was still there that because of wrong this burden was laid upon him. But his soul had adjusted to the inevitable as it hadn't at first.

The boy lay still looking out upon a new life in which everything had to be readjusted to the idea of him and his new limitations. Before this he had thought no height wasn't his for the climbing. Now the heights were his, but he wouldn't climb because his presence might mar the heights themselves. It was wrong, unfair, that things should be so; but they were so, and as long as sin and wrong existed in the world they would be so.

He must look upon life as he'd looked upon every contest through his education. There were always hard things to be borne, but that only made the conquest greater. He must face this thing and win.

And what had he lost that had been his before? Not the beautiful girl, his heart's idol all these years. She was still there, alive and well, and more beautiful than ever. His devotion might yet stand between her and harm if need arose. True, he'd lost the hope of companionship with her, but that had been a day's growth. He'd never had much of it before or expected it when he came north. It would have been a glory and joy beyond expression, but one could live without those things and be true. Some reason for it all existed somewhere in the infinite, he was sure.

The ordinary boy wouldn't philosophize in this way, but Michael had never been an ordinary boy. His soul had always been open to the universe and optimistic in the most trying surroundings. He'd come out of the hardest struggle his soul had yet met, but he'd come out a man. The lines about his mouth weren't there the day before and spoke of strength and self-control. New depths were in his eyes as of one who'd looked down and seen things unspeakable, having to number himself with the lowly.

While he lay there trying to take in the change that had come to him, he suddenly thought of his childhood companions, the little waifs like him who came from the earth's refuse. They'd loved him. He recalled slowly, laboriously, incidents from his early history. Many were dim and uncertain, but little kindnesses stood out. A bad cut on his foot once and how Buck had bathed it and bound it in dirty rags, doing double duty with the newspapers for several days to save his friend from stepping. A bitter cold night back as far as he could remember when he'd had bad luck and come among the others supperless and almost freezing. Buck had shared a crust and found a warm boiler room where they crawled out of sight and slept. Other incidents, more blurred in his memory, but enough to recall how loyal the little gang had been to him. He saw once more their faces when they heard he was going to college, blanched with horror at the separation, lighting with pleasure when he promised to return!

The years, how they'd changed and separated! Where were they, these who really belonged to him? What had the years done to them? And he had a duty to them. How had he been in the city all these hours and not even thought of looking for those loyal souls who stood by him faithfully when they were mere babies? He must go at once. He'd lost his head over attempting to reach things that weren't for him, and this shock had come to set him straight.

Gravely he rose at last, these thoughts surging through his brain.

The heat, the stifling air, his recent struggling, and the exhausting stupor made him reel dizzily as he stood. But his mettle was up now, and he set his lips and went about making himself neat. He longed for a dip in the crystal waters of the college lake. The tiny washbowl in his room proved a poor substitute with its tepid water and diminutive towel.

He went out and breakfasted carefully and then, with his map in his pocket, started out to find his old haunts.

Chapter 8

Thirteen years in New York had brought many changes. Some of the well-remembered landmarks were gone, with new buildings in their places. A prosperous-looking saloon, palatial in its entrance, marked the corner where he used to sell papers. It had been a corner grocery store. Saloons! Always and everywhere were saloons! Michael looked at them wonderingly. He'd forgotten them in his exile, for the college influence had barred them from its vicinity.

The boy Mickey had been familiar with saloons, looking upon them as a necessary evil, where drinking fathers spent the money that should have bought their children food. He'd been in and out of them selling his papers, warming his feet, and getting a crust now and then from an uneaten bit on the lunch counter. Sometimes there had been glasses to drain, but Mickey with his observing eyes had early decided he would have none of the stuff that sent men home to curse their children.

College influence, while little had been said on the subject, had filled the boy with horror for saloons and drunkards. He stood appalled now as he turned at last into an alley where familiar objects, doorsteps, cellars, met his gaze, with grog shops along the way and taking command of every corner.

A strange feeling came over him as long-forgotten sights awoke his memory. Was this really the place, and was that opening beyond the third step the blind alley where Jane used to live? Things were so much dirtier, so much worse in every way than he remembered them. He hurried on, not noticing the attention he was attracting from the wretched children in the gutters, though he scanned them eagerly, with the wild idea that Buck and the rest might be among them.

Yes, the alley was there, dark and ill-smelling as ever, and in its dim recesses on a dirty step a woman's figure hunched—a figure he knew at once. Who was she? What had they called her? Sally? Aunt Sal?

He hurried up to where she sat looking at him. Her gray hair straggled down on her dirty cotton dress open at the neck over shriveled yellow skin; soiled old hands hung over slatternly garments; stockingless feet were stuck into a tattered pair of men's shoes. Nothing seemed changed since he saw her last, except the hair had been black then and the skin not so wrinkled. Aunt Sally had always been good-natured, even when she was drunk; her husband was always drunk also when he came home, but never good-natured. The boy recalled these things as he stood looking down at the wreck of a woman before him.

The bleary eyes looked up unknowing, half resentful of his intrusion.

"Aunt Sally!" cried the boyish voice. "Aren't you Aunt Sally?"

The woman looked surprised. "I be," she said thickly, "but wot's that to youse? I beant no hant o' yourn."

"Don't you remember Mickey?" he asked almost anxiously, for now the feeling had seized him that he must make her remember. He must find out if he could whether anything was known of his origin. Perhaps she could help him.

Perhaps, after all, he might trace his family and find at least no disgrace upon him.

"Mickey!" the woman repeated dully. She shook her head. "Wot's Mickey?"

"Don't you remember Mickey, the little boy who sold papers and brought you water sometimes? Once you gave me a drink of soup from your kettle. Think!"

A dim perception entered the sodden eyes.

"Thur was a Mickey long ago," she mused. "He had hair like a h'angel, bless the sweet chile. But he got shot an' never come back. That war long ago."

Michael took off his hat, and the little light in the dark alley seemed to catch and tangle in the gleam of his hair.

The old woman started as though she'd seen a vision. "The saints preserve us!" she cried aghast, shrinking back into her doorway with raised hands. "An' who be yez? Yeh looks enough like the b'y to be the father of 'im. He'd hair loike the verra sunshine itself. Who be yez? Spake quick. Be ye man er angel?"

Something in the woman's tone went to the lonely boy's heart, even while he recoiled from the repulsive creature before him.

"I'm just Mickey, the boy, grown a little older," he said gently, "and I've come back to see the place where I used to live and find the people I used to know."

"Y've lost yer way thin, fer shure!" said the woman, slightly recovering her equilibrium. "The loikes uv youse nivver lived in dis place. Fer ef yous ain't angel, you's gintulmun, an' no gintulmun ivver cum from the loikes o' this. An' besoides, the b'y Mickey, I tel'd yez, was shot an' nivver comed back no more. He's loikely up wid de angels where he b'longs."

"Yes, I was shot," said Michael, "but I wasn't killed. A good man sent me to college, and I've just graduated and come back to look up my friends."

"Frinds, is it, ye'll be afther a findin'? Thin ye'd bist look ilsewhar, fer thur's no one in this alley fit to be frinds with the loikes uv you. Ef that's wot they does with b'ys at colidge, a pity 'tis more uv um can't git shot an' go there. But ef all youse tell is thrue, moi advice to yez is, juist bate it as hoird as ivver yez kin out'n yere, an' don't yez nivver set oies on this alley agin. Ye'd better stay to colidge all the days uv yer loife than set fut here agin, fer juist let 'em got holt uv yez an' they'll spile yer pretty face. Look thar!" she pointed toward a wreck of humanity that reeled into the alley. "Would yez loike to be loike that? My mon come home loike that ivvery day of his loife, rist his bones, an' he nivver knowed whin he died."

Maudlin tears rolled down the poor creature's cheeks, for they could be no tears of affection. Her man's departure from this life could have been only a relief. Michael recoiled from the sight with a sickening sadness. Nevertheless, he meant to find out if this woman knew anything of his old friends or of his origin. He rallied his forces to answer her.

"I don't have to be like that," he said. "I've come to look up my friends, and I want you to tell me if you know anything about my parents. Did you ever hear anything about me? Did anybody know who I was or how I came to be here?"

The old woman tried to gather her scattered faculties, but she shook her grizzled head. "I ain't nivver laid oies on yez before, an' how cud I know whar yez cum from, ner how yez cam to be here?"

He perceived it would require patience to extract information from this source.

"Try to think," he said more gently. "Can you remember if anyone ever belonged to the little boy they called Mickey? Was there ever any mother or father or—anybody that belonged to him at all?"

Again she shook her head. "Nivver as Oi knows on. They said he just comed a wee babby to the coourt a wanderin' with the other childer, with scarce a rag to his back, an' a smile on him like the archangel, and some said as how he nivver had no father ner mother, but dthrapped sthraight frum the place where de angels live."

"But did no one take care of him or ever try to find out about him?"

"Foind out, is it? Whist! An' who would tak toime to find out whin ther's so miny uv their own. Mickey was allus welcome to a bite an' a sup ef any uv us had it by. There wuz old Granny Bane with the rheumatiks. She gave him a bed an' a bite now an' agin, till she died, an' afther that he made out to shift fer hisse'f. He was a moighty indepindint babby."

"But had he no other name? Mickey what? What was his whole name?"

The old woman only stared stupidly.

"Didn't he have any other name?" There was almost despair in his tone.

Another shake of the head. "Just Mickey!" Her eyes grew dull again.

"Can you tell me if any other people living here now used to know Mickey? Any other men or women who might remember?"

"How kin Oi tell?" snarled the woman impatiently. "Oi can't be bothered."

Michael stood in troubled silence, while the woman turned her head to watch a neighbor coming down the street with a basket in her hand. Her visitor seemed to interest her no longer. She called out some rough ribaldry to the woman, who glanced up fiercely and deigned no further reply. Then Michael tried again.

"Could you tell me about the boys who used to go with Mickey?"

"No, Oi can't," she answered crossly. "Oi can't be bothered. Oi don't know who they was."

"There were Jimmie and Sam and Bobs and Buck. Surely you remember Buck—and little Janie. Janie who died after Mickey went away?"

The bleared eyes turned full upon him again. "Janie? Fine, Oi remimber Janie. They had a white hurse to her, foiner'n any ivver cum to the coourt before. The b'ys stayed up two noights selling to git the money fur it, an' Buck he stayed stiddy while she was aloive. Pity she doied."

"Where's Buck?" demanded Michael with a sudden twinge of his heartstrings that seemed to bring back the old love and loyalty to his friend. Buck had needed him perhaps all these years, and he hadn't known.

"That's whot the police would like fer yez to answer, I'm thinkin'!" laughed old Sal. "They wanted him bad fer breakin' into a house an' mos' killin' the lady an' gittin' aff wid de jewl'ry. He beat it dat noight, an' ain't none o' us seen him these two year. He were a slick one. He were awful smart at breakin' an' stealin'. Mebbe Jimmie knows, but Jimmie, he's in jail, serving his time fer shootin' a man in the hand durin' a dhrunken fight. Jimmie, he's no good. Never wuz. He's jest like his foither. Bobs, he got both legs cut aff, bein' runned over by a big truck, and he doied in the horspittle. Bobs, he were better dead. He'd uv gone loike the rist. Sam, he's round these parts mostly nights. Ye'll hey to come at noight ef yez want to see him. Mebbe he knows more 'bout Buck'n he'll tell."

Sick at heart, Michael put question after question but got no more information, and the old woman showed signs of impatience again. Carefully noting what she said about Sam and getting a few facts as to the best time and place to find him, Michael turned and walked sadly out of the alley. He didn't see old Sal's alert eyes following him nor the keen expression on her face as she stretched her neck to see which way he turned as he left the alley. As soon as he was out of sight, she shuffled down from her doorstep to the corner and peered after him through the morning sunshine. Then she went slowly back to her doorstep.

"Now whut in the divil could he be a wantin' wid Buck' an' Sammie?" she muttered to herself. "All that story 'bout his bein' Mickey was puttin' it on my eye. I'll giv warnin' to Sammie t'night, an' ef Buck's in these pairts he better git out

West some'res. The police uv got onto 'im. But hoiwiver did they know he knowed Mickey? Poor little angel Mickey! I guv him the shtaight about Bobs an' Jimmie, fer they wuz beyant his troublin', but he'll niver foind Sammie from the directin' I sayed."

Michael, sad, horror-filled, conscience-stricken, found a restaurant and ate his dinner, thinking meanwhile what he could do for the boys. Could he visit Jimmie in prison and make his life more comfortable in little ways? Could he plan something for him when he came out? Could he help Sam? The old woman had said little about Sam's condition. Michael thought he might likely by this time have built up a nice little business. Perhaps he had a prosperous newsstand in some frequented place. He looked forward eagerly to meeting him again. Sam had always been a silent child dependent on the rest, but he was one of the little gang, and Michael's heart warmed toward his former comrade. He surely wouldn't find him so loathsome and repulsive as old Sal. She made him heartsick. Just to think of drinking soup from her dirty kettle! How could he have done it? Yet he knew no better life then, and he was hungry and a child.

So Michael mused and with a great heart hunger to know what had become of Buck. Could he and Sam together plan some way to find Buck and help him out of his trouble? How could Buck have done anything so dreadful? And yet even as he thought it he remembered that "pinching" hadn't been a crime in his childhood days, not unless one was found out. How had these principles, or lack of principles, been replaced gradually in his own life without his realizing it? It was strange and wonderful. Practically now he, Michael, had been made into a new creature since he left New York, and so gradually and pleasantly he hadn't realized it.

Yet, as he marveled, a thought shot through him that perhaps it hadn't been a good thing, this making him into a new creature, with new desires and aims and hopes that could never be fulfilled. Perhaps he'd have been happier, better off, if he'd never been taken out of that environment and brought to appreciate another one where he didn't belong and could never stay, since that old environment was the one where he must stay whether he would or not. He put the thought from him as unworthy at once; yet its sharpness lingered and with it a vision of Starr's face as he'd seen her two nights before in her father's home, before he knew the door of that home was shut upon him forever.

Michael passed the day wandering about the city, trying to piece together his old knowledge with the new and know the city in which he'd come to dwell.

It was nearing midnight, when Michael, by old Sal's advice and utterly fearless in his ignorance, entered the court where he had spent his babyhood.

The alley was dark and murky in the humid summer night. But unlike the morning hours it was alive with a writhing, chattering, fighting mass of humanity. Doorways overflowed. The narrow alley itself seemed fairly thronging with noisy, unhappy men and women. Hoarse laughs mingled with rough cursing, pierced with an occasional scream. Stifling odors lurked in cellar doorways and struck one full in the face unawares. Curses seemed to be the setting for all conversation, whether angry or jolly. Babies tumbled in the gutter, and older children fought over some garbage scrap.

Appalled, Michael halted and almost turned back. Then, remembering this was where he'd come from—where he belonged—and that his duty, his obligation, was to find his friends, he went steadily forward.

There sat old Sal, a belligerent gleam in her sodden eyes. Four men on a step opposite, with a candle between them, were playing cards. Sal muttered a word as Michael approached, and the candle was extinguished. It looked as if one had carelessly knocked it onto the pavement, but the glare flickered into darkness, and Michael could no longer see the men's faces. He wondered if one of them was Sam. But when he rubbed his eyes and looked again the four men were gone, and two children occupied the step, holding a sleeping baby between them and staring at him in openmouthed admiration.

The weird blinking light of the distant streetlamp, the noise and confusion, the odors and curses filled him anew with a desire to flee, but he wouldn't let himself turn back. Never had Michael turned from his duty out of fear or dislike of anything.

He tried to enter into conversation with old Sal again, but she ignored him. She'd taken "a wee drapth" and was alert and suspicious. In fact, the whole alley was alert for this elegant stranger who was none of theirs and must have come to spy on someone. He wanted Sam; therefore Sam was hidden well and at that moment playing a crafty game in the back of a cellar on top of an old beer barrel, by the light of a wavering candle, well guarded by sentinels along the way. Michael could have no more found him than a needle in a haystack the size of New York.

He wandered for two hours through the alley, seeing sights long since forgotten, hearing words unspeakable, following suggestions of interested bystanders, always coming back without finding Sam. He hadn't yet understood he wasn't intended to find Sam. He had taken these people into his confidence as he'd always taken everyone into his confidence, and they were playing him false. If they had lived on Fifth Avenue, he wouldn't have expected them to be interested in him and his plans and desires. But these were his very own people, at least the "ownest" he had in the world, and among them he'd once moved freely, confidently. He saw no reason why they'd have changed toward him, though he felt the antagonism in the atmosphere as the night wore on, even as he felt it in the Endicott house the day before.

Heartsick and baffled, at last he took his way slowly, looking back many times and leaving many messages for Sam. He felt as if he simply couldn't return to even so uncomfortable a bed as the one in his new lodgings without finding some clue to his old comrades.

Standing at the corner of the alley opposite the saloon's flaunting lights, he looked back at the swarming darkness of the alley, and his heart filled with a great wave of pity, love, and sorrow. Almost at his feet in a dark shadow of a doorway a tiny white-faced boy crouched fast asleep on the stone threshold. He thought of little Bobs and his own barren childhood, and a mist came before his eyes as he looked up at the sky where the very stars seemed small and far away.

"Oh, God!" he said under his breath. "Oh, God! I must do something for them!"

And then, as if the opportunity came with the prayer, there reeled into view three or four men and a woman.

The woman was talking in a high frightened voice and protesting. The men caught hold of her roughly, laughing and flinging out coarse jests. Then another man came stealing from the darkness of the alley and joined the group, seizing the woman by the shoulders and speaking words too vile for repetition. In terror the girl turned, for Michael could see, now she was nearer, that she was only a young girl and pretty. Instantly he thought of Starr, and his soul rose in mighty wrath that any man would treat any girl as he'd seen these do. Then the girl screamed and struggled to get away, crying, "It ain't true! Lem'me go! I won't go with you—"

Instantly Michael was upon them, his powerful arms and body dashing the men right and left. And because of the suddenness of the attack coming from this unexpected quarter— for Michael had stood somewhat in the shadow—and because of the cowardliness of all bullies, for the moment, he prevailed against all four, long enough for the girl to slip like a wraith from their grasp and disappear into the shadows.

Then when the men, dazed from surprise, though not seriously hurt, discovered their prey was gone and a stranger from the higher walks of life had frustrated their plans, they fell upon him in their wrath.

Michael, brave always and well trained in athletics, parried their blows for an instant. But the man who had come from the shadows, whose face was evil, stole up behind and stabbed him in the shoulder. A sudden faintness made him less able to defend himself. He felt he was losing his senses, and the next blow from one of the men sent him reeling into the street where he fell heavily, striking his head against the curb. A loud cry of murder was heard in a woman's shrill voice, the padded rush of the villains into their holes, the distant ring of a policeman's whistle, and then all was as quiet as a city night could be. Michael lay white and still with his face looking up to the faint pitying moon so far away and his beautiful hair wet with blood flowing out on the pavement. There he lay on the edge of the world that was his own and would not own him. He had come to his own, and his own received him not.

Chapter 9

*M*ichael awoke in the hospital with a bandage around his head and a stinging pain in his shoulder whenever he tried to move.

Back in his inner consciousness there sounded the last words he had heard before he fell, but he couldn't connect them with anything at first: "Hit him again, Sam!"

Those were the words. What did they mean? Had he heard them or merely dreamed them? And where was he?

A glance about the long room with its rows of white beds, each with an occupant, answered his question. He closed his eyes again to be away from all those other eyes and think. Sam! He'd been looking for Sam. Had Sam then come at last? Had Sam hit him? Had Sam recognized him? Or was it another Sam?

But something was wrong with his head, and he couldn't think. He put up his right arm to feel the bandage, and the pain in his shoulder stung again. Somehow to his feverish fancy it seemed the sting of Mrs. Endicott's words to him. He dropped his hand feebly, and the nurse gave him something in a spoon. Then, half dreaming, he fell asleep, with a vision of Starr's face as he'd seen her last.

Three weeks he lay on that narrow white bed and learned to face the battalion of eyes from the other narrow beds around him; to distinguish the quiet sound of the marble-lined room from the rumble of the unknown city without. And when the rumble was the loudest, his head ached with the thought of the alley and the horrible sights and sounds that seemed written in letters of fire across his spirit.

He learned to look upon the quiet monotonous world of ministrations as a haven from the world outside into which he must presently go, and in his weakened condition he shrank from the new life. It seemed filled with disappointments and sorrow.

But one night a man in his ward died and was carried silent and covered from the room. Some of his last moaning utterances had reached his fellow sufferers' ears with a vision of his life and home, and his mortal agony for the past, now that he was leaving it all.

That night Michael couldn't sleep, for the court, the alley, and the whole sunken humanity were pressing upon his heart. It seemed his burden that he must give up his life's hopes to bear. And there he had it out with himself and accepted whatever should come to be his duty.

Meanwhile the wound on his head was healed, the golden halo had covered the scar, and the cut in his shoulder, which had been only a flesh wound, was doing nicely. Michael was allowed to sit up and then to be about the room for a day or two.

In those days of his sitting up, when the sun crept in for an hour each day and reached his hair, the other men of the ward began to notice him. He seemed to them set apart, one lifted above what held them to sin and earth. His countenance spoke of strength and self-control, two things many of them lacked, either through constant sinning or constant fighting with poverty and trouble. So, as he began to get about, they sent for him to come to their bedsides. As they talked, one and another poured out his separate tale of sorrow and woe, till Michael felt he could bear no more. He longed for power to help, to put these wretched men on their feet again to lead a new life, to crush some of the demons in human form who were grinding them down to earth. Oh, for money and knowledge and authority!

One man had lost both legs in a defective machine he was running in a factory. He was a skilled workman with a wife and three children. But he was useless now at his trade. No one wanted a man with no legs. He might be better dead. Damages? No hope of that. He'd accepted three hundred dollars to sign a release. He had to. His wife and children were starving, and they must have the money then or perish. There was no other way. Besides, what hope had he in fighting a great corporation? He was a poor man, a stranger in this country, with no friends. The company had been plenty willing to swear it was the man's fault.

Another had tried to asphyxiate himself by turning on the gas in his wretched little boardinghouse room. He'd lost his position because of ill health, and the firm wished to put a younger man in his place. He almost succeeded in taking himself out of this life.

Next to him was one horribly burned by molten metal he'd been compelled to carry without adequate precautions. It was a cheaper method of handling the stuff, and men cost less than machinery. You could always get more men.

The man across from him was wasted away from insufficient food. He'd been out of work for months, and what little money he could pick up in odd jobs had gone mostly to his wife and children.

And so it was throughout the ward. On almost every life sin—somebody's sin—had left its mark. One or two cheery souls, though poor, were blest with friends and a home of some kind and were looking forward to a speedy restoration, but these were the exception. Nearly all the others blamed someone else for their unhappy condition, and in nearly every case someone else was undoubtedly to blame, even though in most cases each individual had been somewhat responsible.

All this Michael gradually learned, as he began his practical

study of sociology. As he learned story after story and formu-
lated the facts of each, he came to three conclusions: First,
there wasn't enough room in the city for these people to have a
fair chance at life's beautiful things. Second, the people with
the good things were getting them all for themselves and didn't
care a straw whether others went without. Third, somebody
should be doing something about it, and why not he?

Of course it was absurd for a mere boy just out of college,
with scarcely a cent to his name—and not a whole name to
call his own—to think of attacking the problem of the people
single-handed. But still he felt he was called to do it and
meant to try.

He had no idea whether anybody else had seen it this way or
not. He'd read a little of city missions and charitable enterprises, but they scarcely reached his inner consciousness. His
impression gathered from such desultory reading had been that
the effort was sporadic and ineffective. And so, in his gigantic
ignorance and egotism, yet with his sensitivity to the inward
call, Michael set himself to espouse the cause of the people.

Wasn't he one of them? Hadn't he been born there that he
might be one of them and know what they had to suffer?
Weren't they his kindred so far as he had any kindred? Hadn't
he been educated and brought into contact with higher things
so he might know what these other human souls might be if
they had the opportunity? If he'd known more he would have
added "and if they would." But he didn't; he supposed all souls
were as willing to be uplifted as he'd been.

Michael went out from the hospital feeling that his life-
work was before him. The solemn pledge he'd taken as a child
to return and help his former companions became a voluntary
pledge of his young manhood. He knew little about the matter, but he felt much, and he was determined to do, wherever
the way opened. He had no doubt the way would open.

"Now, young man, take care of yourself," said the doctor in

parting from his patient a few days later, "and, for the land's sake, keep away from back alleys at night. When you know a little more about New York, you'll learn it's best to keep far away from such places. Don't fool around thinking you can convert any of those blackguards. They need to be blown up, every one of them, and the place obliterated. Mind, I say, and keep away from them."

Michael smiled and thanked the doctor and walked unsteadily down the hospital steps on feet that were strangely wobbly for him. But he didn't intend to obey the doctor. He had been turning the matter over in his mind and had a plan. And that night about ten o'clock he went back to the alley.

Old Sal was sitting on her doorstep, a little more intoxicated than the last time, and the young man's sudden appearance beside her startled her into an Irish howl.

"The saints preserve us!" she cried, tottering to her feet. "He's cum back to us agin, shure he has! There's no killin' him! He's an angel shure. B'ys, rin! Bate it! The angel's here again!"

There was a sound of scurrying feet, and the place seemed to clear suddenly of the children that had been underfoot. One or two scowling men, or curious women in whose eyes the light of life had died and been left unburied, peered from dark doorways.

Michael stood quietly until Sal's howling had subsided, and then he spoke in a clear tone.

"Can you tell me if Sam has been around here tonight? Is he anywhere near here now?"

There was no answer for a minute, but someone growled out that he might and then he might not have been. Someone else said he'd just gone away, but they didn't know where. Michael perceived it was a good deal as it had been before.

"I've brought a message for him, a letter," he said, and he spoke so that anyone nearby might hear. "Will you give it to him when he comes? He'll want to see it, I'm sure. It's important. I think he'll be glad to get it. It contains good news about an old friend of his."

He held out the letter courteously to old Sal, and she looked at its white crispness as though it had been a message from the lower regions calling her to judgment. A letter, white, square-cornered and clean, with clear, firm inscription, had never come before her gaze. Old Sal had never learned to read. The writing meant nothing to her, but the whole letter represented a mystic communication from another world.

Instinctively the neighbors gathered to look at the letter, and Sal, seeing herself the center of observation, reached forward a dirty hand wrapped in a corner of her apron and took the envelope as though it had been hot, eyeing it fearfully.

Then, bowing and touching his hat to her as though she'd been a queen, Michael turned and walked out of the alley.

Old Sal stood watching him, a kind of wistful wonder in her bleary eyes. No gentleman had ever tipped his hat to her, and no man had ever done her reverence. From her childhood she'd been brought up to forfeit the respect of men. Perhaps she'd never realized she might have been anything but what she was and that men might have honored her.

The neighbors, too, were awed for the moment and stood watching in silence.

Then, when Michael turned the corner out of sight, Sal exclaimed, "Now that's the angel, shure! No gintlemin would ivver uv tipped his 'at to the loikes of Sal. Saints presarve us! That we should hev an angel in this alley!"

When Michael reached his lodging, he found that he was trembling so from weakness and excitement that he could scarcely drag himself up the three flights to his room. So had his splendid strength been reduced by trouble and the fever that came with his wounds.

He lay down weakly and tried to think. Now he'd done his best to find Sam. If Sam didn't come in answer to his letter, he must wait until he found him. He wouldn't give up. So he fell asleep with the burden on his heart.

The letter was as follows:

Dear Sam,

You can't have forgotten Mickey who slept with you in the boiler room and with whom you shared your crusts. You remember I promised when I went away to college I'd come back and try to make things better for you all? And now I've come and am anxious to find the fellows and see what we can do together to make life better in the old alley and make up for some of the hard times when we were children. I've been down to the alley but can get no trace of you. I spent the best part of one night hunting you, and then a slight accident put me in the hospital for a few days; but I'm well now and am anxious to find you all. I want to talk over old times and find out where Buck and Jim are and hear all about Janie and little Bobs.

I'm leaving this letter with Aunt Sally, hoping she'll give it to you. I've given my address below and would be glad to have you come and see me at my room. If you prefer I'll meet you wherever you say, and we'll go together and eat something to celebrate.

Hoping to hear from you very soon, I am as always,

Your brother and friend,
Mickey

A few days later the postman brought a begrimed envelope addressed in pencil to the door. Michael with sinking heart opened it. It read:

MicKY ef yo be reely hym cum to KelLys karner at 10 tumoroW nite. Ef you are mIcK youz thee old whissel an doante bring no une wit yer Ef yO du I wunt be thar.

SAM

Seated on his lumpy bed Michael puzzled this out, word by word, until he made fairly good sense of it. He was to go to Kelly's corner. How the words stirred his memory. Kelly's corner was beyond the first turn of the alley, at the extreme end of an alley within an alley, and had no outlet except through Kelly's saloon. Only the "gang" knew the name, "Kelly's corner," for it wasn't really a corner at all, only a pocket or hiding place so titled by Buck for his own and "de kids'" private purpose. If Michael had been inclined to be a coward since his recent usage in the alley, he'd have kept away from Kelly's corner. Once in there alone with enemies, no policeman's club or hospital ambulance would ever come to help. The things that happened at Kelly's corner never got into the newspapers.

Memory and instinct made this clear to Michael, and if he needed no other warning, those words in the letter about not bringing anyone with him were sufficient to make him wise.

Yet Michael never so much as thought of not keeping the appointment. His business was to find Sam, and it mattered as little to him now that danger stood in the way as it had the day he flung his neglected body in front of Starr Endicott and saved her from the assassin's bullet. He would go, of course, and alone. Neither did it occur to him to leave his name and whereabouts at the police station to be searched for in case he didn't turn up in a reasonable time. It was all in the day's work, and Michael thought no more about the possible peril he was facing than he'd thought of broken limbs and bloody noses before a football scrimmage.

Something else in the letter stirred old memories. The whistle! Of course he hadn't forgotten that, although he hadn't used it much among his college companions. It was a strange, weird, penetrating sound between a call and whistle. He and Buck had made it up as a signal. When Michael went to college, he'd held it sacred as belonging to his old friends, and never, unless alone in the woods where only the birds and the trees could hear, had he let its echoes ring. Sometimes he'd startled the mockingbirds with it, and once he let it ring into the midst of his astonished comrades in Florida when he was hidden from their view and they didn't know who made the sound. He tried it now softly, and then louder, until he knew he could still give it.

The next night at precisely ten o'clock Michael's ringing step sounded down the alley—firm, decisive, secure. Such assurance Daniel must have had as he faced the lions, and so went the three Hebrew children into the fiery furnace.

"It's him! It's the angel!" whispered old Sal, who was watching. "Oi tould yez he'd come fer shure!"

"He's got his nerve with him!" murmured a girl with bold eyes and a coarse kind of beauty, as she drew farther back into the shadows. "He ain't comin' out again so pretty, I guess. Not if Sam don't like. Mebbe he ain't comin' out 'tall!"

"Angels has ways, me darlint!" chuckled Sal. "He'll come back al roight—ye'll see!"

On walked Michael, down the alley to the narrow opening that to the uninitiated wasn't an opening between the build-ings, and slipped in the old way. He'd thought it out in the night. He was sure he knew just how far beyond Sal's house it was. On into the fetid air of the close dark place, the air struck him in the face like a hot, wet blanket.

All was still when he reached the point known as Kelly's corner. It had been so as he remembered it—the place of plots, the hatching of murders and robberies. Had it so changed that it was still tonight? He hesitated for an instant. Should he wait awhile or knock on some door? Would it be any use to call?

But the instinct of the slums was upon him again, his birthright. It seemed to drop upon him from the atmosphere, a sort of stealthy patience. He would wait. Something would come. He must do as he had with the forest birds when he wished to watch their habits. He must stand still unafraid and show he was harmless.

So he stood three, perhaps five minutes. Then softly at first and gradually growing clearer, he gave the call he'd given years before, a barefoot, hungry child in that spot many times.

The echo died away. Nothing made him know a group of curious alley dwellers huddled at the mouth of the trap in which he stood, watching with eyes accustomed to the darkness, to see what would happen—to block his escape if escape should be attempted.

Then out of the silence a sigh seemed to come, and out of the shadows one shadow unfolded and came forward till it stood beside him. Still Michael didn't stir but softly, through half-open lips, breathed the signal once more.

Sibilant, rougher, with a hint of menace as it issued forth, the signal was answered this time, and with a thrill of wonder the mantle of the old life fell upon Michael once more. He was Mickey—only grown more wise. Almost the old vernacular came to his tongue.

"Hi! Sam! That you?"

The figure in the darkness seemed to stiffen with sudden attention. The voice was like, and yet not like, the Mickey of old.

"Wot youse want?" questioned a voice gruffly.

"I want you, Sam. I want to see if you look as you used to, and I want to know about the boys. Can't we go where there's light and talk a little? I've been days hunting you. I've come back because I promised. You expected me to come back someday, didn't you, Sam?"

Michael was surprised to find how eager he was for the answer to this question.

"Aw, what ye givin' us?" responded the suspicious Sam. "D'youse s'pose I b'lieve all that gag about yer comin' here to he'p we'uns? Wot would a guy like youse wid all dem togs an' all dem fine looks want wid us? Youse has got above us. Youse ain't no good to us no more."

Sam scratched a match on his trousers and lit an old pipe he held between his teeth. But as the match flared up and showed his own face, a lowering brow, shifty eyes, a swarthy, unkempt visage, sullen and sly, the eyes weren't looking at the pipe but up at the face above him which shone out white and fine in the little gleam in the dark court. The watchers crowding at the opening saw his face and almost imagined soft shadowy wings behind him. Thus with old Sal's help Michael got the name again, "the Angel." And thus he became "the angel of the alley."

"Sam!" he said, and his voice was very gentle, although he was conscious of two more shadows of men behind him and perhaps more lurking in the dark corners. "Sam, if you remember me you'll know I couldn't forget, and I do care. I came back to find you. I've always meant to come, all the time I was in college. I've had it in mind to come back here and make some of the hard things easier for"—he hesitated—"for us all."

"How did youse figger youse was goin' to do that?" Sam asked, his eyes narrowing on Michael, as he purposely struck another match to watch the effect of his words.

Then Michael's smile lit up his face, and Sam, however much he may have pretended to doubt, knew in his heart this was the same Mickey of old. There was no mistaking that smile.

"I'll need you to help me figure that out, Sam. That's why I was so anxious to find you."

A curious grunt from behind Michael warned him the audience was being amused at Sam's expense. Sam's brows were lowering.

"Humph!" he said, ungraciously striking a third match in time to watch Michael's face. "Where's yer pile?"

"What?"

"Got the dough?"

"Oh," said Michael, "no, I haven't got money, Sam. I've only my education."

"An' wot good's it, I'd like to know. Tell me those?"

"So much good I can't tell it in one short talk," answered Michael steadily. "We'll have to get better acquainted, and then I hope I can make you understand how it's helped. Now tell me about the others. Where's Buck?"

There was a dead silence.

"It's hard to say!" Sam muttered at last.

"Don't you know? Haven't you any idea, Sam? I'd so like to hunt him up."

The question seemed to have produced tension in the atmosphere. Michael felt it.

"I might, an' then agin' I might not," answered Sam in the tone that barred further questions.

"Couldn't you and I find him and—and—help him, Sam? Aunt Sally said he was in trouble."

Another match was scratched and held close to his face, while Sam's narrow eyes seemed to pierce his very soul before he answered with an ugly laugh.

"Oh, he don't need none o' your help, you bet. He's lit out. You don't need to worry 'bout Buck. He kin take car' o' hisse'f every time."

"But won't he come back sometime?"

"Can't say. Hard to tell."

"And Jim?" Michael's voice was sad.

"Jim, he's doin' time."

"I'm sorry!" said Michael.

A strange hush came over the dark group. Now why should this odd chap be sorry? No one else cared, unless it might be Jim, and Jim was caught. It was nothing to them.

"Now tell me about Janie—and little Bobs—" The questioner paused. His voice was low.

"Aw, cut it out!" snarled Sam irritably. "Don't come any high strikes on their account. They're dead, an' you can't dig 'em up an' weep over 'em. Hustle up an' tell us wot yer wantin' to do."

"Well, Sam," said Michael, trying to ignore the natural repulsion he felt at his onetime friend's last words, "suppose you take lunch with me tomorrow at twelve? Then we can talk over old times. I'll tell you about my life, and you must tell me what you're doing."

Sam was silent from sheer astonishment. Take lunch? Never in his life had he been invited out to lunch. Nor had he any desire for an invitation now.

"Where?" he asked after a silence so long Michael began to fear he wasn't going to answer.

Michael named a place not far away. He'd selected it that morning, It was clean, yet not too clean. The fare was far from princely, but it would do. And the locality was none too respectable. Michael was enough of a slum child still to know his guest would never go with him to a respectable restaurant; moreover, he wouldn't have the wardrobe or the manners. He awaited Sam's answer breathlessly.

Sam gave an odd little laugh as if taken off guard. The place named seemed so harmless, and the whole matter of the invitation took on the form of a great joke.

"Well, I might," he drawled. "I won't make no promises, but I might, an' then again I might not. It's jes' as it happens. Ef I ain't there by twelve sharp you needn't wait. Jes' go ahead an' eat. I wouldn't want to spoil your digestion fer my movements."

"I'll wait!" said Michael. "You'll come, Sam. I know you will. Good night!"

And then he did an extraordinary thing. He put out his clean, strong hand, warm and healthy in the keenness of love, found the hardened grimy hand of his onetime companion, and gripped it in a hearty grasp.

Sam started back with the instant suspicion of attack and then stood ashamed and still. The grip of that firm, strong hand, the touch of brotherhood, a touch such as had never come to his life before since he was a little child, completed the work the smile had begun, and Sam knew the real Mickey was before him.

Then Michael walked swiftly down that narrow passage, at the opening of which the human shadows scattered silently and fled, to watch from other furtive doorways, down through the alley unmolested and out into the street again.

"The saints presarve us! Wot did I tell yez?" whispered Sal. "It's the angel all right, fer shure."

"I wonder wot he done to Sam," murmured the girl. "He's got his nerve all right, he sure has. Ain't he beautiful!"

Chapter 10

*M*ichael went early to his lunch party. He was divided between wondering if his strange guest would appear and, if he did, what he should talk about and how he would pilot him through the embarrassing experience of the meal. One thing he was determined upon. He meant to find out, if possible, whether Sam knew anything about his, Michael's, origin. It was scarcely likely, and yet Sam might have heard some talk by older people in the neighborhood. His one great longing was to find out and clear his name of shame, if possible.

Another thing troubled Michael. He wasn't sure he'd know Sam even if he came. The glimpse he'd caught the night before when the matches were struck wasn't illuminating. He had a dim idea Sam was below medium height, with a thin, sallow face; small, narrow eyes; slouching gait; and a head not wide enough from front to back. He had a feeling Sam couldn't see all that should be seen. Sam didn't understand about education. Could he ever make him understand?

Sam came shuffling along at ten minutes after twelve. His sense of dignity wouldn't have allowed him to be on time. Besides, he wanted to see if Michael would wait as he'd said. It was part of testing him—not to prove he was really Mickey, but to see what stuff he was made of and how much he'd meant what he said. Michael was there, standing anxiously outside the eating-house. He didn't enjoy the surroundings or the attention he was attracting. He was too well dressed for that locality, but these were his oldest clothes. He would have considered them shabby at college. He was getting worried his plan had failed. Then Sam slouched along, his hat drawn down, his hands in his pockets, wearing an air of indifference that almost amounted to effrontery. He greeted Michael as if they'd had no previous arrangement and met by chance. Nothing about his manner showed he'd come late to test him, but Michael knew intuitively it was so.

"Shall we go in now?" said Michael, smiling happily. He was glad Sam had come, repulsive in appearance though he was, hard of countenance and unfriendly in manner. He felt he was getting on a little in finding and helping his old friends and perhaps learning more of his own history.

"Aw, I donno's I care 'bout it!" drawled Sam, as if he hadn't intended going in all along and hadn't been anticipating the "feed" all morning.

"Yes, you better," said Michael, putting a friendly hand on Sam's shoulder. If he felt a repugnance to touching the tattered, greasy coat, he controlled it, remembering how he'd once worn garments far more tattered and filthy. His desire to uplift made him forget everything else.

It wasn't that Michael was so filled with love for this miserable creature who used to be his friend or so desired to renew old associations after long years of separation. It was the terrible need, the conditions, that appealed to his spirit because of what had once been done for him. It had come upon him without his knowledge, with the revival of old scenes and memories. But as with workers for humanity, it had gone so deeply into his soul as to make him forget there was even such a thing as sacrifice.

They passed into the restaurant: Michael in his well-made clothing and with his strikingly handsome face and gold hair attracting at once every eye in the place; Sam with an insolent air of assurance to cover a sudden embarrassment of pride at the company he was in.

Michael gave a generous order and talked pleasantly as they

waited. Sam sat in low-browed silence, watching him furtively, almost disconcertingly.

When they reached the course of three kinds of pie and a dab of dirty-looking pink ice cream professing to be fresh strawberry, Michael looked keenly at his guest and asked, "What're you doing now, Sam? In business for yourself?"

Sam's eyes narrowed until they were almost eclipsed, though a steel glitter could be seen beneath the colorless lashes. A mask, impenetrable as lead, seemed to settle over his face, which had been gradually relaxing during the meal into a half-indulgent grin of interest in his odd host.

"Yas, I'm in business fer myself," he drawled at last, after scrutinizing the other's face to be sure of no underlying motive for the question.

"Newsstand?" asked Michael.

"Not eggs-act-ly!"

"What line?"

Sam finished his mince pie and began on the pumpkin before he answered. "Wal, there's sev'ral!"

"Is that so? Got more than one string to your bow? That's a good thing. You're better off than I am. I haven't looked around for a job yet. I thought I'd get at it tomorrow. I wanted to look you fellows up first before I got tied down to anything where I couldn't get off when I wanted to. Perhaps you can put me onto something. How about it?"

Michael hadn't once thought of going to Endicott for the position and help offered him, since the setting down he'd received from Mrs. Endicott. The time appointed for his going to Endicott's office was long since passed. He hadn't even turned the matter over in his mind since that awful night of agony and renunciation. Mrs. Endicott had told him her husband "had done enough for him," and he realized this was true. He would trouble him no more. Sometime perhaps the world would turn around so he could repay Endicott's kindness that he might not repay in money, but until then Michael would keep out of his way. It was the one little rag of pride he allowed himself from the shattering of his hopes.

Sam narrowed his eyes and looked Michael through, then slowly widened them again, with an expression of real interest.

"Say! Do you mean it?" he asked doubtfully. "Be you straight goods? Would you come back into de gang an' not snitch on us ner nothin'?"

"I'm straight goods, Sam, and I won't snitch!" said Michael quickly. He knew he could hope for no fellow's confidence if he "snitched."

"Wal, say, I've a notion to tell yeh!"

Sam attacked his ice cream. "How would a bluff game strike you?" he asked as the last mouthful of cream disappeared. He reached for the fresh cup of coffee the waiter had just set down.

"What sort?" asked Michael, wondering what he was coming on in the way of revelation, but resolving not to be horrified at anything. Sam mustn't suspect until he could understand the difference education had made in the way of looking at things.

"Wal, there's diffrunt ways. Cripple's purty good. Foot all tied up in bloody rags, arm an' hand tied up, a couple o' old crutches. I could lend the clo'es. They'd be short fer yeh, but that'd be all the better gag. We cud swap, an' I'd do the gen'l-man act awhile." He looked covetously at Michael's handsome brown tweeds. "Den you goes fom house to house, er you stands on de corner—"

"Begging!" said Michael aghast. His eyes were on his plate, and he was trying to control his voice, but something of his horror crept into his tones.

Sam felt it and hastened on apologetically. "Er ef you want to go it one better, keep on yer good cloes an' have the asthma bad. I know a feller what'll teach you how an' sell you the whistles to put in yer mouth. You've no notion how it works.

You just go around in the subbubs tellin' you've only been out of the 'orspittal two days an' you walked all this way to get work an' couldn't get it, an' you want five cents to get back— see? Why, I know a feller—course he's been at it fer years an' has his regular beats—folks don't seem to remember—and he can work the ground over 'bout once in six months er so, and he's made high's thirty-eight dollars in a day at asthma work."

Sam paused triumphant to see what effect the statement had on his friend, but Michael's face was toward his coffee cup.

"Seems sort of small business for a man!" he said at last, his voice steady with control. "Don't believe I'd be good at that. Haven't you got something that's real work?"

Sam's eyes narrowed. "Ef I thought you was up to it," he murmured. "You'd be great with that angel face o' yourn. Nobody'd ever suspect you. You could wear them clo'es, too. But it's work all right, an' mighty resky. Ef I thought you was up to it—"

He continued to study Michael, and Michael, with innate instinct, felt his heart beat in discouraged thumps. What new deviltry was Sam about to propose?

"You used to be game, all right!" murmured Sam. "You never used to scare easy. Wal, I'll tell you," he said in answer to Michael's questioning eyes which searched his sharp wizened face.

"You see, it's a reg'ler business, an' you hev to learn. But I'd give you pinters—all you'd need to know. I'm pretty slick myself. There's tools to open things, an' you hev to be ready to 'xplain how you come thur an' jolly up a parlor maid per'aps. It's easy to hev made a mistake in the house er be a gas man er a plumber wot the boss sent up to look at the pipes. But night work's best pay after you get onto things. Thur's houses where you ken lay your han's on things goin' into the thousands an' lots ov um easy to get rid of without anybody findin' out. There's Buck—he used to be great at it. He taught the gang. The day he lit out, he bagged a bit o' glass wuth tree tousand dollars, 'sides a whole handful of fivers an' tens wot he found lyin' on a dressin' table pretty as you please. Buck, he were a slick one at it. He'd be pleased to know you'd took up the work—"

Sam paused and eyed Michael with the first friendly gleam he'd shown in his eyes, and Michael, with his heart in a tumult of emotions and the quick color flooding brow and cheek, held himself in check. He mustn't speak too hastily. Perhaps he hadn't understood Sam's meaning.

"Where is Buck?" Michael looked Sam straight in the eye. The small pupils seemed to contract and shut out even his gaze.

"They ain't never got a trace of Buck," he said.

"But don't you know?" Something in Michael's look demanded an answer.

"I might, an' I might not."

Michael was still for several seconds watching Sam, each trying to understand the other.

"Do you think he'll come back where I can see him?" he asked at length.

"He might, an' he might not. 'T depends. Ef you was in th' bizness, he might. It's hard to say. 'T depends."

Michael watched Sam again thoughtfully.

"Tell me more about the business," he said at last, his lips compressed, his brows drawn into a frown of intensity.

"Thur ain't much more t' tell," said Sam, still sullen. "I ain't sure you're up to it."

"What do you mean by that?"

"Ain't sure you got de sand. You might turn faint and snitch." Sam leaned forward and spoke in low rapid sentences. "Wen we'd got a big haul, 'sposen you'd got into de house an' done de pinchin', and we got the stuff safe hid, an' you got tuk up? Would you snitch? Er would you take your pill like a man?

That's what I'd want to be sure. Mickey would 'a' stood by the gang, but you—you've had a edicashun! They might go soft at college. I ain't much use fer edicated persons myself. But I'll give you a show ef you promise stiff not to snitch. We've gotta big game on tonight up on Madison Avenue, an' we're a man short. Dere's dough in it if we make it go all right. Rich man. Girl goin' out to a party tonight. She's goin' to wear some dimons wuth a penny. Hed it in de paper. Brung 'em home fom de bank this mornin'. One o' de gang watched de feller come out o' de bank. It's all straight so fur. It's a pretty big haul to let you in de first try, an' you'll hev to run all de risks. But ef you show your game we'll make it a bargain."

Michael held himself tensely and fought the desire to choke the fellow. He tried to remember he was the same Sam who had once divided a crust with him and whom he'd come to help and reflected that he might have been as bad himself if he hadn't been taken from the terrible environment of the slums and shown a better way. He knew that if for one fraction of a second he showed his horror at the evil plot or tried to stop it, all hope of reaching Sam, Buck, or the others was ended—and with it all hope of finding any stray links to his own history. Besides, though honor was strong in him and he'd never "snitch" on his companions, it would certainly be better to find out as much as possible about the scheme. There might be other ways of stopping such things besides "snitching."

Then suddenly his heart almost stopped beating. Madison Avenue! Sam had said Madison Avenue and a girl! What if they were planning to take Starr's jewels? He knew very little about such matters except what he'd read. It didn't occur to him that Starr wasn't yet "out" in society; that she would be too young to wear costly jewels and have her costume put in the paper. He only knew his heart was throbbing again painfully and that the fellow before him seemed too vile to live longer on the same earth with little, exquisite Starr.

He was quite still when Sam had finished. His face was white with emotion, and his eyes were blazing blue flames when he raised them to look at Sam. Then he became aware that his answer was awaited.

"Sam, do you mean burglary?" He tried to keep his voice low and steady as he spoke, but he felt as if he'd shouted the last word. The restaurant was almost empty now, and the waiters had retired behind the scenes amid a clatter of dishes.

"That's about as pretty a word as you can call it, I guess," said Sam, drawing back with a snarl as he saw the light in Michael's eyes.

Michael looked him through, and if a glance can burn, then surely Sam's soul shrank scorching into itself. But it was so brief that the brain keen only to earthly things hadn't analyzed it. Michael dropped his glance to the table again and began playing with his spoon and trying to get calm with a deep breath as he used to when he knew a hard spot in a ball game was coming.

"Well, why don't you speak? You 'fraid?" he said with a sneer a devil from the pit might have given.

Then Michael sat up calmly. His heart was beating steadily now, and he was facing his adversary.

"No! I'm not afraid, Sam, if there were any good reason for going. But you know I never could feel comfortable in getting my living off somebody else. It doesn't seem fair to the other fellow. They've got a right to the things they own, and I haven't. And because I might be smart enough to catch them napping and sneak away with what they prize doesn't make it right, either. Now that girl probably thinks a lot of her diamonds, you see, and it doesn't seem quite the manly thing for a big strong fellow like me to get them away from her, does it? Of course you may think differently, but I'd rather do some good hard work that would keep my muscles trim than to live off someone else.

"There's a pretty gray moss that grows where I went to college. It floats along a little seed blown in the air first and lodges on a tree limb and begins to fasten itself into the bark and grow and suck life from the big tree. It doesn't seem much at first, and it seems as if the big tree might spare enough juice to the little moss. But wait a few years and see what happens. The moss grows and drapes itself in long festoons all over that tree, and the first thing you know, that tree has lost its green leaves and stands up stark and dead with nothing on its bare branches but that old gray moss which has to die, too, because it has nothing to live on any longer. It never learned to gather any juice for itself. They call the moss a parasite. I couldn't be a human parasite, Sam. You may feel differently about it, but I really couldn't."

Michael's eyes had grown dreamy and lost their fire as he remembered the dear South and dead sentinel pines with their waving gray festoons against the blue sky. As he talked he saw the great outdoors again where he'd wandered so many years free and happy, free from humanity's burdens that pressed sorely now. A great longing to fly back to it all, away from the sorrow and degradation and shame, filled his heart, leaped into his eyes, caught and fascinated the attention of the listening Sam, who understood little of the peroration. He'd never heard of a parasite. He didn't know he'd always been a human parasite. He was merely astonished and fascinated by the passion and appeal in Michael's face as he spoke.

"Say!" he said in a tone almost of admiration. "Is that wot edicashun done fer you?"

"Perhaps," said Michael pleasantly, "though I think I always felt a bit that way, Sam. I just didn't know how to say it."

"Wal, you allus was odd!" muttered Sam half apologetically. "I couldn't see it that way myself, as you say, but o' course it's your fun'ral! Ef you kin scratch up enough grub bein' a tree, why, that's your lookout. Moss is good 'nough fer me fer de present."

Michael beamed his wonderful smile on Sam. "Perhaps you'll see it my way someday, Sam, and then we can get a job together!"

There was so much comradery in the tone and so much brilliancy in the smile that Sam forgot to be sullen.

"Wal, mebbe," he chuckled, "but I don't see no edicashun comin' my way dis late day, so I guess I'll git along de way I be."

"It isn't too late yet, Sam. There's more than one way of getting an education. It doesn't always come through college."

After a little more talk, in which Sam promised to find out if Michael could visit Jim in his temporary retirement from the law-abiding world and Michael promised to visit Sam in the alley again at an appointed time, the two separated.

Then Michael went forth to reconnoiter and to guard the Endicott house.

With no thought of any personal danger, Michael laid his plans. Before sundown he was on hand, having considered all visible and invisible means of ingress to the house. He watched from a suitable distance all who came and went. He saw Mr. Endicott come home. He waited till the evening drew near when a luxurious limousine stopped before the door, assuring himself only Mrs. Endicott had gone out. A little later Mr. Endicott also left the house. Starr hadn't gone out. He felt he needed doubly to watch now as she was alone with only the servants.

Up and down he walked. No one passed the Endicott house unwatched by him. None came forth or went in without his noting it.

The evening passed, and the master and mistress of the house returned. One by one the lights went out. Even the servants' rooms were dark at last. The night deepened, and the stars thickened overhead.

The policeman's whistle sounded through the quiet streets, and the city seemed to be sinking into a brief repose. It was long past midnight, and still Michael kept up his patrol. Up this side of the street, down that, around the corner, through the alley at the back where "de kids" had stood in silent respect toward his window years ago, back to the avenue again and on around. With his cheery whistle and steady ringing step he awakened no suspicion, even when he came near a policeman. Besides, no lurkers of the dark would steal out while he was so noisily in the neighborhood.

And so he watched the night through, till morning broke and sunshine flooded the window of the room where Starr, unconscious of his vigil, lay sleeping.

Busy milk wagons were making their rounds, and sleepy workmen with dinner pails slung over their arms were striding to their day's work through the morning coolness, as Michael turned his steps toward his lodging.

Broad morning was upon them, and deeds of darkness could be no more. The night was over. Nothing had happened. Starr was safe. He went home and to sleep well pleased. He might not companion with her, but it was his privilege to guard her from unsuspected evils. That was one joy that couldn't be taken from him by the taint upon him. Perhaps his being a child of the slums might yet help guard her life from harm.

Chapter 11

$\mathcal{T}$he first week in September Michael, passing through a crowded thoroughfare, came face-to-face with Mr. Endicott.

The days had passed into weeks, and Michael hadn't gone near his benefactor. He'd felt he must drop out of his old friend's life until he could show his gratitude for the past. Meanwhile he hadn't been idle. His winning smile and clear eyes had been his passport, and after a few preliminary experiences he'd secured a position as salesman in a large department store. His college diploma and a letter from the college president were his references. He wasn't earning much, just enough to pay his absolute expenses and a bit over. But he was gaining experience.

This Saturday morning of the first week of September, he'd come to the store as usual but found that because of a firm member's sudden death the store would be closed for the day.

He was wondering how to spend his holiday and wishing he might get out and breathe the open air under waving trees and listen to the birds and water and wind. He was half tempted to squander a few cents and go to Coney Island or up the Hudson, anywhere to get out of the grinding, noisy, tempestuous city. Its sin and burden pressed on his heart night and day because of that from which he'd been saved and yet couldn't save others.

Then out of a doorway rushed a man toward a waiting automobile and almost knocked Michael over in his progress.

"Oh! It's you, young man! At last! Well, I'd like to know

what you've done with yourself all these weeks and why you didn't keep your appointment with me."

"Oh!" said Michael, pleasure and shame striving together in his face. He could see the man wasn't angry and was relieved to find him.

"Where are you going, son?" Endicott's tone had already changed from gruffness to kindly welcome. "Jump in and run down to the wharf with me while you give an account of yourself. I'm going down to see Mrs. Endicott off to Europe. She's taking Starr over to school this winter. I'm late already, so come on."

Michael seemed to have no choice and stepped into the car, which whirled through the maze of humanity and machinery toward the regions where the oceangoing steamers harbored.

His heart was in a tumult at once, both of embarrassed joy to be with the man who'd done so much for him and of eager anticipation. Starr! Would he see Starr again? That thought was uppermost in his mind. He hadn't yet realized she was going away for a long time.

All spring he'd kept guard over the house in Madison Avenue. Not all night, of course, but hovering about there now and then, and nightly for two weeks after he'd talked with Sam. Always he walked that way before retiring and looked toward the window where a soft light burned. Then they'd gone to the seashore and the mountains, and the house had put on solemn shutters and lain asleep. Michael knew from a stray paragraph in the society column of the daily paper he happened to read.

Toward the end of August, he'd made a round through Madison Avenue every night to see if they'd returned home, and for a week the shutters had been down and the lights burning as of old. It was good to know his charge was back safely. And now he was to see her.

"Well! Give an account of yourself. Were you trying to keep

out of my sight? Why didn't you come to my office?"

Michael looked him straight in the eye with his honest, clear gaze that showed no sowing of wild oats, no dissipation or desire to escape friendly espionage. He decided in a flash that this man should never know the blow his beautiful, haughty wife had dealt him. What she said was true, and he would give the real reason why he hadn't come.

"Because I thought you'd done for me far more than I deserved already, and I didn't wish to be any further burden to you."

"The dickens you did!" exclaimed Endicott. "You good-for-nothing rascal! Didn't you know you'd be more of a burden running off like that without a trace so I could hunt you up, than if you'd done as I told you? Here I've been worrying unnecessarily about you. I thought you'd fallen among thieves or gone to the dogs. Don't you know it's unpardonable to run off from a man who's told you he wants to see you? I thought I made you understand I had more than a passing interest in your welfare!"

The color came into the fine, strong face and a pained expression in his eyes.

"I'm sorry, sir. I didn't think of it that way. I thought you felt some kind of an obligation. I never felt so, but you said you did, and I thought if I got out of your way I wouldn't trouble you anymore."

"Trouble me! Why, son, I like to be troubled once in a while by something besides getting money and spending it. You never gave me a shadow of trouble, except these last weeks when you disappeared and I couldn't do anything for you. You've somehow crept into my life, and I can't get you out. I don't want to. But, boy, if you felt that way, what made you come to New York at all? You didn't feel that way the night you came to my house to dinner."

Michael's eyes owned this was true, but his firm lips showed he would never betray the real reason for the change.

"I—didn't—realize—sir!"

"Realize? Realize what?"

"I didn't realize the difference between my station and yours, sir. There was nothing during my years in school to make me know. I'm a child of the slums"—unconsciously he drifted into words from Mrs. Endicott's speech—"and you belong to a fine old family. I don't know what terrible things are in my blood. You have riches and a name beyond reproach." He saw the words in an article he'd read the evening before and felt they fitted the man and the occasion. He didn't know he was quoting. They'd become part of his thoughts.

"I might make the riches if I tried hard." He held up his head proudly. "But I could never make the name. I will always be a child of the slums, no matter what I do!"

"Child of the fiddlesticks!" interrupted Endicott. "Wherever did you get that rot? It sounds as if you've been attending society functions and listening to their twaddle. It doesn't matter what you're the child of, if you've a mind to be a man. This is a free country, son, and you can be and climb where you please. Tell me—where did you get all these ideas?"

Michael looked down. "In a number of places."

"Where?"

"For one thing, I've been down to the alley where I used to live."

The eyes were looking into his now, and Endicott felt a strange swelling of pride that he'd had a hand in the making of this young man.

"Well?"

"I know what you've taken me from—I can never be what you are!"

"Therefore you won't try to be anything? Is that it?"

"Oh, no! I'll try to be all I can, but—I don't belong with you. I'm of another class—"

"Oh, bosh! Cut that out, son! Real men don't talk like that. You're a better man now than any of the pedigreed dudes I know of. As for taints in the blood, I could tell you about some of the sons of great men who have taints as bad as any child of the slums. Young man, you can be whatever you set out to be in this world! Remember that."

"Everyone doesn't feel that way," said Michael with conviction, though he was conscious of great pleasure in Endicott's hearty words.

"Who, for instance?" said Endicott, looking at him sharply.

Michael was silent.

"Who?" asked the insistent voice once more.

"The world!"

"The world is brainless. You can make the world think what you like, son. Remember that! Here we are. Would you like to come aboard?"

But Michael stood back.

"I'll wait here," he said gravely. He realized Mrs. Endicott would be there. He mustn't intrude, not even to see Starr. Besides, she'd made it a point of honor for him to keep away from her daughter. He had no choice but to obey.

"Very well," said Endicott, "but see you don't lose yourself again. I want to see you about something. I'll not be long. It must be nearly time for starting." He hurried away, and Michael stood on the edge of the throng looking up at the great floating village.

It was his first view of an oceangoing steamer at close range, and everything about it interested him. He wished he might have gone aboard and looked the vessel over. He'd like to know about the engines and see the cabins and especially the steerage he'd read so much about. But perhaps he'd have another opportunity. He'd go to Ellis Island, too, and see the emigrants as they entered the country, seeking a new home where they'd been led to expect to find comfort and plenty of work. Finding none, most of them landed inevitably in the city slums, where the population was already congested and where vice and disease preyed upon them. Michael had been spending enough time in the alleys of the metropolis to be deeply interested in the city's problems and deeply pained by its sorrows.

But he wasn't thinking altogether of the masses and the classes as he stood in the sunlight and gazed at the great vessel about to plow its way over the waters. He was realizing that somewhere within those many windowed cabins was a bright-faced girl, the only one of womankind in the earth his tender thoughts had hovered about. Would he catch a glimpse of her face before she left for the winter? She was going to school, her father said. How could they bear to send her across the water from them? A whole winter was a long time, and yet it would pass. Thirteen years had passed since he left New York, and he was back. It wouldn't be as long as that. She would return and need him perhaps. He would be there and ready when he was needed.

The lips were set firmly, with the patient, fearless lines of a soldier in the boy's face, and rugged strength showed forth. If he'd been born in aristocratic circles he would have been the idol of society, the spoiled of all who knew him. Even now those in sight were staring at him, and more than one pair of marine glasses from the first cabin deck were pointed at him; but he stood deep in his thoughts and utterly unconscious of his attraction.

It was only a moment before the first warning came, and people crowded on the wharf side of the decks, while others hurried down the gangplank. Michael watched the confusion with eagerness, his eyes searching the decks for Starr.

When the last warning was given, as the gangplank was about to be hauled up, Mr. Endicott hurried down, and Michael suddenly saw her face in the crowd on the deck above, with her mother's haughtily pretty face just behind her.

Without realizing what he was doing, Michael moved through the crowd until he stood close behind Starr's father. Then all at once he became aware that her eyes were upon him, and she recognized him.

He lifted his hat and stood in reverent attitude, his eyes glowing eloquently, his face paying her tribute as plainly as words could have. The noonday sun burnished his hair with its aureole flame, and more than one of the passengers called attention to the sight.

"See that man down there!" exclaimed a woman behind Mrs. Endicott. "Isn't he magnificent! He has a head and shoulders like a young god!" She spoke as if her acquaintance with gods was wide, and her neighbors turned to look.

"See, Mama," whispered Starr, glowing with pleasure. "They're talking about Michael."

Then the eyes turned sharply and recognized him. "You don't mean to tell me that upstart has dared to come down and see us off. The impudence! I'm glad your father had enough sense not to bring him on board. He'd probably have come if he'd let him. Come away, Starr. He simply shall not look at you that way!"

"What! Come away while Papa is standing there watching us out of sight? I simply couldn't. What would Papa think? And, besides, I don't see why Michael shouldn't come if he likes. I think it was nice of him. I wonder why he hasn't been to the house to explain why he never came for that horseback ride."

"You're a silly, ignorant girl, or you'd understand he has no business coming to our house, and he knows it. I want you to stop looking in that direction at once. I simply won't have him devouring you with his eyes that way. I'd like to go back and tell him what I think of him. Starr, stop, I tell you!"

But the noise of the starting drowned her words, and Starr, her cheeks like roses, was waving a handkerchief and smiling and throwing kisses. The kisses were for her father, but the smiles, the glances, and the waving bit of cambric were for Michael, and they all traveled through the air together, drenching the bright uncovered head of the boy with sweetness. His eyes gave her greeting and thanks and parting all in one in that brief moment, and her graceful form and dainty vivid face were engraved on his memory in quick sweet blows of pain, as he realized she was going from him.

Slowly the great vessel glided out upon the waters and grew smaller and smaller. The crowd on the wharf was breaking away and hurrying back to business or home or society. Still Michael stood gazing, with that illumined expression on his face.

Endicott, a mist on his own glasses at parting from his beloved baby, saw the boy's face as it were the face of an angel and was half startled, turning away embarrassedly as though he'd intruded upon a soul at prayer; then he looked again.

"Come, son!" he said huskily. "It's over! We better be getting back. Step in."

The ride to the office was a silent one. Somehow Endicott didn't feel like talking. There had been some annoying differences between him and his wife, and a strange belated regret that he'd let Starr go away for a foreign education was eating into his heart. Michael, on his part, was reliving the passing of the vessel and the blessing of the parting.

Back in the office, however, all was different. Among the familiar walls and gloomy desks and chairs, Endicott was himself and talked business.

"What are you doing with yourself? Working? What at? H'm! How'd you get there? Like it? Satisfied to do that all your life? You're not? Well, what's your line? Any ambitions? You should have got some notion in college of what you're fit for. Have you thought what you'd like to do in the world?"

Michael hesitated, then looked up with his clear, direct, challenging gaze.

"Two things," he said. "I want to earn money and buy some land in the country, and I want to know about laws."

"Do you mean you want to be a lawyer?"

"Yes."

"What makes you think you'd be a success as a lawyer?"

"Oh, I might not be a success, but I need to know law. I want to try to stop some things that shouldn't be."

"H'm!" grunted Endicott disapprovingly. "Don't try the reform game; it doesn't pay. But if you feel that way you'll probably be all right to start. That'll work itself off and be a good foundation. There's no reason why you should not be a lawyer if you choose, but you can't study law selling calico. You might get there someday, if you stick to your ambition. But you'd be pretty old before you were ready to practice if you started at the calico counter and worked your way up through everything you came to. Well, I can get you into a law office right away. How soon can you honorably get away from where you are? Two weeks? Well, just wait a minute."

Endicott called up a number on the telephone by his side, and there followed a conversation, brief, pointed, but in terms Michael could barely follow. He gathered that a lawyer named Holt, a friend of Mr. Endicott's, was being asked to take him into his office to read law.

"It's all right, son," said Endicott as he hung up the receiver and whirled around from the phone. "You're to present yourself at the office as soon as you're free. This is the address—" He hurriedly scribbled something on a card and handed it to him.

"Oh, thank you!" said Michael. "But I didn't mean to have you take any more trouble for me. I can't be dependent on you any longer. You've done so much for me."

"Bosh!" said Endicott. "I'm not taking any trouble. And you're not dependent on me. Be as independent as you like. You're not quite twenty-one, are you? Well, I told you you were my boy until you were of age, and I suppose there's nothing to hinder me doing as I will with my own. All I've done for you so far has paid well, and I feel the investment was a good one. You'll get a small salary for some office work while you're studying, so after you're twenty-one, you can be on your own if you like. Till then I claim the privilege of giving you a few orders. Now that's settled. Where are you stopping? I don't intend to lose sight of you again."

Michael gave him the street and number. Endicott frowned.

"That's not a good place. I don't like the neighborhood. If you're going to be a lawyer, you must start in right. Here, try this place. Tell the woman I sent you. One of my clerks used to board there."

He handed Michael another address.

"Won't that cost a lot?" asked Michael, studying the card.

"No more than you can afford," said Endicott, "and remember, I'm giving orders until your majority."

Michael beamed his brilliant smile at his benefactor.

"It's like a real father!" said the boy, deeply moved. "I can never repay you. I can never forget it."

"Well, don't!" said Endicott. "Let's turn to the other thing. What do you want land for?"

Michael's face sobered instantly.

"For an experiment I want to try," he said without hesitation, and then his eyes lit up. "I can do it now, soon, perhaps, if I work hard. You see, I studied agriculture in college."

"The dickens you did!" exclaimed Endicott. "Why did you do that?"

"Well, it was there, and I could, and I wanted to know about it."

"H'm!" said Endicott. "I wonder what some of my pedigreed million-dollar friends' sons would think of that? Well, go on."

"Why, that's all," said Michael, laughing happily. "I studied it, and I want to try it and see what I can do with it. I want to buy a farm."

"How would you manage to be a farmer and a lawyer both?"

"Well, I thought there might be a little time after hours to work, and I could tell others how—"

"Oh, I see; you want to be a gentleman farmer," said Endicott, laughing. "I understand that's expensive business."

"I think I could make it pay, sir," said Michael, shutting his lips with his firm challenge. "I'd like to try."

Endicott looked at him quizzically for a minute and then, whirling around in his office chair, he reached out his hand to a pigeonhole and took out a deed.

"I've a mind to let you try," said Endicott, chuckling as if it were a good joke. "Here's a little farm down in Jersey. It's swampy and thick with mosquitoes. I understand it won't grow a beanstalk. There are twelve acres and a tumbledown house on it. I had to take it in settlement of a mortgage. The man's dead, and there's nothing but the farm to lay hands on. He hadn't even a chick or a child to leave his debt to. I don't want the farm and can't sell it without a lot of trouble. I'll give it to you. You may consider it a birthday present. If you'll pay the taxes, I'll be glad to get it off my hands. That'll be something for you to be independent about."

He touched a bell, and a boy appeared.

"Take this to Jowett and tell him to have a deed made out to Michael Endicott and attend to the property transfer, nominal sum. Understand?"

The boy said, "Yes, sir," and disappeared with the paper.

"But I can't take a present like that from you after all you've done for me," gasped Michael, a granite determination showing in his blue eyes.

"Nonsense," said Endicott. "Other men give their sons automobiles when they come of age. May I not give you a farm if I like? Besides, it's of no account. I want to get rid of it, and I want to see what you'll make of it. I'd like to amuse myself seeing you try your experiment."

"If you'll let me pay you for it little by little."

"Suit yourself after you've become a great lawyer," said Endicott, laughing, "but not till then—remember. There, cut it out, son! I don't want to be thanked. Here's the description of the place and directions how to get there. It isn't many miles away. If you've got a half holiday, run down and look it over. It'll keep you out of mischief. There's nothing like an ambition to keep people out of mischief. Run along now—I haven't another minute to spare. But mind you turn up at Holt's office this day in two weeks and report to me afterward how you like it. I don't want to lose sight of you again."

Another man entered on business, cutting short the interview, and Michael, bestowing an agonizingly happy grip on Endicott's hand and a brilliant smile, took his directions and hurried out into the street.

Chapter 12

*W*ith the precious paper in his hand, Michael hurried to the DesBrosses Ferry. Would there be a train? It was almost two o'clock. He'd had no lunch, but what of that? He had in his heart what made mere eating seem unnecessary. The experiences of the past two hours had lifted him above earthly things. And a farm, a real farm! Could it be true? Had his wish come true so soon? He could scarcely wait for the car to carry him or the boat to puff its way across the water. He felt as if he must fly to see his new possession. And Mr. Endicott had said he might pay for it sometime when he got to be a great lawyer. He had no doubt he would get there if such a thing were possible, and, anyhow, he meant to pay for that ground. Meanwhile it was his. He wasn't a poor nobody after all. He owned land and a house.

His face was a mingling of delightful emotions as he stood by the ferry rail and let his imagination leap ahead of him. The day was perfect. It had rained the night before, and everything, even the air, seemed newly washed for a fresh trail at living. The sunlight shimmered on the water, and every wavelet sparkled like a jewel. Michael forgot for the moment the sorrow and misery of the crowded city he was leaving behind him. For this afternoon at least, he was a boy again wandering off into the open.

His train was being called as he stepped from the ferry. He hurried aboard and was soon speeding through the open country, with glimpses of the sea, as the train neared the beach. They passed beautiful resorts, private villas, great hotels, and miles of cottages set in a green terrace with glowing autumn flowers in boxes or bordering the paths.

Michael watched everything with interest. This was the land of his new possession. Whatever was growing here would likely grow on his place if properly planted and cared for. Before this, flowers had had little part in his farming scheme, but as soon as he saw the brilliant display he resolved to have some also. And flowers would sell as well as, if not better than, vegetables if properly marketed.

That vivid hedge of scarlet and gold—he thought they were called dahlias—would take up little room and make his new place beautiful. Farther on, one great white cottage spread its veranda wings on either side to a tall fringe of pink, white, and crimson cosmos. Then a rambling gray stone piece of quaint architecture, with low sloping roofs of mossy green and velvet lawn creeping down even to the white beach sands, was set about with flaming scarlet sage. It was a revelation to the boy who had never seen the like.

Nature in its wildness and original beauty had been in Florida; New York was all pavements and buildings with a window box here and there. He as yet knew nothing of country homes in their luxury and perfection, except from magazine pictures. All along he was picking out features he meant someday to transfer to his farm.

After three he reached the station and walked a good fifteen minutes to the farm, but every step was a delight.

Pearl Beach, they called the station. The beach was half a mile from the railroad, and an odd straggling town, mostly cottages and a few stores, hovered between railroad and beach. A river, broad and shallow, wound about the village and lost itself in the ocean's wideness.

Here and there a white sail flew across its gleaming center, and fishermen in little boats sat at their idle task. What if his land should touch this bonny stream!

Too eager to wait for investigation, he stopped a passing stranger and questioned him. Yes, the river was salt. It had tides with the sea, too. They had great fishing and sailing, and some preferred bathing there to the ocean. Yes, Old Orchard Farm was on its bank. It had a river frontage of several hundred feet, but it was over a mile back from the beach.

The stranger wanted to linger and gossip about the death of the former owner of Old Orchard and its probable fate now that the mortgage had been foreclosed, but Michael, with a happy light in his eyes, thanked him courteously and hurried on. He felt like a bird set free. He breathed in the strong salt air with delight.

And the city's burden came to him again, the city with all its noise and folly and sin; with its smells and heat and lack of air; with its crowded, suffering, awful humanity, herded together like cattle and living in conditions worse than the beasts of the fields. If he could only bring them out here, some of them at least, and show them what God's earth was like! Ah!

His heart beat wildly at the thought! It wasn't new. He'd harbored it ever since his first visit to the alley. It was his great secret, his much-hoped-for experiment. This little farm would open the way. Money would be needed, of course, and where would it come from? But he could work. He was strong. He would give his young life for his people—save them from their ignorance and despair. At least he could save some; even one would be worthwhile.

So he mused as he hurried on, eyes and mind open to all he saw.

No fence stood in front of Old Orchard Farm. A white road bordered with goldenrod and wild asters met the scraggly grass that matted and tangled itself beneath the gnarled apple trees. A grassy rutted wagon track curved itself between the trees up to the house set far back from the road. A passing man identified the place for Michael.

The house was of weather-beaten unpainted clapboards, its roof of curled and mossy shingles, doubtless leaking, and patched here and there. A crazy veranda ambled across the front. Inside he found a long, low room with an old-fashioned chimney place wide enough to sit in; a square south room that must have been a dining room because of the painted cupboard with empty shelves gazing between half-open doors; and a small kitchen, not much more than a shed. In the long room a staircase twisted up to the four rooms under the leaky roof. It was all empty and desolate, except for an old cot bed and a broken chair. The floors had a sagging, shaky appearance. The doors quaked when opened. The windows were cobwebby and dreary. Yet it looked to the new householder's eyes like a palace. He saw it in light of future possibilities and gloried in it. That chimney place. How would it look with a great log burning in it and a rug and rocking chair before it?

What would Aunt Sally, perhaps, say to it when he got it fixed up? Could he ever coax her to leave her dirty doorstep and her drink and come out here to live? And how would he manage it all if he could? There would have to be something to feed her with and buy the rug and the rocking chair. And first of all there would have to be a bathtub. Aunt Sally would need to be purified before she could enter the portals of this ideal cottage, when he'd made it as he wanted it to be. Paint and paper would make wonderful transformations, for he'd often helped remodel the college rooms during summer vacations. He'd watched the workmen and finally taken a hand. This habit of watching and helping had taught him many things. But where were paper and paint and time coming from? Ah, well, leave that to the future. He would find a way. Yesterday he didn't have the house or the land for it to stand on. It had come, and the rest would follow in their time.

He went happily about planning for a bathroom. They

would need water power. He had seen windmills on other places he passed. That was perhaps the solution, but windmills cost money. Still—all in good time.

A tumbledown barn and chicken house stood in the back near a scraggly attempt at a garden: a strawberry bed overgrown with weeds, a sickly cabbage lifting its head bravely, a gaunt row of currant bushes, another of raspberries. A broken fence was just beyond that, with a stretch of soggy bog land to the right. Then the farm trailed off into desolation, ending in a charming grove of thick trees down by the river's bank.

Michael surveyed it carefully, noted the exposure of the land, kicked the sandy soil to examine its unpromising state, walked all around the bog, and tried to remember what he'd read about cranberry bogs. He wondered if the saltwater came up here—was it good or bad for cranberries? And he wondered if cowpeas grew in Jersey and if they'd do for a fertilizing crop as they did in Florida. Then he walked through the lovely woods, smelling the breath of pines. They weren't like the giant pines of the South but were sweeter and more beautiful in their form.

He went down to the river's brink and looked across. Not a soul was in sight, and nothing moved except a distant sail fleeing out to the sea. He remembered what the man had said about bathing and, yielding to an irresistible impulse, was soon swimming out across the water. To propel himself with strong, graceful strokes through the water gave him a new lease on life. A bird shot up into the air with a wild sweet note, and he felt like answering to its melody. He whistled softly in imitation of its voice, and the bird answered, and again and again they called across the water.

But a look toward the west where the water was crimsoning already with the setting sun warned him his time was short. He swam back to the sheltered nook where he'd left his clothes, and improvising a towel from his handkerchief, he dressed rapidly. The last train left at seven. If he didn't wish to spend the night in his new, uninhabitable abode, he must make good time. It was later than he'd thought, and he wanted to go back to the station by way of the beach if possible, though it was out of his way. He must stand on the shore once, look out across it, and know how it looked near his own house.

He hurried through the grove and across the farm to the eastern edge. Looking beyond the broken fence that marked the bounds of the bog and over the waste of salt grass, he could see the white waves tumbling to get past one another. He took the fence at a bound, made good time over the uncertain footing of the marsh grass, and was soon standing on the broad smooth beach with the open stretch of ocean before him.

It was the first time he'd ever stood on the seashore, and the awe that filled him was great. But beyond any other sensation came the thought that Starr, his beautiful Starr, was out there on that vast ocean, tossing in a tiny boat. For now the great steamer that had seemed so large and palatial had dwindled in his mind to a frail toy, and he was filled with a nameless fear for her. His little Starr out there on that fearful deep, with only that cold-eyed mother to take care of her. A wild desire to fly to her and bring her back possessed him, a thrilling, awesome something he'd never known before. He stood speechless before it.

Then he looked up and said aloud, "Oh, God, I love her!"

He faced the thought with solemn joy and pain for an instant, then turned and fled from it down the purpling sands, fleeing, yet carrying his secret with him.

All the way home the new thought surged over him: He loved her, and she could never be his. It was beautiful, but it was agonizing. He recalled how beautiful she was as she waved farewell. And some of her smiles were for him, he was sure. He knew the kisses were for her father, and yet they were blown freely his way, and she looked pleased at his presence. He saw the same look in her eyes she wore that day in the college chapel when she threw precaution to the wind and put her arms about his neck and kissed him. His young heart thrilled with a deep joy over the memory of it. It was wonderful that she'd done it, when he was what he was, a child of the slums! The words seemed burned upon his soul now, part of his life. He wasn't worthy of her, not worthy to receive her favor.

Yet he closed his eyes, leaning his hand against the window frame as the train hurried along, and saw again the bright lovely face, the dainty fingers blowing kisses, the lips wreathed in smiles, and knew some of the farewell was surely meant for him. He forgot the beautiful villas along the way, forgot to watch for the lights or care how the cottages looked at evening. Whenever the track veered toward the sea and gave a glimpse of gray sky and yawning ocean with an occasional point of light to make the darkness blacker, he seemed to know and, opening his eyes, strained to look across it. Out there in the blackness somewhere was his Starr, and he might not go to her or she come to him. That gray, impassable sky and sea of impossibility would always lie between them.

As he neared New York, however, these thoughts dropped from him. Standing on the ferryboat, with the city's million twinkling lights and the looming blackness of buildings towering against the illumined sky, the people called to him. Over there in the darkness, swarming in the fetid atmosphere of a crowded court, were thousands like him—yes, for he was one of them. He belonged there. They were his kind, and he must help them!

Then his mind went to the farm and his plans, and he entered back into the grind of life and assumed its burden with the sweet pain of his secret locked in his heart.

Chapter 13

"Sam, have you ever been in the country?"

Michael asked the question. They were sitting in a small, dreary room he could afford to rent in a house on the edge of the alley. Not that he'd moved there! He couldn't have endured life if he'd had to spend it in that atmosphere. He still kept his little fourth-floor back in the dismally respectable street. He hadn't gone to the place Endicott recommended, because he found the difference he'd have to pay would enable him to rent this room near the alley. For his purposes this seemed necessary now.

The weather was growing too cold for him to meet with his new old acquaintances of the alley outside, and it was little better indoors even if he could have endured the dirt and squalor of those apartments that would have been open to him. Besides, he had a great longing to show them something brighter than their own forlorn houses.

A settlement house a few blocks away hadn't drawn the dwellers in this particular alley. They were sunken too low, perhaps, or the settlement workers had found more hopeful quarters in which to work, for the city was wide and deep and dark. Michael knew little about the settlement house. He'd read of such things and had glanced shyly toward its workers now and then. But as yet he knew none of them, though they'd heard of the "angel-man of the alley" and were curious to check him out.

But Michael's enterprise and ways of working were his own. He had reached back into his childhood years and found out from his inner consciousness what he'd needed then, and now he was going to try to give it to some other "kids" as forlorn and friendless as he'd been. He couldn't do much, but what he could do he would, and as soon as possible.

So he'd rented this tiny room and purified it. He'd compelled Sam to help him. And that compelling was almost a modern miracle, wrought by radiant smiles and a firm grip on Sam's shoulder when he told him what he wanted done.

Together they'd swept and scrubbed and scraped the dirt from that room.

"I don't see what you're makin' sech a fuss about dirt fer!" grumbled Sam as he arose from his knees after scrubbing the floor for the fourth time. "It's what we're all made of, dey say, an' nobuddy'll know de diffrunce."

"Just see if they won't, Sam," Michael said as he polished off the door he'd been cleaning. "See there—how nice that looks! You didn't know that paint was gray, did you? It looked brown before; it was so thick with dirt. Now we're ready for paint and paper!"

With soap and water they'd worked night after night till very late, and Sam actually let a well-planned, promising raid go by because he was so interested in what he was doing and was ashamed to tell Michael of the plan.

Sam had never helped paper a room; in fact, he'd probably never seen a room with clean, fresh paper on its walls, unless in some house he'd entered unlawfully. When this one was arrayed at last in its newness, he stood back and surveyed it in awe.

Michael had chosen paper the color of sunshine, for the court, the alley, the room, and even the souls of the people were dark. They must have light and brightness if he would win them to better things. Besides, the paper was only five cents a roll, the cheapest he could find in the city. Michael had learned during college vacations how to put it on. He made Sam wash and wash his hands before he handled the delicate paper.

"De paper'll jest git dirty right away," Sam said, grumbling, though he washed his hands and his eyes glowed as they used to when a child at a rare "find" in the gutter.

"Wot'll you do when it gits dirty?" demanded Sam.

"Put on some clean," said Michael. "Besides, we must learn to have clean hands and keep it clean. I wish we had some curtains. They had thin white curtains at college."

"Are you makin' a college fer us?" Sam asked sharply.

"Well, in a way, perhaps. You know I want you to have all the advantages I had as far as I can get them."

Sam only whistled and looked perplexed, but he was doing more serious thinking than he'd ever done.

So the two had worked and planned, and now tonight the work was about finished. The walls reflected the yellow of the sunshine, and the woodwork was painted white enamel. Michael had just put on the last gleaming coat.

"We can give it another coat when it looks a little dirty," he'd remarked to Sam.

"Dey better hev dere han's clean," Sam, frowning, had replied.

The floor was painted gray. There was no rug. Michael felt its lack and meant to remedy it as soon as possible, but rugs cost money. A small coal stove was set up and polished till it shone, and a fire was laid ready to start. They hadn't needed it while they were working hard. The furniture was a wooden table painted gray with a cover of bright cretonne, two wooden chairs, and three boxes. Michael had collected these furnishings carefully and economically, for he had to sacrifice many small comforts to get them.

On the walls were two or three good pictures fastened by brass tacks and some of the gray moss and pine branches from Michael's room. In the central wall appeared one of Michael's beloved college pennants. Those who entered the room understood it to be the symbol of what made the difference between them and "the angel," and they looked at it reverently.

At the windows two lengths of snowy cheesecloth, crudely hemmed by Michael, were tacked up in pleats with brass-headed tacks and tied back with narrow yellow ribbons. This had been the last touch, and Sam sat looking thoughtfully at the stiff angular bows when Michael asked if he'd ever been in the country.

"Sure!" said Sam scornfully. "Went wid de Fresh Air folks wen I were a kid."

"What did you think of it?"

"Don't tink much! Too empty. Nothin' doin'! Good 'nough fer kids. Never again fer me."

Three months had passed since Michael had made his memorable first visit to Old Orchard Farm. For weeks he'd worked shoulder to shoulder every evening with Sam, and as yet no word of that plan nearest his heart had been spoken. This was his first attempt to open the subject.

That Sam had developed a certain respect and fondness for him he was sure, though it was never expressed in words. Always he either objected to any plan Michael suggested or was extremely indifferent and wouldn't promise to be on hand. He was almost always there, however, and Michael had realized Sam was proud of his friendship and at least somewhat interested in his plans to better the court.

"Other things in the country make up for the city's stir," said Michael thoughtfully.

This was the first unpractical conversation he'd tried to hold with Sam. He'd been leading him up through the various stages from dirt and degradation, by means of soap and water, then paper and paint, and now they'd reached the doorway of nature's school. Michael wanted to introduce Sam to the great outdoors. For, though Sam had lived all his life outdoors, it had been a world of brick walls and stone pavements, with little sky and almost no water. Not a green thing in sight, not a bird or a beast except of burden. The first lesson waited in a paper bundle under the table. *Will Sam take it?* Michael wondered as he rose and brought it out, unwrapping the papers carefully, while Sam watched and pretended to whistle, not to show too much curiosity.

"What things?" he asked at last.

"Things like this," answered Michael, setting out on the table an earthen pot containing a scarlet geranium in bloom.

It glowed forth its brilliant torch at once and gave just the touch to the clean room Michael had hoped it would. He stood back, surveying it proudly, and then looked at Sam to see if the lesson had been understood. He expected to see a scornful expression on the hardened sallow face of the slum boy, but instead Sam was gazing openmouthed, with unmitigated admiration.

"Say! Dat's all right!" he exclaimed. "Where'd you make de raise? Say! Dat makes de paper an' paint show up fine!"

Then he rose from the box he'd been sitting on and went and stood before the flower.

"Say! I wisht Jim cud see dat!" he exclaimed after a long silence, and something in his face brought the quick moisture to Michael's eyes.

It was only a common red geranium bought for fifteen cents, but it had touched with its miracle of bright life the young burglar's hardened soul and opened his vision to higher things. And in that moment his heart turned to his old companion who was uncomplainingly taking the punishment which rightfully belonged to the whole gang.

"We'll take him one tomorrow," said Michael in a voice husky with feeling. It was the first time Sam had voluntarily mentioned Jim, and he'd seemed so loath to take Michael to see him in jail that Michael had ceased to speak of the matter.

"There's another one like this where I bought this one. I couldn't tell which to take; they were both pretty. We'll get it the first thing in the morning before anybody else snaps it up, and then when could we get in to see Jim? Would they let us in after my office hours, or would we have to wait till Sunday? You look after that, will you? I might get off at four o'clock if that's not too late."

"Dey'll let us in on Sunday ef you ask, I reckon," said Sam, much moved. "But it's awful dark in prison. It won't live, will it? Only one streak o' sun shines in Jim's cell a few minutes every day."

"Oh, I think it'll live," said Michael hastily, a strange choking sensation in his throat at the thought of his onetime companion shut in a dark prison.

Of course, he deserved to be there. He'd broken the laws, but then no one had ever made him understand how wrong it was. If someone had only tried, Jim might never have done what put him in prison.

"I'm sure it'll live," he said again cheerfully. "I've heard geraniums are hardy. The man told me they would live all winter in the cellar if you brought them up again in the spring."

"Jim'll be out again in de spring," Sam said softly. It was the first sign of anything like emotion in Sam.

"Isn't that good!" said Michael heartily. "I wonder what we can do to make it pleasant for him when he comes back to the world. We'll bring him to this room, of course, but in the spring this'll be getting warm. And that makes me think of what I was talking about a minute ago. There's so much more in the country than in the city!"

"More?" questioned Sam.

"Yes, things like this to look at. Growing things you get to love and understand. There's a river that sparkles and talks as it runs. Trees that laugh and whisper when the wind plays in their branches. And wonderful birds, live breaths of air with music inside that make splendid friends when you're lonely. I know, for I made lots of bird friends when I went away from you all to college. You know, I was pretty lonely at first."

Sam looked at him with keen wonder and a lighting of his face that made him almost attractive and sent the cunning in his eyes slinking out of sight. Had this fine greathearted creature really missed his old friends when he went away? Did he really need them still with his education—and—difference? It was food for thought.

"Then there's the sky, so much of it," went on Michael, "and so wide and blue, with soft white clouds sometimes. They make you feel rested when you look at them floating through the blue and never seeming tired—not even when there's a storm and they have to hurry. And there's the sunset. Sam, I don't believe you ever saw the sunset, not right, anyway. You don't have sunsets here in the city; it just gets dark. You should have seen one I saw not long ago. I mean to take you there someday, and we'll watch it together. I want to see if it'll do the same thing to you it did to me."

Sam looked at him in awe, for Michael wore his exalted look. And when he spoke like that Sam feared perhaps he was, as old Sal said, more angel than man.

"Then there's the earth, covered with green—plenty to lie in if you want to—and it smells so good. And there's so much air—enough to breathe your lungs full and nothing disagreeable in it, no ugly smells or sounds. And things are growing everywhere. Oh, Sam! Wouldn't you like to make things like this grow?"

Sam nodded and reached out hesitantly to touch the velvet of a green leaf.

"You'll go with me, Sam, to the country sometime, won't you? I've got a plan, and I'll need you to help me carry it out. Will you go?"

"Sure!" said Sam in quite a different voice from any reluctant assent he'd ever given. "Sure, I'll go!"

"Thank you, Sam," said Michael, more moved than he dared show. "And now that's settled I want to talk about this room. I'm having five kids here tomorrow early in the evening. I told them I'd show them how to whittle boats, and we're going to sail them in the scrub bucket. They're about the age you and I were when I went away to school. Perhaps I'll teach them a letter or two of the alphabet if they seem interested. They should know how to read, Sam."

"I never learned to read—" muttered Sam half belligerently.

"That so?" said Michael, as if it were a matter of small moment. "Well, what if you were to come in and help me with the boats? Then you could pick it up when I teach them. You might want to use it someday. It's good to know how, and a man learns things quickly, you know."

Sam nodded.

"I don't know's I care 'bout it," he said indifferently, but Michael saw he intended to come.

"Well, after the kids have gone—I won't keep them late—I wonder if you'd like to bring some of the fellows in to see this?"

Michael glanced around the room.

"I have some pictures of alligators I think they might like to see. I'll bring them down if you say so."

"Sure!" said Sam, trying to hide his pleasure.

"Then tomorrow morning I'm going to let the woman who lives in the cellar under Aunt Sally's room bring her sewing here and work all day. She makes buttonholes in vests. It's so dark in her room she can't see, and she's almost ruined her eyes working by candlelight."

"She'll mess it all up!" grumbled Sam. "An' she might let other folks in, an' they'd pinch the picters an' the posy."

"No, she won't do that. I've talked to her about it. The room is to be hers for the day, and she's to keep it looking just as nice as it did when she found it. She'll only bring her work over and go home for her dinner. She's to keep the fire going so it will be warm at night, and she's to try it for a day and see how it goes. I think she'll keep her promise. We'll try her anyway."

Sam nodded as to a superior officer who nevertheless was awfully foolish. "Mebbe!"

"Sam, do you think it would be nice to bring Aunt Sally over now a few minutes?"

"No," said Sam shortly, "she's too dirty. She'd put her fingers on de wall first thing—"

"But, Sam, I think she should come—and first. She's the one who helped me find you—"

Sam looked sharply at Michael and wondered if he suspected how long that same Aunt Sally had frustrated his efforts to find his friends.

"We could tell her not to touch things, perhaps—"

"Wal, you lemme tell her. Here! I'll go fix her up an' bring her now." And Sam hurried out of the room.

In a few minutes he returned with Aunt Sally. But it was a transformed Aunt Sally. Her face had been scrubbed in a circle out as far as her ears, and her scraggy gray hair was twisted in a tight knot at the back of her neck. Her hands were several shades cleaner than Michael had ever seen them, and her shoes were tied. She wore a small three-cornered plaid shawl over her shoulders and entered cautiously as if afraid to come. Her hands were clasped high across her breast. She'd evidently been severely threatened against touching anything.

"The saints be praised!" she exclaimed warmly after she'd looked around in silence. "To think I'd ivver see the loikes uv this in de alley. It lukes loike a palace. Mickey, ye're an angel, me b'y! An' a rale kurtin, to be sure! I ain't seen a kurtin in the alley since I cummed. An' will ye luke at the purty posy a blowin' as foine as ye plaze! Me mither had the loike in her cottage window when I was a leetle gal! Aw, me pure auld mither!"

And suddenly, to Michael's amazement and Sam's disgust, old Sal sat down on the one chair and wept aloud, with the tears streaming down her seamed, sin-scarred face. Sam was for putting her out at once, but Michael soothed her with his cheery voice, making her tell of her old home in Ireland and the kind mother she'd loved, though it was long years since she'd thought of her.

With rare skill he drew from her the picture of the Irish cottage with its thatched roof, peat fire, and well-swept hearth; the table with the white cloth; the cat in the rocking chair; the curtain starched stiffly at the window; the bright posy on the deep window ledge; and, last, the little girl with clean pinafore and curly hair who kissed her mother every morning and trotted off to school. But that was before the father died and the potatoes failed. The school days were soon over, and the little girl with her mother came to America. The mother died on the way over, and the child fell into evil hands. That was the story, and as it was told, Michael's face grew tender and wistful. Would that he knew so much of his history as that!

But Sam stood by dumbstruck, trying to imagine this old woman as the bright rosy child she told about. Sam was passing through a sort of mental and moral earthquake.

"Perhaps someday we'll find another little house in the country where you can go and live," said Michael. "But, meanwhile, suppose you go and see if you can't make your room look like this one. You scrub it up, and perhaps Sam and I will come over and put some pretty paper on the walls for you. Would you like that? How about it, Sam?"

"Sure!" said Sam rather grudgingly. He hadn't much faith in Aunt Sally and didn't see what Michael wanted with her anyway, but he was loyal to Michael.

Irish blessings mingled with tears and garnished with curses in an extraordinary way were showered upon Michael.

At last, when he could stand no more, Sam said, "Aw, cut it out, Sal. You go home an' scrub. Come on now!" And he bundled her off in a hurry.

Late as it was, old Sal lit a fire and by the light of a tallow candle got down on her stiff old knees and began to scrub. It seemed nothing short of a miracle that her room could ever look like the one she'd just seen; but if scrubbing could do anything toward it, scrub she would. She hadn't thought of scrubbing her room for ten years. She hadn't seemed to care. But tonight, as she worked with her trembling, drink-shaken hands, the memory of her childhood home was before her vision, and she worked with all her might.

So the light and cheeriness of the little white room in the dark alley began to work. It was named "the angel's quarters," and to be invited within its charmed walls was an honor all coveted as time passed. And that was how Michael began the salvation of his native alley.

Chapter 14

*M*ichael had been with the new law firm three months and was getting accustomed to the violent contrast between the day spent in the atmosphere of low-voiced, quiet-stepping, earnest men, who moved about in their environment of polished floors, Oriental rugs, leather chairs, and walls with leather-covered law books, and the evening spent down in the alley where his bare white and gold room made the only tolerable spot in the neighborhood.

He was still occupying the fourth-floor back at his original boardinghouse and had seen Mr. Endicott briefly three or four times, but nothing had been said about his lodgings.

One morning he came to the desk set apart for him in the law office and found a letter lying there for him.

> *Son, your board is paid at the address given below, up to the day you are twenty-one. If you don't get the benefit, it will go to waste. Mrs. Semple will make you quite comfortable, and I desire you to move to her house at once. If you feel any obligation toward me, this is the way to discharge it. Hope you are well.*
>
> > *Yours,*
> > *Delevan Endicott.*

Michael's heart beat faster with varied emotions. It was pleasant to have someone care, and of course if Mr. Endicott wished it so much he would manage somehow—perhaps he could get some night work or copying to do—but he'd never let him bear his expenses.

He hurried off at the noon hour to find his benefactor and make this plain with due gratitude. He found, however, that it wasn't so easy to change the man's mind, once made up. Endicott wouldn't hear of any change in arrangements. He had paid the board for the remaining months of Michael's minority and maintained his right to do so if he chose. Neither would he let Michael refund him any of the amount.

So Michael moved, bag and baggage, and found the change good. The regular, well-cooked meals increased his appetite, which had been going back on him for some time under his economical regime, and the larger room with better outlook and more air, to say nothing of a comfortable bed with adjoining bathroom, and plenty of heat and light, made life seem more worthwhile. Besides, he now came in pleasant contact with other boarders, and a large parlor with easy chairs boasted an old-fashioned square piano which still retained much of its original sweet tone.

Mrs. Semple had a daughter, Hester, an earnest, gray-eyed girl with soft brown hair and a firm chin, who had taken an art course at Cooper Institute and painted very good pictures which didn't sell. Hester played the piano—not very well, but well enough to make it enjoyable to a lonely boy who'd known no music in his life except the birds or his own whistle. She played hymns on Sunday after church while they waited for dinner to be ready, and evenings after supper she played other things—old ballads and tender melodies from old masters simplified for her ability. Michael sometimes lingered a half hour before hurrying to the alley, joining his rich natural tenor with her light, pretty soprano. Sometimes Will French, a young fellow who was in the same law office and also boarded at Mrs. Semple's, stayed awhile and sang bass. It made it seem more as if Michael were living in a home.

All this time, Michael was carrying on his quiet work in the alley, saying nothing about it to anybody. In the first place, he felt shy about it because of his personal connection with the place. Not that he wished to hide his origin from his employers, but he felt he owed it to Mr. Endicott, who had recommended him, to be as respectable as possible. And so long as they neither knew nor cared it didn't matter. Then it never occurred to Michael he was doing anything remarkable with his little white room in the darkness of the sin stronghold.

Night after night, he gathered his newsboys and taught them whittling, basketry, reading, arithmetic, and geography, with a little philosophy and botany thrown in unawares. Night after night, the older fellows dropped in, one or two at a time, and listened to the stories Michael told—of college life and games they were interested in or nature and his experiences in finding an alligator or a serpent or watching some bird. He never realized he was preparing in the school of experience to be a magnificent public speaker. With an audience as difficult as any he could have found in the whole city, he managed to hold them every time.

And the favorite theme often was agriculture. He would bring a new little plant to the room, set it up, and show it to them, and then talk about soil conditions and how plants were being improved. He would usually take time at noon to read some article on agriculture and review it for their benefit.

They heard all about Burbank and his wonderful experiments in making plants grow and develop, and as they listened, they gathered around the blossom Michael had just brought to them and gazed with wonder at it. A flower was a strange enough sight in that court, but when they heard the stories, it became filled with new interest. For a while they forgot their evil plotting and were lifted above themselves.

Another night he talked on fertilizers and how one crop would sometimes give out something another crop needed later. Gradually, because he talked about things he was interested in, he gave these sons of ignorance a dim knowledge of and interest in the culture of life and the tilling of the ground, preparing them for what he'd hardly dared put into words even to himself.

One day he took Sam down to Old Orchard. It was the week before Christmas. They'd made their second visit to Jim the week before, and he'd spoken of the spring when he would get out into the world again. He seemed to be planning to get even with those who had confined him for his wrongdoing. Michael's heart was filled with anxiety for him.

Something about Jim appealed to Michael from the beginning. He'd first seen him standing behind his cell grating, a great unkempt hulk of a fellow with fiery red hair and brown eyes that roved restlessly through the corridor. He would have been handsome except for his weak chin. Jim had melted almost to tears on seeing the scarlet geranium they brought him on that first visit, and he seemed to care more about his old comrade "Mickey's" appearance than Sam had.

Jim was to get out in April. If only he had someplace to go!

Michael and Sam talked about it on the way down. Sam seemed to think Jim would find it pretty hard to leave New York. Sam himself wasn't much interested in Michael's continued hints about going to the country.

"Nothin' doin' " was his constant refrain when Michael tried to tell him how much better it would be if some of the city's congested part could be spread out into the country—especially for the poor people who would have a greater opportunity for success in life.

But Sam was impressed with the wideness of the landscape on his first long trip out of the city. As Michael unfolded to him the story of the gift of the farm and his own hopes for it, Sam left off his scorn and gave replies that showed he was thinking about it.

"Say!" he said suddenly. "Ef Buck was to come back, would you let him live down to your place an' help do all them things you're plannin'?"

"I surely would. Say, Sam—do you or do you not know where Buck is?"

Sam gazed thoughtfully out of the window. Then he looked down at his feet and nodded his head slowly.

"I thought so!" said Michael eagerly. "Sam, is he in hiding for something he's done?"

Sam nodded his head again, even more slowly and cautiously.

"Sam, will you send him a message from me?"

Another nod.

"Tell him I love him," Michael breathed the words eagerly. His heart remembered kindness from Buck more than anything else in his sad childhood. "Tell him I want him—I need him! Tell him I want him to make an appointment to meet me somewhere so we can talk over this plan of mine. I want him to go in with me and help me make that farm into a fit place to take people who haven't the right kind of homes, where they can have honest work and good air and be happy! Will you tell him?"

And Sam nodded his head emphatically.

"An' Jim'll help, too, ef Buck goes. That's dead sure!" Sam volunteered.

"And, Sam, I'm counting on you!"

"Sure thing!" said Sam.

Michael tramped all over the place with Sam, showing him everything and telling all his plans. He was very familiar with his land now. He'd planned the bog for a cranberry patch and already negotiated for the bushes. He'd trimmed up the berry bushes in the garden himself during his holiday trips and arranged with a fisherman to dump a few shellfish haulings on one field where he thought that kind of fertilizer would be effective. He'd determined to use his hundred-dollar graduation present in fertilizer and seed. It wouldn't go far, but it would be a beginning. The work he'd have to get some other way. He would have little time to put toward it himself until late in the summer probably, and a great deal should be done in the early spring. He would have to be content to go slow, of course, and must remember that unskilled labor was always expensive and wasteful; still, it would likely be all he could get. Just how he would feed and house even unskilled labor was a problem yet to be solved.

It was a day of many revelations to Sam. For one thing, even the bare snowy stretch of wide country had taken on a new interest to him since Michael had been telling all these wonderful things about the earth. Sam's brain, which up to this time had never busied itself with anything except how to get other men's goods from them, had suddenly awakened to the wonders of the world.

He spotted a colony of cocoons on the underside of leaves and twigs. "Say, ain't dem some o' de critters you was showin' de fellers t'other night?"

And Michael fell upon them eagerly. They happened to be rare specimens, and he knew from college experience that such could be sold to advantage to the museums. He showed Sam how to remove them without injuring them. A little farther on they came to a wild growth of holly, loaded with berries and burnished thorny foliage, and near at hand a mistletoe bough with tiny white transparent berries.

"Ain't dem wot dey sell for Chris'sum greens?" Sam's city eyes picked them out at once.

"Of course," said Michael, delighted. "How did I miss them before? We'll take a lot back with us and see if we can get any price for it. Whatever we get we'll devote to making the house livable. Holly and mistletoe should have a good market about now. That's another idea! Why not cultivate a lot of this stuff right in this tract of land? It seems to grow without any trouble. See! There are lots of little bushes. We'll encourage them, Sam. And say, Sam, if you hadn't come along I might never have thought of that. You see, I needed you."

Sam grunted in a pleased way.

When they reached the house, it looked even more desolate in the snowy stretch of setting than with the grass about it. Michael's heart sank.

"I don't know if we can ever do anything with the old shack," he said, shaking his head. "It looks worse than I thought."

" 'Tain't so bad," said Sam cheerfully. "Guess it's water-tight." He peered through the dusty windowpane where he'd cleared a spot with his coat sleeve. "Looks dry inside. 'Twould be a heap better'n sleepin' on de pavement fer some. Dat fire hole would take in a lot o' wood, an' I guess dere's plenty round de place without robbin' de woods none."

Michael led him to the seashore and bade him look. He wanted to see what effect it would have upon him. The coast swept wild and bleak in the cold December day, and Sam shivered in his thin garments. A look of awe and fear came into his face. He turned his back on it.

"Too big!" he said sullenly, and Michael understood that the sea in its vastness oppressed him.

"Yes, there's a good deal of it," he admitted, "but after all, it's sort of like the geranium flower."

Sam turned back and looked.

"H'm! I don't see nothin' like!" he grunted despairingly.

"Why, it's wonderful! It's beyond us! We couldn't make it. Look at that motion! See the white tossing rim of the waves! See that soft green-gray! Isn't it just the color of the little down on the geranium leaf? See the silver light playing back and forth, and look how it reaches as far as you can see. Now doesn't it make you feel a little as it did when you first looked at the geranium?"

Sam looked in vain. "Not fer mine!" he shrugged. "Gimme the posy every time."

They walked in silence along the beach toward the flowing

of the river, and Sam eyed the ocean furtively as if he feared it might run up and engulf them suddenly when they weren't looking. He'd seen the ocean from wharves, of course, and once stole a ride in a pilot boat out into the deep a little way. But he'd never been alone with the whole sea at once as this seemed. It was too vast for him to comprehend. Still, in a misty way, he knew what Michael was trying to make him understand, and it stirred him uncomfortably.

They hired a little boat, and Michael with strong strokes rowed them back to the farm, straight into the sunset. The sky was purple and gold that night and empurpled the golden river, whose ripples blended into pink and lavender and green. Sam sat huddled in the boat's prow facing it all. Michael had planned that. The oars dipped quietly, and Sam's small eyes widened and took it all in. The sun slipped lower in a crimson ball, and a flood of crimson light broke through the purple and gold for a moment and left a thin, clear line of flame behind.

"Dere!" exclaimed Sam, pointing excitedly. "Dat's like de posy. I kin see that all right!"

Michael rested on his oars and looked back at the sunset, well pleased with this day's work.

They left the boat at a little landing where its owner had promised to get it and walked back through the wood, gathering holly branches and mistletoe. When they reached the city, Michael found a good market for it and received enough for what he'd brought to more than cover the price of the trip. Best of all, Sam was as pleased with the bargain as if it were for his personal benefit.

When they parted, Sam wore a mistletoe sprig in his ragged buttonhole, and Michael carried holly branches back to his boarding place. Most of this he gave to Hester Semple to decorate the parlor with, but one fine branch he kept and carried to his room and fastened over his mirror.

After gazing at it, he selected a spray containing several fine large berries, cut it off, and packed it carefully in a tiny box. This without name or clue to sender, he addressed in printing letters to Starr. Mr. Endicott had asked him to mail a letter to her as he passed by the box the last time he'd been in the office, and without his intention, the address had been burned into his memory. He hadn't expected to use it, but there could be no harm, surely, in sending the girl this bit of Christmas greeting out of a world of possible people. She would never know he sent it, and perhaps it would please her to get a piece of Christmas holly from home. She might think her father had sent it. It didn't matter, and it helped him think he might send this much of his thoughts over the water to her. He thought about how she would look when she opened the box. But whether she was pleased or not he could only surmise, for she would never know to thank him. Ah, well, it was as near as he dared hope for touching life's happiness. He must be glad for what he might have and try to work and forget the rest.

Chapter 15

*N*ow about this time the law firm where Michael worked became deeply interested in their new boy. He studied hard and seemed to know what he was about all day. They saw signs of extraordinary talent in him. Once or twice, thinking to make life pleasant for him, they invited him to their club or to some evening's entertainment, and always Michael had courteously declined, saying he had an engagement for the evening. They casually questioned Will French, the other student, who was a happy-go-lucky and in the office because his father wished him to study something and not because he wanted to. Will said Michael went out every evening and came in late. Mrs. Semple had remarked she often didn't know whether he came in at all until she saw him at breakfast.

This report and a weariness about the eyes some mornings led the firm's senior member to look into Michael's affairs. The natural inference was that Michael was getting into social life too deeply, perhaps wasting the hours in late revelry when he should have been sleeping. Mr. Holt liked Michael and dreaded seeing signs of dissipation appear on that fine face. He asked Will French to make friends with him and find out if he could where he spent his evenings. Will agreed and at once entered on his mission with a zeal beyond all baffling.

"Hello, Endicott!" called Will as Michael reached the front door on his way to his mission that same evening. "Where're you going? Wait, can't you, and I'll walk along with you? I was going to ask if you wouldn't go to a show with me this evening. I haven't anything on for tonight, and it's slow."

As he spoke he seized his coat and hat, which he'd purposely left in the hall, and put them on.

"Thank you," said Michael as they went out together. "I'd be glad to go with you, but I have something that can't be put off."

"Well, go tomorrow night with me, will you? I like you and think we should be friends."

Will's idea was they'd get to talking at a show and he could find out a good deal. He thought it must be a girl. He'd told the senior Holt it was a girl, of course, and he wouldn't take long to spot her. It must be either a girl or revelry to take the fellow out every night in the week so late.

"Well, I'm sorry," said Michael, "but I'm afraid I have an engagement every night. It's rather a permanent job I'm engaged in. What do you do with your evenings?"

Will described parties and entertainments he had been invited to and nice girls he knew, hinting he might introduce Michael if he was so inclined. Michael talked on, leading his unsuspecting companion further from the subject of his own evenings. Finally they came to a corner, and Michael halted.

"I turn here," he said. "Which way do you go?"

"Why, I turn, too," said Will, laughing. "That is, if you don't object. I'm out for a walk, and I don't care much what I do. If I'm not welcome, just tell me and I'll clear out."

"Of course you're quite welcome," said Michael. "I'm glad to have company, but the quarter I'm walking to isn't pleasant for a walk, and indeed you mightn't like to return alone even early in the evening if you walk far. I had an unpleasant encounter myself once, but I know the ways of the place now, and it's different."

Will eyed him curiously. "Am I allowed to ask where we're going?" he asked in a comical tone.

Michael laughed. "Certainly. If you're bound to go, I'll have to tell you all about it. But I strongly advise you to turn back now, for it isn't a savory neighborhood, and I don't believe you'll care for it."

" 'Where thou goest I will go,' " replied Will, mocking. "My curiosity is aroused. I'll certainly go. If it's safe for you, it is for me. My good looks aren't nearly as valuable as yours or so noticeable. And since I have no valuables in the world, I can't be knocked down for booty."

"You see, they all know me," explained Michael.

"Oh, they do! And can't you introduce me? Or don't you like to?"

"I suppose I can, if you really want me to, but I'm afraid you'll turn and run when you see them. They're not very— handsome. They're not what you're used to. You wouldn't want to know them."

"But you do."

"I had to," said Michael desperately. "They needed some-thing, and I had to help them!"

Up to now Will was sure Michael had fallen into the hands of sharpers. But something in his tone made him turn and look, and he saw Michael's face uplifted in the streetlight, glowing with an earnestness that surprised and awed him.

"Look here, man," he said. "Tell me who they are and what you're doing anyway."

Michael told him a few words, saying little about himself or his first reason for being interested in the alley. There were a few neglected newsboys, mere kids. He was trying to teach them a few things, reading and figures and a little manual training. Something to make life more than suffering and sin.

"Is it settlement work?" Will asked, puzzled and interested.

"No, there's a settlement, but it's too far away and has too big a district to reach this alley. It's just my own little work."

"Who pays you for it?"

"Who pays me?"

"Yes, who's behind the enterprise? Who forks over the

funds and pays you for your job?"

Michael laughed long and loud. "Well, now, I hadn't thought about pay, but I guess the kids do. You can't think how they enjoy it all."

"H'm!" said Will. "I think I'll go along and see how you do it. I won't scare 'em out, will I?"

"Well, now I hadn't thought of that. In fact, I didn't suppose you'd care to go all the way, but if you think you do, I guess it'll be all right."

"Not a very warm welcome, I must say," laughed Will, "but I'm going just the same. You get me in, and I'll guarantee not to scare the crowd. Have any time left over from your studies for amusement? If you do I might come in on that. I can do tricks."

"Can you?" said Michael, looking at his unbidden guest doubtfully. "Well, we'll see. I'm afraid you'll be disappointed. It's very informal. Sometimes we don't get beyond the first step in a lesson. Sometimes I have to stop and tell stories."

"Good!" said Will. "I'd like to hear you."

"Oh, you wouldn't enjoy it, but there are a few books there. You might read if you get tired looking around the room."

And so Michael and his guest entered the yellow and white room together. Michael lit the gas, and Will blinked in amazement.

Coming through the alley to the room had taken away Will's exclamatory powers and exhausted his vocabulary. The room in its white simplicity, immaculately kept and constantly in touch with fresh paint to hide any stray finger marks, stood out in startling contrast with the regions round about it. Will took it all in: paint, paper, and pictures. The tiny stove glowing warmly, the improvised seats, the blackboard in the corner, and the bits of life in the geranium, butterfly cocoons, and birds' nests. Then he looked at Michael, tall and fine and embarrassed, in the center of it all.

"Great Scott!" he exclaimed. "Is this an enchanted island, or am I in my right mind?"

But before he received an answer, they heard clattering young feet and a tumult outside the door. Then the boys entered, eager, panting but decorous, some with clean faces, most of them with clean hands or moderately so, all with their caps off in homage to their prince. Michael welcomed them as if he stood in a luxurious drawing room on Fifth Avenue and these were his guests.

He introduced them, and Will greeted them chummily. They stood off from him at first with suspicion, huddled together in a group near Michael. But later, when the chalkboard lesson was over and Michael was showing a set of pictures, Will sat down in a corner with a string from his pocket and began showing two of the boldest some tricks. This took at once. When he added a little sleight of hand, pulling pennies from their hair, pockets, and hands, and letting them keep them after the game was over, they were ready to accept him into their inner circle at once.

But when Sam, unaccountably late that night, sidled in alone, he looked at the stranger with belligerence. Michael introduced him as his friend, and Sam's eyes glinted with a jealous light. Sam didn't like Michael to have any friends of that sort. This new man wore shiny boots, fine new clothes, and well-brushed hair and manipulated a smooth handkerchief with fingers as white as any gentleman's.

To be sure, Michael was like that. But he belonged to them, and his clothes made him no worse. Who was this intruder? A gentleman? All gentlemen were natural enemies to Sam.

"Come outside," said Sam to Michael gruffly, ignoring the white hand Will held out cordially.

Michael saw something was on his mind. "Will, can you amuse these kids a minute while I step out? I won't be long."

"Sure!" said Will heartily. He hadn't had such a time in

months, and what a story he'd have to tell the senior partner in the morning.

"Ever try to lift a fellow's hand off the top of his head? Here, kid, sit in that chair and put your right hand flat on the top of your head. Now, sonny, you lift it off. Pull with all your might. That's it—"

Michael's eyes shone, and even Sam grinned surreptitiously.

"He'll do," he said to Sam as they went out. "He was lonesome this evening and wanted to come along with me."

Lonesome! A fellow like that! It gave Sam a new idea to think about. Did people with money and education and used to living in clothes like that get lonesome? Sam looked more kindly back at Will as he closed the door.

Alone in the dark cold entry, where the wind whistled up from the river and every crack seemed to conduct a blast, Sam and Michael talked in low tones.

"Say, he's lit out!" Sam's tone conveyed dismay as well as apology.

Michael guessed at once whom he meant. "Buck?"

Sam grunted assent.

"When?"

"Day er so ago. I tuk yer word to 'im, but he'd gone. Lef' word he had a big deal on, an' ef if it came troo all right 'e'd send fer us. You see it wan't safe round 'ere no more. The police was onto his game. Thur wan't no more hidin' fer him. He was powerful sorry not to see you. He'd always thought a heap o' Mickey!"

"How long had he known I was here?" Michael's face was grave in the darkness. Why hadn't Buck sent him word? Made some appointment?

"Since you first cum back."

"Why—oh, Sam, why didn't he let me come and see him?"

"It warn't safe," said Sam earnestly. "Sure thing, it warn't! 'Sides—"

"Besides what, Sam?"

" 'Sides, he knowed you had edicashun, an' he knowed how you looked on his way o' livin'. He didn't know but—"

"You mean he didn't trust me, Sam?"

Sam felt the keen eyes upon him even in the darkness. "Naw, he didn't tink you'd snitch on him ner nothin', but he didn't know if you'd tink you had to do some tings what might kick it all up wid him. You'd ben out o' tings fer years, an' you didn't know de ways o' de city. 'Sides, he ain't seed you like I done—"

"I see," said Michael. "I understand. It's a long time, and of course he only knows what you've told him, and if there was danger—but, oh, Sam, I wish he could go down to Old Orchard. Did you ever tell him about it and my plans?"

"Sure ting I did. Tole 'im all you tole me. He said 'twar all right. Ef he comes out on dis deal he'll be back in a while, an' he'll go down dere ef you want him. He said he'd bring a little wad back to make things go ef dis deal went troo."

"Do you know what the deal is, Sam?"

"Sure!"

"Is it dis— Is it"—he paused for a word that would convey his meaning and yet not offend—"is it. . .dangerous, Sam?"

"Sure!" admitted Sam solemnly as though it hurt him to pain his friend.

"Do you mean it will make more hiding for him?"

"Sure!" emphatically grave.

"I wish he hadn't gone!" There was sharp pain in Michael's voice.

"I wisht so, too!" said Sam with a little choke. "Mebbe 'twon't come off after all. Mebbe it'll git blocked. Mebbe he'll come back."

The anxiety in Sam's tone touched Michael, but another thought struck him.

"Sam," he said, plucking at the other's sleeve in the darkness, "tell me—what was Buck doing—before he went away? Was it all straight? Was he in the same business with you?"

Sam breathed heavily but didn't answer. At last with difficulty he answered a gruff "Nope!"

"What was it, Sam? Won't you tell me?"

"It would be snitchin'."

"Not to me, Sam. You know I belong to you all."

"But you've got new notions."

"Yes," admitted Michael. "I can't help that, but I don't go back on you, do I?"

"No, you don't go back on we'uns, thet's so. But you don't like we'uns doin's."

"Never mind. Tell me, Sam. I think I must know."

"He kep a gamin' den—"

"Oh, Sam!" Michael's voice was stricken, and his great athletic hand gripped Sam's hard skinny one, and Sam in the darkness gripped back.

"I knowed you'd feel thet way," he mourned as if the fault were all in his telling. "I wisht I hadn't 'a' tole yer."

"Never mind, Sam. You couldn't help it, and I suppose I wouldn't have known the difference myself if I hadn't gone away. We mustn't judge Buck harshly. He'll see it the other way in time."

Sam straightened perceptibly. Something in this speech put him in the same class with Michael. He'd never had qualms of conscience concerning gambling, but now he found himself arrayed against it almost unawares.

"I guess mebbe!" he said comfortingly and then sought to change the subject. "Say, is dat guy in dere goin' along to de farm?"

"Who?"

"Why, dat ike you lef' in de room. Is he goin' down 'long when we's go?"

"Oh, Will French! No, Sam. He doesn't know anything

about it yet. I may tell him sometime, but he doesn't need that. He's studying to be a lawyer. Perhaps someday if he gets interested he'll help do what I want for the alley and all the other alleys in the city—make better laws and see that they're enforced."

"Laws!" said Sam in a startled voice. "What laws?" Laws were his natural enemies.

"Laws for better tenement houses, more room and more windows, better air, cleaner streets, room for grass and flowers, pure milk and meat, less crowding and dirt. Understand?"

It was the first time Michael had gone so deep into his plans with Sam, and he longed now to have his comradeship in this hope, too.

"Oh, sure!" said Sam, relieved he hadn't mentioned laws about gambling dens and pickpockets.

Sam might be willing to reform his own course in Michael's brilliant wake, but as yet he hadn't reached the point where he cared to see vice and dishonesty swept off the globe.

They went slowly back to the white room to find Will French leading a chorus of youngsters in the latest popular melody while they kept time with an awkward shuffle of their ill-shod feet.

"Cut it out, kids," Sam growled. "You scratch de floor."

Will French subsided with apologies. "I never thought of the floor, Endicott. Say, you should have a gymnasium and a swimming pool here."

Michael laughed.

"I wish we had, but I'd start on a bathroom. We need that first of all."

"Well, let's get one," said Will eagerly. "That wouldn't cost so much. We could get some people to contribute a little. I know a man with a big plumbing establishment. He'd do a little something. I mean to tell him about it. Is there any place it could be put?"

Sam followed them, listening, wondering, as they stepped into the hall to see the little dark hole which might with ingenuity be converted into a bathroom. While he leaned back against the doorjamb, hands in his pockets, he studied the newcomer's face.

"Guess dat guy's all right," he reassured Michael as he helped him turn the lights out a little later.

Will was waiting on the doorstep, whistling a new tune to his admiring following. He'd caught "de kids."

"I say, Endicott," he said as they walked up the noisy midnight street and turned into the avenue. "Why don't you get Hester to go down there and sing sometime? Sunday afternoon. She'd go. Ask her."

And that night was the beginning of outside help for Michael's mission.

Hester fell into the habit of going down Sunday afternoons, and soon she had an eager following of sad-eyed women and eager little children, and Will French spent his leisure hours hunting up tricks and games and puzzles for the kids.

Meanwhile, the account he'd given Holt and Holt of the way Michael spent his evenings was not without fruit.

About a week after Will's first visit to the alley, the senior Mr. Holt paused beside Michael's desk one afternoon before leaving the office and laid a bit of paper in his hand.

"French tells me you're interested in work in the slums," he said in the same tone he used to give Michael an order for his daily routine. "I'd like to help a little if you can use that." He left before Michael had fully comprehended what he'd said. The young man looked down at the paper and saw it was a check made out to him for one hundred dollars!

With a quick exclamation of gratitude he was on his feet and out in the hall after his employer.

"That's all right, Endicott. I don't get as much time as I'd like to look after the charities, and when I see a good thing I like to give it a boost. Call on me if you need money for any special scheme. And I'll mention it to some of my clients occasionally," said the old lawyer, pleased with Michael's gratitude.

He did, and the clients responded. Every little while a ten-dollar bill or a five, and now and then a check for fifty, would find its way to Michael's desk—for Will French, thoroughly interested, kept Holt and Holt well informed concerning what was needed.

Chapter 16

*B*efore winter was over Michael put in the bathroom, bought a plow and other farm implements, and secured the services of a man who lived near Old Orchard to do some early plowing and planting. He bought seeds and fertilizer, enough at least to start his experiment, and toward spring he took advantage of a holiday, and with Sam and a carpenter went down to the farm and patched up the old house.

After that a few cots, some boxes for chairs and tables, some cheap comforters for cool nights, some dishes and cooking utensils from the ten-cent store, and the place would be ready for his alley-community when he dared bring them down. A canvas cot and a wadded comforter would be luxury to any of them. The only question was, would they be contented out of the city?

Michael had read many articles about taking the poor of the cities into the country, and he knew experience had shown they were in most cases miserable to get back again. He believed this might be different with the right conditions. In the first place, they must have an environment full of new interest to replace the city's rush, and then they must have some great object they would be eager to attain. He felt, too, that they should be prepared beforehand for their new life.

To this end he had spent two or three hours a week the last six months with five or six young fellows Sam had called in. He had brought the agricultural papers to the room and made much of the illustrations. The boys as a rule couldn't read, so he read to them, or rather translated into their own slangful

English. He told them what wonders had been attained by farming the right way. As these fellows had little idea of farming in any way, or little knowledge of farm products except what came to them through the markets in their very worst forms, he carried in cabbages, apples, and other fruits and vegetables for their inspection.

One night he brought several gnarled, green-skinned, sour, speckled apples. He called attention to them very carefully. Because an apple was a treat, however poor it might be, he asked them to notice the flavor as they ate. Then he produced some magnificent specimens of apples, crimson and yellow, with polished skins and delicious flavor, and set them in a row on the table beside more little speckled apples. They looked like a sunset beside a ditch. The young men gathered around the beautiful apples, touching their shiny streaks as if they might be painted and listening to the story of their development from the ugly specimens they had just been eating. When the perfect apples were cut up, each one enjoyed the delicious fruit with new understanding.

Other nights, with Will and Hester's help, Michael demonstrated potatoes and other vegetables, with regular lessons on how to get the best results with these products. Hester served a tasty refreshment from roasted potatoes, cooked just right, and showed the difference between the soggy potatoes full of dry rot and those grown under the right conditions. Occasionally a cup of coffee or some delicate sandwiches accompanied a demonstration of lettuce or celery or cold cabbage in the form of slaw, and the light refreshments served with the agricultural lessons became a pleasant feature of Michael's evenings. More and more young fellows dropped in to listen to the lesson and enjoy the plentiful "eats" as they called them. When they reached the lessons on peas and beans, the split-pea soup and rich bean soup were well appreciated.

Not that all took the lessons with equal enthusiasm, but

toward spring Michael felt that his original five with Sam as their leader would do fairly intelligent work on the farm. They were told the story often, until they were eager to know if they might be among the pioneers in the work.

Will French faithfully reported the condition of the work, and more friends and clients of the office would stop at Michael's desk, chat with him briefly about the work, and always leave something to help it along. Michael's eyes shone, and his heart beat high with hopes in these days.

But he still had further work to do before his crude apprentices were ready to be sent out into the wilds of nature.

Michael began one evening to tell them of the beauty and wonder of the world. He used a cocoon to illustrate, and for three evenings they watched with bated breath the strange little roll, almost doubting Michael's veracity, yet full of curiosity. Then one night it burst its bonds and floated up into the white ceiling, its pale green, gorgeously marked wings captivating their hearts in a way no years could ever make them forget. It was the miracle of life, and they'd never seen or heard of it.

Another night he brought a singing bird in a cage and pictures of wild birds. He taught them the ways of the birds they would see in New Jersey, how to tell their songs apart, where to look for their nests—all the odd things a bird lover knows and that Michael through roaming about the woods knew by heart. The bird in its cage stayed in the yellow and white room and, strange to say, thrived, becoming a joy and wonder to visitors and a marvel to those who lived in the court. Its continuous brilliant song burst forth from a heart that seemed too full of happiness and must bubble over into music. The kids and even the older fellows felt a proprietorship in it and liked to stand beneath the cage and call to it as it answered "peep" and watched them through the gilded bars.

One night, with the help of Will French, who had some

wealthy friends, Michael borrowed a large picture of a sunset and told them about the sunlight and its effects on growing things and the wonder of its departure for the night.

By this time they would listen in awed silence to anything Michael said, though the picture was perhaps one too many for most of them. Sam, however, heard with approval and afterward laid his finger reverently on the picture's crimson, purple, and gold. Sam understood, for he'd seen the real thing. Then he turned to the others.

"Say, fellers, it's aw-right. You wait till yer see one. Fine ez silk an' twicet as nateral."

So the work went on. Spring was coming and with it the end of Jim's "term" and the beginning of Michael's farm experiment.

Meanwhile Michael was working hard at his law and studying half the night when he returned from the alley work. If he hadn't had an iron constitution and thirteen years of healthy outdoor life, with plenty of sleep and exercise and good food, he couldn't have stood it. As it was, the hard work was good for him, for it kept him from brooding about himself and his hopeless love of the little girl far across the water.

Some weeks after Christmas a brief note from Starr had come, with his name written in her hand and the address in her father's.

Dear Michael,

I'm almost sure I'm indebted to you for the lovely holly sprig that reached me on Christmas. I've tried to think who the sender might be, for I didn't know the writing, or rather printing. But today it fell down from over the picture where I had fastened it on the wall, and I noticed for the first time "A Happy Christmas" in the tiny letters of the message cut or scratched on the underside of the stem. The letters reminded me of you and the charming surprises you used to send me long ago from Florida when I was a little girl. Then all at once I was sure you had sent the holly, so I'm sitting right down to write and thank you for it.

You see, I was very lonesome and homesick that Christmas morning, for most of the girls in the school had gone home for Christmas. Mama had meant to come and take me to Paris for the holidays, but she wrote she wasn't well and couldn't come, so I knew I'd have to be here by myself. I was feeling very sad even with the presents Mama sent me, until I opened the box and saw the dear holly berries that cheered me up and made me think of home. I kept it on my desk all day so the bright berries would make me feel Christmassy.

And just before dinner that night, what do you think happened? Why, my dear daddy came to surprise me, and we took the loveliest trip together to Venice, Florence, and Rome. It was beautiful! I wish you could have been along and seen everything. I know you'd have enjoyed it. I mustn't take the time to write about it because I should be studying. This is a very pleasant place and a good school, but I'd rather be at home, and I'll be glad when I'm finished and allowed to come back to my own country.

Thanking you ever so much for the pretty Christmas reminder, for you see I'm sure you sent it, and wishing you a belated Happy New Year, I am

Your friend,
Starr Delevan Endicott

Michael read and reread the letter, treasured the thoughts and visions it brought him, pondered whether he might answer, and decided he had no right. Then he put it away with his own heartache, plunging into his work with redoubled energy and taking an antidote of so many pages of Blackstone when his thoughts lingered on forbidden subjects. So the winter fled, and spring came stealing on apace.

Chapter 17

*A*s Michael had no definite knowledge of either his exact age or birth month, no day could be set for his coming of age. His own memory of how many summers and winters he had passed showed he was about seven years old at the time of the shooting. If that was correct it would make him between nineteen and twenty at the time of his graduation.

On the first day of July following his first winter in New York, Michael received a brief letter from Mr. Endicott, containing a check for a thousand dollars, with congratulations on his majority and a request that he call at the office the next day.

Michael, eager, grateful, overwhelmed, was on hand at the appointed minute.

The wealthy businessman, whose banking affairs had long since righted themselves, turned from his multifarious duties and rested his eyes on the young fellow, listening half-amused to his eager thanks.

The young man in truth was a sight to rest weary eyes.

The winter in New York had put new lines on his face and deepened the wells of his blue eyes. They were the work of care and wit and suffering but had made a man's face out of a boy's fresh countenance. Power showed in the fine brow, strength in the firm, well-molded chin, and both kindness and unselfishness in his pleasant lips. The city barber had been artist enough not to cut the glorious hair too short, while yet giving it the latest clean-cut curve behind the ears and on the neck. By instinct Michael's hands were well cared for. Endicott's tailor had looked out for the rest.

"That's all right, son," Endicott cut Michael's sentence short. "I'm pleased with the way you've been doing. Holt tells me he never had a more promising student in his office. He says you're cut out for the law, and you're going to be a success. But what's this they tell me about you spending your evenings in the slums? I don't like the sound of that. Better cut that out."

Michael began to tell in earnest protesting words of what he was trying to do, but Endicott put up an impatient hand.

"That's all very well, son. I've no doubt they appreciate your help and all that, and it's been commendable of you to give your time. But now you owe yourself and the world something. You've got to turn out a great lawyer and prove to the world that people from that district are worth helping. That's the best way in the long run to help those people. Give them into somebody else's hands now. You've done your part. When you get to be a rich man you can give them something now and then if you like, but it's time to cut out the work now. That sort of thing might be popular in a political leader, but you've got your way to make. It's time you gave your evenings to culture and to going out into society. Here's a list of concerts and lectures for next winter. You should go to them all. I'm sorry I didn't think of it this winter, but perhaps it was as well not to go too deep at the start. You should waste no more time, though. I've applied for season tickets for those things on that list, and you'll receive them in due time. An art exhibit or two will have good things to see. You've got to see and hear everything if you want to be a thoroughly educated man. I said a word or two about you here and there, and I think you'll receive some invitations worth accepting pretty soon. You'll need a dress suit, and I sent word to the tailor about it this morning when it occurred to me—"

"But," said Michael, amazed and perturbed, "I don't belong in society. People don't want someone like me there. If they knew they wouldn't ask me."

"Bosh! Didn't I tell you to cut that out? People don't know, and you've no need to tell them. They think you're a distant relative of mine if they think anything about it, and you're not to tell them you're not. You owe it to me to keep still about it. If I guarantee you're all right, that should suit anybody."

"I couldn't go where people thought I was more than I was," said Michael, head up, eyes shining, his firmest expression on his mouth, but trouble in his eyes. It was hard to go against his benefactor.

"You got all those foolish notions from working down there in the slums. You've got a false idea of yourself and a false notion of right and wrong. It's high time you stopped going there. After you've been to a dance or two and a few theater suppers, and you're acquainted with some nice girls who'll invite you to their house parties, you'll forget you ever had anything to do with the slums. I insist you give up that work at once. Promise me you won't go near the place again. Write them a letter—"

"I couldn't do that!" said Michael, his face expressive of anguish fighting with duty.

"Couldn't! Nonsense. There's no such word. I want you to do it. Haven't I proved my right to make that request?"

"You have," said Michael, dropping his sorrowing eyes slowly and taking out the folded check from his pocket.

"You have the right to ask it, but I have no right to do what you ask. I've begun the work, and it wouldn't be right to stop it. Indeed, I couldn't. If you knew what it means to those fellows—but I can't keep this if you feel that way! I was going to use it for the work—but now—"

Michael's pauses were eloquent. Endicott was deeply touched, but he wouldn't show it. He was used to having his own way, and it irritated him, while it pleased him somehow, to have Michael so determined. As Michael stopped talking, he laid the check on the desk.

"Nonsense!" said Endicott. "This has nothing to do with the check. That was your birthday present. Use it as you like. What I've given, I've given and won't take back even if I have nothing more to do with you from this time forth. I have no objection to your giving away as much money as you can spare to benevolent institutions, but I do object to your wasting your time and reputation in such low places. It will injure you eventually. I want you to take your evenings for society and lectures and concerts—"

"I'll go to the concerts and lectures gladly," said Michael gravely. "I can see they'll be fine for me, and I thank you very much for the opportunity. But that won't hinder my work. It begins always rather late in the evening, and there are other times—"

"You've no business staying out in places like that after the hour decent amusements close."

Michael refrained from saying he'd noticed society ladies returning from balls and entertainments several times on his way home.

"I simply can't have it if I'm to stand behind you."

"I'm sorry," said Michael. "You won't ever know how sorry I am. It was so good to know I had somebody who cared a little for me. I'll miss it very much. It's been almost like having a real father. Do you mean you'll have to give up the— fatherliness?"

Endicott's voice shook with mingled emotions. This young upstart, who professed to be so grateful and for whom he'd done so much, wouldn't actually run the risk of angering him— for the sake of a few wretched beings and a sentimental feeling he belonged in the slums and should do something for them!

"It means I won't do anything I planned to do for you, if you persist in refusing my reasonable request. Listen, young man—"

Michael noticed with pain that he'd dropped the customary "son" from his conversation, and it gave him an odd sensation of having been cut off from the earth.

"I planned—"

The keen eyes searched the face before him, and the man's voice took on an insinuating tone—the tone he used when he wished to buy up some political pull, that never failed to buy his man. Yet even as he spoke he felt that here was a man he couldn't buy.

"I planned to do a good many things for you. You'll be through your studies soon and be ready to set up for yourself. Had you thought ahead enough to know whether you'd like a partnership in some old firm or whether you want to set up for yourself?"

Michael's voice was grave and troubled, but he answered at once. "I'd like to set up for myself, sir. There are things I must do, and I don't know if a partner would feel as I do about them."

"Very well," said Endicott with satisfaction. He could only be pleased with the straightforward, decided way in which the boy was going ahead and shaping his own life. It showed he had character. There was nothing Mr. Endicott prized more than character—or what he called character.

"When you get ready to set up for yourself, and I don't think that will be so many years off from what I hear, I'll provide you an office, fully furnished, in the city's most desirable quarter and start you off as you should be started in order to win. I'll introduce you to some of my best friends and send lucrative business your way, with great corporations that will bring you into immediate prominence. Then I'll propose your name for membership in two or three good clubs. Now I'll do those things because I believe you have it in you to make good, but you'll need the boosting. Every man in this city does. Genius alone can't work you to the top, but I can give you what you need, and I mean to do it. But I feel that you should comply with the conditions."

There was a deep silence in the room. Michael was struggling to master his voice, but when he spoke, it was husky with suppressed feeling.

"It's a great plan," he said. "It's just like you. Thank you, sir, for the thought, with all my heart. It grieves me more than anything I ever had to do to say no to you, but I cannot do as you ask. I cannot give up what I'm trying to do. I feel it would be wrong for me. I feel it is imperative, sir!"

"Cannot! You're like all the upstart reformers, filled with conceit. You think no one else can do the work but you! I'll pay someone to do what you're doing! Will that satisfy you?"

Michael shook his head slowly.

"No one could do it for pay," he said with conviction. "It must be done from—perhaps it's love—I don't know. But no one was doing it, and I must, for they are my people!"

As he said this the young man lifted his head with his angel-proud look that defied a universe to set him from his purpose, and Endicott, while he secretly revelled in the boy's firmness and purpose, yet writhed that he couldn't control this strength as he would.

"Your people! Bosh! You don't even know that! You may be the son of the richest man in New York for all you know."

"The more shame mine, then, if he left me where you found me! Mr. Endicott, have you ever been down in the alley where I used to live? Do you know the conditions down there?"

"No, and I don't want to go. And, what's more, I don't want you to go again. Whatever you were or are, you should see that you're mine now. Why, how do you know you weren't kidnapped for a ransom and the game went awry? There are a thousand possible explanations for your presence there. You may have been lost—"

"Then haven't I a debt to the people I lived with?"

"Oh, poppycock!" exclaimed the man angrily. "We'd better

close the conversation. You understand how I feel. If you think it over and change your mind, come back and tell me within the week. I sail Saturday for Europe. I may not be back for three or four months. If you don't make up your mind before I go, you can write to me here at the office, and my secretary will forward it. You've disappointed me beyond anything I could have dreamed. I'm sure when you think it over you'll see how wrong you are and change your mind. Until then, good-bye!"

Michael arose dismissed, but he couldn't go that way.

"I won't change my mind," he said sadly, "but it's terrible not to have you understand. Won't you let me tell you about it? Won't you let me explain?"

"No, I don't want to hear any explanations. There's only one thing for me to understand, and that is that you think more of a set of vagabonds in an alley than you do of my request!"

"No! That's not true!" said Michael. "I think more of you than of any living man. I don't believe I could love you more if you were my own father. I would give my life for you this minute."

"An old word somewhere says, 'To obey is better than sacrifice.' Most people think they'd rather be great heroes than do simple everyday things demanded of them. The test doesn't always prove they would."

Michael's head went up almost haughtily, but great tears were in his eyes. Endicott dropped his own gaze from that sorrowful face. He knew his words were false and cruel. He knew Michael wouldn't hesitate a second to give his life. But the man couldn't bear to be withstood.

"If you feel that way I cannot take this!" Michael held out the check sadly, proudly.

"As you please!" snapped Endicott. "There's the wastebasket. Put it in if you like. It isn't mine any longer. You may spend it as you please. My conditions have nothing to do with what is past. If you don't prize my gift to you, by all means throw it away."

With a glance that would have broken Endicott's heart if he hadn't been too stubborn to look up, Michael slowly folded the check and put it back in his pocket.

"I do prize it," he said, "and I prize it because you gave it to me. It meant and always will mean a great deal to me."

"Hmph!"

"Perhaps I should tell you one more thing," Michael said hesitantly. "The farm. I'm using it in my work for those people. Perhaps you won't approve of that."

"I have nothing further to do with the farm. You bought it, I believe. You wanted to pay for it when you were earning enough money. That time hasn't come, so nothing more need be said. It's your farm, and you may use it as a pleasure park for pigs if you like. I don't go back on my bargains. Good afternoon."

Endicott turned to the phone, took up the receiver, and called up a number. Michael saw the conversation was ended. Slowly, with heavy step and heavier heart, he left the office.

New lines of sadness were etched on Michael's face that day. And when he went down to the alley that evening, he was so gentle with the kids that they looked at him more than once with a new kind of awe and wonder. It was the gentleness of sacrifice for them, bringing with it the pain of love.

Old Sal, who came over to "look in" that evening, as she put it, shook her head as she stumped back to her rejuvenated room with its gaudy flowered wall, bit of white curtain, and flowerpot in the window, all the work of Michael and his follower Sam.

"I'm thinkin' he'll disuppeer one o' these days. Ye'll wake up, an' he'll be gahn. He's not of this worrld. He'll sprid his wings an' fly away. He's a man-angel, thet's wot he is!"

Michael went home that night and wrote a letter to Mr.

Endicott that would have broken a heart of stone, telling his inmost thought, showing his love and anguish in every sentence, and setting forth simply and unassumingly the wonderful work he was doing in the alley.

But though he waited anxiously day after day, he received no reply. Endicott read every word of the letter and fairly gloated over the boy's strength, but he was too stubborn to let it be known. Also, he rather enjoyed the test to which he was putting him.

Michael watched the outgoing vessels on Saturday, looked up the passenger lists, went down to the wharf, and tried to see him before he sailed. But for some reason he couldn't get in touch with him.

Standing sadly on the wharf as the vessel sailed, he caught sight of Endicott. Though he was sure he had been seen, he received no sign of recognition and turned away heartsick, feeling as if he had for conscience's sake stabbed one who loved him.

Chapter 18

Those were trying days for Michael. The weather had turned suddenly warm. The office was sometimes stifling. The daily routine got on his nerves, he who never knew he had nerves. He ached that Starr was gone from him—forever—and now he had by his own word cut loose from the man who was like a father to him—forever! He saw no hope in the future.

About that time, too, another sorrow came to him. He was glancing over the paper one morning on his way to the office, and his eye fell on the following item:

LONE TRAIN BANDIT HURT IN FIGHT
AFTER GETTING LOOT
CAPTURED BY CONDUCTOR AFTER RIFLING MAILBAGS
ON UNION PACIFIC EXPRESS

Topeka, Kan., July 20—A daring bandit was captured last night after he robbed the mail car on the Union Pacific train that left Kansas City for Denver at ten o'clock.

The train, known as the Denver Express, carrying heavy mail, was just leaving Kansas City when a man ran across the depot platform and leaped into the mail car through the open door. The clerk in charge faced the man, who aimed a revolver at him. He was commanded to bind and gag his five associates, and he obeyed. The robber went through the registered pouches, stuffing the packages into his pockets. Then he commanded the clerk to untie his comrades.

At Bonner Springs, where the train stopped briefly, the

*robber ordered the men to continue their work so as not to
attract the attention of persons at the station. When the train
reached Lawrence, the robber dropped from the car and ran
toward the rear of the train. The conductor summoned two
Lawrence policemen, and all three followed. After a quick race
and a struggle, during which his arm was broken, the robber
was captured. He appears to be an old offender New York
police have been searching for in vain for the past ten months.
He is known in the city's lower districts as "Fighting Buck"
and has a list of offenses against him too numerous to mention.*

Michael didn't know why he'd noticed the article or read it
through to the finish. He didn't care to read that kind of thing;
yet lately all crime and criminals held a sorrowful fascination
for him. "It's what I might have done if I'd stayed in the alley,"
he would tell himself when he heard of some terrible crime
being committed.

But when he reached the end of the article and saw Buck's
name his heart seemed to stand still. Buck! The one old comrade he'd loved the most, who had loved and sacrificed for
him; to whom he'd written and sent money; whose brain was
brighter and heart was bigger than the others'; for whom he'd
searched in vain and found only to lose before he saw him;
whom he'd hoped yet to find and save. Buck had done this
and was caught. And a government offense, too—robbing the
mailbags! It would mean long, hard service. It would mean
many years before Michael could help him to the right kind
of life, if ever.

He asked permission to leave the office that afternoon and
took the train down to the farm where Sam had been staying
for some weeks. He read the article to him, hoping Sam
would say there was some mistake and would know Buck was
safe. But Sam listened, his countenance lowering. When the
reading was finished he swore a great oath, such as he'd never

uttered in Michael's presence, and Michael knew the story must be true.

Nothing could be done now; the law must have its course. But Michael's heart was heavy with the weight of what might have been if he could have found Buck sooner. The next day he secured permission to begin his vacation at once and, in spite of his presence being needed at Old Orchard, took the train for Kansas. He felt he must see Buck at once.

All during the long dismal ride, Michael's heart was beating over and over with the story of his own life. *I might have done this thing. I would have dared and thought it brave if I hadn't been taught better. I might be even now in jail with a broken arm and a useless life. The story of my crime might be bandied through the country in the newspapers if it hadn't been for Mr. Endicott—and little Starr! And yet I've hurt his feelings and alienated his great kindness by refusing his request. Was there no other way?*

Always his conscience answered, "There was no other way!"

Michael, armed with a letter from the senior Holt to a powerful member of Western municipal affairs, found entrance to Buck in his miserable confinement possible. He dawned upon his onetime friend, out of the cell's darkness, as an angel of light. Indeed, Buck, waking from a feverish sleep on his hard cot, moaning and cursing with the pain from his arm, started up and looked at him with awe and horror! The light from the corridor caught the gold in Michael's hair, and Buck thought some new terror had befallen him, and the Death Angel was summoning him to a final judgment for his misdeeds.

But Michael met his old friend with tenderness and a few phrases that had expressed their childish loyalty. Weakened by fever and pain, and above all his defeat and capture, Buck broke down and wept, and Michael wept with him.

"It might have been me instead of you, Buck. If I'd stayed behind, I'd have done all those things. I see it clearly. I might have been living here and you out free. Buck, if it could give you my chance in life and help you see it all as I do, I'd gladly lie here and take your place."

"Mickey! Mickey!" cried Buck. "It's me own Mickey! You was allus willin' to take de rubs! But, Mickey, ef you'd hed de trainin' you'd hev made de fine robber! You'd hev been a peach an' no mistake!"

Michael had found a soft spot in the warden's heart and succeeded in doing some little things for Buck's comfort. He hunted up the chaplain and secured a promise from him to teach Buck to read and write and to read to Buck all letters he received, until he could read them himself. He sent a pot of roses with buds in full bloom to perfume the dark cell, and he promised to write often.

Buck could only say over and over, "Oh, Mickey! Mickey! Ef we wos oney kids again! Oh, Mickey, I'll git out o' here yit an' find ye. Ye'll not be ashamed o' me. Ef I oney hadn't a bungled de job. It was a bum job, Mickey! A bum job!"

Michael saw little use in talking to Buck about his sin. Buck had nothing to build on in morals. To be loyal to his friends and do his "work" so he wouldn't get caught were the only articles in his creed. To get ahead of the rich, to take from them what was theirs if he could, regardless of life or consequences, that was virtue. The rich were enemies; they must outwit him or lose. If they died, it was "all in the day's work" and their loss. When his turn came he'd take his medicine calmly. But Buck's trouble now was that he'd "bungled the job." He'd disgraced his profession. Things had been going against him lately, and he was "down on his luck."

Michael left the West feeling the time allotted him with Buck was too short for what he wanted to do for him; yet he felt it was worth the journey. Buck appreciated his sympathy, even if he didn't have an adequate sense of his sinfulness. Michael had talked and pitied and tried to make Buck see, but in vain, and Michael went home to hope and write and try to educate Buck through sheer love. It was all he saw to do.

About this time, Michael began receiving money in small sums anonymously through the mail. "For your work," the first was labeled, and the remittances that followed had no inscriptions. They weren't always addressed in the same hand, and he never knew the writing. Sometimes there would be a ten-dollar bill, sometimes a twenty and often more, and they came irregularly, enclosed in a thin, inner envelope of foreign-looking paper.

Michael wondered if Starr could have sent them, but that was impossible, for she knew nothing of his work, and they were always postmarked New York. He discovered that such thin foreign-looking envelopes could be bought in New York, and after that he abandoned trying to solve the mystery. It was probably some eccentric, kind person who didn't wish to be known. He accepted the help gladly and broadened his plans for the farm accordingly.

Sam and his five friends had gone down early in the spring, bunking in the old house and enjoying the outing immensely. Under Sam's captaincy and the tutelage of an old farmer Michael had found, who couldn't work much himself but could direct, the work had gone forward.

Michael came down Saturdays and such ends of afternoons as he could get. Many mistakes were made through ignorance, and no less than five times the whole gang went on strike until Michael returned to settle some dispute between the new scientific farming he'd taught them and some old superstition or clumsy practice of the farmer's. But on the whole they did tolerably good work.

The farm community had been meanwhile increasing. Michael picked them up in the alley, or they came to him and asked to be taken on for a trial. They'd heard of the experiment through Sam or one of the boys who had returned to the city for a day on some errand.

One glorious summer morning Michael took ten small newsboys down to pick wild strawberries for the day, and they came back dirty, tired, strawberry streaked, and happy, loudly praising Old Orchard as if it were a heaven. After that, Michael had no trouble transplanting anyone he wished to take with him.

He found a poor wretch lately moved with his family to one of the crowded tenements in the alley. He was sodden in drink and going to pieces fast. Michael sobered him up, found he used to be a master carpenter, and quickly transplanted him to Old Orchard, family and all.

Under the skilled carpenter's hand, tents and, later, one-room shacks or bungalows sprang up. Michael bought lumber and found apprentices to help, and the carpenter repaired barns, outhouses, and fences or built shacks, whenever the head of affairs saw fit to need another.

The only person in the whole alley Michael invited in vain to the farm was old Sally. She steadily refused to leave her brightly papered room, curtained window, and geranium. It symbolized "ould Ireland" to her, and she felt afraid of Michael's new place. It seemed like a door to heaven, from which she felt barred by her life and some nameless terror in her thoughts. She wasn't ready to leave her bit of life and take chances even for Michael. And so she sat on her doorstep and watched the alley dwellers come and go, listening with interest to each new account of the farm, but never willing to see for herself. Perhaps the secret of her hesitation went deeper than superstition. She had learned Old Orchard had no rum shop around the corner. Old Sally couldn't risk it, so she stayed at home.

But the carpenter's wife was glad to cook for the men during the busy days of planting and weeding and harvesting, and the community grew. Two or three other men came down with their families and helped the carpenter build little houses, with a tiny garden in back and a flower bed in front. They could see the distant sea from their tiny porches and the river winding its salty silver way around. It was a great change from the alley. Not all could stand it, but most of them bore the summer test well. When winter set its white distance upon them, chilled the flowers to slumber, and stopped the labor, the testing time would come, and Michael was thinking about that.

He began hunting out helpers for his purposes. He found a man skilled in agricultural arts and secured his services to hold a regular school during the winter for the men. He found a poor student at Princeton who could run up on the train daily and give simple lessons in reading and arithmetic. He impressed it upon Sam and the other young men that unless they could read for themselves enough to keep up with new discoveries, other farmers would get ahead of them and grow bigger potatoes and sweeter corn. He talked eagerly with them about what they were going to do and how the place was going to grow, until he felt as if they owned the earth and meant to show the world how well they were running it. In short, he poured his own spirit of enthusiasm into them and made the hard summer of unaccustomed labor one great game.

When the proceeds from their first simple crops came in from selling products they didn't need, Michael carefully divided it among his workmen. At his wish they went in a body, and each started a bank account at the town's national bank. It was an absurdly small amount, but it made the workers feel like millionaires. Word of the successes reached the city, and more people came down, until by fall thirty-eight men, women, and children were living on the farm.

Of course that made little appreciable difference in the alley's population, for as soon as one family moved out another moved in, and there was plenty of room for Michael's work to go on. Nevertheless, thirty-eight souls were on the way to a better knowledge of life, with clean, wholesome surroundings and a chance to learn how to read and work.

The carpenter was set to build more tiny houses for the next summer's campaign. The tents were folded away. The spring wheat was in. The fall plowing and fertilizing were completed and whatever else should be done to a farm for its winter sleep. Half a dozen cows were introduced into the settlement, and a roomy chicken house and run were built. Sam set about studying incubators and teaching his helpers. Then when the cranberries were picked, the community settled down to its study.

The Princeton student and the agricultural student grew deeply interested in their motley school and found a young woman who traveled down every afternoon for compensation and taught a kindergarten. Many of the prematurely grown-up mothers came with delight and profit and incidentally learned how to be better, cleaner, wiser mothers. The young woman of her own accord added a cooking school for the women and girls.

Once a week Michael brought someone from New York to amuse these poor childish people. And so the winter passed.

Once a wealthy friend of Mr. Holt asked to see the place. After going around the farm and making himself friendly by roasting chestnuts around the open fire in the "big house," as the original cottage was called, he returned to New York praising Michael. A few days later he mailed Michael the deed of the adjoining farm of one hundred acres, and Michael, radiant, realized his dreams for his downtrodden people were coming true. There would be room enough now for many years to come for the people he needed to bring down.

Of course this hadn't been done without discouragements. Some in the community had proved unmanageable, or unwilling to work; some had run away or smuggled in whiskey. There had been two or three incipient fights, and more than double the number of disappointing enterprises, but the work was going on.

And still no word came from Mr. Endicott.

Michael was holding well with his employers, who were beginning to talk to him of a partnership with them when he was finished. He had far outstripped French in his studies and seemed to master everything he touched with an eagerness that showed great intellectual appetite.

He still kept up his evening work in the room in the alley, though he divided his labors somewhat with Will French, Hester Semple, and others who heard of the work and offered their services. It had almost become a little settlement or mission in itself. The one room had become two and a bath, then the whole first floor with a small gymnasium. Will French led enthusiastically in this, and Hester had done many things for the little children and women. The next people for Michael's farm were always being prepared and were spoken of as "eligibles" by the workers.

Hester Semple had proved a valuable assistant, ready with suggestions, tireless, and as fervent as Michael. Night after night, the three toiled and came home happily together. The association with the two was sweet to Michael, whose heart was famished for friends and relations who "belonged." But Michael never thought to look on Hester in any other light than friend and fellow worker.

Will and Michael were coming home from the office one afternoon, talking eagerly of the progress at the farm.

"When you get married, Endicott," said Will, "you must build a handsome bungalow or something for your summer home, down there on the knoll overlooking the river where you can see the sea in the distance."

Michael grew sober at once. "I don't expect ever to be married, Will," he said after a pause, with one of his faraway looks and his chin up.

"The dickens!" said Will, stopping in his walk. "She hasn't

refused you?"

"Refused me? Who? What do you mean?"

"Why, Hester. She hasn't turned you down, old chap?"

"Hester! Why, Will, you never thought—you don't think she ever thought—?"

"Well, I didn't know," said Will, embarrassed. "It looked pretty much like it sometimes. There didn't seem much show for me. I've thought lately you'd settled it and were engaged sure."

"Oh, Will," said Michael in a tone that showed his soul was moved to its depth.

"I say, old chap!" said Will. "I'm fiercely sorry I've butted into your affairs. I never dreamed you'd feel like this. Since I have, though, will you give me a good send-off with Hester? Sort of bless-you-my-son, and tell me you don't mind if I go ahead and try my luck."

"With all my heart, Will. I never thought of it, but I believe it would be great for you both. You seem sort of made for each other."

"It's awfully good of you to say so," said Will, "but I'm afraid Hester doesn't think so. She's taken up with you."

"Not at all!" said Michael eagerly. "Not in the least. I've never noticed it. I'm sure she likes you best."

So from that night Michael almost always had some excuse for staying later at the room or for going somewhere else for a while so he'd have to leave them partway home, and Hester and Will from then on walked together more. Thus Michael took his lonely way, cut off from even this friendly group.

And summer and winter made the second year of the Old Orchard community.

Then the following spring Starr Endicott and her mother came home, and things began to happen.

Chapter 19

Starr was eighteen and very beautiful when she returned. Society was made at once aware of her presence.

Michael, whose heart was alert to know of her and find out where Mr. Endicott was, saw the first notice in the paper.

Three times Endicott crossed the water to visit his wife and daughter during their stay abroad, and every time Michael knew and anxiously awaited some sign of his return. He'd read the society columns for two years now solely to see any news of the Endicott family, and he was growing wondrously wise in society's ways. He had also come to know society a little in another way.

Shortly after his last interview with Endicott, Emily Holt, daughter of the senior member of the Holt and Holt firm, had invited Michael to dine with her father and her. Following this had come an invitation to a house party at the Holts' country seat. This came in the busy season of the farmwork, but Michael, eager to please his employers, took a couple of days off and went. He enjoyed the good times to the full. He renewed his tennis, at which he'd been a master, and his rowing and riding, in both of which he excelled. Also, he met some pleasant people who accepted him for the splendid fellow he appeared and didn't ask who he was. Men of his looks and bearing didn't come their way every day, and Michael was good company wherever he went.

In the evenings, though, Michael was at a loss. He couldn't dance or make small talk. He was too intensely in earnest for society's ways, and they didn't understand. He could talk about books he'd read and what he thought, but they were great thoughts and not good form for a frivolous company to dwell upon. One didn't want an economics problem or a deep philosophical question thrust upon one at a dance. Michael became a delightful but difficult proposition for the girls present, each one undertaking to teach him how to talk in society, but each failing. At last Emily Holt set out to give him gentle hints on light conversation and found herself deep in a discussion of Wordsworth's poems, about which she knew nothing and in which Michael's weary soul had been steeping itself lately.

Emily retired in laughing defeat finally and advised her protégé to take a course on modern novels. Michael, always serious, took her at her word and proceeded to do so, but his course ended after two or three weeks. He found them far from his taste, most too vividly portraying his alley's sins in high life. Michael had enough of that in real life and felt he couldn't stand the strain of modern fiction, so he returned to Wordsworth and found soothing mental stimulus.

Other invitations followed; some he accepted, and some he declined. Still, the handsome, independent young Adonis was in great demand despite his peculiar habit of always being in earnest about everything. Perhaps they liked him and ran after him more because of his inaccessibility and because he was doing something in the world. For it was being whispered about among those who knew—and perhaps Emily Holt originated it—that Michael would be brilliant in doing worthwhile things someday.

The tickets Endicott promised had arrived in due time, and anxious to please his benefactor, even in his alienation, Michael faithfully attended concerts and lectures and enjoyed them fully. He borrowed from his sleep, rather than from his work or study. And so he grew in knowledge and love of the arts.

Matters stood thus when Starr appeared on the scene. The

young girl made her debut that winter, and the papers were filled with her picture and the activities given in her honor. She dined and danced day and night, and no debutante ever received the critics' higher praise for beauty, grace, and charm.

Michael read them all, carefully cut out and preserved a few pleasant things written about her, looked at the pictures, and turned from the pomp and pride to the snapshot of her on horseback in the park with her groom, which she sent to him when she was a little girl. That was his alone, but these others belonged to the world in which he had no part.

From all this society Michael now held aloof. He received many invitations, for he was growing more popular every day; but he declined them all. His honor kept him from going anywhere Starr was sure to be. He had a right, of course, and it would have been somehow pleasant for her to see he was welcome in her world. But her mother's biting words always appeared before his mental vision as she put him down from her glorified world into shame and sin and sorrow. He felt that Starr was so far above him he mustn't hurt her by coming too near. And so in deference to his vow when his unworthiness was first presented to him, he stayed away.

As Starr heard more of his conquests in her world, she wondered and was piqued that he didn't come near her. And one day, meeting him by chance on Fifth Avenue, she greeted him graciously and invited him to call.

Michael thanked her with his quiet manner, while his heart was in a tumult over her beauty and her smiles that blossomed out in the old childish ways—only more beautifully, it seemed to him. He went in the strength of that smile many days, but he didn't call.

The days passed into weeks and months, and still he didn't appear, and Starr, hearing more of his growing inaccessibility, determined to show the others she could draw him out of his shell. She humbled her Endicott pride and wrote him a charming note asking him to call on an afternoon when she and her mother held court. But Michael, though he treasured the note, wrote a courteous but decided refusal.

This angered Starr so much she decided to cut him out of her good graces entirely. And indeed her social activities scarcely gave her time for remembering old friends. In occasional odd moments when she thought of him at all, it was with a vague disappointment that he, too, with all her other childhood things, hadn't turned out to be what she had thought.

But she met him face-to-face one Sunday afternoon walking on the avenue with one of many young men who eagerly attended her. He was slender and handsome, with dark eyes and hair and a reckless mouth. Jaded lines had already formed around his eyes and lips. His name was Stuyvesant Carter. Michael recognized him at once from his picture in the papers the week before as leader with Starr of the cotillion. Seeing him with her in the sunny afternoon was like a cloud of trouble looming on a perfect day. He searched the man before him to the depths and then looked at the beautiful, innocent, happy face.

Michael was walking with Hester Semple, who in her broadcloth tailored suit and black plumed hat looked pretty and distinguished walking beside him. His own garments always seemed to set him off as if designed especially for him, and many watched him as he passed by.

Had it been a moment later, or even three minutes before, Will French would have been with them, and Michael would have been obviously a third member of the party, for he was careful in these days to let them both know he considered that they belonged together. But Will had stopped a moment to speak to a business acquaintance, and Hester and Michael were walking slowly ahead until he rejoined them.

"Look!" said Hester excitedly. "Isn't that the pretty Miss

Endicott whose picture's in the papers so much? I'm sure it must be, though she's ten times prettier than her pictures."

But Michael was already looking with all his soul in his eyes.

As they came opposite, he lifted his hat with such marked deference to Starr that Stuyvesant Carter looked at him insolently, with a careless motion of his own hand toward his hat. But Starr, with brilliant cheeks and her eyes looking straight at Michael, continued her conversation with her companion and never by a flickering eyelash recognized her former friend.

Hester was so taken up with looking at the society beauty that she never noticed Michael's lifted hat until they were passed. Then Will French joined them breezily.

"She's a peach, isn't she?" he breathed as he took his place beside Hester, and Michael dropped behind. "But I suppose it'll rub off. They say most of those swells aren't real."

"I think she's real!" declared Hester. "She has sweet eyes and a charming smile. The color on her cheeks wasn't painted on. I just love her. I'd like to know her. She certainly is beautiful and doesn't look a bit spoiled. Did you ever see such eyes?"

"They aren't half as nice as a pair of gray ones I know," said Will, looking at them as they were lifted smiling to his.

"Will, you mustn't say such things—on the street—anyway—and Michael just behind. Why, where is Michael? Oh, he's dropped behind and is walking slowly. Will, does Michael know Miss Endicott? I never thought about their names being the same. But he lifted his hat to her—and she simply stared blankly at him as if she'd never seen him before."

"The little snob!" said Will indignantly. "I told you they were all artificial. I believe they're some kind of relation or other. Come to think of it—I believe old Endicott introduced Michael into our office. Maybe she hasn't seen him in a long time and has forgotten him."

"No one who has known Michael could ever forget him," said Hester with conviction.

"No, I suppose that's so," said Will, looking at her wistfully.

After this meeting Michael kept more aloof from even small entrances into society and gave more of his time to study and to work among the poor.

So the winter passed in a round of festivities, transplanted for a few weeks to Palm Beach, back to New York, then to Tuxedo Park for the summer—and Michael knew but had no part in it. Now she had cut him out of her life herself, and he might not even cherish her bright smiles and words of the past. She didn't wish to know him. It was right and best—but agony!

Michael grew pale that year and looked more like the man-angel than ever as he came and went in the alley. Old Sally from her doorstep, drawing nearer to her own end, saw it first and called daily attention to Michael's spirit-look as he passed.

One evening early in spring, Michael was starting home weary and unusually discouraged. Sam had gone down to the farm with Jim to prepare for the spring work and find out how things were going and what was needed from the city. Jim was developing into a tolerably dependable fellow except for his hot temper, and Michael missed them from the alley work, for the rooms were crowded now every night. True, Hester and Will were faithful, but they were so much taken up with one another these days that he didn't like to trouble them with unusual cases, and he had no one with whom to counsel. Several things had been going awry, and he was sad.

Hester and Will were ahead, walking slowly as usual.

Michael locked the door with a sigh and turned to follow them, when he saw in the shadows on the other side of the court two figures steal from an opening between the houses and move along toward the end of the alley. Something in their demeanor made Michael watch them. As they neared the end of the alley toward the street they paused a moment, and one figure stole back. He thought he recognized her as a girl cursed with more than the usual amount of beauty. She disappeared into the dark tenement, but, after looking back, the other kept on toward the street. Michael quickened his steps and reached the corner at about the same time, crossing as the other man passed the light and looking full in his face.

To his surprise he saw that the man was Stuyvesant Carter!

With an exclamation of disgust and horror, Michael stepped in the man's path and blocked his passage.

"What are you doing here?" he asked in tones that would have made a brave man tremble.

Stuyvesant Carter glared at him, drew his hat down over his eyes, and snarled, "Get out of my way, or you'll be sorry! I'm probably doing the same thing you're doing here!"

"Probably not!" said Michael. "You know you can mean no good to a girl like the one you were just with. Come down here again at your peril! And if I hear of you having anything to do with that girl, I'll have the whole thing made public."

"Indeed!" said Carter. "Is she your girl? I think not. And who are you anyway?"

"You'll find out if you come down here again!" said Michael, his fingers fairly aching to grip the gentlemanly villain before him. "Now get out of here at once, or you may not be able to walk out."

"I'll get out when I like!" sneered the other, nevertheless backing away through the opening given him. After reaching a safe distance, he added tauntingly, "And I'll come back when I like, too."

"Very well—I'll be ready for you, Mr. Carter!"

Michael's tones were clear and distinct and could be heard two blocks away in the city night. Hearing his real name spoken fearlessly in such an environment, Carter slid away as if he'd suddenly been erased from the scene.

"Who was dat guy?" asked a small voice at Michael's elbow.

Hester and Will were far down the street in the other direction and had forgotten Michael.

Michael turned and saw one of his smallest "kids" crouching in the shadow beside him.

"Why, Tony, are you here yet? You should have been asleep long ago."

"Was dat de guy wot comes to see Lizzie?"

"See here, Tony—what do you know about this?"

Tony proceeded to unfold a tale that made Michael's heart sick.

"Lizzie, she's got swell sence she went away to work to a res'trant at de sheeshole. She ain't leavin' her ma hev her wages, an' she wears fierce cloes, like de swells!" finished Tony solemnly as if these were the worst of all he'd told.

So Michael sent Tony to his rest and went home with a heavy heart, to wake and think through the night what he should do to save his bright beautiful Starr from the clutches of this human vampire.

When morning dawned Michael knew—he would go to Mr. Endicott and tell him the whole story. Starr's father could and would protect her better than he could.

As early as he could he hurried to carry out his purpose. But on arriving at Mr. Endicott's office he was told the gentleman had sailed for Austria and would be absent some weeks, even months, perhaps, if his business didn't mature rapidly.

Michael asked for the address, but when he reached his desk again and tried to frame a letter to convey the truth convincingly to the absent father, who couldn't read it for more than a week at least and would then be thousands of miles away, he gave it up as useless. Something more effectual must be done quickly.

First he must have facts. He couldn't do anything until he knew without a doubt that what he feared was true. If he could have told Mr. Endicott, all would have been different;

he could investigate if he saw fit. Michael might have left the matter in his hands. But he couldn't tell him.

If he could go to some other male family member with the warning, he must be very sure of his ground before he spoke. If there were no such male friend or relative he must do something else—what? He shrank from thinking.

So, with the sources open to a keen lawyer, he took steps to ferret out the life and doings of Stuyvesant Carter and, needless to say, unearthed a lot of information so sickening he felt almost helpless before it. It was appalling—and more so because of the man's rank and station. If he had been raised in the slums one might have expected it—but this!

The second day, Michael, haggard and worn with the responsibility, started out to find that useful male Endicott relative. There seemed to be no such person. The third morning he came to the office determined to tell the whole story to the senior Mr. Holt and ask his advice and aid in protecting Starr. But to his dismay he found the man had been taken seriously ill with heart trouble, and it might be weeks before he could return to the office.

Deeply grieved and baffled, the young man tried to think what to do next. The junior Mr. Holt had never encouraged confidences and wouldn't likely help in this matter. He must do something himself.

And now Michael faced two alternatives. Only two people could he tell the story to: Starr and her mother!

Tell Starr all he knew he could not. To tell her anything of this story would be gall and wormwood! To drop a hint that would blacken another man's character would place him in an awkward position. To think of doing it was like tearing out his heart for her to trample upon.

Yet Michael would rather face a thousand bristling cannons in battle than meet the mother on her own ground and tell her what he had to tell, while her steel-cold eyes pierced him through with scorn and unbelief. He felt he would fail if he went to her.

At last he wrote a note to Starr:

Dear Miss Endicott:
  Can you let me have a brief interview at your convenience and as soon as possible? I have a favor to ask of you which I earnestly hope you will grant.

Sincerely yours,
Michael

He sent the note off with fear and trembling. He had carefully considered every word, and yet it haunted him that he might have written differently. Would she grant the interview? If she didn't, what should he do?

The next day he received a ceremonious note on creamy paper crested with a silver star monogrammed in blue.

  Miss Endicott will receive Mr. Endicott tomorrow morning at eleven.

A shiver ran through him as he read and then consigned the elegant communication to his wastebasket. It wasn't from his Starr. It was from a stranger. Yet the subtle perfume stealing from the envelope reminded him of her. On second thought he drew it forth again and put it in his pocket. After all she'd granted the interview, and this paper was part of her daily life; it had come from her, and she had written and sent it to him. It was precious.

Starr had been more than usually thoughtful when she read Michael's note. It pleased her that at last she'd brought him to her feet, though not for the world would she let him know. Doubtless he wished her influence for some position he would have asked of her father if he'd been at home. Starr knew nothing of the alienation between her father and Michael. But Michael should pay for his request, in humility at least. So she sent her cool stab.

But Michael didn't look humiliated as he entered the library where Starr had chosen to receive him. His manner was grave and assured, and he made no sign of the tumult it gave him to see her thus in her own home again where the luxury enhanced her womanliness and charm.

He came forward to greet her as if she hadn't cut him dead the last time they met, and Starr, as she regarded him, was struck with wonder over the exalted beauty of manhood that was his unique inheritance.

"Thank you for letting me come," he said. "I won't intrude long upon your time—"

Starr had a strange fearful sensation he would slip away from her again before she was willing.

"Oh, that's all right," she said graciously. "Won't you sit down? I'm always glad to do a favor for a childhood friend."

She had rehearsed that sentence many times in her mind, and it was meant to convey reproach and indifference. But as she fluttered into a great leather chair, she felt her voice was trembling, and she'd miserably failed in what she'd meant to do. She felt strangely ashamed of her attitude, with those two clear eyes looking straight at her. It reminded her of how he'd looked when he told her in the Florida chapel long ago that nobody but she had ever kissed him—and she had kissed him then. Suppose he was going to ask her to do it again! The thought made her cheeks rosy, and her society air deserted her. But of course he wouldn't do that. It was a crazy thought. What was the matter with her anyway, and why did she feel so unnerved? Then Michael spoke.

"May I ask if you know a man by the name of Stuyvesant Carter?"

Starr looked startled and then stiffened slightly.

"I do!" she answered graciously. "He's one of my intimate friends. Can he do something for you that you'd like my intercession?"

Starr smiled graciously. She thought she understood the reason for Michael's call now and was pleased to think how easily she could grant his request. The idea of introducing them was stimulating. She was pondering what a handsome pair of men they were and so different from each other.

But Michael's clear voice startled her again out of her complacence.

"Thank God there isn't!" he said, and his tone made Starr sit up and put on all her dignity.

"Indeed!" she said with asperity, her eyes flashing.

"Pardon me, Miss Endicott," Michael said sadly. "You don't understand my feeling!"

"I certainly do not." Starr had inherited her icicle sentences from her mother.

"And I cannot explain," he went on sadly. "I must ask you to take it on trust. The favor I've come to ask is this—that you won't have anything further to do with that young man until your father's return. I know this may seem strange to you. But, believe me, if you understood, you wouldn't hesitate to do what I've asked."

Michael held her with his look and earnest tones. She couldn't speak from sheer astonishment at his audacity. Then she froze him with a look copied from her mother's haughty manner.

"And what reason can you give for such an extraordinary request?" she asked at last, when his look compelled an answer.

"I cannot give you a reason," he said gravely. "You must trust me that this is best. Your father will explain to you when he comes."

Another pause, and then Starr asked, "And you really think I'd grant such a ridiculous request which implies a lack of trust in the character of one of my warmest friends?"

"I most earnestly hope you will," answered Michael.

In spite of her hauteur she was impressed by Michael's manner. His grave tones and serious eyes told her heart that here was something extraordinary; at least she gave Michael credit for thinking there was.

"I certainly won't do anything of the kind without good reason for it." Starr's tone was determined and cold.

"And I can give you no reason beyond telling you he isn't the kind of man a friend of yours should be."

"What do you mean?"

"Please don't ask me. Please trust me and give me your promise. At least wait until I can write your father."

Starr rose with a look of her father's stubbornness now in her pretty face.

"I wish to be told," she demanded angrily.

"You wouldn't wish it if you knew," he answered.

She looked at him steadily for a full moment, then tossed her head and said, "I must decline your request, Mr. Endicott. You'll excuse me. I have a luncheon engagement now."

She stood aside for him to go out the door.

He rose with pleading still in his eyes. "You'll write to your father and tell him what I've said? You'll wait until you hear from him?"

"It's impossible, Mr. Endicott." Starr's tone was freezing now, and he could see she was very angry. "Mr. Carter is my friend!" she flung at him as he passed her into the hall.

Another anguishing night brought Michael face-to-face with the necessity for an interview with Starr's mother.

Taking his cue from the hour Starr had set for his call, he went a little before eleven o'clock and sent up the card of the firm with his name written below, for he doubted he would obtain an interview if the lady thought he might be there on his own business.

Mrs. Endicott probably didn't recognize the former "Mickey" under the title written below his most respectable law firm's name. Any representative of Holt and Holt was to be recognized, of course. She came down within a half hour, graciously with lorgnette in hand, until she reached the center of the reception room where he was put to await her. Then Michael arose, almost from the same spot where she had addressed him nearly four years before, the halo of the morning shining through the window on his hair. With a start and stiffening of her form, she recognized him.

"Oh, it's you!" Her tone argued ill for Michael's mission, but with grave and gentle bearing he began.

"Madam, I beg your pardon for the intrusion. I wouldn't have come if there'd been another way. I tried to find Mr. Endicott but was told he'd sailed—"

"You needn't waste your time and mine. I'll do nothing for you. As I told you before, if I remember, I think far too much already has been done for you, and I never felt you had the slightest claim on our bounty. I refuse to hear any hard-luck stories."

Michael's face was a study. Indignation and shame struggled with a sudden sense of the ridiculous. What he did was laugh—a rich, clear, musical laugh that stopped the lady's tirade better than anything else could have.

"Well! Really! Have you come to insult me?" she said angrily. "I'll call a servant." She stepped toward the bell.

"Madam, I beg your pardon," said Michael, grave at once. "I intended no insult and haven't come to ask a favor. I came because of a serious matter, perhaps a grave danger to your home, which I thought you should know about."

"Indeed! Well, make haste," said Mrs. Endicott, half mollified. "My time is valuable. Is someone planning to rob the house?"

Michael looked straight in her face and told her briefly a

few facts, delicately worded, forcefully put, which would have convinced the heart of any true mother that the man before her had only pure motives.

Not so this mother. The more Michael talked, the stiffer, haughtier, more hateful grew her stare. Then he paused, not wishing to overwhelm her with his facts.

"How could you possibly know these things," she remarked, "unless you were in the same places where you claim Mr. Carter has been? But, oh, I forgot! Your former home was there, and so you must have many friends among—ah—those people!" She punctuated the last two words with a contemptuous look through the lorgnette.

"But, my dear fellow," she went on in her patronizing manner, "you should never trust those people. Of course you don't understand that, having been away from them so many years among respectable folks, but they really don't know what the truth is. I doubt there's any foundation for all you've been telling me."

"Madam, I've looked into the matter and know every word I've told you is true. Two of the city's most noted detectives have been investigating. I wouldn't have come if I hadn't had indisputable facts to give you."

Mrs. Endicott arose, still holding the lorgnette to her eyes, though she showed the interview was drawing to a close.

"Then, young man," she said, "I must tell you the things you've been saying are not considered proper to speak of before ladies in respectable society. I remember your low origin and lack of breeding and forgive what I would otherwise consider an insult. Further, it isn't considered honorable to investigate a gentleman's private life too closely. All young men sow their wild oats and are probably none the worse for it. In fact, if a man hasn't seen life, he isn't worth much. It's his own affair and not your business. I must ask you not to say anything of this to anyone. Not a word! My husband would be deeply outraged to know a friend of his daughter's, a man of refinement and position, had been the object of scandal by one who should honor anyone he honors. I can't spare any more time this morning."

"But, madam! You certainly don't mean you won't investigate this matter for yourself? You wouldn't let your daughter accept such a man as her friend?"

The lorgnette came into play again, but its stare was ineffectual upon Michael's pale, earnest face. His deep eyes lit with horror at this monstrous woman who seemed devoid of mother-love.

"It's none of your business what I mean. You've done what you thought was your duty by telling me. Now put the matter entirely out of your mind. Desist at once!"

With a final stare, she swept out of the room and up the broad staircase. Michael, watching her until she was out of sight, left the house with bowed head and burdened heart to write a letter to Starr's father. The letter would have performed its mission where his other efforts had failed, but because of a sudden and unexpected change of address, it just missed him at every stopping place as it traveled its silent, unfruitful way about the world after him, never getting anywhere until too late.

Chapter 20

Starr was very angry when Michael left her. There was perhaps more hurt pride and pique in her anger than she'd have owned. He hadn't succumbed to her charms; he hadn't seemed to notice her as other men did; he had even lost the look of admiration he used to wear when they were boy and girl. He'd refused to tell her what she had a great curiosity to know.

She was sure that if Michael would tell her what he had against Stuyvesant Carter she could explain it. Her head was almost turned by now with the adoration she'd received. She thought she knew almost everything Stuyvesant Carter had ever done. He was a fluent talker and had spent many hours detailing incidents and anecdotes of his eventful career to her. He had raced a good deal and still had several expensive racing cars. There was nothing very dreadful about that except it was dangerous. He used to gamble a great deal, but he promised he'd never do it again because she thought it unrefined. Of course it wasn't as if he didn't have plenty of money, and her mother had told her all young men did those things. No, not her father, of course, for he'd been unusual, but times were different now. Young men were expected to be a little wild. It was the influence of college life and a progressive age, she supposed. It didn't do any harm. They always settled down and made good husbands after marriage. Michael didn't understand these things. He'd spent many years in Florida with a dear old professor and a lot of good little boys and was unacquainted with the world's ways.

Thus she reasoned, though Michael's warning troubled her. Finally she decided to go to the best source of information and ask Carter himself.

So three days after Michael's visit, when Carter dropped in to ask her to go to the opera that evening instead of something else they'd planned, she laughingly questioned him.

"What in the world can you ever have done, Mr. Carter, that would make you unfit company for me?"

She asked the question lightly, though her eyes watched his face closely as she waited for the answer.

The blood rolled in dark waves over his handsome face, and his brows grew dark with anger, half hiding the start of almost fear with which he regarded her.

"What do you mean, Starr?" He looked at her keenly and couldn't tell if she were in earnest or not.

"Just that," she said, half mocking, half serious. "Tell me what you've been doing that would make you unfit company for me? Someone has been trying to make me promise to have nothing to do with you, and I want to know what it means."

"Who's been doing that?" Dangerous lights flickered in the dark eyes, lights that showed the brutality of the coward and the evildoer.

"Oh, a man! But if you look like that, I won't tell you anything more about it. I don't think I like you now. You look as if you could eat me. You make me think there must be something to it."

Quick to take the warning, the young man brought his face under control and broke into an artificial laugh. Suddenly he understood, and fear entered his heart. There was nothing like being bold and taking the bull by the horns.

"I'll wager I can explain the riddle for you," he said airily. "I lost my way the other evening coming home late. There had been some mistake, and my car didn't come to the club for me. I started on foot, leaving word for it to overtake me." He lied as he went along. He'd had a short lifetime of practice and did it easily. "I was thinking about you and how soon I dared ask you a certain question, when all at once I noticed things seemed unfamiliar. I turned to go back but couldn't tell which way I'd turned at the last corner—you see what a dangerous influence you have on me—and I wandered deeper into things. It wasn't a very savory neighborhood, and I wanted to get out as soon as possible. I suspected it wasn't even safe down there alone at that hour of the night. I was hesitating under a streetlight close to a dark alley, trying to decide the quickest way out and what I should do to find a policeman. Suddenly, out of the dark, loomed a great tall brute with the strangest-looking yellow hair and a body that looked as if he could play football with the universe. He charged me with having come down there to visit his girl.

"Well, of course the situation wasn't very pleasant. I tried to explain I was lost and had never been down in that quarter before and didn't even know his girl. But he wouldn't listen to anything and began threatening me. Then I took out my card and handed it to him, unwisely, of course—but then I'm wholly unused to such situations. I explained to him who I was and of course I wouldn't want to see his girl, even if I'd be so mean and all that. But that fellow wouldn't take a word of it. He threw the card on the sidewalk, ground his heel into it, and used all sorts of evil language I can't repeat. Finally, after I thought he was going to put me in the ditch and pummel me, he let me go, shouting after me that if I ever came near his girl again he'd publish it in the newspapers. Then of course I understood what a foolish thing I'd done in giving him my card. But it was too late. I told him as politely as I knew how that if he'd show me the way to get home I'd never trouble him again. He finally let me go."

Starr's eyes were all this time searching his face. "Was the man intoxicated?"

"Oh, I presume so, more or less. They all are down there, though I'd say he wasn't of the slums himself. He was well-dressed and probably angry I'd discovered him in such haunts."

"When did this happen?"

"About a week ago."

"Why didn't you tell me about it before?"

"Oh, I didn't want to distress you. Besides, I've had my mind too full of other things. Starr, darling, you must have seen all these weeks how much I love you and how I've only been waiting for the opportunity to ask you to be my wife."

Starr was in a measure prepared for this proposal: Her mother had instructed her that the alliance was wholly acceptable, even desirable. She herself was quite taken up with this handsome admirer who flattered her hourly and showered attentions upon her until she felt quite content with herself, the world, and him. Starr had a spice of daring that liked what she thought to be Carter's wildness and energy, and she'd made up her mind to accept him.

One week later the society papers announced the engagement, and the world was in a flutter over the many functions immediately set up in their honor.

Michael, at his desk in the busy office, read and bowed his head in anguish. His bright, beautiful Starr, to be sacrificed to a beast like that! Would that he might save her again to life and happiness!

For the next few days Michael went about in a state that almost bordered on the frantic. His pale face looked drawn, and his eyes burned like live coals. People turned to look after him on the street and exclaimed, "Why, look at that man!" Yet he seemed more like an avenging angel dropped down for some terrible errand than like a plain, ordinary man.

Mr. Holt noticed it and spoke to him about it. "You should drop work and take a good vacation, Endicott. You're in bad shape. You'll break down and be ill. If I were in your place

I'd cancel the rent of that office and not try to start out for yourself until fall. It'll repay you in the end. You're taking things too seriously."

But Michael smiled and shook his head. He was to open his own office the following week. It was ready with its simple furnishings, in marked contrast to the rooms that would have been his if he'd acceded to his benefactor's request. But Michael had lost interest in office and work alike, and the room seemed now only a refuge from men's eyes where he might hide with his great sorrow and try to study out some way to save Starr. Surely her father would do something when he received his letter! It was long past time for an answer. But then perhaps he was already doing something, though he was unwilling to afford Michael the satisfaction of knowing it.

He gave much thought to sending a cablegram, telling the story to the father while telling nothing to the world, but abandoned the idea.

Sam came up from the farm and saw Michael's face and was worried.

"Say, pard, wot yer bin doin' t' yersef? Better come down t' th' farm an' git a bit o' fresh air."

The only two people who didn't notice the change in Michael's appearance were Hester and Will. They were too much engrossed in each other by this time to notice even Michael. They usually left the rooms in the alley earlier than Michael and went home by themselves.

They left him thus one night about three weeks after Starr's engagement had been announced. Michael stayed in the room for an hour after everyone else had gone. He was expecting Sam to return. Sam had been up from the farm several times lately, and this time without any apparent reason he had lingered in the city. He hadn't been to the room that night except for ten minutes early in the evening when he mumbled something about a little business and said he would be back before Michael left.

Michael sat for a long time, his elbow on the table, his head in his hands. He'd thought of a way that might prevent Starr from throwing away her happiness. The morning paper had hinted of plans for a speedy wedding. It was rumored that Miss Endicott would marry as soon as her father reached home. Michael was desperate. The father might arrive too late for him to speak with him. He'd begun to know it was hard to convince people of the evil of those they'd chosen as friends. It would take time.

There was a way. He might have the whole story published in the papers. A public scandal would doubtless delay if not stop this alliance, but a public scandal that touched Mr. Carter would also touch and bring into publicity the girl whose life was almost linked with his. Not until the last resort would Michael bring about that publicity. That such a move on his part would beget him the eternal enmity of the entire Endicott family he didn't doubt, but that factor didn't figure in Michael's calculations. He wasn't working for himself in this. Nothing that ever happened could make things right for him, he felt, and what was his life, or good name even, beside Starr's happiness?

Wearily, at last, his problem unsolved, he got up and turned out the lights. As he was locking the door, his attention was arrested by two figures standing between him and the street-light at the end of the alley. It was a man and a woman, and the woman seemed to be clinging to the man and pleading with him.

Such sights weren't uncommon in the alley. Some poor woman often thus appealed to what used to be good in the man she married, to get him to stay away from the saloon or give her a little of his money to buy food for the children.

More than once in such instances Michael had successfully added his influence to the wife's and convinced the man to go quietly home.

He put the key hastily in his pocket and hurried toward the two.

"You won't never go back to her!" he heard the woman cry fiercely. "You promised me—"

"Shut up, will you? I don't care what I promised," said the man in a guarded voice Michael felt sure he'd heard before.

"I won't shut up! I'll holler ef you go, so the police'll come. You've got a right to stay with me. You won't do me wrong, ner you won't go back to that stuck-up piece. You're mine, I say, and you promised!"

With a curse the man struck her a cruel blow across the mouth and tried to tear her clinging hands away from his coat, but they only clung more fiercely.

Michael sprang to the woman's side like a panther.

"Look out!" he said in clear tones. "You can't strike a woman!" His voice was low and calm and sounded as it had on the ball field when he was giving directions to his team at some crisis in the game.

"Who says I can't?" snarled the man, and now Michael was sure he knew the voice.

Then the wretch struck the woman between her eyes, and she fell heavily to the ground.

Like a flash Michael's arm went out and felled the man. In the same breath, from the shadows sprang Sam's slender, wiry figure flinging itself upon the man on the ground who with angry imprecations was struggling to his feet. His hand had gone to an inner pocket as he fell, and in a moment more came a flash of light, and Michael felt a bullet whiz by his ear. Nothing but the swerving of the struggling figures saved it from going through his brain. In that instant it occurred to Michael that was what had been intended. The conviction that the man had also recognized him gave strength to his arm as he wrenched the revolver from the would-be assassin's hand. Nobody knew better than Michael how easy it would be to plead "self-defense" if the fellow got into trouble. A man in young Carter's position with wealth and friends galore needn't fear wiping an unknown fellow out of existence, whose friends with few exceptions were toughs and jailbirds and ex-criminals.

As he gave Carter's wrist the twist that sent the revolver to the ground beside the unconscious woman, Michael heard the hurried footsteps of the law officer accompanied by a curious motley crowd who had heard the pistol shot and come to see any new excitement life offered. He suddenly realized how bad matters would look for Sam if he were found in the embrace of one of society's pets who would surely tell a tale to clear himself regardless of others. Michael had no care for himself. The police about that quarter knew him well and were acquainted with his work. They looked upon him with almost more respect than they did the priests and deaconesses who went about their errands of mercy; for Michael's spirit-look of being more than man and the stories attached to his name in the alley filled them with a worshipful awe. There was little likelihood of trouble for Michael with the officers he knew. But Sam was another proposition. His past life hadn't been virtuous, and lately he'd been in New Jersey so much he was little known and would be suspected of causing the trouble. Besides, the woman lay unconscious at their feet.

With a mighty effort Michael now reached forth and plucked Sam, struggling fiercely, from his antagonist's arms and put him behind him in the doorway, standing firmly in front. Carter, thus released, sprawled in the road; then taking advantage of the momentary release he struggled to his feet and fled in the opposite direction from which the officers approached.

"Let me go! I gotta get 'm!" muttered Sam, pushing fiercely to get by Michael.

"No, Sam, stay where you are and keep quiet. You'll gain

nothing by running after him. You'll only get into trouble yourself."

"I don't care what happens to me!" said Sam. "I'll kill him. He stole my girl!"

But Michael stood before him like a wall.

"Yes, Sam, my poor fellow, I know," said Michael gently, sadly. "I know, Sam. He stole mine, too!"

Sam subsided as if he'd been struck, a low awful curse upon his lips, his face pale and baleful. •

"You, too?" The yearning tenderness went to Michael's heart like sweet salve, even in the stressful moment. They were brothers in sorrow, and their brotherhood saved Sam from committing a crime.

Then the police and crowds swept up breathless.

"What does all this mean?" panted a policeman, touching his cap respectfully to Michael. "Someone been shooting?"

He stooped and peered into the pale face of the still-unconscious woman and then looked suspiciously toward Sam standing sullenly behind Michael.

"He's all right," said Michael with a smile, throwing an arm across Sam's shoulder. "He only came in to help me when he saw I was having a hard time. The fellow made off in that direction." Michael pointed after Carter, whose form had disappeared in the darkness.

"Any of the gang?" asked the officer as he hurried away.

"No!" said Michael. "He doesn't belong here!"

One officer hurried away accompanied by a crowd; the other stayed to look after the woman. He touched the woman with his foot as he might have tapped a dying dog to see if any life remained. A low growl like a fierce animal came from Sam's closed lips.

Michael put a warning hand on his arm. "Steady, Sam, steady!" he murmured and went himself and lifted the girl's pretty head from its stony pillow.

"I think you'd better send for the ambulance," he said to the officer. "She's had a heavy blow on her head. I arrived just in time to see the beginning of the trouble—"

"Ain't she dead?" asked the officer indifferently. "Best get her into her house. Don't reckon they want to mess up the hospital with such cattle as this."

Michael caught the fierce gleam in Sam's eyes. A second more would have seen the officer lying beside the girl in the road and a double tragedy to the night's record, for Sam was crouched and moving stealthily like a cat toward the officer's back, a look of almost insane fury upon his small, thin face. Michael's steady voice recalled him to sanity, as many times in the midst of a game he'd put self-control and courage into his teammates' hearts.

"Sam, could you come here and hold her head a minute, while I try to get some water? Yes, officer, I think she's living, and she should be taken to the hospital as soon as possible. Please give the call at once."

The officer sauntered off to do his bidding. Michael and Sam began working over the unconscious girl, and the crowd stood idly waiting until the ambulance rattled up. They watched with awe as the woman's form was lifted in, and Michael and Sam climbed up on the front seat with the driver and rode off. Then they drifted away to their beds, and the street settled into the brief night respite.

The two young men waited at the hospital an hour until a white-capped nurse came to tell them Lizzie had recovered consciousness, and there was hope of her life. Then they went out into the late night.

"Sam, you're coming home with me tonight!" Michael put his arm affectionately around Sam's shoulders. "You never would come before, but you must come tonight."

And Sam, looking into the other's face, saw something in Michael's suffering eyes that made him yield.

"I ain't fit!" Sam murmured as they walked along. It was Sam's first hint that he wasn't every whit as good as Michael, and Michael with rare tact had never by a glance let Sam know how much he wished to have him cleaner and more suitably garbed.

"Oh, we'll make that all right!" said Michael, thankful that at last the time had come for presenting the neat garments he'd purchased some weeks before as a gift for Sam.

The dawn was hovering in the east when Michael led Sam up to his room and, throwing wide the door of his private bathroom, told Sam to take a hot bath; it would make him feel better.

While Sam was thus engaged, Michael bundled up Sam's old garments and, stealing to the back hall window, landed them neatly on top of the ash barrel in the court below. Sam's clothes might see the alley again by way of the ash man, but never on Sam's back.

Late that same morning Sam, clothed and in a new and righter mind than ever in his life, walked down with Michael to breakfast and was introduced as "my friend Mr. Casey" to the landlady, who was hovering about the now-deserted breakfast table. He looked every inch a respectable citizen. Not handsome and distinguished like Michael, of course, but proper as a guest at Mrs. Semple's breakfast table.

Michael explained that an accident had detained them late the night before. Mrs. Semple gave special orders for a nice breakfast to be served to Mr. Endicott and his friend and said it wasn't any trouble at all.

People always thought it was no trouble to do things for Michael.

While they ate, Michael arranged with Sam to take a trip out to see Buck.

"I was expecting to go this morning," he said. "I'd made my plans. They write me that Buck's getting uneasy and they wish I'd come. But now"—he looked at Sam—"I think I should stay here awhile. Could you go in my place? I must attend to some things here."

Sam's face grew dark with sympathy. He understood.

"I'll keep you informed about Lizzie," went on Michael with delicate intuition, "and anyway, you couldn't see her for some time. I think if you try, you could help Buck as much as I. He needs to understand that breaking laws is all wrong, that it doesn't pay in the end and there has to be a penalty—you know. You can make him see things in a new way if you try. Will you go, Sam?"

"I'll go," said Sam.

Michael knew he'd do his best. Sam's changed viewpoint might have more effect on Buck than anything Michael could say. For it was an open secret between Sam and Michael now that Sam stood for a new order of things and the old life, so far as he was concerned, had been put away.

So Sam was taken safely away from the danger spot, and Michael stayed to face his sorrow and the problem of how to save Starr.

Chapter 21

The papers the next morning announced that Mr. Stuyvesant Carter, while taking a shortcut through the city's lower quarter, had been cruelly attacked, beaten, and robbed and barely escaped with his life.

He was lying in his rooms under a trained nurse's care and recovering as rapidly as could be expected from the shock.

Reading it the next morning after seeing Sam off to Kansas, Michael lifted his head with that quiet show of indignation. He knew the message must have been telephoned to the paper by Carter himself shortly after he escaped from the police. He saw just how easy it was for him to give out any report he chose. Money and influence would buy even the public press. It would be little use to try to refute anything he chose to tell about himself.

The days following were to Michael one long blur of trouble. He haunted Mr. Endicott's office in hopes of getting news of his return, but they told him the last letters had been very uncertain. He might come quickly or might be delayed a month or even longer, and a cablegram might not reach him much sooner than a letter, as he was traveling from place to place.

After three days of this agony, knowing the enemy would soon be recovering from his bruises and be about again, he reluctantly wrote a note to Starr.

My dear Miss Endicott,
  At the risk of offending you, I feel I must try again to save

you from what I feel can only be great misery. The young man we were speaking of has twice to my knowledge visited a young woman of the slums within the last month and has even since your engagement been maintaining an intimacy with her which can only insult you. Though you may not believe me, it gives me greater pain to tell you this than anything I ever had to do before. I've tried every way I know to communicate with your father but have thus far failed. I hope that if you won't take my word for it, you'll at least find some trustworthy intimate family friend you can confide in, who'll investigate this matter for you and give you his candid opinion of the young man. I can furnish such a man with information as to where to get the facts. I know that what I've said is true. I beg for the sake of your future happiness that you'll discover for yourself.

Michael

To this note, within two days, he received a condescending reply.

Michael,

I'm very sorry you've used means so low to accomplish your end, whatever that may be. It's beyond me to imagine what possible motive you can have for all this ridiculous calumny you're trying to cast on one who's shown a noble spirit toward you.

Mr. Carter has fully explained to me his presence at that girl's home, and because I don't like for anyone to think evil of the man I'm to marry, I'm taking the trouble to explain to you. The young woman is a former maid of Mr. Carter's mother, and she's deeply attached to her. She does up Mrs. Carter's fine laces, and Mr. Carter has twice been the bearer of laces to be laundered, because his mother was afraid to trust such valuable pieces to a servant.

*I hope you'll now understand the terrible things you've tried
to say against Mr. Carter are false. Such things are called
blackmail and bring terrible consequences in court, I'm told, if
they become known, so I must warn you never to do anything
like this again. It's dangerous. If my father were at home he'd
explain it to you. Of course, having been in that out-of-the-
way Florida place for so long you don't understand these
things. But for Papa's sake I wouldn't like you to get into
trouble in any way.*

*I must say one more thing: Mr. Carter tells me he saw you
down in that questionable neighborhood and that you are
yourself interested in this girl. When this is the case, it seems
strange you should have thought so ill of him.*

Trusting you'll cause me no further annoyance in this matter,

S. D. Endicott

When Michael had read this, he bowed himself on his desk
as one stricken unto death. To read such words from the one
he loved better than his own soul was terrible! And he might
never let her know these things said of him were false. She
would probably have the idea always that his presence in that
alley was shameful to him. So far as his personal part in the
danger to her was concerned, he was from now on powerless
to help her. If she thought such things of him—if she'd really
been made to believe them—then of course she could credit
nothing he told her. Some higher power than his would have
to save her if she was to be saved.

To do Starr justice, she was very much stirred by Michael's
note and after a night of wakefulness and thought had taken
the letter to her mother. Not that Starr turned naturally to her
most unnatural mother for help in personal matters usually,
but she seemed to have no one else. If only her father were
home! She thought of cabling him, but what could she say in
a brief message? How could she make him understand? And

then the world was always standing by to peer over one's shoulder when one sent a message. She couldn't hope to escape the public eye.

She considered showing Michael's note to Morton, her faithful nurse, but Morton, wise in many things, wouldn't understand this matter and would be powerless to help her. So Starr went to her mother.

Mrs. Endicott, shrewd to perfection, masked her indignation under a proper show of horror and told Starr of course it wasn't true; but equally of course it must be investigated. She gave her word she'd do so immediately, and her daughter needn't think further of it. Then she sent at once for Carter, holding a brief consultation with him, and at the end called Starr and cheerfully gave the version of the story she wrote to Michael.

Stuyvesant Carter could be very alluring when he tried, and he chose to try. The stakes were a fortune, a noble name, and a very pretty girl he was as much in love with at present as he'd ever been, in his checkered career, with any girl.

Moreover his nature held revenge long. He delighted turning the story on the man who pretended to be so righteous and dared give him orders about a poor, worthless slum girl. He set his cunning intellect to devise a scheme for catching his adversary in his own net. He found a powerful ally in the mother of the girl he was to marry.

For reasons of ambition Mrs. Endicott desired an alliance with the Carter house, and she was determined nothing should upset her plans for her only daughter's marriage.

She knew that if her husband returned and heard any hint of the story about Carter, he would at once end any relations between him and Starr. It would be mortifying to have the arrangements balked after things had gone so far. And there was that hateful Mrs. Waterman, setting her cap for him so odiously everywhere, even since the engagement had been announced. Mrs. Endicott would risk nothing. Therefore she planned with the young people for an early marriage. She was anxious to have everything so cut-and-dried and matters gone so far that her husband couldn't upset them when he returned. Finally she cabled him asking him to set a positive date for his homecoming as the young people wished an early wedding. He cabled back a date not so far off, for in truth, though he'd received none of Michael's warnings, he was uneasy about his daughter's engagement. Carter had seemed all right, and he saw no reason to demur when his wife wrote that the young people had come to an understanding; but he hadn't thought the marriage would be soon. He was troubled at losing the one bright treasure of his home, when he'd just got her back again from her European education. He felt it was unfortunate that imperative business had called him abroad almost as soon as she returned. He was in haste to be back.

But when his wife followed her cable message with a letter speaking of an immediate marriage and setting a date only four days after his arrival, he cabled her to set no date until his return, which would be as soon as possible.

Mrs. Endicott had planned well, however. The invitations had been sent out that morning. She thought it unnecessary to cable again but wrote:

> *I'm sorry, but your message came too late. The invitations are out now and arrangements going forward. I knew you wouldn't want to stop Starr's plans, and she seems to have her heart set on being married at once. Dear Stuyvesant finds it urgent to take an ocean trip, and he cannot bear the thought of going without his wife. I don't see how things could be held off now. We'd be the laughingstock of society, and I'm sure you wouldn't want me to endure that. And Starr, dear child, is childishly happy over her arrangements. She's only anxious to have you properly home in time, so do hurry and get an earlier boat if possible.*

Over this letter Mr. Endicott frowned and looked troubled. His wife had always taken things in her own hands when she would. But concerning Starr they'd never agreed, though he'd let her have her way about everything else. It was like her to get this marriage fixed up while he was away. Of course it must be all right, but so sudden! And his little Starr! His one little girl!

Then, with his usual abrupt action, he put the letter in his inner pocket and hurried his business as much as possible to take an even earlier boat. And he finally succeeded by working night and day and leaving several important matters to go as they would.

The papers at last announced that Mr. Delevan Endicott, abroad for three months on business, had sailed for home and would reach New York nearly a week before the date set for the wedding. The papers also were filled with elaborate foreshadowings of what that event would likely mean to society.

And Michael, knowing he must suffer and endure to the end of it, if perchance he might yet save her in some miraculous way, read every word and knew the day and hour of the boat's probable arrival. He planned to meet the boat himself. If possible he'd go out on the pilot and meet his man before he landed.

Then the silence of the great deep fell about the traveler, and the day passed with the waiting one in the city and preparations hurried forward by skilled workers. The Endicott home was filled with comers and goers who brought silks and satins and costly laces and jewels from around the world.

Over the machinery she set going, Mrs. Endicott presided with the calmness and positive determination of one who had a great purpose in view and meant to carry it out. Not a detail escaped her vigilant eye; not an item was forgotten of the million necessities the world expected and she must have forthcoming. Anything to make the wedding unique, artistic, or perfect must be carried out. This was her highest opportunity to shine, and Mrs. Endicott intended to make the most of it. Not that she hadn't shone throughout her worldly career, but she knew that with her daughter's marriage, her own life would reach its zenith point and then decline. This event must be remembered in the annals of the future so long as New York married and was given in marriage. Starr's wedding must surpass all others in wonder, beauty, and elegance.

So she planned, wrought, carried out, and day by day the gleam in her eyes indicated she was nearing triumph.

It didn't disturb her when the steamer was overdue one day and then two. Starr, even amid the festivities in her honor, found time to worry about her father, but the wife only found cause for congratulations. She felt her crucial time was coming when her husband reached home. If Michael had carried out his threats, or if breath of the stories concerning Carter's life reached him, there would be trouble against which she had no power.

Not until the third morning with still no news of the vessel did Mrs. Endicott feel uneasy. It would be awkward to have to delay the ceremony, and of course it wouldn't do to have it without the bride's father when he was hurrying to be present. If he would arrive just in time so much the better, but late—ah—that would be dreadful! She tightened her lips and looked like a Napoleon saying, *There shall be no Alps!* In like manner she would have said if she could, *There shall be no sea if I wish it.*

But her anxiety was only manifested by closer vigilance over her helpers as hourly the preparations glided to their finish.

Starr grew nervous and couldn't sleep, hovering from room to room in the daytime looking out the windows or telephoning the steamship company for news. Her fiancé found her unsatisfactory, and no plans he proposed for her diversion pleased her. Dark rings appeared under her eyes, and she looked at him with a troubled expression sometimes when she should have been laughing in the midst of pleasures.

Starr deeply loved her father, and some vague presentiment of coming trouble seemed to shadow life. Now and then Michael's face with its great, true eyes and pleading expression came between her and Carter's face, blurring its handsome lines, and then indefinite questions haunted her. What if those terrible things Michael had said were true? Was she sure? At such times she saw a weakness in the lines about Carter's eyes and mouth.

But she was unused to studying character and had no guide to help her in her lonely problem of choosing, for already she'd learned that her mother's ways and hers weren't the same, and her father didn't come. When he came it would be all right. It had to be, for there was no turning back now. The wedding was two days off.

Michael, in his new office, acknowledged to himself he couldn't work. He'd done all he could and awaited a report of that vessel. When it landed he hoped to be the first man on board; in fact, he'd arranged to meet it before it landed. But it didn't come! Would it be prevented until the day was put off? Would that improve matters? And could he accomplish anything with Mr. Endicott if he had time? Wasn't he foolish to try? Mr. Endicott was already angry with him for another reason. His wife and Starr and that scoundrel Carter would tell all sorts of stories. Of course he would believe theirs over his! He groaned aloud sometimes, alone in his office, and wished he could fling himself between Starr and evil once for all—give his life for hers. Gladly he'd do it if it would do any good. Yet there was no way.

And then came news. The vessel had been heard from many miles out at sea, with a propeller broken and laboring along at great disadvantage. But if all went well she would reach her dock at noon the following day—eight hours before the wedding!

Starr heard, and her face blossomed into smiles. All would go well. She telephoned the steamship company later, and her fears were allayed by their assurances.

Mrs. Endicott heard the news with relief. Her husband would scarcely have time to find out anything. She must prevent his seeing Michael before the ceremony.

The young man heard, and his heart beat wildly. Would there be enough time to save Starr?

Noon the next day came, but the steamer hadn't landed, though the news from her was good. She would be in before night, for sure. Mr. Endicott would be in time for the wedding, but that and no more. He sent reassurances to his family, and they were going forward happily in the whirl of last things.

But Michael in his lonely office hung up the telephone receiver with a heavy heart. There would be no time to save Starr. Everything was against him. Even if he could get speech with Mr. Endicott, which was doubtful now, would the man listen at this the last minute? Of course his wife and daughter and her fiancé could easily persuade him all was well and Michael a jealous fool!

As he sat thus with bowed head before his desk, he heard footsteps along the stone floor of the corridor outside. They halted at his door, and hesitating fingers fumbled with the knob. He looked up frowning and was about to send any chance client away, explaining he was too occupied now to be interrupted, when the face of the woman opening the door caught his attention.

Chapter 22

*I*t was Lizzie, with her baby in her arms—the girl he had defended in the alley, whose face he'd seen lying white and unconscious in the moonlight, looking ghastly enough with the dark hair flung back against the harsh stone pillow.

The face was white now but softened with motherhood. The bold, handsome features had taken on a gentleness, though passion and unrest glowed and burned in her dark eyes.

She stood looking at Michael after she closed the door and held the baby close as if she feared someone might be there wanting to take it from her.

As Michael watched her, fascinated, cut to the heart by the suffering in her eyes, he was reminded of an exquisite Madonna he'd seen in an exhibit not long ago. The draperies had been dainty and cloudlike, and the face refined in its beauty, but the eyes had held the same sorrowful mother-anguish. It passed through his mind that this girl and he were kin because of a mutual torture. His face softened, and he felt a great pity for her.

His eyes wandered to the upturned face of the baby wrapped in the shabby shawl against its mother's breast. It was a beautiful sleeping face, with a look of the spirit world from which it had recently come, a little stranger soul.

Why had the baby come? To make one more of the swarming mass of sinful wretches crowding the alley? Would those cherub lips half-parted now in a seraphic smile live to pour forth blasphemous curses as he'd heard from even very small children in the alley? Would that tiny seashell hand, resting so trustingly against the coarse cloth of its mother's raiment, looking like a rosebud gone astray, live to break open safes and take their contents? Would the soft round body, whose tender curves showed pitifully beneath the thin old shawl, grow up to lie in the gutter someday? The problem of the people had never come to Michael so forcibly, so terribly as in that moment before Lizzie spoke.

"Be you a real lawyer?" she asked. "Kin you tell what the law is 'bout folks and thin's?"

Michael smiled and rose to give her a chair as courteously as if she'd been born a lady.

"Sit down," he said. "Yes, I'm a lawyer. What can I do for you?"

"I s'pose you charge a lot," said the girl, glancing around the room. "You've got thin's fixed fine as silk here. But I'll pay anythin' you ast ef it takes me a lifetime to do it, ef you'll jest tell me how I kin git my rights."

"Your rights?" questioned Michael sadly. Poor child! Had she any rights in the universe that he could help her get? The only rights he knew for such as she were room in a quiet graveyard and a chance to be forgotten.

"Say, ain't it against the law fer a man to marry a woman when he's already got one wife?"

"It is," said Michael, "unless he gets a divorce."

"Well, I ain't goin' to give him no divorce, you bet!" said the girl fiercely. "I worked hard enough to get a real marriage, an' I ain't goin' to give up no fash'nable swell. I'm's good's she is, an' I've got my rights, an I'll hev 'em. An' besides, there's baby!" Her face softened and took on a love-light, and immediately Michael was reminded of the Madonna picture again. "I've got to think o' him!"

Michael marveled to see the girl revelling in the little helpless burden who had added to her sorrow.

"Tell me about it." His voice was gentle. He recalled suddenly that this was Sam's girl. Poor Sam, too! The world was a terrible tangled mess of trouble.

"Well, there ain't much to tell that counts—only he kep' comp'ny with me, an' I wouldn't hev ennythin' else but a real marriage, an' so he giv' in, an' we had a couple o' rooms in a respectable house an' hed it fine till he had to go away on business, he said. I never b'leeved that. Why, he was downright rich. He's a real swell, you know. What kind o' business cud he have?" Lizzie straightened herself proudly and held her head high.

"About whom are you talking?" asked Michael.

"Why, my husband, 'course, Mr. Sty-ve-zant Carter. You ken see his name in the paper real often. He didn't want me to know his real name. He hed me call him Dan Hunt fer two months, but I caught on, an' he was real mad fer a while. He said his ma didn't like the match, an' he didn't want folks to know he'd got married; it might hurt him with some of his swell friends—"

"You don't mean to tell me Mr. Stuyvesant Carter married you!" said Michael incredulously.

"Sure!" said Lizzie proudly. "Married me jest like enny swell; got me a dimon ring an' a silk-lined suit an' a willer plume an' everythin'." She held up a grimy hand on which Michael saw a showy glitter of jewelry.

"Do you have anything to show for it?" asked Michael, expecting her to say no. "Do you have any certificate or paper to prove you were married according to law?"

"Sure!" said Lizzie triumphantly, drawing forth a crumpled roll from the folds of her dress and smoothing it out before his astonished eyes.

There it was, a printed wedding certificate, in blue and gold with a colored picture of two clasped hands under a white dove with a gold ring in its beak. Beneath was an idealized boat with silken sails bearing two people down a rose-lined river of life; and the whole was bordered with orange blossoms. It was one of those old-fashioned affairs country ministers gave their parishioners in years gone by and can still be found in some dusty corners of a forgotten drawer in country bookstores. But Michael recognized at once that it was a real certificate. He read it carefully. The blanks were filled in, the marriage date she gave was there, and the bridegroom's name, though evidently written in a disguised hand, could be deciphered as "Sty. Carter." Michael didn't recognize the names of the witnesses or the officiating minister.

"How do you happen to have Mr. Carter's real name here when you say he married you under an assumed name?" he asked, moving his finger over the blurred name that had evidently been scratched out and written over again.

"I made him put it in after I found out who he was," said Lizzie. "He couldn't come it over me thet-a-way. He was awful gone on me then, an' I cud do most ennythin' with him. It was 'fore she cum home from Europe! She jes' went fer him an' turned his head. Ef I'd a knowed in time I'd gone an' tole her, but land sakes! I don't s'pose 'twould a done much good. I would a-ben to her before—only I was fool 'nough to promise him I wouldn't say nothin' to her ef he'd keep away from her. You see I needed money awful bad fer baby. He don't take to livin' awful good. He cries a lot, an' I hed to hev thin's fer 'im, so I threatened him ef he didn't do sompin' I'd tell her, an' he up an' forked over, but not till I promised. But now they say the papers is tellin' he's to marry her tonight, an' I gotta stop it somehow. I got my rights an' baby's to look after, promise er no promise. Kin I get him arrested?"

"I'm not sure what you can do until I look into the matter," Michael said gravely. Would the paper he held help or not, in his mission to Starr's father? And would it be too late? His heavy heart couldn't answer.

"Do you know these witnesses?"

"Sure," said Lizzie. "They're all swells. They come down with him when he come to be married. I never seen 'em again, but they was real jolly an' nice. They gave me a bokay of real roses an' a bracelet made like a snake with green glass eyes."

"And the minister? Which is his church?"

"I'm sure I donno," said Lizzie. "I never ast. He come along an' was ez jolly ez enny of 'em. He drank more'n all of 'em put together. He was awful game fer a preacher."

Michael's heart sank. Was this a genuine marriage? Could anything be proved? He questioned the girl carefully and then sent her on her way, promising to do all in his power to help her and arranging to let her know as soon as possible if she could do anything.

That was a busy afternoon for Michael. The steamer's arrival was forgotten. His telephone rang vainly on the desk to a silent room. He was out tramping over the city searching for the witnesses and minister who had signed Lizzie's marriage certificate.

Meanwhile the afternoon papers came out with a glowing account of the wedding that was to be, headed by pictures of Starr and Mr. Carter, for the wedding was a great event in society circles.

On her way back to the alley, confident Michael, the angel of the alley, would do something for her, Lizzie heard the boys crying the afternoon edition of the paper and was seized with a desire to see if her husband's picture would be in again. She could ill spare the penny she spent for it, but what was money in a case like this? Michael would do something for her, and she would have more money. Besides, if worse came to worst she would go to the fine lady and threaten to make it all public, and she would give her money.

Lizzie had had more advantages than most of her class in the alley. She'd worked in a seashore restaurant several summers and could read a little. From the newspaper account she gathered enough to rouse her half-soothed frenzy. Her eyes flashed fire as she went about her dark tenement room making the baby comfortable. His feeble wail and sweet eyes looking into hers only fanned the fury of her flame. She determined not to wait for Michael but to go on her own at once to that girl who was stealing her husband, her baby's father, and tell her what she was doing.

With the cunning of her kind, Lizzie dressed herself in her best: a soiled pink silk shirtwaist with elbow sleeves, a spotted and torn black skirt that showed a tattered orange silk petticoat beneath its ungainly length, a wide white hat, with soiled and draggled willow plume of Alice blue, and high-heeled pumps run over on their uppers. If she'd only known she looked ten times better in the old shawl she wore to Michael's office—but she took great satisfaction in being able to dress appropriately when she went to the swells.

The poor baby she wrapped in his soiled best and pinned a large untidy pink satin bow on the back of his dirty blanket. Then she started on her mission.

Now Starr had just heard her father's vessel would dock in a little over an hour, and her heart was light and happy. All her misgivings seemed to flee away, now that he was coming. She flew from one room to another like a wild bird, trilling snatches of a song and looking prettier than ever.

"Aw, the wee sweet bairnie!" murmured the old Scottish nurse. "If only her man will be gude to her."

Some special bit of Starr's attire for the evening hadn't arrived. She was in a twitter of expectancy about it, to be sure it pleased her. When she heard the bell she rushed to the head of the stairs and halfway down to see if it had come, and the servant opened the door to Lizzie and her baby.

One second more and the door would have closed hopelessly on poor Lizzie, for no servant in that house would have admitted such a creature to their lady's presence a few hours before her wedding. But Starr, poised halfway on the landing, called, "What is it, Graves—someone to see me?"

"But she's not the sort of person—Miss Starr!" protested Graves with the door only open a crack now.

"Never mind, Graves—I'll see her for a minute. I can't deny

anyone on my wedding day, you know, and Father almost safely here. Show her into the little reception room." She smiled a ravishing smile on the devoted Graves.

So with many qualms of conscience and misgivings as to what the mistress would say if she found out, Graves ushered Lizzie and her baby to the room indicated, and Starr fluttered down to see her. So it was Starr's own doing that Lizzie came into her presence on that eventful afternoon.

"Oh, what a sweet baby!" exclaimed Starr. "Is he yours?" Lizzie's fierce eyes softened.

"Sit down and tell me who you are. Wait—I'll have some tea brought for you. You look tired. Won't you let me give that sweet baby a little white shawl of mine? I'm to be married tonight, and I'd like to give him a wedding present," she said merrily, and Morton was sent for the shawl and another servant for the tea, while Starr amused herself by making the baby crow at her.

Lizzie sat in wonder. She almost forgot her errand, watching this sweet girl in her lovely attire making much of her baby.

But when the tea had been brought and the soft white wool shawl wrapped around the smiling baby, Starr said again, "Now please tell me who you are and what you've come for. I can give you only a minute or two more. This is a busy day, you know."

Lizzie's brow darkened.

"I'm Mrs. Carter!" she said, drawing herself up with conscious pride.

"Carter?" said Starr politely.

"Yes, I'm the wife of the man you're goin' to marry tonight, an' this is his child. I thought I'd come an' tell you 'fore 'twas too late. I thought ef you had enny goodness in you, you'd put a stop to this an' give me my rights, an' you seem to hev some heart. Can't you call it off? You wouldn't want to take my husband away from me, would you? You can get plenty others, an' I'm jest a plain workin' girl, an' he's mine anyhow, an' this is his kid."

Starr had started to her feet, her eyes wide, her hand fluttering to her heart.

"Stop!" she cried. "You must be crazy to say such things. My poor girl, you've made a great mistake. Your husband is some other Mr. Carter. My Mr. Carter is not that kind of man. He's never been married—"

"Yes, he has!" interposed Lizzie fiercely. "He's married all right, an' I got the c'tif'ct all right, too—only I couldn't bring it this time cause I lef' it with my lawyer. But you can see it ef you want to, with his name all straight. Sty-ve-zant Carter, all writ out. I see to it he writ it himself. I kin read meself pretty good, so I knowed."

"I'm very sorry for you," said Starr sweetly, though her heart was beating violently in spite of trying to be calm and get rid of this wretched imposter without making a scene before the servants. "I'm very sorry, but you've made a great mistake. I can't do anything for you now. But later when I return to New York, if you look me up, I'll try to do something for the baby."

Lizzie stood erect in the middle of the room, her face slowly changing to a stony stare, her eyes fairly blazing with anger.

"De yer mean ter tell me yer a-goin' t' marry my husban' ez ef nothin' happened? Ain't yer ter ast him ef it's true ner nothin'? Ain't yer goin' t' find out what's true 'bout him? 'R d' ye want 'im so bad ye don't care who yer hurt or wot he is, so long's he makes a big splurge before folks? Ain't you a-goin' ter ast him 'bout it?"

"Oh, why, certainly," said Starr. "I'll ask him, but I know you're mistaken. Now really I have to say good afternoon. I haven't another minute to spare. You must go!"

"I won't stir a step till you promise you'll ast him straight away. Ain't you got no telyphone? Well, you kin call him up an' ast him why he didn't never speak to you of his wife Lizzie and where he was the evenin' of Augus' four. That's the date of the c'tif'ct! Tell him you seen me, an' then see wot he says. Tell him my lawyer is a-goin' to fix him ef he goes on.

It'll be in all the papers tomorrer mornin' ef he goes on. An' you kin say I won't never consent to no divorce; they ain't respectable, an' I got to think o' that on baby's account."

"If you'll go quietly away now and say nothing about this to anyone, I'll tell Mr. Carter all about you," said Starr, her voice trembling with an effort at self-control.

"D' ye promus you will?"

"Certainly," said Starr with dignity.

"Will ye do it straight off?"

"Yes, if you'll go at once."

"Cross yer heart?"

"What?"

"Cross yer heart ye will? Thet's a sort o' oath t' make yer keep yer promus," explained Lizzie.

"A lady needs no such thing to make her keep her promise. Don't you know ladies always keep their promises?"

"I wasn't so sure!" said Lizzie. "You can't most allus tell—'t's bes' to be on the safe side. Will yer promus me yer won't marry him ef ye find out he's my husband?"

"Most certainly I won't marry him if he's already married. Now go, please, at once. I haven't a minute to spare. If you don't go at once, I can't have time to call him up."

"You sure I kin trust you?"

Starr turned on the girl such a gaze of mingled dignity and indignation that her eye quailed before it.

"Well, I s'pose I gotta," she said, dropping her eyes before Starr's righteous wrath. "But no weddin' bells fer yer tonight ef yer keep yer promus. So long!"

Starr shuddered as the girl passed her. The whiff of un-washed garments, stale cooking, and undefinable tenement odor sickened her. Must she let this creature have a hold even momentarily upon her last few hours? Yet she knew she must; she wouldn't rest until she'd been reassured by Carter's voice and the explanation he would surely give her. She rushed upstairs to her private phone, locking the door on even her old nurse, and called up the phone in Carter's private apartments.

Without admitting it to herself, she had been troubled all afternoon because she hadn't heard from Carter. Her flowers had come—magnificent in their costliness and arrangement—and everything he was to attend to was done. But no word had come from him. It was unlike him.

She knew he'd given a dinner the evening before to his old friends who were to be his ushers and that the festivities would have lasted late. He probably hadn't arisen very early, but it was drawing toward the wedding hour now. She intended to begin dressing at once after phoning him. It was strange she hadn't heard from him.

After much delay an unknown voice answered the phone and told her Mr. Carter couldn't come now. She asked who it was but got no response, except that Mr. Carter couldn't come now. The voice had a muffled, thick sound. "Tell him to call me then as soon as possible," she said, and the voice answered, "Awright!"

Reluctantly she hung up the receiver and called Morton to help her dress. She preferred to get the matter out of the way before she went about the pretty ceremony and with an ill grace and troubled thoughts submitted herself to her nurse's hands. The coarse beauty of Lizzie's face haunted her. It reminded her of an actress Carter had once openly admired. She found herself shuddering inwardly every time she recalled Lizzie's harsh voice and uncouth sentences.

She paid little heed to dressing and let Morton do as she would, starting nervously when the phone bell rang or anyone tapped at her door.

A message came from her father finally. He hoped to be with her in less than an hour, and no word had come from Carter! Why didn't he know she would be anxious? What could have kept him from his usual greeting to her—and on their wedding day!

Suddenly, in the midst of Morton's draping of the wedding

veil she was trying in various ways to see how to put on at the last minute, Starr started up from her chair.

"I cannot stand this, Mortie. That will do for now. I must telephone Mr. Carter. I can't understand why he doesn't call me."

"Oh, but the poor man is that busy!" murmured Morton as she hurried obediently out of the room. "Now mind you don't muss that beautiful veil."

But after a half hour of attempting to reach Carter, Starr suddenly appeared in her door, calling for her faithful nurse again.

"Mortie!" she called excitedly. "Come here quick! I've ordered the electric. It's at the door now. Put on your big cloak and come with me! I've got to see Mr. Carter at once, and I can't get him on the phone."

"But, Miss Starr!" protested Morton. "You've no time to go anywhere now, and look at your pretty veil!"

"Never mind the veil, Mortie. I'm going. Hurry. I can't stop to explain. I'll tell you on the way. We'll be back before anyone misses us."

"But your mama, Miss Starr! She'll be very angry with me!"

"Mama mustn't know. And anyway I must go. Come—if you won't come with me I'm going alone."

With these words Starr grasped a great cloak of dark green velvet, threw it over her white bridal robes, and hurried down the stairs.

"Oh, Miss Starr, darlin'," moaned Morton, looking hurriedly around for a cloak. "You'll spoil yer veil sure! Wait till I take it off'n ye."

But Starr had opened the front door and was already getting into the luxurious car that stood outside.

Chapter 23

*M*ichael, as he searched, kept crying in his heart, *Oh, God! Do something to save her! Do something to save my little Starr!*

The prayer prayed itself without apparent thought or volition on his part, as he went from place to place, searching out what he needed to know. At last toward six o'clock, his chain of evidence led him to the door of Stuyvesant Carter's apartments.

After some delay the door was opened a little by a servant who stared at him blankly but finally admitted that the three men whose names he mentioned were inside. He also said Mr. Carter was in but couldn't be seen.

He closed the door on the visitor and went inside to see if any of the others would come out. An altercation ensued in loud, unsteady tones. At last the door opened again, and a fast-looking young man who admitted himself to be Theodore Brooks slid out and closed it carefully behind him. The air that came with him was thick with tobacco smoke and heavy with liquor, and Michael's one glimpse into the room showed a strange radiance of some peculiar light that glowed into the dusky hall.

The heavy-eyed youth braced against the wall looked into Michael's face with an impudent laugh.

"Well, parson, what's the grouch? Are you the devil or an angel sent to bring retribution?"

He ended with a silly laugh that told the young lawyer's experienced ear that the young man had been drinking heavily. And this was the man whose name was signed as Rev.

Theodore Brooks, D.D., on the tawdry marriage certificate Michael held in his hand. His heart sank at the futility of the task.

"Are you a minister?" asked Michael.

"Am I a minister?" drawled young Brooks. "M—mi—m—m—m'nster! Well, now, that gets my goat! Say, boys, he wants t' know 'f I'm a m—min'ster! Min-ster of what? Min-ster plen—p'ten'sherry?"

"Did you ever perform a marriage?" asked Michael sharply to stop the loud guffaw reechoing through the apartment's polished corridors.

"P'form a m'riage, d' ye say? No, but I'm goin' t' perform 't a marriage tonight 'f the dead wakes up in time. Goin' t' be bes' man. Say, boys! Got 'im 'wake yet? Gettin' late!"

Michael in despair took hold of the other's arm and tried to explain what he wanted to know. Finally he succeeded in bringing the matter into the fellow's comprehension.

"Wedding, oh, yes, I 'member, peach of a girl! Stuyvy awfully fond of her. No harm meant. Good joke! Yes, I borr'wed Grand'f'ther Brooks's old gown 'n' ban's. Awf'lly good disguise! No harm meant—on'y good joke—girl awf'lly set on getting married. Stuyvy wanted t' please 'er—awfully good joke!"

"A ghastly joke, I should say, sir!" said Michael sternly.

And then the door was flung open by hands from inside, loud angry voices protesting while another hand sought unavailingly to close the door again. But Michael came and planted himself in the open door and stood like an avenging angel calling to judgment. The scene revealed to him was too horrifying for words.

A long banquet table stood in the midst of the handsomely furnished room. Amid the scattered remains of the feast—napkins under the table, upset glasses still dripping their ruby contents down the damask tablecloth, broken china, scattered plates and silver—stood a handsome silver coffin, within which, pallid and deathlike, lay the handsome form of the evening's bridegroom. Around the casket in sconces burned tall tapers, casting their spectral light over the scene.

Distributed about the room—lounging in chairs, fast asleep on the couches, lying under the table, fighting by the doorway, one standing on a velvet chair raising an unsteady glass of wine and attempting a drinking song—were ten young men, the flowers of society, the expected ushers of the evening's wedding.

Michael, with his pale face, his golden hair aflame in the flickering candlelight, his eyes full of shocked indignation, stood for a moment surveying the scene and all at once knew his prayer was answered. There would be no wedding that night.

"Is this another of your ghastly jokes?" He turned to Brooks who stood by as master of ceremonies, undisturbed by the stranger's presence.

"That's just what it is," stuttered Brooks, "a j–j–joke, a p–p–p–pract'cal joke. No harm meant, only Stuyvy's hard to wake up. Never did like gettin' up in the mornin'. Wake 'im up, boys! Wake 'im up! Time to get dressed for the wedding!"

"Has anyone sent word to Miss Endicott?"

"Sent word to Mish Endicott? No, I'd 'no's they have. Think she'd care to come? Say, boys, that's a good joke. This old fellow—don't know who he is—devil 'n' all his angels p'raps—he s'gests we send word to Mish Endicott t' come t' th' fun'ral."

"I said nothing of the kind," said Michael fiercely. "Have you no sense of decency? Go and wash your face and try to realize what you've been doing. Have someone telephone for a doctor. I'll go and tell the family." Michael strode out of the room to perform the hardest task ever.

He didn't wait for the elevator but ran down the stairs, trying to steady his thoughts and realize the horror through which he'd just passed.

As he started down the last flight, he heard the elevator

door *clang* below. As it shot past him he glimpsed white garments and a face with eyes he knew. He stopped short and looked upward. Was it—could it be? No, of course not. He was foolish. He turned and compelled his feet to hurry down the rest of the stairs. But at the door his worst fears were confirmed, for there stood the electric car, and the Endicott chauffeur's familiar face assured him someone of the family had just gone to the ghastly spectacle upstairs.

In sudden panic he turned and fled up the stairs. He couldn't wait for elevators now. He wished for a protecting angel's wings, that he might reach her before she saw that horrible sight.

Yet even as he started he knew he must be too late.

Starr stopped startled in the open doorway, with Morton, protesting, apprehensive, behind her. The soft cloak slid down the satin of her gown and left her revealed in all her wedding whiteness, her eyes like stars, her beautiful face flushed. Then the eyes rested on the coffin and its deathlike occupant, and her face went white as her dress, while horror grew in her eyes.

Brooks, more nearly sober than the rest, saw her first and hastened to do the honors.

"Say, boys, she's come!" he shouted. "Bride's come. Git up, Bobby Trascom. Don't yer know ye mustn't lie down when there's a lady present—Van—get out from under that table. Help me pick up these things. Place's a mess. Glad to see you, Mish Endicott." He bowed low and staggered as he recovered himself.

Starr turned toward him. "Mr. Brooks," she said in a tone that sobered him somewhat, "what does it mean? Is he dead?"

"Not at all, not at all, Mish Endicott," he tried to say gravely. "Have him all right in plenty time. Just a little joke, Mish Endicott. He's merely shlightly intoxicated."

But Starr heard no more. With a stifled cry and a groping motion of her white-clad arms, she crumpled into a white heap at her horrified nurse's feet. As she fell Michael appeared at the door, like the rescuing angel he was, and with one withering glance at the huddled group of men, he gathered her in his arms and sped down the stairs, faithful Morton puffing after him. Neither of them noticed a man who got out of the elevator just before Starr fell and, walking rapidly toward the open door, saw the whole action. In a moment more Mr. Endicott stood in the door surveying the scene before him with stern, wrathful countenance.

Like a dash of cold water, his appearance brought several participants in the disgraceful scene to their senses. A few questions and he had the whole shameful story: the stag dinner growing into a midnight orgy; the foolish dare and its reckless acceptance by the already intoxicated bridegroom; the drugged drinks; and the practical joke carried out by brains long under the influence of liquor. Carter's men who had protested had been bound and gagged in the back room. The jokers had found no trouble in securing the necessary tools to carry out their joke. Money will buy anything, even an undertaker for a living man. The promise of secrecy and the generous fees brought all they needed. Then when the ghastly work was completed and the unconscious bridegroom lying in state in his coffin amid the debris of the table, they drowned the horror of their deed in deeper drinking.

Mr. Endicott turned from the scene, his soul filled with loathing and horror.

He'd reached home to find the house in a tumult and Starr gone. Morton, going out the door after her young mistress, had whispered to the butler their destination and that they would return at once. She suspected it would be best for someone to know.

Mr. Endicott ordered the runabout and hastened after them, arriving a moment or two later. Michael had just vanished up the apartment stairs as he entered the lower hallway. The vague indefinite trouble that had filled his mind concerning his daughter's marriage to a man he little knew, except by reputation, crystallized into trouble, clear and distinct, as he hurried after his daughter. Something terrible must have come to Starr, or she would never have hurried away almost alone at such a time.

The electric car was gone by the time Mr. Endicott reached the lower hall again, and he was forced to go back alone as he came, without further explanation than what he could see. But he had time in the rapid trip to become profoundly thankful the disgraceful scene he'd left had occurred before and not after his daughter's marriage. Whatever circumstances might excuse the reckless victim of his comrades' joke, the fact remained that a man who could fall victim to such a joke was not the companion for his daughter's life—she who had been guarded at every possible point and loved as the apple of his eye. He dared not think yet about the perpetrators of this gruesome sport. No punishment seemed too great for such. And she, his little Starr, had looked upon that shameful scene and seen the man she expected to marry lying as one dead! It was too awful! And what had it done to her? Had it killed her? Had the shock unsettled her mind? The journey to his home seemed longer than his whole ocean voyage. Oh, why hadn't he let business go to the winds and come back long ago to shield his little girl!

Meanwhile, Michael, his precious burden in his arms, had stepped into the waiting car, motioning Morton to follow and sit in the opposite seat. The delicate Paris frock trailed unnoticed underfoot, and the veil's rare lace fell back from the white face. But neither Michael nor the nurse thought of satin and lace now, as they bent anxiously over the girl to see if she still breathed.

All the way to her home Michael held the lovely bride in his arms, feeling her weight no more than a feather, thankful he might bear her away from the danger that had threatened her life. He wished he might carry her to the ends of the earth and never stop until he had her safe from all harm. His heart thrilled wildly with the touch of her sweetness, even while he bent over her to watch for returning consciousness.

But she didn't become conscious before she reached the house. His strong arms held her as gently as though she'd been a baby as he stepped carefully out and carried her to her own room, laying her upon the white bed, where two hours before the delicate wedding garments had been spread for her to put on. Then he stood back, looked reverently on her dear face, and turned away. In the hall he met her mother, and her face was fairly disfigured with sudden recognition of him.

"What! Is it you have dared come into this house? The impertinence! I'll report your doings to my husband. He'll be very angry. You're at the bottom of this whole business! You'll be dealt with as you deserve!"

She hissed the words after him as Michael descended the stairs with bowed head and closed lips. It didn't matter now what she said or thought of him. Starr was saved!

He was about to go into the world again, away from her, from even knowing how she came out of her swoon. He had no further right there. His duty was done. He'd been allowed to save her when she needed him!

But as he reached the door, it opened, and Mr. Endicott hurried in.

He paused for an instant.

"Son! It was you who brought her home!" he said, as if that conviction had just been revealed to his perturbed mind. "Son, I'm obliged. Sit here till I come. I want to speak with you."

The doctor came with a nurse, and Michael sat and listened to the distant voices in her room. He gathered from the sounds that Starr was conscious, was better.

Until then no one had thought of the wedding or the guests

who would be gathering. Something must be done. So, as the organ sounded forth the wedding march—for by some blunder the bride's signal was given to the organist when the Endicott car drew up at the church—Michael, bareheaded, hat in hand, walked gravely up the aisle. Unconscious of the eyes and the astonished whispers of "Who is he? Isn't he magnificent? What does it mean? I thought the ushers were to come first?" he stood calmly in the chancel and faced the wondering audience.

If an angel had come from heaven and interfered with their wedding they couldn't have been more astonished. As he stood beneath the soft lights in front of the wall of living green and blossoms, with his pale face and dignity, they forgot to study the fashion of his coat and sat awed before his beautiful face. For tonight Michael wore the look of transport with chin uplifted, glowing eyes, and countenance that showed the spirit shining through.

The organist looked down and instinctively hushed his music. Had he made some mistake? Then Michael spoke. Doubtless he should have gone to the minister who was to perform the ceremony and given him the message, but Michael little knew the ways of weddings. It was the first he'd ever attended, and he went straight to the point.

"Because of the sudden, serious illness of the groom," he said, "it will be impossible for the ceremony to go on at this time. The bride's family asks that you'll kindly excuse them from further intrusion or explanation this evening."

Inclining his head slightly to the breathless audience, Michael passed down the aisle and out, and the organist, by tremendous self-control, kept on playing softly until the excited people who had drifted usherless into the church got themselves out into their carriages.

Michael walked out into the night, bareheaded still, his eyes lifted to the stars shining far above the city, and said softly, reverently, "Oh, God! Oh, God!"

Chapter 24

Following hard upon the interrupted wedding came other events. These helped hush matters and gave the world a plausible reason why the ceremony didn't come off as soon as the groom was convalescent from what was easily attributed to the many banquets and entertainments preceding a society wedding.

During that eventful night, while Starr lay like a crushed lily torn from its stem, her mother, after a stormy scene with her husband, in which he made it plain what kind of man she wanted her daughter to marry, and during which she saw the fall of her greatest social ambitions, was suddenly felled by a stroke.

The papers next morning told the news as sympathetically as a paper can tell one's innermost secrets. It praised the ability of the woman who had so successfully arranged for what had promised to be the greatest wedding of the season, if not of all seasons, and upon whose overtaxed strength the last straw had been laid in the bridegroom's illness. It stated that of course the wedding would be delayed indefinitely, as nothing could be thought of while the bride's mother lay in such a crucial state.

For a week daily bulletins of her condition were published in more and more remote corners of the paper, until the ripple made in the stream of life passed, and no further mention was made except when they sent for some famous specialist, took her to the shore to try the sea air, and brought her home again.

But all the time the woman lay locked in rigid silence. Only her cold eyes followed whoever entered her room. She gave no sign of knowing what they said or caring who came near.

Her husband's earnest pleas, Starr's tears, drew from her no expression that could even be imagined from a fluttering eyelash. Nothing but that stony stare, that almost unseeing gaze, followed wherever one moved. It was a living death.

And when one day the release came and the eyes were closed forever from this world, it was a sad relief to both husband and daughter. Starr and her father stole away to an old New England farmhouse where Mr. Endicott's elderly maiden sister still lived in the old family homestead. She was a soft-spoken woman with plain gray dresses and soft white laces at wrists and neck and ruched about her sweet old face above her silver hair.

Starr hadn't been there since she was a child, and her sad heart found her aunt's home restful. She stayed there through the fall and until after the first of the year, while her father came and went as business dictated, and the Endicott home on Madison Avenue remained closed except for the caretakers.

Meanwhile Carter had discreetly escorted his mother to Europe and was supposed by the papers to be returning almost immediately. Not a breath of gossip, strange to say, stole forth. Everything seemed arranged to quiet any suspicion that might arise.

Early in the fall he returned to town, but Starr was still in New England. No one knew of the estrangement between them. Their immediate friends were away from town still, and everything seemed natural in the order of decency. Of course people couldn't be married at once after a death in the family.

No one but the two families knew of Carter's repeated attempts to reconcile with Starr; of his feeble endeavor to explain; of her continued refusal to see him and the decided letter she wrote him after he had written her the most abject apology he knew how to frame. Nor did anyone else know of her father's interview with the young man, wherein he was told some facts about himself more plainly than anyone even in his boyhood ever dared tell him. Mr. Endicott agreed to keep silence for Starr's sake, provided the young man created no gossip about the matter, until the intended wedding was forgotten and other events had taken the minds of society from their particular case.

Carter, for his sake, didn't care to let the story get abroad and sullenly acceded to the command. He didn't, however, think it necessary to make himself entirely miserable while abroad, and some more than once spoke his name in company with that of a young and dashing divorcée. Some even thought he returned to America sooner than he intended in order to travel on the same steamer she was taking. But those whispers hadn't yet crossed the water, and even if they had, such things were too common to cause much comment.

Then, one Monday morning, the papers were filled with horror over a terrible automobile accident, in which a party of seven, of whom the young divorcée was one and Stuyvesant Carter was another, went over an embankment sixty feet in height, the car landing upside down on the rocks below and killing every member of the party. The paper also stated that Mr. Theodore Brooks, intimate friend of Carter's, who was to have been best man at the wedding some months previous, postponed because of the sudden illness and death of the bride's mother, was in the party.

Thus ended the career of Stuyvesant Carter, and thus the world never knew exactly why Starr Endicott did not become Mrs. Carter.

From the moment he left after delivering his message in the church, Michael saw no more of the Endicotts. He longed to call and inquire for Starr; to get some reconciling word from her father; to ask if there wasn't some little thing he might be trusted to do for them. But he knew his place wasn't there, and his company wasn't desired. Neither would he write, for even a note from him could seem to Starr a reminder of the terrible things she'd witnessed, that is, if anybody told her he had brought her home.

One solace alone he allowed himself. Nightly as he went home late he would walk far out of his way to pass the house and look up at her window; and always it comforted him to see the dim radiance of her soft night-light. Behind those windows she lay asleep, the dear girl he was permitted to carry to her home and safety, when she had almost reached the brink of destruction.

About a week after the fateful wedding day, Michael received a brief note from Starr.

> My dear Mr. Endicott:
> I wish to thank you for your trouble in bringing me home last week. I cannot understand how you were there at that time. Also, I'm deeply grateful for your kindness in making the announcement at the church.
>
> Very sincerely,
> S. D. E.

Michael felt the covert question in that phrase: "I cannot understand how you were there at that time." She thought, perhaps, that to carry his point and stop the marriage he had had a hand in that miserable business! Well, let her think it. It wasn't his place to explain and could matter little to her what she believed about him. As well to let it rest. He belonged out of her world and would never try to force his way into it.

And so with the pale face lingering from the hard days of tension, Michael went on, straining every nerve in his work. He kept the alley room open nightly even during hot weather and stayed in constant touch with the farm, which was now fairly on its feet and almost earning its own living. Contributions still kept coming to him quietly here and there, though, and helped in the many new plans growing out of the many new necessities.

The carpenter had built and built, until bungalows of one or two and three rooms dotted about the farm for rent at a low price to the workers. It had become a community by itself, spoken of as "Old Orchard Farms" and well respected in the neighborhood. In truth the motley company Michael and Sam gathered there had done far better in the way of law and orderliness than either had hoped. They seemed to take pride in letting nothing that could hurt "the boss's" reputation as a landowner be charged to them. If by chance any sordid being came into their midst who couldn't see matters in that light, the rest promptly taught him better or put him out.

And now the whole front yard was aflame with brilliant flowers in their season. The orchard had been pruned and trimmed and grafted, and in spring showed forth in pink and white splendor. At all seasons the grassy drive wound its way up to the old house, through a vista of green or brown branches.

Michael had thought for some time of rebuilding the old house—for what he didn't know. He didn't hope to use it except as a transitory dwelling; yet he wanted to have it as he dreamed it out. It might be needed someday, and now was the time to get it ready. So one day he took an architect down to stay overnight and get an idea of the surroundings, and a few weeks later he had a plan for how the old house could be made into a beautiful new house and yet keep the original outlines. The carpenter, pleased with doing something really fine, undertook the work and was moving it forward rapidly.

The main walls were to be built around with old stone bought from the ruins of a desolated barn. Some of the stone was rusty, golden, and green in lovely mellow tones; some was gray with age and mossy in places; and now and then a dead black stone strengthened the whole coloring. There would be wide, low windows everywhere, letting the sunlight in, with some nestled in the sloping roof to be stained green like the moss that would grow on them someday. A piazza would extend across the entire front with rough stone pillars and a stone-paved floor up to which the orchard grass would grow in a gentle terrace.

Sam and his helpers were already starting rose vines to train about the trellises and pillars. Sam had elected to call it Rose Cottage. Who would ever have suspected Sam of having poetry in his nature?

The great stone fireplace with its ancient crane and place to sit inside was to be retained and built about with more stone. The partitions between the original sitting room and hall were to be torn down, making one living room with the fireplace as center, a window at one side looking toward the sea, and a deep seat with bookcases in the corner. Heavy beams would be put in the ceiling to support it, and fine wood used in the wainscoting and paneling, with rough soft-toned plaster between and above. The floors would be smooth, well-fitted hardwood boards.

A gable would be added on the morning side of the house for a dining room, all windows, with an ocean view on one side and the river on the other. Upstairs would be four bedrooms and a bathroom, with white wainscoting halfway up and delicately vined or tinted papers above.

Michael enjoyed going down to look at the house and watch the progress, as the whole community did. They called it "the boss's cottage," and after work at night men, women, and children stopped by to see what had been done during the day. In it they saw their highest dreams coming true for the man they loved because he'd helped them to a future of possibilities. Each one wondered if he would ever get to the place where he could build himself a house like that and resolved secretly to try for it; always the work went better the next day after the visit.

But, after all, Michael would turn from his house with an empty ache in his heart. What was it for? Not for him. It wasn't likely he would ever spend happy hours there. He wasn't like other men. He must take his happiness in making others happy.

But one day, as he watched the laborers, he suddenly

wanted Starr to see it, to know what she would think of it and if she'd like it. Sometime, in the changing of the world, she might chance that way, and he would have an opportunity to show her the house he built—for her! Not that he'd ever tell her the last. She must never know she was the only one in the world he could ever care for. That would seem a great presumption in her eyes. But there would be no harm in showing her the house, and he would make it now as beautiful as if she were to occupy it, with the hope that she might one day see and approve it.

As the work neared its completion, he watched more carefully, matching tints in rooms and always bringing some new idea or finding some bit of furniture that would fit into a certain niche. In that way he cheated the lonely ache in his heart and made believe he was happy.

And another winter drew its white mantle about its shoulders and prepared to face the blast.

It was a bitter winter for the poor, for everything was high, and unskilled labor was poorly paid. Sickness and death lurked in the milk supply, the food supply, the unsanitary tenements about the alley, which, because it hadn't been so bad as some other districts, had been left uncondemned. Yet it was bad enough, and Michael's hands were full keeping his people alive and trying to keep some of them from sinning. For always where misery exists, so does more sinning.

Old Sal sat shivering on her doorstep with her tattered shawl about her shoulders or peered from her muslin-curtained window to see the dirty white hearse, with its pink-winged angel atop, pass slowly in and out with some little fragment of humanity. She knew her turn would come one day to leave it all and go. Then she turned back to her little room which had become the only heaven she knew and solaced herself with the contents of a black bottle!

Chapter 25

During the years of his labor in the alley Michael had become better known among workers for the poor, and he found strength in their brotherhood, though he kept mainly to his own corner and had little time to visit other fields. But he'd formed pleasant distant friendships and met prominent men interested in reforms of all sorts.

He was hurrying back to his boarding place one evening late in January, thinking again of how to reach the masses and help them live in decency so they might stand some chance of being good as well as being alive.

At the crossing of another avenue he met a man whose eloquence as a public speaker was only equaled by his tireless work among men.

"Good evening, Endicott," he said cordially, halting. "I wonder if you're not the very man I want. Will you do me a favor? I'm in great straits and no time to hunt up anybody."

"Anything I can do, sir. I'm at your service," said Michael.

"Good! Thank you! Are you free this evening for an hour?"

"I can be," said Michael, smiling. The other man's hearty greeting and warm "thank you" cheered his lonely heart.

"Well, then, you'll take my place at Madison Square Garden tonight, won't you? I've just had a telegram that my mother's very ill, perhaps dying, and I must go at once. I'm on my way to the station now. I thought Patton would be at his rooms and help me out, but they tell me he's out of town on a lecture tour."

"Take your place?" said Michael, aghast. "That I could

never do, sir! What were you going to do?"

"Why, there's a mass meeting at Madison Square Garden. We're trying to get more playgrounds and roof gardens for poor children, you know. I was to speak about the tenement district and give people a general idea of the need. I'm sure you're well acquainted with the subject. They're expecting some men who can give generously if they're touched the right way. You're very good to help me out. You'll excuse me if I hurry on. It's almost train time. I want to catch the six o'clock express west."

"But, sir, I couldn't do that. I'm not a public speaker—I never addressed a large audience in my life! Isn't there someone else I could get for you?"

While he was speaking, a vision of the church filled with the fashionable world, waiting for a wedding that didn't materialize, came strangely to his thoughts.

"Oh, that doesn't make the slightest difference in the world! You know the subject from A to Z, and I don't know another available soul tonight who does. Just tell them what you know. You needn't talk long; it'll be all right anyway. Just smile your smile, and they'll give all right. Good night, and thank you from my heart! I must take this cab." He hailed a passing cab and sprang inside, calling out above the city's noise, "It's at eight o'clock. Don't worry! You'll come out all right. It'll be good practice for your business."

Michael stood still in the middle of the crowded pavement and looked after the departing cab in dismay. He felt utterly inadequate to fill the situation and tried to think of someone else. There seemed no one used to speaking who knew the subject. The few who knew were either out of town or at some distance. He didn't know how to reach them in time. Besides, Michael wouldn't shirk a situation no matter how trying it was to him. It was one of the first principles he was taught in football, and before he reached his boarding place, his chin was up, his lips set.

Will French coaxed it out of him after dinner and laughed and slapped him on the shoulder. Will was engaged to Hester now and was outrageously happy.

"Good work, old fellow! You've got your chance. Now give it to 'em! I don't know anybody who can do it better. I'd like to bring a millionaire or two to hear you. You've been there—now tell 'em! Don't frown like that, old fellow. You've got the chance of your life. Why don't you tell 'em about the tenement in the alley?"

Michael's face cleared. "I hadn't thought of it, Will. Do you think I could? It isn't exactly on the subject. I understood from him I was to speak of the tenement in relation to the playground."

"The very thing," said Will. "Didn't he tell you to say what you knew? Well, give it to 'em straight, and you'll see those rich old fellows open their eyes. Some of 'em own some of those old rickety shacks and probably don't know what they own. Tell 'em. Perhaps the old man who owns our tenement will be there! Who knows?"

"By the way," said Michael, his face alight, "did I tell you Milborn told me the other day they think they're on the track of the real owner of the tenement? The agent let out something the last time they talked with him, and they think they may discover who he is, though he's hidden himself well behind agents for years. If we can find out who he is, we may help him understand the great need for him to make a few changes."

"Yes, a few changes!" said Will, sneering. "Tear down the whole rotten death trap and build a new one with light and air and a chance for human beings to live! Give it to 'em, old man! He may be there tonight."

"I believe I will," said Michael thoughtfully, and he went up to his room and locked the door.

When he came out again, Will, waiting to accompany him to the meeting, saw in his eyes the look of the dreamer, the man who sees into the future and prophesies. He knew Michael wouldn't fail in his speech that night. He gave a knowing look to Hester as she came out to go with him, and Hester understood. They walked behind him quietly or speaking in low tones. They felt the pride and anxiety of the moment as much as if they were going to make the speech. The angel in the man had dominated them also.

Now Starr had come down with her father for a week's shopping the last time he ran up to his sister's, and on this particular evening she had claimed her father's society.

"Can't you stay at home, Daddy dear?" she asked. "I don't want to go to Aunt Frances's 'quiet little evening' one bit. I told her you needed me tonight since we have only a day or two before I go back."

Aunt Frances was Starr's mother's sister and, as the servants of the two families agreed, "Just like her, only more so." Starr had never been quite happy in her company.

"Come with me for a while, daughter. I'm sorry I can't stay at home all evening, but I promised I'd drop into a charitable meeting at Madison Square for a few minutes. We won't need to stay long, and if you're with me, it'll be easier to get away."

"Agreed!" said Starr and got ready quickly.

So the roll of martial music poured forth from the fine instruments secured for the occasion, and the evening's leaders and speakers, with the presidents of this society or that army or settlement or organization for the relief and benefit of the poor, filed onto the great platform. And Starr and her father occupied prominent seats in the vast audience and joined in the enthusiasm that spread like a wave before the great American flag that burst out in brilliant electric lights of red and white and blue.

Michael entered with the others, as calmly as though he'd

spent his life preparing for the public platform. There was fire in his eyes, the fire of passion for the people of the slums who were his kin. He looked over the audience with a throb of joy to think he had such a mighty opportunity. His pulses weren't stirred, because he had no self-consciousness. His subject was to live before the people; he was nothing at all. He had no fear about telling them, if that was all they wanted. Sentences burning with the blood of souls had been pouring through his mind since he'd decided to talk of his people. He was only in a hurry to begin lest they wouldn't give him time to tell all he knew! Could he ever tell it? It was endless as eternity.

With a strange stirring of her heart, Starr recognized him. She felt the color stealing into her face. She thought her father must notice it and glanced at him, but he was deep in conversation about some banking business. So she sat and watched Michael during the opening exercises and wondered how he came to be there and what his position was. Did lawyers get paid for doing something to help along charitable institutions? She supposed so. He was probably given a seat on the platform for his pains.

Yet she couldn't help thinking how fine he looked sitting there in the center, the place of honor, it seemed. He was taller than the others, sitting or standing, and his fine form and bearing made him quite noticeable. Starr could hear women about her whispering to their escorts: "Who is he?" Her heart gave strange little throbs that she knew. It seemed odd to her that seeing him now took her back to that morning in Florida when she'd kissed him in the chapel. The memory seemed sweet and tender, and she dwelt upon it, while she watched him gazing calmly over the audience, rising and moving to let another pass him, bowing and smiling to a noted judge who leaned over to grasp his hand. Did young lawyers like that get to know noted judges? And wherever did he get his grace? Rhythm and beauty were in his every motion. Starr had never had such an opportunity to observe him before, for in the sea of faces she knew hers would be lost, and she might watch him at will.

"Daddy, did you know Michael was up there?" she asked after awhile when her father's friend returned to his seat.

"Michael? No, where? On the platform? I wonder what in the world he's doing there? He must be mixed up in this thing somehow. I understand he's stuck at his mission work. I tried to stop him several years ago. Told him it would ruin his prospects, but he was too stubborn to give up. So he's here!"

Mr. Endicott searched out Michael and studied the face keenly, looking in vain for any marks of degradation or fast living. The head was lifted with its conquering look; the eyes shone forth like jewels. *Michael was a man, a son—to be proud of,* he told himself and breathed a heavy sigh. That was one time his stubbornness hadn't conquered, and he found himself glad it hadn't.

The opening exercises were mere preliminary speeches and resolutions, mixed with music and the introduction of the city's mayor and one or two other notables who said a few apathetic words commending the work and retired on their laurels.

"I understand this Dr. Glidden who's to speak is quite eloquent," said Starr's father as the president got up to introduce the evening speaker. "The man just talking with me says he's worth hearing. If he's tiresome we'll slip out. I wonder which one he is? He must be the man with the iron-gray hair over there."

"Oh, I don't want to go out," said Starr. "I like it. I never was in a great meeting like this. I like to hear them cheer."

Her cheeks were rosy, for in her heart she found she longed to stay there and watch Michael a little longer.

"I'm sorry to tell you our friend and advertised speaker was called away by the sudden and serious illness of his mother and left for the West on the six o'clock express," said the chairman.

Sounds of disappointment swept over the audience, and some men reached for their hats.

"Well, now that's a pity," whispered Endicott. "I guess we better go before they slip in some dry old substitute. I've been seen here—that's enough."

But Starr laid a hand on her father's arm.

"Wait a little, Daddy," she said softly.

"But he's sent a substitute," went on the chairman, "a man he says is a hundred times better able to talk on the subject than he. He spoke to me from the station phone just before he left and told me he felt you'd all agree he did well to go when you heard the man he sent in his place. I have the pleasure of introducing to you Mr. Michael Endicott, who will speak to you this evening on the needs of the tenement dwellers—Mr. Endicott."

Amid the silence that ensued after the feebly polite applause Michael rose. For an instant he stood, looking at the audience, and a strange subtle thrill ran over the assembly.

Then Michael, measuring the spacious hall, flung his clear, beautiful voice out into it and reached its uttermost bounds.

"Did you know that in this city now are 71,877 totally dark rooms? Some of them are connected with an air shaft twenty-eight inches wide and seventy feet deep, and many have no access to even a dark shaft. And did you know these rooms are the only place in the world for thousands of little children, unless they stay in the street?"

The sentence shot through the audience like a deliberate lightning bolt, crashing through the hearers' hearts and tearing away every vestige of their complacency. The people sat up and took notice. Starr trembled—she didn't know why.

"There's a tenement with rooms like this—a dumbbell tenement, it's called—in the alley where, for no reason I know, I was born."

"Oh!" The sound swept over the listeners in a great wave like a sob of protest. Men and women raised their opera glasses and looked at the speaker again. They asked one another who he was and settled down to hear what more he had to say.

Then Michael told of three dark little rooms in "his" tenement where a family of eight, accustomed to better things, had been forced by circumstances to make their home and where tuberculosis germs had been growing in the dark, until the whole family was infected. He spoke of a ten-year-old girl, living in one of these rooms, pushed down on the street by a playmate, an accident thought nothing of in a healthy child; but in this child it produced tubercular meningitis, and after two days of agony the child died. He told of a delicate girl, who with her brother were the sole wage earners of the family, working all day and sewing far into the night to make clothes for the brothers and sisters, who had fallen prey to the white plague. He told instance after instance of sickness and death from the terrible conditions in this one tenement.

Then a refined-looking woman in the audience, who had dropped in with her husband on the way to some other gathering, drew her mantle about her shoulders with a shiver and whispered: "Really, Charles, it can't be healthy to have such terrible things in the city where we live. Germs could get out and float around to us. Such low creatures should be cleaned out of a decent community. Do let's go now. I can't listen to another word. I won't enjoy the reception."

But the husband sat frowning and listening to the end of the speech, granting her whisper the single growl: "Don't be a fool, Selina!"

On Michael went, taking his audience with him through room after room of "his" tenement, showing them horrors they'd never dreamed. He gave them an occasional glimmer of light when he told of a curtained window with fifteen minutes of morning sun, where a little cripple watched for her sunbeam and pushed her pot of geraniums along the sill to benefit from its brief shining. He brought laughter from the audience over the wit of some poor creatures in trying situations, showing a sense of humor wasn't lacking in "the other half." And he set them weeping over a baby's funeral.

He told them how hard the workers were trying to improve the terrible conditions; how cruelly slow this tenement's owner was even to cut windows into dark air shafts; how so far it had been impossible to discover the name of the building's true owner, because he had for years hidden behind agents who held the building in trust.

The speech closed in a mighty appeal to the people of New York to rise up and wipe out this curse of the tenements and build in their places light, airy, clean, wholesome dwellings, where people might live and work and learn life's lessons aright, and where sin could find no dark hole in which to hatch its loathsome offspring.

As Michael sat down amid a burst of applause given few speakers, another man stepped to the front of the platform. The cheers were hushed somewhat, only to swell and burst forth again, for this man was one of the city's great minds and always welcome on any platform. He'd been asked to make the final appeal for funds for the playgrounds. It was considered a great stroke of luck by the committee to secure him.

"My friends," he said when the hush came at last and he could be heard, "I appreciate your feelings. I'd like to spend the remainder of the night applauding the man who has just finished speaking."

The clamor showed signs of breaking forth again.

"This man has spoken from his heart. And he knows what he speaks about, for he's lived in those tenement rooms, like the children for whom he pleads. I'm told he's given every evening for four years out of a busy life, just opening into great promise, to help his people. Listening to him has reminded me of Lanier's wonderful poem 'The Marshes of Glynn.' Do you recall it?

Ye spread and span like the catholic man who hath
  mightily won
God out of knowledge, and good out of infinite pain,
  and sight out of blindness, and purity out of a stain.

Let us get to work at once and do our duty. I see you don't need urging. My friends, if such a man as this, a prince among men, can come out of the slums, then the slums are surely worth redeeming."

The audience thundered and clamored, and women sobbed openly, while the ushers hurried about collecting the eager offerings. Michael had won the day, and everybody was ready to give. It helped get the burden of such conditions off their consciences.

Starr sat through the whole speech with glowing cheeks and wet lashes. Her heart throbbed with wonder and personal pride in Michael. Somehow the years between seemed to drop away, and she saw before her the boy who had described the Florida sunset and filled her with childish admiration over his beautiful thoughts. His story appealed to her. The lives of the little ones he'd been telling about were like his poor neglected existence before her father took him up—the little lonely life offered freely to save her own.

She forgot all that had passed between: her anger at his not coming to ride; after her return from abroad, his not calling or accepting her invitations; her rage at his interference in her affairs. Her persistent folly now seemed unspeakable. She was ashamed of herself. The tears streamed unnoticed down her cheeks.

When the speeches were over and the applause had subsided, Starr turned to her father, her face aglow, her lashes still wet. Her father had been silent and absorbed. His face was inscrutable now. He could mask his emotions even to those who knew him best.

"Daddy dear," whispered Starr, "couldn't we buy that tenement and rebuild it? I'd love to give those children happy homes."

Endicott turned and looked at his treasured child, her lovely face eager now. She had infinite faith in her father's ability to purchase anything she wanted. The father himself was deeply stirred. He looked at her searchingly at first, then tenderly, but his voice was almost gruff.

"H'm! I'll see about it!"

"Couldn't you let Michael know now, Daddy? I think it would be such a help to him to know his speech has done some good." The voice was sweet and appealing. "Couldn't you send him word by an usher?"

"H'm! I suppose I could." Endicott took out his fountain pen and a business card and began to write.

"You don't suppose, Daddy, that the owner will object to selling? There won't be any trouble about it that way, will there?"

"No, I don't think there'll be any trouble."

Endicott slipped the card into an envelope he found in his pocket and, calling an usher, asked him to take it to the platform to Michael. What he had written was this:

> *I suppose you've been talking about my property. Pull the tenement down if you like and build a model one. I'll foot the bills.*
>
> *D. E.*

When Michael, surprised at receiving a communication on the platform, tore the envelope open and read, his face fairly blazed with glory. Starr was watching him, and her heart gave an odd throb of pleasure at the light in his eyes. The next instant he was on his feet and, with a whispered word to the chairman, came to the front of the platform. He raised his hand and brought instant silence.

"I have good news. May I share it with you? The owner of the tenement is in this house and has sent word he'll tear it down and build a model one in its place!"

The ring in Michael's voice and the light on his face equalled a dozen votes of thanks. The audience rose to its feet and cheered.

"Daddy! Oh, Daddy! Are you the owner?" Astonishment, reproof, excuse, and forgiveness mingled in Starr's voice.

"Come, Starr," said her father abruptly, "we'd better go home. This is a hot, noisy place, and I'm tired."

"Daddy dear! Of course you didn't know how things were!" said Starr sweetly. "You didn't, did you, Daddy?"

"No, I didn't know," said Endicott evasively, "that Michael has a great gift of gab! Would you like to stop and have an ice somewhere, daughter?"

"No, Daddy, I'd rather go home and plan how to make over that tenement. I don't believe I'd enjoy an ice after what I've heard tonight. Why do some people have so much more than others to start with?"

"H'm! Deep question, child. Better not trouble your brains with it."

Starr saw that her father, though deeply moved, didn't wish to discuss the matter.

The next day Michael called at Endicott's office but didn't find him in and wrote a letter out of his joyful heart, asking permission to call and thank his benefactor and talk over plans. The following day he received a curt reply.

Son—Make your plans to suit yourself. Don't spare expense within reason. No thanks needed. I did it for Starr. You made a good speech.

Michael choked down his disappointment over this rebuff. He wasn't forgiven yet. He might not enter into communion again, but he was beloved. He couldn't help feeling that, because of the "Son" that began the communication. And the grudging praise his speech received was more to Michael than all the adulation people had showered upon him since the meeting. But Starr! He did it for Starr! She wanted it! She was perhaps there! How else would she have known? The thought thrilled him. Oh, if he might have seen her! But then perhaps he couldn't have told his story, so it was just as well. But Starr was interested in his plans! How wonderful for her to work with him even in this indirect way. Oh, if someday—!

But here Michael shut down his thoughts and went to work.

Chapter 26

Late in January Michael was taking his nightly walk homeward by way of the Endicott home. He was convinced Starr was still away from home, for he'd seen no lights now for several weeks in the room he knew was hers. But there was always the chance she might have returned.

He was nearing the house when he saw from the opposite direction a man turn the corner and with halting gait walk slowly toward the house and pause before the steps. Something familiar in the man's attitude caused Michael to hasten his steps, and coming closer he found it was Mr. Endicott looking up the steps of his home as if they were a difficult hill he must climb.

Michael stopped beside him, saying good evening, the thrill of his voice conveying his joy in the meeting.

"Is that you, son?" asked the older man, swaying slightly toward him. "I'm glad you came. I feel strangely dizzy. I wish you'd help me in."

Michael's arm went about the other's shoulders at once, and his ready strength almost lifted his benefactor up the steps. He opened the night latch with the key handed him and, without waiting to call a servant, helped Mr. Endicott up to his room and to his bed.

The man sank back wearily with a sigh and closed his eyes, then suddenly roused himself.

"Thank you, son, and will you send a message to Starr that I cannot come tonight as I promised? Tell her I'll likely be all right tomorrow and will try to come then. You'll find the address at the head of the telephone list in the hall. I guess you'll have to phone for the doctor. I don't feel like myself. Something must be wrong. I think I've taken a heavy cold."

Michael hurried to the phone and called the physician, begging him to come at once, for he could see Mr. Endicott was very ill. Then his voice trembled as he gave the message to Western Union over the phone. It seemed almost like talking to Starr, though he sent the telegram in her father's name.

The message sent, he hurried back to the sick man, who seemed to have fallen into a stupor. His face was flushed and hot, the veins in his temples and neck throbbing rapidly. In all his healthy life Michael had seen little of illness, but he recognized it now and knew it must be a violent attack. If only he knew something to do until the doctor arrived!

Hot water used to be the universal remedy for all diseases at college. The matron always had someone bring hot water when anyone was ill. Michael went downstairs to find a servant, but they must all be asleep, for he'd been unusually late in leaving the alley that night.

He found that the bathroom would supply hot water, however, so he undressed his patient, wrapped him in a blanket, and placed his feet in hot water. But the patient showed signs of faintness and couldn't sit up. A footbath under such conditions was difficult to administer. The unaccustomed nurse got his patient into bed again with difficulty and was wondering what to do next when the doctor arrived.

Michael watched the doctor's grave face as he examined the sick man. He knew his intuition was right. Mr. Endicott was seriously ill. At last the doctor stepped out of the room and motioned Michael to follow him.

"Are you a relative, young man?" he asked, looking at Michael keenly.

"No, only someone who's very much indebted to him."

"Well, it's lucky for him if you feel that indebtedness now.

Do you know what's the matter with him?"

"No," said Michael. "He looks pretty sick to me. What is it?"

"Smallpox!" said the doctor. "And a case at that." He noted there was no blanching of panic in the young man's face, no hint of movement to leave the room. The man wasn't a coward anyway.

"How long have you been with him?" he asked abruptly.

"Since I telephoned you," said Michael. "I happened to be passing the house and saw him trying to get up the steps alone. He was dizzy, he said, and seemed glad to have me help him."

"Have you ever been vaccinated?"

"No," said Michael indifferently.

"The wisest thing for you would be to get out of the room at once and let me vaccinate you. I'll try to send a nurse to look after him as soon as possible. Where's the family? Not at home? The servants will probably scatter as soon as they learn what's the matter. A pity he wasn't taken to the hospital, but it's hardly safe to move him now. He's a very sick man, and there's only one chance in a hundred of saving him. You've run some big risks, taking care of him this way."

"Any bigger than you're running, doctor?" Michael smiled gravely.

"H'm! Well, it's my business, and I don't suppose it's yours. People are paid for those things. Come and get out of this room, or I won't answer for the consequences."

"The consequences will have to answer for themselves, doctor. I'm staying here till somebody better comes to nurse him."

Michael's eyes didn't flinch as he said this.

"Suppose you take the disease?"

Michael smiled one of his brilliant smiles. "Why, then I will, but I'll stay well long enough to take care of him until the nurse comes."

"You might die!"

"Of course."

"Well, it's my duty to tell you you'd probably be throwing your life away, for there's only a chance he won't die."

"Not throwing it away if I helped him suffer a little less. And you said there's a chance. If I didn't stay, could he miss that chance?"

"Probably."

"Can I do anything to help or ease him?"

"Yes."

"Then I stay. I should stay anyway until someone comes. I couldn't leave him this way."

"Very well, then. I'm proud to know a man like you. There's plenty to be done. Let's get to work."

The hour that followed was filled with instructions, and Michael had no time to think what would become of work or anything. He only knew this was the present duty and went forward in it step by step. Before the doctor left, he vaccinated Michael and gave him careful directions on how to take all necessary precautions for his own safety. But he knew from the lofty look in the young man's face that these were secondary considerations. The patient's needs came first.

The doctor roused the servants, told them what had happened, and tried to persuade them to stay quietly in their places, assuring them he'd see they ran no risks if they obeyed his directions. But they all panicked and gathered their effects, like the Arabs of old who folded their tents and stole away in the night. Before morning Michael and his patient were alone in the house.

Early in the morning the doctor called. He hadn't secured a nurse yet. Could Michael hold the fort a few hours longer? He'd relieve him sooner if possible, but experienced nurses for contagious cases were hard to get just now. There was a great deal of sickness. He might get one this morning, but it was doubtful. He had telephoned everywhere.

Of course Michael would hold the fort.

The doctor gave explicit directions, asked questions, and promised to call as soon as possible.

Michael, alone in the great silence that the occasional babble of a delirious person emphasizes in an otherwise empty house, began to think of things that must be done. Fortunately a telephone was in the room. He wouldn't have to leave his patient alone. He called Will French and told him in a few words what had happened; laughed pleasantly at Will's fears for him; asked him to look after the alley work and attend to one or two matters connected with the office work which couldn't be put off. Then he called Sam at the farm, for Michael had long ago found it necessary to have a telephone put in at Old Orchard.

The sound of Sam's voice cheered his heart. After Michael explained briefly his present position as nurse for the head of the Endicott house who lay sick with smallpox, Sam responded with a "Fer de lub o' Mike!"

When Michael had finished his directions to Sam and received his partner's promise to do everything as Michael would have done it, Sam broke out with: "Say, does dat guy know what he's takin' off'n you?"

"Who? Mr. Endicott? No, Sam, he doesn't know anything. He's delirious."

"Umm!" grunted Sam, deeply troubled. "Well, he better fin' out wen he gets hisself agin, er there'll be sompin' comin' to him."

"He's done a great deal for me, Sam."

"Umm! Well, you're gettin' it back on him sure thing now. Say, you t' care o' yerse'f, Mickey! We all can't do nothin' w'th'ut yer. You lemme know every day how you be."

"Sure, Sam!" responded Michael, deeply touched by the choking in Sam's voice. "Don't worry. I'm sound as a nut. Nothing'll happen to me. The doctor vaccinated me, and I won't catch it. You look after things for me, and I'll be on deck again someday, all the better for the rest."

Michael sat back in the chair after hanging up the receiver, his eyes glistening with moisture. To think the day had come when Sam cared like that! It was a miracle.

Michael returned to the bed to look after his patient. After doing everything the doctor had said, he decided to reconnoiter for some breakfast. There must be something in the house to eat even with the servants gone, and he should keep up his strength.

It was late in the morning, nearly half-past ten. The young man hurried downstairs and began to search the pantry. He didn't want to be away long from the upper room. Once, as he was looking in the refrigerator for butter and milk, he thought he heard a sound at the front door. But then all seemed still, so he hurriedly put a few things on a tray and carried them upstairs. He might not be able to come down again for several hours. But when he reached the top of the stairs he heard a voice, not his patient's, but a woman's voice, sweet and troubled.

"Daddy! Oh, Daddy dear! Why don't you speak to your little girl? What's the matter? Can't you understand me? Your face and your hands are so hot—they burn me. Daddy dear!"

It was Starr's voice, and Michael's heart stood still with the thrill of it—and the instant horror of it. Starr was in the room of death with her father. She was exposed to the terrible contagion—she, the beautiful treasure of his heart!

He set the tray on the hall table and hurried to the door.

She sat on the side of the bed, her arms about her father's unconscious form and her head buried in his neck, sobbing.

For an instant Michael was frozen with horror at her danger. If she'd wanted to take the disease she couldn't have found a more certain way.

The next instant his senses returned and without thinking

he sprang forward and caught her up in his arms, bearing her from the room and setting her down at the bathroom door.

"Oh, Starr! What have you done!" he said, a catch in his voice like a sob.

Starr, frightened, struggling, sobbing, turned and looked at him.

"Michael! Why are you here? What's wrong with my father?"

"Go wash your hands and face quickly with this antiseptic soap," he commanded, alert now and dealing out the things the doctor had given for his own safety. "And here! Rinse your mouth with this quickly, and gargle your throat! Then go and change your things as quick as you can. Your father has the smallpox, and you have been in there close to him."

"The smallpox!"

"Hurry!" ordered Michael, handing her the soap and turning on the hot water.

Starr obeyed because people did when he spoke in that tone, but her frightened eyes sought his face for some reassurance.

"The smallpox! Oh, Michael! How dreadful! But how do you know? Has the doctor been here? And how did you happen to be here?"

"I was passing last night when your father came home, and he asked me to help him in. Yes, the doctor was here and will come again soon and bring a nurse. Now hurry! You must get far away from this room!"

"But I'm not going away!" said Starr stubbornly. "I'm staying by my father. He'll want me."

"Your father would be distressed beyond measure if he knew you were exposed to such a terrible danger. He'd much rather you go away at once. Besides, he's delirious, and your presence can't do him any good now. You must take care of yourself, so that when he gets well you'll be well, too, and can help him back to health."

"But you're staying."

"It doesn't matter about me," said Michael. "There's no one to care. Besides, I'm a man and strong. I don't think I'll take the disease. Now please take off those things you wore in there and get something clean that hasn't been in the room and go away from here as quickly you can."

Michael had barely persuaded her to take precautions when the doctor arrived with a nurse and the promise of another before night.

He scolded Starr for her foolishness in going into her father's room. He had been the family physician ever since she was born, knew her well, and took the privilege of scolding when he liked. Starr succumbed meekly. But one thing she wouldn't do, and that was leave the house while her father remained in critical condition. The doctor frowned and scolded but finally agreed to let her stay. And indeed it was perhaps the only choice, for she had undoubtedly been exposed to the disease and was subject to quarantine. There seemed to be no place she could safely go where she could be comfortable, and the house was large enough for two or three parties to remain in quarantine in several detachments.

There was another question. The nurses would have their hands full with their patient. Someone must stay in the house to look after things, see they needed nothing, and prepare meals. Starr, of course, knew nothing about cooking, and Michael's experience was limited to roasting sweet potatoes around a college bonfire and cooking eggs and coffee at the fireplace on the farm. But a good cook to stay in a plague-stricken dwelling would be difficult to find, so the doctor decided to attempt the willing services of these two. Starr was established in her own room upstairs, which could be shut away from the front part of the house by a short passageway and two doors, with access to the lower floor by means of the back stairs. And Michael made a bed of the soft couch in the reception room, where he'd twice passed through trying experiences. Great curtains kept constantly wet with antiseptics shut away the sickroom and adjoining apartments from the rest of the house.

Michael was to place such supplies as were needed at the head of the stairs, just outside the curtains, and the nurses would pass all dishes through an antiseptic bath before sending them downstairs again. The electric bells and telephones in the house enabled them to communicate without danger of infection.

Starr was at once vaccinated, and the two young people received many precautions and orders with medicine and a strict regime. Even then the doctor shook his head. If those two beautiful faces should have to pass through that dread disease, his heart would break. Whatever skill and science could do to prevent that should be done.

So the house settled down to a daily routine—the busy city humming outside, but no more a part of them than if they were living in a tomb. The warning card on the door sent the neighbors scurrying off in a panic to Palm Beach or Europe, and even the strangers passed by on the other side. The grocery boy and the milkman left their orders hurriedly on the front steps, and Michael and Starr might almost have used the street for an exercise ground—so deserted it had become.

But they didn't need to go farther than the front door, for they had a lovely side and backyard, screened from the street by a high wall, where they could walk when they weren't too busy with their work—which for their unskilled hands was laborious. Nevertheless, the orders were strict, and every day they went out for a couple of hours at least. To keep from getting chilled, Michael invented games when tired of walking, and twice after a new snowfall they went out and threw snowballs, coming in with glowing faces and shining eyes, to change wet garments and hurry back to their kitchen work.

But this was after the first few serious days were passed, and the doctor had given them hope that if all went well, the patient had a good chance of pulling through.

They settled into their new life like two children who had known each other a long time. All the years between were as if they hadn't been. They made their blunders, were merry over their work, and grew into each other's companionship. Their cooking ideas were primitive, and if they couldn't have ordered things from caterers, they and the nurses might have starved. But with telephoning the nurses for directions and studying the recipes on the boxes of cornstarch and farina and oatmeal and the like that they found in the pantry, they were learning day by day to do a little more.

And then one blessed day the dear nurse Morton walked in and took off her things and stayed. Morton had paid a long-delayed visit to her old father in Scotland that winter. But when she saw in the papers the notice of the calamity that had befallen the house of her past employer, she packed her trunk and took the first steamer back to America. Her baby and her baby's father needed her, and nothing could keep Morton away after that.

Her coming relieved the situation, for though she'd never been a fancy cook, she knew all about good old-fashioned Scottish dishes, and from the first hour took up her station in the kitchen. Comfort and order reigned at once, and Starr and Michael had time on their hands not spent in eating, sleeping, working, or exercise.

Then they read together, for the library was filled with treasures of literature, many of which Michael had never had access to except through public libraries. But a book in hand is more satisfying when one has a bit of leisure in a busy life. Starr had been reading more than ever this winter with her aunt and enjoyed the pleasant companionship of a book together.

Then some hours Starr played softly and sang, for the piano was far from the sickroom and couldn't be heard upstairs. Indeed, if it hadn't been for the anxious struggle going on up there, these two would have had a beautiful time.

For, unknown to them, they were growing daily to delight in each other's presence. Even Michael, who had long ago laid down the lines for his life and never expected to be more to Starr than friend and protector, didn't realize where this intimate companionship was leading. When he thought of it at all, it seemed a precious solace for his years of loneliness, to be enjoyed fully and treasured in the barrenness that must surely follow.

Upstairs the fight continued daily, until at last one morning the doctor told them it was won, that the patient, though very much enfeebled, would live and slowly regain his strength.

That was a happy morning. The two caught each other's hands and whirled around the dining room when they heard it, and Morton came in with her sleeves rolled up and her eyes like two blue lakes blurred with raindrops in the sunlight.

The next morning the doctor looked the two over before he went upstairs and set a limit to their quarantine. If they kept on doing well they would be reasonably safe from taking the disease. It would be a miracle, almost, if neither took it; but it looked as if they'd be all right.

Now they had been so absorbed in one another that they'd thought little about taking the disease themselves. If either had been in the house with nothing to do but brood, it might have been the sole topic of thought. But their healthy busy hours had helped the good work on.

One bright morning, while waiting for the doctor to come, Michael was glancing over the morning paper, and Starr was trying a new song that had just arrived in the previous evening's mail.

Suddenly Michael exclaimed in dismay, and Starr, turning

on the piano stool, saw him staring out the window, his face pale and drawn.

"What is it?" she asked in quick, sympathetic tones.

Michael turned to look at her vivid beauty, his heart thrilling with the sound of her voice, and suddenly felt the gulf between them. What he'd read in the paper had shaken him from his dream and brought him back to the reality of what he was.

The paper reported Buck's escape from jail. Michael was greatly troubled for Buck and instantly recalled he belonged in Buck's class and not in Starr's charmed circle here.

He looked at the girl with serious, tender eyes that seemed less intimate than in these weeks. She sensed the difference at once.

He showed her the item.

Starr's face softened with sympathy, then expressed indignation. "He was one of those people in your tenements you've been trying to help?" she asked, trying to understand his look. "He should have been ashamed to get into jail after you were helping him. Wasn't he a worthless fellow?"

"No," said Michael in quick defense, "he never had a chance. And he wasn't just one of those people; he was the one. He was the boy who took care of me when I was a little fellow. He shared everything he had—a hard crust, a warm cellar floor. I think he loved me—"

Something in Michael's face and voice warned Starr to tread lightly.

"Tell me about him," she said softly.

So Michael, his eyes tender, his voice gentle, because she cared to know, told her of Buck. When he finished, her eyes were wet with tears, and she looked so sweet he had to avert his own eyes to keep from taking the lovely vision into his arms and kissing her. It was a strange, wild impulse and frightened him. Suppose someday he forgot himself and let her see how he dared love her? That must never be. He must watch himself. Her sweet friendship to him must never be broken by his word, look, or action.

And from that morning his manner changed, subtly, intangibly—but changed.

They read and talked together, and Michael opened his heart to her as never before about the alley, his farm community, and his hopes for his people. Starr listened and entered eagerly into his plans, yet felt the change, and her troubled spirit didn't know what it was.

Chapter 27

$\mathcal{A}$ ll this while Michael communicated daily with Sam, as well as Will French, who with Hester's help had kept the alley rooms going, though they reported the leader was sorely missed.

Sam reported daily progress with the house and about two weeks before Michael's release from quarantine announced its completion, even to papering the walls and oiling the floors.

A fire had been burning in the furnace and fireplaces for several weeks, so the plaster was thoroughly dry. Michael planned for Starr and her father to go straight to the farm as soon as they were free to leave the house.

To this end Hester and Will were given daily commissions to purchase this or that article of furniture, until at last Michael felt the house would be habitable for Starr and her precious invalid.

During the winter Michael had purchased rugs and charming, suitable furniture for the house he was building. He'd already selected the important things and knew he could trust Hester's taste for the rest. For some reason he'd never said much to Starr about Hester or Will, perhaps because they had always seemed to belong to one another and thus set apart from his life.

But one morning Starr entered the library where Michael was telephoning Hester about some last purchases she was making and overheard these words: "All right, Hester, you'll know best, but I think you better make it a dozen instead of half. It's better to have too many than too few, and we might have company."

Now, of course, Starr couldn't know dishes were being discussed. In fact, she didn't stop to think what they were talking about; she only knew he called this other girl "Hester." She suddenly realized that during these weeks, although she addressed him as Michael, he avoided using any name for her, except on one or two occasions, substituting pronouns whenever possible. She hadn't noticed this before, but when she heard that "Hester" in his pleasant tones, she wondered. Who was Hester? And why was she Hestered so carelessly as though he had a right? Was Michael engaged to her? Why hadn't she thought of it before? Of course it would be natural. This other girl had been down in his dear alley, working shoulder to shoulder with him all these years, and he must love her.

Starr's bright morning suddenly clouded over with darkness, and though she tried to hide it even from herself, her spirit was heavy with something she didn't understand.

That evening Michael came into the library unexpectedly. He'd been out in the kitchen helping Morton open a box that was stuck. He found the room dark but thought he heard a soft sound like sobbing in one corner.

"Starr!" he said. "Starr, is that you?"

He didn't know he'd called her by her name, though she knew very well. She kept still an instant and then rose from the crumpled heap in the corner of the leather couch where she'd dropped in the dark to cry out the strange ache of her heart. She thought Michael was safely in the kitchen for a while.

"Why, yes, Michael!" she said in a broken voice, though struggling to make it natural.

Michael stepped to the doorway and turned on the hall lights so he could see her figure standing in the shadow. Then he stepped over to her, his whole heart yearning over her, but with great control.

"What's the matter—dear?" He breathed the last word almost under his breath. He didn't realize he'd spoken it aloud.

It seemed to envelope her with a deep tenderness, breaking her partial self-control. She sobbed again before she could speak.

Oh, if he only dared take that dear form into his arms and comfort her! But he had no right!

Michael stood still and struggled with his heart, standing near her, yet not touching her.

"My dear!" he breathed to himself, in love and self-restraint.

But she didn't hear the breath. She was struggling on her own, remembering that Hester girl and her own duty. She mustn't let him see how she felt, not for anything in the world. He was kind and tender. He had always been. He'd denied himself to stay with them in their need because of his gratitude toward her father for all he'd done for him. He breathed that "dear" as he would have to any tenement child in trouble. Oh, she understood, even while she let the word comfort her lonely heart. But why had she been left to trifle with a handsome scoundrel? Why hadn't she been worthy to win the love of a great man like this one?

At last, in her sweet voice she burst forth: "Oh, Michael, you've been so good to me—to us, I mean—staying here all these weeks and not showing any impatience when you had great work to do. I've just been thinking how horrid I was to you last winter—the things I said and wrote to you—and how I treated you when you were trying to save me from an awful fate! I'm so ashamed—and so thankful! I realized tonight what I owe you, and I can't ever thank you. Can you forgive me for the horrid way I acted and for passing you on the street that Sunday without speaking to you—I'm so ashamed! Will you forgive me?"

She put out her hands with a pathetic motion toward him in the room's half-light, and he took them in his warm ones and held them, his whole frame thrilling with her sweet touch.

"Forgive you, little Starr!" he breathed. "I never blamed you—"

And there's no telling what might not have happened if the doctor hadn't arrived just then to complete arrangements for their going to the farm.

When Michael returned from letting the doctor out, Starr had fled upstairs to her room. When they met the next morning, the bustle of preparation was upon them, and each cast shy smiling glances toward the other. Starr knew she was forgiven, but she also knew a wall stood between them that hadn't before, and her heart ached with the knowledge. Nevertheless, it was a happy morning, and one couldn't be miserable in Michael's company, with her father recovering rapidly and the prospect of going with him into the beautiful outdoors in a few hours.

Michael prepared to go with a look of solemn joy. Solemn because the wonderful companionship he'd had alone with Starr would soon end. Joyful because he could be with her still and know she'd escaped the terrible disease. Besides, he might always serve her, and they were friends now, not enemies—that was a great deal!

Old Orchard stood on tiptoe that lovely spring morning when the party came down. The winding road to the cottage was arched with bursting bloom, for the apple trees had decorated for the occasion and made a canopy of pink and white for Starr to pass beneath.

Not a soul was in sight as they drove up to the cottage, except Sam, standing respectfully to receive them in front of the piazza, and Lizzie, vanishing around the corner of the cottage with her boy toddling after—Lizzie had come down to be a waitress at Rose Cottage for the summer. But every soul on the farm was watching at a safe distance. Sam, without breathing a word, had conveyed to them all that those coming as their guests were beloved of Michael, their angel-hearted man. They stood in silent, adoring groups behind a row of thick hedges and watched them arrive, glorying in the beauty of the one they called in their hearts "the boss's girl."

The room stood wide and inviting to receive them. A fire of logs burned on the great hearth, and a deep leather chair sat before it, with a smaller rocker at one side and a sumptuous leather couch for the invalid on the other side, where the light of the flames wouldn't strike the eyes, yet the warmth would reach him. Soft greens and browns were blended in the silk pillows piled on the couch and on the seats that appeared here and there about the walls as if they grew by nature. The bookcase was filled with Michael's favorites—Will French had seen to this—and a few books were scattered on the big table where a green shaded lamp of unique design, a magazine, and a chair at just the right angle suggested a pleasant evening hour. Two or three pictures adorned the walls; Michael had selected these as he learned more about art from his study at the exhibits.

"Oh!" exclaimed Starr. "How lovely! It's a real home!"

It will probably be Michael and Hester's someday, she thought. But she wouldn't let shadows spoil her good time now, for it was her good time, and she had a right to it. She, too, was happy that she and Michael were friends—the kind of friends that can never be enemies again.

The invalid sank into the couch cushions with a pleased · light in his eyes. "Son, this is all right. I'm glad you bought the farm."

Michael turned with a look of love to the only father he'd ever known. It was good to be reconciled with him and know he was on the road to health once more.

The doctor who had come down with them looked about with satisfaction.

"I see you're fixed," he said to Endicott. "I wouldn't mind being in your shoes myself. Wish I could stay and help you enjoy yourself. If I had a pair of children like those, I'd give up work and buy a farm alongside and settle down for life."

The days at the farm passed in a charmed existence for Starr and her father. Everything they needed seemed to come as if by magic. Starr's every wish was anticipated, and Lizzie waited upon her devotedly, never by even a look trying to win recognition. Starr, keen in her remembrances, knew and appreciated this.

After the first two days Michael was back and forth in the city. His business, growing steadily before his temporary retirement from the world, had piled up and was awaiting his attention. His work in the alley called loudly for him every night. Yet he came down to the farm often and spent his Sundays there.

One Saturday evening about three weeks after arriving at the farm, they were all seated cozily in the cottage living room. The invalid was resting on the couch in the shadow, with Starr seated close beside him, the firelight glowing on her face, her hand in her father's. Michael sat by the table with a fresh magazine he was about to read to them when a knock came at the door. Opening the door, Michael found Sam standing on the piazza, and another dark form huddled behind him.

"Come out here, can't yer! Buck's here!" whispered Sam.

"Buck!" Michael spoke the word with a joyful ring that thrilled Starr's heart with sympathy as she sat listening, her ears alert with interest.

"I'm so glad!" said Michael's vibrant voice again, with real welcome. "Come in, Buck. I have a friend here who knows all about you. No, don't be afraid. You're safe. What? Well, we'll turn the light out and sit in the firelight. You can go over in that corner by the fireplace. No one will see you. The shades are down."

Michael's voice was low, and he stood inside the doorway.

There was dissent in a low whisper outside, and then Sam's voice growled, "Go in, Buck, ef he says so." And Buck reluctantly entered, followed by Sam.

Buck was dressed in an old suit of Sam's, with his hands and face washed and hair combed. Sam had imbibed ideas and wasn't slow to impart them. But Buck stood dark and frowning against the closed door; his eyes, like black coals in a setting of snow, darted about the room in restless vigilance. His body wore the habitual air of crouching alertness. He started slightly when anyone moved or spoke to him.

Michael went quickly over to the table and turned down the lamp.

"You won't mind sitting in the firelight, will you?" he said to Starr in a low tone, and her eyes told him she understood.

"Come over here, Buck," said Michael, motioning toward the sheltered corner of the other side of the fireplace from where Starr was sitting. "This is one of my friends, Miss Endicott, Mr. Endicott. Will you excuse us if we sit here and talk a few minutes? Miss Endicott, you remember my telling you about Buck?"

Starr, with sudden inspiration, stood up and crossed to where the dark-browed Buck stood frowning and embarrassed in the chimney corner and put out her hand to him. Buck looked at it in dismay and didn't stir.

"Why don't yer shake?" whispered Sam.

Then with a grunt of astonishment Buck put out his rough hand and for the first time held a lady's hand in his. The hunted eyes looked up startled to Starr's. And somehow Starr, with her smile and her eyes and her gentle manner, unknowingly conveyed a thought from Browning's poem to Buck! Poor, neglected, sinful Buck!

All I could never be,
    All men ignored in me,
This, I was worth to God, whose wheel the pitcher shaped.

And Michael, looking on, knew what she'd done and blessed her in his heart.

Buck sat down in the chimney corner, half in shadow with the lights from the great log flaring over his face. The shades were drawn, the doors closed. He was surrounded by friendly faces. For a few minutes the eyes ceased roving around the room and rested on Starr's sweet face as she quietly held her father's hand. It was a sight Buck's eyes had never rested upon in his whole checkered existence, and for the moment he let the sweet wonder of it filter into his dark, scarred soul with blessed healing. Then he looked from Starr to Michael's face nearby, joyous at Buck's coming, anxious with the outcome, and for a moment the heavy lines in forehead and brow that Buck had worn since babyhood softened with a tender look. Perhaps 'tis given once to even the lowest soul to see, no matter how far fallen, just what he might have been.

They had been sitting thus for about fifteen minutes, talking quietly. Michael intended to take Buck upstairs soon and question him, but first he wanted time to think what to do. Then suddenly a loud knock startled them all, and as Michael rose to go to the door there followed the resounding clatter of the tongs falling on the hearth.

A voice with a knife edge to it cut through the room and made them shiver.

"Good evening, Mr. Endicott! I'm sorry to trouble you, but I've come on an unpleasant errand. We're after an escaped criminal, and he was seen entering your door a few minutes ago. Of course I know your good heart. You take 'em all in, but this one is a jailbird. You'll excuse me if I take him off your hands. I'll try to do it as quietly as possible."

The big, blustery voice ceased, and Michael, looking at the sinister gleam of metal in the hands of the men accompanying the county sheriff, knew the crisis was upon him. The man, impatient, was already pushing past him into the room. It was no use resisting. He flung the door wide and turned with the saddest look Starr had ever seen on a man's face.

"I know," he said, his voice filled with sorrow. "But—he was one I loved!"

"Wasted love, Mr. Endicott. Wasted love. Not one of 'em worth it!" growled the big man walking in.

Then Michael turned and faced the group around the fireplace and, looking from one to another, paled with amazement, for Buck wasn't among them!

Starr sat beside her father in the same attitude she'd held throughout the last fifteen minutes, his hand in hers, her face turned, startled, toward the door and something inscrutable in her eyes. Sam stood close to the fireplace, the tongs he'd just picked up in his hands and a look of sullen rage on his face. Nowhere in the whole room was a sign of Buck, and there seemed no spot where he could hide. The dining room door was in the opposite wall, and behind it could be heard the cheerful clatter of clearing the table. If Buck had escaped that way there would have been an outcry from Morton or the maid. Every window's shade was closely drawn.

The sheriff looked suspiciously at Michael whose blank face showed he had no part in making way with the outlaw. The man behind him looked sharply around and finished with a curious gaze at Starr. Starr, rightly interpreting the scene, rose to the occasion.

"Would they like to look behind this couch?" she said, moving quickly to the other side of the fireplace over toward the window, with a warning glance toward Sam.

Then while the men searched in vain around the room, in

the chimney closet and behind the furniture, she stood beside the corner window.

Michael had arranged for the windows to have springs worked by pressing a button like some car windows, so a touch would send them up at will.

Only Sam saw Starr's hand slide under the curtain and unfasten the catch at the top—then quickly down and touch the button in the windowsill. The window went up noiselessly, and in a moment the curtain was moving out, puffed by the soft spring breeze, and Starr had returned to her father's side.

"I can't understand it," Michael said. "He was here a moment ago!"

The sheriff, nosing about the fireplace, turned and stepped over to the window, sliding up the shade and peering out into the dark orchard.

"H'm! That's where he went, boys. After him, quick! We should have posted a watch at each window as well as at the back. Thank you, Mr. Endicott! Sorry to trouble you. Good night!" And the sheriff clattered after his men.

Sam quickly pulled down the window, fastened it, and gazed with almost worshipful understanding at Starr.

"Isn't that fire getting pretty hot for such a warm night?" said Starr, pushing back the hair from her forehead and bright cheeks. "Sam, suppose you get a little water and pour over the log. I think we won't need any more fire tonight anyway."

And Sam hastened to obey, his mouth stretching in a broad grin as he went out the door.

"She'd make a peach of a burglar," he remarked to himself as he filled a bucket with water and hurried back to the fire.

Michael, in his strait between law and love, was deeply troubled and had followed the men out into the dark orchard.

"Daddy, I think you'd better get up to your room. This excitement has been too much for you," Starr said.

But Mr. Endicott demurred. He had been interested in the

drama enacted before him and wanted to sit up and see the end of it. He was inclined to blame Michael for bringing such a fellow into Starr's presence.

But Starr laughingly bundled him off to bed and sat for an hour reading to him, her heart in a flutter to know how things came out. She wondered if Sam understood and put out the fire and if she could safely give him any broader hint.

At midnight, Michael lay awake with a troubled spirit, wondering if he might have done anything for Buck if he'd only done it in time—and been right to do.

Cautiously a man stole out of the orchard's darkness until he stood close to the old chimney. Then softly on the midnight summer air came a peculiar sibilant sound, clear, piercing, yet blending with the night and leaving no trace of its origin. One couldn't tell where it came from. But Michael, keeping his vigil, heard and rose up on his elbow. Was Buck calling him? It came again, softer this time but distinct. Michael sprang from his bed and threw on his garments. That call should never go unanswered!

Stealthily, in the moonlight, a dark figure stole forth from the chimney top, climbed down on the ladder that had been tilted against it, helped lay the ladder back in the deep grass and, joining the figure on the ground, crept toward the river where a boat waited.

Buck lay down in the bottom of the boat, covered with a piece of sacking, and Sam took up the oars when a long, sibilant whistle like a night bird floated through the air. Buck started up and turned suspicious eyes on Sam.

"What's that?"

"It's Mickey, I reckon," said Sam reverently. "He couldn't sleep. He's huntin' yer!"

Buck lay down with a sound like a moan, and the boat took up its silent glide toward safety.

"It's fierce ter leave him this a-way!" muttered Buck. "Youse tell him, won't yer, an' her—she's a ly-dy, she is. She's all right! Tell her Buck'll do ez much fer her someday ef he ever gits the chance."

"In doin' fer her you'd be doin' fer him, I spekullate," said Sam after a long pause.

"So?" said Buck.

"So," answered Sam. And that was how Sam told Buck of Starr's identity.

Now Starr, from her darkened window beside the chimney, had watched the whole thing. She waited until she saw Michael come slowly, sadly back from his fruitless search through the dawning mist alone, with bowed head, and her heart ached for the problem filling him with sorrow.

Chapter 28

Starr was coming to the city on the early morning train with Michael to shop for summer clothes. She was leaving in a few days to be bridesmaid at the wedding of an old school friend who lived out West, and she told herself she wanted the pleasure of this trip to town with Michael. She treasured each beautiful day filled with precious experiences, like jewels to be strung on memory's chain, with a vague unrest lest some future event might snatch them from her forever.

She wished she had refused her friend's pleading, but the friend had delayed the wedding until Starr could leave her father, and her father had also insisted she have the rest and change after the winter's ordeal. So Starr seemed to have to go, much as she preferred to stay. She had vowed to herself that she would return at once after the wedding despite the family's pleas to stay all summer with them. She sensed that the days of her companionship with Michael might be short, and she must make the most of them. It might never be the same again. She wasn't even sure her father would remain all summer at the farm as Michael urged.

This morning she was happy about going with Michael. The sea seemed to sparkle with a thousand gems as the train swept along. Michael told her of his first coming to see the farm and pointed out the flowers along the way. She assured him Old Orchard was far prettier than any of them, now that the roses were beginning to bud. It would soon be Rose Cottage indeed!

Then the talk fell on Buck and his brief visit.

"I wonder where he can be and what he's doing," said Michael, sighing. "If he only could have stayed longer for me to talk with him. I believe I could have persuaded him to a better way. But it's a mystery how he got away with those men watching the house."

Starr, her cheeks rosy, her eyes shining mischievously, looked up at him. "Didn't you suspect where he was hiding?"

Michael looked at her with a sudden start and smiled into her eyes. "Why, no. Did you?"

"Of course. I knew all the time. Do you think it was dreadful for me not to tell? I couldn't bear to have him caught before you'd had a chance to help him and when he was so good to you as a little boy. Besides, I saw his face, that terrible, hunted look. There wasn't anything really wrong in my opening that window and throwing them off the track, was there?"

"Did you open the window?"

Starr nodded saucily. "Yes, and Sam saw me do it. Sam knew all about it. Buck went up the chimney right through that hot fire. Didn't you hear the tongs fall down? He went like a flash before you opened the door, and one foot was still in sight when that sheriff came in. I was so afraid he'd see it. Was it wrong?"

"I suppose it was," he said sadly. "The law must be maintained. It can't be set aside for one fellow who's touched one's heart by some childhood action. But right or wrong I can't help being glad you cared to do something for poor Buck."

"I think I did it mostly for—you," she said softly, her eyes still down.

For answer, Michael reached out his hand, took her small gloved one lying in her lap, and pressed it for an instant. Then, as if a mighty power were forcing him, he laid it gently down again and drew his hand away.

Starr felt the pressure of that strong hand and its message through long days afterward, and more than once it gave her courage and cheer. Come what may, she had a true friend.

They spoke no more till the train swept into the station and they'd hurried through the crowd and were standing on the front of the ferryboat. The water sparkled before them, and the whole stirring city spread before their gaze, with the light from the cross on Trinity Church steeple sending its glory in their faces.

"Look!" said Michael, pointing. "Do you remember the poem we were reading the other night—Wordsworth's 'Upon Westminster Bridge'? Doesn't it fit this scene perfectly? I've often thought of it when I was coming across in the mornings. To look over there at the beauty, one would never dream of all the horror and suffering within those streets. It's beautiful now. Listen! Do you remember it?

> *"Earth has not anything to show more fair:*
> *Dull would he be of soul who could pass by*
> *A sight so touching in its majesty:*
> *This City now doth like a garment wear*
> *The beauty of the morning; silent, bare,*
> *Ships, towers, domes, theatres, and temples lie*
> *Open unto the fields and to the sky;*
> *All bright and glittering in the smokeless air.*
> *Never did sun more beautifully steep*
> *In his first splendor valley, rock, or hill;*
> *Ne'er saw I, never felt, a calm so deep!*
> *The river glideth at its own sweet will:*
> *Dear God! the very houses seem asleep;*
> *And all that mighty heart is lying still!"*

Starr gazed long at the picture before her, while her companion spoke the beautiful lines word by word.

Michael's hat was off, and the morning sunlight lay on his hair and cheek and brow. Her heart swelled within her as she looked, and tears filled her eyes. She dared not look longer lest she show her deep emotion. The look of him, the words he spoke, and the whole wonderful scene would linger in her memory as long as life should last.

Two days later Starr started west, and life seemed empty for Michael. She was gone from him, but still she would come back. Or would she? How long could he hope to keep her if she did? Sad foreboding filled him, and he worked with strained nerves, for now he knew that right or wrong she was heart of his heart, part of his consciousness. He loved her better than himself, and he saw no hope in forgetting. Yet never would he ask her to share the dishonor of his heritage.

The day before Starr was expected back at Old Orchard, Michael picked up the morning paper and with growing horror read:

BANDIT WOUNDED AS FOUR HOLD UP TRAIN
EXPRESS MESSENGER PROTECTS CASH DURING DESPERATE GUNFIGHT IN CAR

Fort Smith, Ark.—Four bandits bungled the holdup of a Kansas City passenger train, between Hatsfield and Mena, Ark., early today. One was probably fatally wounded and captured, and the others escaped after a battle in which the express messenger exhausted his ammunition and was badly beaten.

When the other robbers escaped, the wounded bandit eluded the conductor and made his way into the sleeper, where he climbed into an empty berth. But he was soon traced by the drops of blood from his wound. The conductor and a brakeman hauled him out and battled with him in the aisle amid passengers' screams. The bandit aimed his revolver at the conductor and fired, but his wrist twisted suddenly, sending the bullet into his own body instead of the conductor's. The wounded bandit received the bullet in his left breast near the heart and will probably die. The express messenger is in the hospital at Mena and may recover.

*If the bandit's bullet had gone as intended it would proba-
bly have wounded one or two women passengers, who at the
sound of trouble had jumped from their berths into the aisle
and were directly in the bullet's path.*

*The captured bandit may prove to be the escaped convict
"Buck," who was serving a long sentence in the state peniten-
tiary and for whom the police have been searching in vain for
the last three months.*

Michael was pale and trembling when he finished reading
the story. Was this then Buck's end? Must he die like that?
Disgrace and sin and death, with no chance to make good?
Michael bowed his head on the table before him, his heart
too heavy to think it out. That evening a telegram arrived
from Arkansas.

*A man named Buck is dying here and calls incessantly for
you. If you wish to see him alive, come at once.*

Michael took the midnight train. Starr had telegraphed her
father she would reach Old Orchard in the morning. It was
hard to go when she was just returning. Michael wondered if
it would always be so now.

Buck roused at Michael's coming and smiled feebly.

"Mickey! I knowed you'd come! I'm done for, pardner. I
ain't long fer here, but I couldn't go 'thout you knowin'. I'd
meant to git jes' this one haul an' git away to some other
country where it was safe. Then I was goin' to try'n keep
straight like you'd want. I would a'got trough all right, but I
seen her—the pretty lady—your girl—standing in the aisle
right ahin' the c'ndct'r, jes' es I wuz pullin' the trigger. I
knowed her right off, an' I couldn't run no resks. I ain't never
bin no bungler at my trade, but I had to bungle this time
'cause I couldn't shoot your girl! So I turned it jes' in time an'
took it mese'f. She seen how 'twas 'ith me that time at your

house, an' she he'ped me git away. I sent her word I'd do the same for her someday. Bless her—an' now—you tell her we're square! I done the bunglin' fer her sake, but I done it fer you too, pard—little pard—Mickey!"

"Oh, Buck!" Michael knelt beside the bed and buried his face in the coverlet. "Oh, Buck! If you'd only had my chance!"

"Never you mind, Mickey! I ain't squealin'. I knows how to take my dose. An' mebbe they'll be some kind of collidge whar I'm goin', an' I kin get a try at yet—don't you fret, little pard—ef I git my chancet, I'll take it fer yer sake!"

The life breath seemed spent with the effort, and Buck sank slowly into unconsciousness and so passed out of a life that had been against him.

After doing the last little things permitted him, Michael sadly returned home.

He reached the city in the morning and spent several hours putting to rights his business affairs. By noon he found himself so weary he took the two o'clock train down to the farm. Sam met him at the station. Sam somehow sensed when to meet him, and the two gripped hands and walked home together across the salt grass. Michael told in low, halting tones what Buck had said. Sam kept his face turned the other way, but once Michael glimpsed it and was sure tears were on his cheeks. To think of Sam shedding tears for anything!

Arriving at the cottage, Sam told him he thought Mr. Endicott was taking his afternoon nap upstairs and Miss Endicott had gone to ride in an auto with some fancy woman who'd called for her.

Being weary and yet unwilling to risk waking Mr. Endicott by going upstairs, Michael asked Sam to bolt the dining room door and give orders not to disturb him for an hour. Then he lay down on the leather couch in the living room. The windows were open around, and the sweet breath of the opening roses stole in with the summer breeze, while the drone of bees and the song sparrow's pure notes lulled him to sleep.

Chapter 29

*M*ichael had slept perhaps an hour when he was roused by voices—a sharp, hateful one with an unpleasant memory in it and a sweet, clear one that went to his soul.

"Sit down here, Aunt Frances. No one's about. Papa's asleep, and Michael hasn't returned yet from a trip out West. You can talk freely."

"Michael, Michael!" sniffed the voice. "Well, that's what I came to talk to you about. I didn't want to say anything where the chauffeur could hear. He's too curious and might tell the servants. I wouldn't have it get out for the world. Your mother would have been mortified about all this, and I can't see what your father is thinking about. He never did seem to have much sense where you were concerned!"

"Aunt Frances!"

"Well, I can't help it. He doesn't. Now take this matter of your being down here, and the thought of your calling that fellow Michael—as if he were a cousin or something! Why, it's disgusting! I hoped you'd stay out West until your father was well enough to go away somewhere with you. But now that you've come back I think you should leave here at once. People will talk, and I don't like it. Why, the fellow will presume on it to be intimate with you—"

Michael suddenly realized he was listening to a conversation not intended for his ears, and yet he couldn't get out of hearing without passing the door in front of which the two women were seated. Both the dining room door and the stairs were on the other side of the room from him, and he would risk being seen by either or both of them if he attempted to cross to them. The windows were screened by wire nailed over the whole length, so he couldn't get out through them. He could only lie still and pretend to be asleep if they discovered him afterward. It was embarrassing but not his choosing.

There was a slight stir outside. Starr had risen and stood with her back to the doorway.

"Aunt Frances! What do you mean? Michael is our honored and respected friend, our protector—our host. Think what he did for Papa! Risked his life!"

"Stuff and nonsense! Risked his life. He took the risk for his own reasons. He knew how to worm himself into the family again."

"Aunt Frances! I won't hear you say such things. Michael is a gentleman, well educated, with the highest ideals and principles. If you knew how self-sacrificing and kind he is!"

"Kind, yes, kind!" sniffed the aunt. "What will you think about it when he asks you to marry him? Will you think he's kind to offer you a share in the inheritance of a nobody—a charity—dependent—a child of the slums? If you stay here you'll have all New York gossiping about you, and then when you're in disgrace—I suppose you'll turn to me to help you out of it."

"Stop!" cried Starr. "I won't listen to another word. What do you mean by disgrace? There could be no disgrace in marrying Michael. The girl who marries him will be the happiest woman in the world. He's good and true and unselfish to the heart's core. But there's no danger of his ever asking me to marry him, Aunt Frances. I'm sure he loves another girl and is engaged to marry her, and she's a nice girl, too. But if it were different, if he were free and asked me to marry him, I would be as proud and glad as if a prince of the highest realm had asked me to share his throne with him. I'd rather marry Michael than any man I ever met, and I don't care in the least whether he's a child of the slums or a child of a king. I know what he is, and he's a prince among men."

"Oh, really! Has it come to this? Then you're in love with him already, and my warning comes too late, does it? Answer me! Do you imagine yourself in love with him?"

"Aunt Frances, you have no right to ask me that question," said Starr steadily, her cheeks red, her eyes bright.

Michael was sitting bolt upright on the couch now, forgetful of his eavesdropping, fairly holding his breath to listen and straining his ears that he might not lose the slightest word. He was devouring the dear little form in the doorway with his eyes, and her words fell on his tired heart like raindrops in a thirsty land, bringing forth the flowers of hope into lovely bloom.

"Well, I do ask it!" snapped the aunt. "Come, answer me—do you love him?"

"That, Aunt Frances, I shall never answer to anybody but Michael. I must refuse to hear another word on this subject."

"Oh, very well, good-bye. I'll leave you to your silly fate, but don't expect me to help you out of trouble if you get into it. I've warned you, and I wash my hands of you."

The angry woman flounced out to her waiting car, but the girl stood still in the doorway.

"Good afternoon, Aunt Frances," she said with dignity. "I shall never ask your help in any way."

Starr watched the car out of sight, tears welling into her eyes and rolling down her cheeks. Michael sat breathless on the couch and tried to think what to do, while his very being was rippling with the joy of her words.

Then she turned and saw him, and he stood up and held out his arms.

"Starr, my little Starr! My darling! Did you mean all you said? Would you really marry me? I've loved you always, Starr, since the first time I saw you as a tiny child. I've loved your soft baby kisses and those you gave me later when you were a little girl and I was an awkward boy. You never knew how dear they were or how I would go to sleep at night dreaming about those kisses on my face. Oh, Starr! Answer me. Did you mean it all? And could you ever love me. You said you would answer that question to no one else but me. Will you answer it now, darling?"

For answer she came and stood inside his arms, her face all tears and smiles, and he folded her within his strong clasp and, stooping, whispered softly, "Starr, little darling—my life—my love—my—wife!"

Three weeks later, when the roses were bursting with bloom over the porch at Rose Cottage and June was everywhere with her richness and beauty, Starr and Michael were married on the piazza under an arch of roses. A favored few of society's cream motored down to Old Orchard to witness the ceremony, and despite her ugly predictions and threats Aunt Frances was among them, smiling and dominating.

"Yes, so sensible of her not to make a fuss with her wedding, when her father is getting back again. Of course she could have come to my house and been married. I begged her to—naturally she shrank from another wedding in connection with the old home—but her father seemed to dread coming into town, so I advised her to go ahead and be married here. Isn't it a charming place? So rustic and simple and quite artistic in its way. Michael had done it all, planned the house and everything, of course, with Starr's help. You know it's quite a large estate, belonging to Michael's great-grandfather once, several hundred acres, and he's used part of it for charitable purposes—has a farm school or something for poor slum people and is teaching them to be decent. I hope they'll be duly grateful. See those roses? Aren't they perfectly dear?"

Thus she chattered to those in the car with her all the way to the farm. To see her going about among the guests and smiling and posing to Michael when he came near, you would have thought she had made the match and never dreamed it was only because Michael, out of his great, forgiving heart, had said, "Oh, forgive her and ask her down. She's your mother's sister, and you'll be glad you did afterward. Never mind what she says. She can't help her ideas. It was her unfortunate upbringing, and she's as much to be pitied as I for my slum education."

The pretty ceremony under the roses was over, and Starr had gone upstairs to change the simple embroidered muslin for her traveling dress and motor coat. Michael and Starr were to take their honeymoon in their own new car, a wedding gift from her father, and Endicott himself was to go to his sister's by rail in Will French's company, to stay during their absence and be picked up by them on their homeward route.

Michael stood among his friends on the piazza giving last directions to Will, who was to look after his law business during his absence. Will was eager to tell his friend how he and Hester planned to be married in the fall and set up housekeeping in a five-room flat that might have been a palace from the light in Will's eyes. Hester was talking with Lizzie, who had edged near the porch with her boy hiding shyly behind her, but the smile Hester threw in Will's direction now and then showed she well knew his subject of conversation.

The whole community had gathered in the orchard in front of the rose arch to watch the wedding ceremony, and many still lingered to see the beloved bride and groom depart.

Suddenly, during Will's eager description of the flat and its prospects, Michael noticed Sam's shy look as he waited anxiously for notice.

"Excuse me, Will. I must see Sam a minute," said Michael, hurrying over to where the man stood.

"Say, Mickey," said Sam shyly, grasping Michael's hand, "me an' Lizzie sort o' made it up as how we'd get tied, an' we thought we'd do it now whiles everybody's at it, an' things is all fixed. Lizzie wanted me to ask you ef you s'posed she'd mind ef we'uns stood thur on the verandy whur yous did, arter you was gone?"

Sam looked at him as if he'd asked for half of Michael's kingdom and scarcely expected to get it, but Michael's face was filled with glory as he clasped his comrade's rough hand heartily.

"Mind! She'd be delighted, Sam! Go ahead. I'm sorry we didn't know it before. We'd have liked to give you a present, but I'll send you the deed to the little white cottage at the head of the lane, the one that looks toward the river and the sunset, you know. Would you two like to live there?"

Sam's eyes grew large with happiness, and a mist came over them as he held tight to the hand enclosing his own and choked and tried to answer.

Amid a shower of roses and cheers, Michael and Starr rode into the sweet June afternoon, alone together at last. And when they had gone beyond the town and were on a stretch of quiet woodsy road, Michael stopped the car and took his bride in his arms.

"Dear," he said as he tenderly kissed her, "I've just been realizing what might have happened if Buck hadn't seen you in time and taken the shot himself—that I might not have you, my life, my dear, precious wife!"

Then Starr looked up with her eyes dewy. "Michael, we must try to save a lot of others for his sake."

And Michael smiled and pressed his lips to hers again with deep, sweet understanding.

When they were riding along again, Michael told her what Sam asked and how another wedding was to follow theirs.

"Oh, Michael!" exclaimed Starr. "Why didn't you tell me sooner! I wish we'd stayed to see them married. Couldn't we turn around now and get there in time if you hurry?"

"We'll try," said Michael, reversing the car.

In an instant more it was shooting back to Old Orchard, arriving just as Sam and Lizzie were shyly taking their places, hand in hand, under the roses, in as near imitation of Michael and Starr as their unaccustomedness could compass.

Jim discovered the car coming up the orchard lane.

"For de lub o' Mike!" he exclaimed aloud. "Ef here don't come Mickey hisse'f and her! Hold up dar, mister preacher. Don't tie de knot till dey gits here!"

And a cheer arose loud and long and echoed through the trees and over the river to the sea. Three cheers for the love of Michael!

Sam and Lizzie bloomed forth with smiles, and the ceremony went forward with alacrity now that the real audience was present.

An hour later, having done their part to make the wedding festivities as joyous as their own had been, Michael and Starr started out again into the waning day, a light on their faces and joy in their hearts.

Starr, her heart full, laid her hand on Michael's and said with shining eyes, "Michael, do you know—I found a name for you. Listen: 'And at that time shall Michael stand up, the great prince which standeth for the children of thy people: and at that time thy people shall be delivered, every one that shall be found written in the book.' Michael, you are my prince!"

And Michael, as he stooped and kissed her, murmured, "My Starr."